Quilting school

READER'S
Learn-As-You-Go Guide
DIGEST

Quilting school

Ann Poe

Contributing Editor

Angela Besley

Reader's
Digest

THE READER'S DIGEST ASSOCIATION, INC.
Pleasantville, New York
Montreal

QUILTING SCHOOL

A READER'S DIGEST BOOK

Designed and edited by Quarto Inc.

First printed in paperback 2002

Library of Congress Cataloging in Publication Data.

Poe, Ann
  Quilting school/ Ann Poe.
  p. cm. - (Reader's Digest learn-as-you-go guides)
  Includes index.
  ISBN 0-89577-471-2 hardcover
  ISBN 0-7621-0412-0 paperback
  1. Quilting-Handbooks, manuals, etc.
  I. Title,   II. Series
TT835.P63 1993
746.46-dc20   92-43792

Senior Editor: *Honor Head*
Editor: *Maggi McCormick*
Publishing Director: *Janet Slingsby*
Art Director: *Moira Clinch*
Senior Art Director: *Amanda Bakhtia*r
Designer: *Sheila Volpe*
Illustrator: *Sally Launder*
Photographers: *Paul Forrester, Chas Wilder*
Picture Researcher: *Carmen Jones*
Picture Manager: *Rebecca Horsewood*

For more information about Reader's Digest products, visit our website at **rd.com**

Printed in China by Leefung-Asco Printers Ltd

4 6 8 10 9 7 5 3 hardcover
2 4 6 8 10 9 7 5 3 1 paperback

CONTENTS

INTRODUCTION

Quilting is easy, and quilting is fun! If you're a beginner, we encourage you to explore the pleasures of quilting. Use this comprehensive book to take some of the mystique out of this ancient, beautiful and very satisfying craft by learning the basic cutting and stitching techniques for all kinds of different quilts. If you're already an accomplished quilter, you'll find this book a useful reference for your library. Experiment with new techniques, and use the projects and the examples of fine historical quilts shown on the following pages for inspiration.

The history of quilting is long and varied. *Quilting School* begins with the Story of Quilts, an introduction to different types of quilts. It includes a visual overview of historical examples, ranging from a spectacular appliquéd Baltimore album quilt to modern Seminole patchwork.

The second section, Quilting Basics, discusses the materials and equipment that you will need to make the projects in the book. It also teaches all the fundamental skills, such as estimating yardage, making templates, marking and cutting fabrics, piecing by hand and machine, joining blocks and adding borders, assembling a quilt top, quilting by hand and machine, and finishing the quilt edges. These

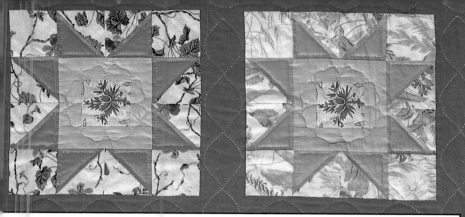

are techniques you will need for making the sampler quilt in the next section, and they will help you stitch many more patchwork and quilting designs, traditional and modern.

The next section, the Sampler Quilt, takes you step-by-step through the stages of making a quilt, from creating nine different blocks to the final binding. Every stage is clearly shown, so that you learn how to make the various blocks, add sashing, make and add a checkered border, and finally mark, quilt, and finish your quilt. If you do the lessons in this section, you will end up with a beautiful sampler quilt in traditional colors.

Extending Your Skills introduces some of the more unusual types of piecing and quilting, including sashiko, trapunto, Italian cording, wholecloth quilting, and English patchwork. Each new skill features full instructions for a simple project.

The Pattern Library illustrates a wide range of the most popular quilting and piecing designs. Use these for your own projects or substitute them for some of the designs used in the sampler quilt.

The final section gives you advice on restoring, caring for, and displaying quilts. A glossary of common patchwork and quilting terms is in the back of the book.

1

The story
of quilts

The story of patchwork and quilting is extensive and intriguing. Techniques are rooted in the practical details of everyday life in times before most people had the leisure to pursue arts and crafts for their own sake. Piecing was a necessary skill, so that leftover dressmaking scraps or the best parts of worn clothing could be used and re-used for economy when fabric was still a precious commodity. People kept

The story of quilts

warm with quilting in clothes and bedcovers; soldiers wore quilted armor and padded jackets for protection.

But human beings are naturally creative and as patchwork and quilting developed, designs began to appear. Rather than piece or stitch haphazardly, sewers began to use particular patterns, which were refined and developed while being handed down from generation to generation. Craftspeople, itinerant workers, and patternmakers spread new ideas to different areas; certain places and peoples developed their own specialized techniques, a process which continues today.

To give you an overview of some of the main types of quilting, we have put together a gallery of fine historical examples, showing the skill and versatility of our ancestors.

Shells, flowers, and interlocking chains have been combined in this wholecloth quilt dating from 1935; the main motifs have been set off by the contrasting checkerboard background texture, worked both straight and diagonally.

This 19th century painting called The Wedding Quilt *by Ralph Hedley, shows women and girls sewing at a quilting bee.*

WHOLECLOTH QUILTING

Wholecloth quilts are not pieced, but are made from a background fabric and decorated with stitched patterns. Wholecloth quilting dates back several hundred years in many traditions, especially in the North of England, Wales, and North America. The fabrics and battings used depended on the materials most easily available in the area. The quilting is often worked in the same color thread as the background fabric, although occasionally a contrast color is used. The traditional quilting stitch is a running stitch, worked through all three layers of top fabric, batting, and backing fabric; the stitch holds the batting in place.

The designs of wholecloth quilts were usually inspired by everyday objects – leaves, flowers, feathers, goose tails and wings, cords, fans, shells. Leaf shapes were often created by drawing using a flat-iron as a template; one side of the iron would be traced, then turned around for the other half of the leaf shape. Because quilting was usually done in groups, it is difficult to know where the traditional designs originated; individual quilters would add their own touches to the chosen patterns.

AMERICAN BLOCK QUILTS

Traditional American quilts were often pieced in square blocks. Stitching one block made the work easily portable, and blocks could be stock-piled until there were enough for a whole quilt top. In the earliest quilts from colonial days, the seams were stitched by hand. With the advent of the sewing machine, the stitching became much quicker, but many quilts are still pieced by hand in blocks.

The range of block designs is phenomenal, many of them with evocative names like Oh Susannah, Goose in the Pond, Rising Star, and Steps to the Altar.

It was customary for an unmarried girl to piece quilt tops and store them in her Hope Chest. When she became engaged, her friends and relatives would join in, add remaining layers of batting and backing, then stretch, stitch, and finish the quilts, helping her get ready for her new life as a married woman.

Despite the wandering appearance of the overall pattern, this quilt is actually made in blocks; pieced blocks of 25 squares alternate with plain white blocks that have had small squares appliquéd in the corners. The design is known as Irish Chain.

AMISH QUILTS

The Amish people take their name from Joseph Amman, a Swiss who was a model of conservatism. When William Penn invited persecuted people to join him in his new land, the Amish went from Switzerland, Germany, and the Alsace to America. Still clinging tenaciously to their clothing styles, traditions, and religious observances from centuries past, the Amish people today live apart from their fellow countrymen and follow a simple way of life.

With this stress on simplicity, it is easy to appreciate the stark beauty of the Amish quilts. Many of them are made from the plain hand-dyed fabrics also used in the traditional Amish clothing. Sometimes large sections of solid-color cloth are used in the quilts instead of pieced blocks. The quilts may have one or more borders and are always quilted with exquisite and intricate designs, sometimes stitched in a contrasting color such as orange or purple. Often the large areas of pure colors are offset by black borders or binding.

The vivid colors, multiple borders, and central diamond of this quilt are all typical features of Amish quilts – finished with exquisite quilting in every section.

ENGLISH PATCHWORK

English patchwork differs dramatically in technique from American patchwork but possesses an equally noble history. The earliest known example dates from 1708. In English patchwork, the fabric pieces are basted over paper shapes, then sewn together to form a simple or complex pattern. As with many other techniques, English patchwork from different eras varies in appearance with the kind of fabrics that were fashionable at the time. When exotic prints were imported in large quantities from the Middle East in the 19th century, patchwork was made from those; when Britain began producing inexpensive cotton print fabrics later on, the appearance of the patchwork changed accordingly.

During Queen Victoria's long reign, patchwork made from pieces of solid colored silk became extremely popular; certain patterns, such as diamonds and hexagons, were especially in vogue. English patchwork has been very useful for social historians because it was often worked in scrap fabrics such as pattern samples from mills. Also, the papers used in the inner templates were often cut from old letters, ledgers, and books, and provide fascinating information when pieced together from unfinished bits of patchwork.

The bright solid colors and geometric design of this quilt, dating from the end of last century, are typical of English patchwork at its height.

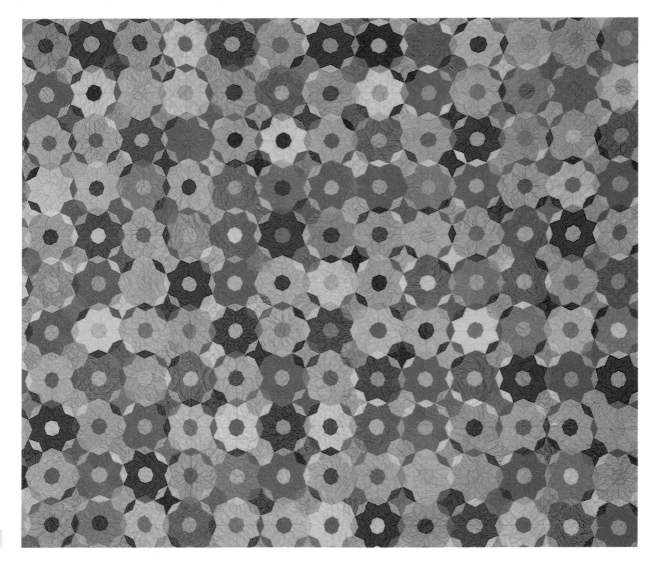

The red dye used on this quilt, dating from the turn of the century, was known as Turkey Red and was one of the most popular colors for this kind of simple appliqué.

APPLIQUÉ

Appliqué has been around for many centuries; the first person to sew a patch on worn clothing was using appliqué. Traditional appliqué in quilts involved arranging fabric shapes – often natural forms such as petals, leaves, berries, animals, or feathers – in a pleasing design on a background. The fabric shapes were then sewn into place with tiny invisible stitches; raw edges were turned under so they didn't fray or were held in place with a decorative stitch.

Early appliqué quilts often used a simple color scheme, perhaps one or two strong colors on a plain white background. Some of these quilts were called turkey quilts because a certain shade of red, known as turkey red, was a popular choice. Another form of applied stitching was crazy quilting – random shapes of patchwork, often made from velvets and other fancy fabrics, were embellished with embroidery, beadwork, and patriotic slogans. Broderie perse was also popular; this method involved cutting motifs from several printed fabrics, arranging and stitching them onto a background fabric, and embellishing the new design, if desired.

A spectacular example of a Baltimore album quilt, featuring many complex and beautifully executed appliqué designs, including many typical garlands and vases of flowers, and several versions of the American eagle.

ALBUM QUILTS

Album, or friendship, quilts are a specialized type of quilt originating in America. The original album quilts were usually done as gifts, perhaps for a wedding or if a friend was moving. These quilts are generally stitched in blocks, but in true album quilts, each block is a different design and often was stitched by a different person. Christmas Cactus and Basket blocks were favorite designs, and occasionally three-dimensional flower motifs were appliquéd; the designs are sometimes breathtakingly detailed. The colors and patterns were usually carefully chosen so that the whole quilt harmonized when assembled; red and green on a white background was a favorite color scheme. On some examples the names of the

SEMINOLE PATCHWORK

The Seminole Indians of Florida developed distinctive patchwork designs in strip-pieced patterned bands. The technique seems to have developed in the late 1800s when the sewing machine became available to them.

The technique involves strip piecing two or more long pieces of fabric and then cutting the new fabric into secondary strips. The secondary strips are then laid out and joined in a new relationship to each other, forming patterned bands which can be quite complex. The Seminoles generally use the bands on garments, but they can be used to create large decorative pieces as well.

Many different geometric patterns can be seen in this striking example of Seminole patchwork, worked in a limited color scheme of bright solid fabrics set off by the black border.

quilters were embroidered on the blocks.

The most spectacular examples of album quilts were done in the Baltimore area, so album quilts are often known as Baltimore quilts. Genuine Baltimore quilts are highly sought after and prized by collectors. Album quilts are still made today; they are popular as community and school projects.

The spiky plant design worked in a solid-colored appliqué on a white background, is typical of Hawaiian Kapa Lau work.

HAWAIIAN APPLIQUÉ

Hawaii has developed its own form of appliqué called Kapa Lau. It is made by stitching one large, carefully shaped piece of fabric onto a plain background. American missionaries showed the islanders how to fold paper and cut it into shapes like simple plants or snowflakes; the unfolded paper was then used as a pattern for cutting the appliqué fabric. Hawaiians soon developed their own designs, and the original small patterns became larger and larger, many of them based on the luxuriant foliage of the island such as pineapples, breadfruit trees, ferns, palms, and paw-paws.

Once the design has been cut out, it is basted to a background fabric and the edges are carefully turned under and stitched down. This is a very time-consuming process, for some of the designs are extremely complicated. Once the appliqué is complete, the area beyond the appliqué is usually quilted with echo quilting – lines of stitching that echo the outline of the appliqué shape.

TRAPUNTO QUILTING

Trapunto, or stuffed, quilting is a specialized technique that involves stitching two layers of fabric together in shaped pockets which can then be stuffed. Stuffing is inserted through the backing fabric (if it is loosely woven) or through a slit which is later sewn closed. Raised appliqué work of this kind is common in ecclesiastical embroidery.

In 18th and 19th century trapunto quilts, most of the quilt would be quilted in the ordinary way, then a central motif or medallion was given an extra layer of stuffing to raise it. It is an effective way to draw attention to a particular part of a design.

This quilt shows an attractive combination of appliqué and quilting in a subtle color scheme; the border of grapes and the delicate outer border provide an attractive frame for the geometric central design.

ITALIAN QUILTING

Italian, or corded, quilting involves threading cords through channels stitched in a double layer of fabric; the corded design stands out in relief from its background. Despite its name, it did not develop solely in Italy; corded quilting is found in artefacts from many Asian and Middle Eastern countries as well as European ones. Wonderful examples have survived from the 18th and 19th centuries in England of whole bedcovers decorated with tiny, elaborate, intricate corded quilting designs.

Linear designs lend themselves well to Italian quilting, but the design can be as fine or as bold as you wish. Modern quilters have experimented using everything from thin yarn to rope for the cording and leather to net for the fabric.

This corded and quilted hat dates from the early 20th century; it was made in Northern India.

2

Quilting basics

aking a traditional quilt is not an activity that can be rushed; that is part of its charm. There are several different stages, from choosing the fabric and working out the design, through cutting, piecing, backing and quilting, to the final finishing by binding the raw edges. The main stages of quilt making have a logical order, and in the pages that follow we take you through them one by one. Occasionally, a stage

Elements of a quilt

may not be necessary; for instance, you will not need to draw a design and make templates if you are using commercial templates, but generally each step will be covered in some way.

But first you'll need to understand the terms that quilters use; like every other art and craft, quilting has its own special vocabulary. Words and phrases like basting, batting, piecing, sashing, setting blocks, and quilt top can all seem strange and bewildering if you're a beginner, but you'll quickly become used to them, and like the stages in quilt making, they are all perfectly logical. On these pages, we introduce you to the common terms for the different parts of a quilt and the various processes involved. The same terms will be used throughout the book.

Piecing or patchwork refers to pieces of fabric cut in specific shapes and then stitched together in a decorative design.

A block is a section of patchwork stitched in a regular shape, usually a square. Traditional quilts are often built up from several individual blocks; the blocks may be identical or may vary in design. In our sampler quilt, we use nine different square block designs.

Binding is the edging of the quilt, and covers all the raw edges neatly. It also contributes to the overall effect of the design. There are several ways of binding quilt edges (see page 98).

Backing fabric provides a neat finish for the back of the quilt; the batting is concealed between it and the quilt top.

Basting is used to hold the three layers of the quilt together; the lines of basting threads, worked in a grid across the quilt (see page 52), hold the layers in place while they are being quilted.

24

A **frame** is used to stretch the fabric while it is being quilted. Frames may be large, so that the whole quilt can be stretched at once, or small enough for one section to be quilted at a time (see page 54).

Quilting *refers to the stitching which passes through all three layers of the quilt (top, batting, and backing); the quilting provides both texture and decoration. Quilting may be done by hand or machine (see page 96).*

A **border** *is a decorative edging of plain fabric or pieced work added around the main quilt area. Borders can be made from one or several fabrics, plain or patterned (see page 150). This is a plain border with a quilted design.*

Sashing *or* **setting strips** *refer to strips of fabric used to separate blocks in a quilt. In some quilt designs, blocks are joined without any sashing so that new patterns are formed (see page 38).*

Batting *is used to pad the quilt, and provides texture and bulk. Various kinds of batting are available to suit different requirements (see page 52).*

While there is plenty of specialized equipment available to help the quilter, not very much of it is essential; most of the tasks of making templates, cutting and piecing fabric, and marking and stitching quilting patterns can be done with general drawing and sewing equipment that you will probably already have in your house. If you are just beginning quilting, start off with the essentials, marked

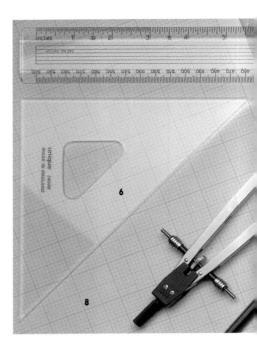

Equipment

with a bullet (•) below; they will provide all that you need to make the projects in this book. As you want to extend your quilting skills, acquire the more specialist items listed: they will save you time as you cut and stitch.

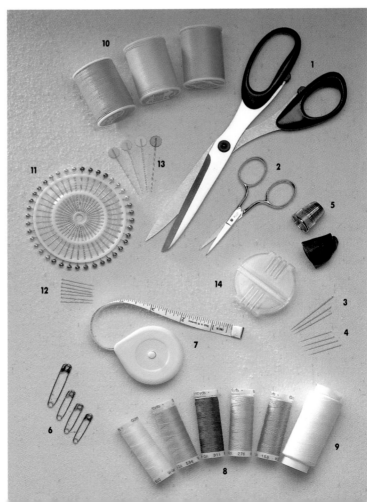

▶ **General sewing equipment**

• **1** Large scissors for cutting fabric
• **2** Small, sharp-pointed embroidery scissors
• **3** Selection of sewing needles
• **4** Quilting needles
• **5** Thimbles
• **6** Safety pins
• **7** Tape measure
• **8** Cotton or polyester sewing thread
• **9** Basting thread
• **10** Quilting thread
• **11** Pins, preferably glass-headed (they are easily visible and can't

accidentally be ironed over)
• **12** Extra-fine pins for silks and satins
• **13** Flat-headed pins (useful when machine-stitching as they don't catch in the foot)
• **14** Beeswax and beeswax holder

Even-feed foot for sewing machine
Sewing machine
Thumble (used on the thumb of your quilting hand)

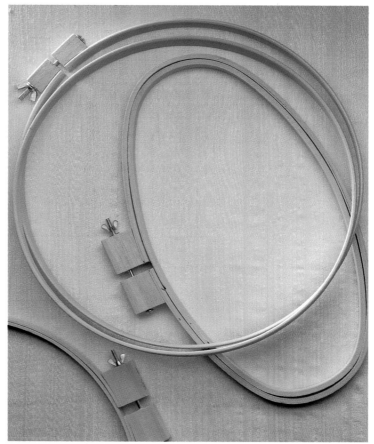

◄ **General drawing equipment**

- **1** *Pencils – both medium-hard and soft, HB and 2B*
- **2** *Pencil sharpener*
- **3** *Eraser*
- **4** *Short and long rulers (12 in. and 24 in.)*
- **5** *Crayons or felt-tip pens*

  6 *Set square*

  7 *Protractor*

  8 *Graph paper*

  9 *Compass*

▼ ► **Frames**

- *Quilting frames (you will only need one type: circular, rectangular, oval, rolling, slate, floor-standing, full-size)*

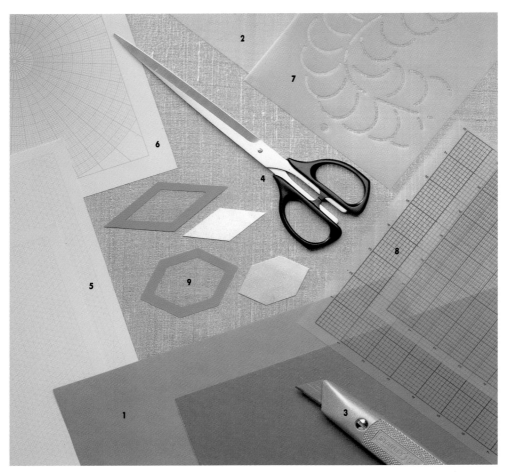

◄ **Templates and template materials**
- **1** Cardboard
- **2** *Plain template plastic*
- **3** *Craft knife*
- **4** *Paper scissors*

5 *Isometric graph paper*

6 *Polar coordinate graph paper*

7 *Quilting templates in different designs*

8 *Sheets of template plastic marked with guide rules*

9 *Window template (for positioning a printed motif accurately within the template shape)*

Patchwork templates in different designs

► **Equipment for cutting accurate fabric patches**
- **1** *Rotary cutter*
- **2** *"Self-healing" specialized cutting mat with cutting guides for templates*

3 *Sandpaper grips (used on the corners of rulers and templates to stop fabric from slipping while you cut)*

4 *45° Kaleidoscope wedge ruler*

5 *Omnigrid (a useful guide for cutting many different templates)*

6 *Multi Miter (a guide for miters of different angles)*

7 *Scrapsaver ruler*

8 *BiRangle for cutting half rectangles*

9 *Magic Star for cutting 8-pointed stars*

10 *Quilter's Rule*

11 *9 inch Circle Wedge*

Quilt and Sew ruler
Easy Angle (for cutting accurate triangles)
Lip edge ruler
Pineapple ruler (measures accurate 45° sections)
Salem ruler (a guide marked with 60° and 45° angles)
Super Seamer ruler (for adding seam allowances to templates and fabric pieces)

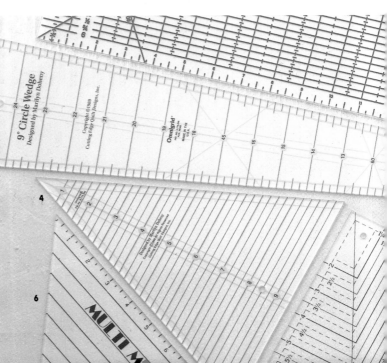

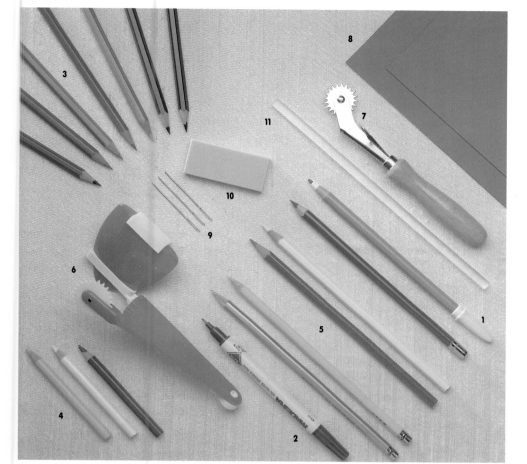

● **1** *Soluble-ink pens (marks can be removed with cold water)*

2 *Fading-ink pen (marks fade gradually when exposed to air)*

3 *Colored pencils*

4 *Cloth markers*

5 *Colored marking pencils*

6 *Tracing wheel with chalk holder*

7 *Prick and pounce wheel*

8 *Dressmaker's carbon paper (available in several colors)*

9 *Blunt tapestry needles*

10 *Fabric eraser (for removing ordinary pencil marks from fabric)*

11 *Quilter's quarter (adds $\frac{1}{4}$ in. to straight edges)*

Bodkin

Silverpoint (pencil-shaped metal implement used for marking fabrics)

Transfer pens (for drawing on transfers)

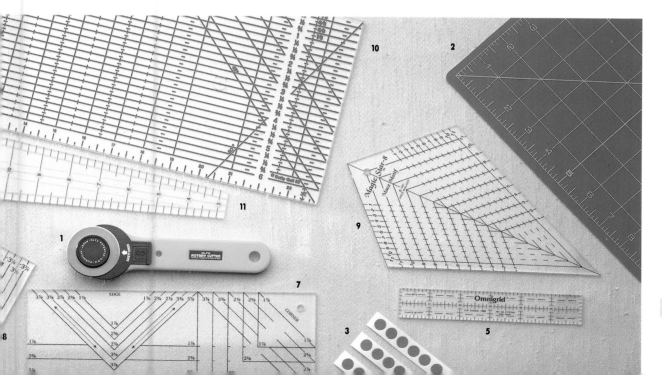

In the early days of patchwork, people would simply use what was available, usually the best parts left in worn-out clothing or bedding. In fact, that was how the whole craft of patchwork began; it was born from necessity, when fabric was expensive and thrift was the order of the day. Nowadays, most of us buy patchwork fabrics new for each project, and there is an endless variety to select from: wool, cotton,

Choosing fabrics

◄ Cotton
All of these fabrics are 100% cotton in different thicknesses. Cottons come in myriad prints and solid colors, and are the ideal quilting fabrics. Polished cotton and chintz have a shiny finish which looks very pretty in plain quilted areas; the glaze is diminished, though, by hot washing, and it makes it more difficult to work the quilting.

synthetics, and novelty fabrics such as lamé, fur, plastic, and leather. In addition, many of these fabrics are available in a multitude of solid colors, prints, and textures, which can make your choice bewildering. How do you decide whether to use solid or printed fabrics? Large or small prints? Should you mix different types of fabric?

Although it seems a very mundane consideration, the first thing to decide is whether the finished article will need to be washed. Obviously, if you are making a quilt for your bed, a pillow cover, or a garment, at some stage the item will need washing, so you will have to use a fully washable fabric. The most suitable is lightweight 100% cotton, which holds its shape well, is washable, and is easy to stitch through several layers if you are quilting. Cotton/polyester blends are available in many pretty solids and prints, but generally they aren't so satisfactory for quilting; they slip around more while you are working on them, can be rather translucent, and are often more difficult to quilt through several layers.

All the fabrics you plan to use in a washable item must be soaked in warm water to pre-shrink them and to test them for color fastness. Light- to medium-colored ones can be washed by machine on a warm cycle, but dark colors are more likely to run and should be washed separately. Rinse the fabric until the water runs clear; if color is still bleeding from it after about six rinses, discard it – it could ruin

◄ Cotton/polyester blends
These fabrics are attractive, but don't have the density or firmness of cotton.

◄ Polyester fabric
Many polyester fabrics are unsuitable for quilting because they are slippery and loosely woven, but others, such as the firm polyester silks shown here, can be used to great effect in patchwork and quilting.

◄ Satin
Satin has a wonderful sheen and can be very dramatic used in stained glass patchwork (see page 108).

many hours of work if it runs when your finished patchwork item is washed. Once the fabric is dry, check whether the grain is straight; the visible horizontal and vertical threads (warp and weft) should be at right angles. If they aren't, gently pull the fabric diagonally to straighten the grain. Then press the fabric to remove the creases caused by washing. If you wash and press your fabrics as soon as you buy them, when inspiration strikes, you're all ready to cut and sew!

Some types of silks and satins can be washed; others have to be dry-cleaned; check with the supplier when you buy them, and don't mix the two types. Generally it's better to use the same kind of fabrics in a patchwork item – for instance, all cottons or all silks – unless you are mixing them for a particular effect. If you want the look of silk without the expense and the washing difficulties, polyester silks are available.

Finally, if you're making something which won't be washed, you can use any fabric. Thick fabrics such as linen, sailcloth and twill are usually too thick to be pieced or quilted successfully, while wool fabrics such as chambray are often too thin and too loosely woven. However, there are plenty of other fabrics to experiment with. Lamé patches here and there on a jacket or wallhanging give a wonderful sparkle; nets and voiles can be layered over other fabrics to create new tones and depths of color; fur fabric and leather could make realistic animals on a child's wall quilt. Exotic silks, satins, and velvets make a rich setting for the embroidery on a crazy quilt.

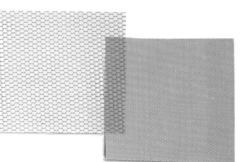

◀ **Silk**

Silk is available in many different weights, weaves, colors, and textures. The firmer weaves are very satisfactory for patchwork; the finer ones can be very slippery. Some silks are woven to produce novel effects, such as heavy slubs; "shot" silk has different colors for the warp and weft threads and shimmers between the two shades.

◀ **Net and voile**

These fabrics aren't firm enough to use for patchwork on their own, but they produce interesting special effects in experimental work.

◀ **Metallic fabric**

Metallic fabrics are generally wholly or partly synthetic, and come in a dazzling variety of finishes. They can be used with conventional patchwork patterns to make exotic items such as evening jackets and glittery bags, but have the drawbacks of other synthetic fabrics. Also, they have a very strong visual impact, so don't overdo them.

GRAIN LINES

Good fabric should have the long grain running parallel to the selvage (the finished edge). Check this before buying, because if the grain is not true your pieces may become distorted. Templates should always be placed straight along the grain. In a woven fabric such as cotton, the long grain is sometimes known as the warp, while the yarn woven across this at a 90° angle is the weft.

O nce you've decided on a patchwork pattern, the next important decision is color. You may want to match or contrast with something in your decor or an outfit, and this may determine the dominant color for your patchwork. Or, you may want the patchwork to have a certain "feel", for instance, a vibrant look, or a soft, gentle effect. Patchwork patterns themselves often suggest to the quilter the kind

Choosing colors

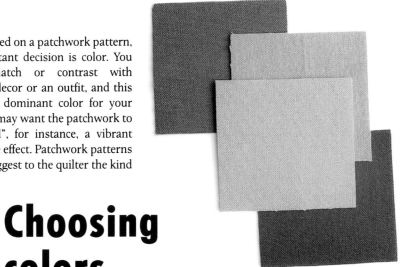

◀ **Shades of one color**
Although we divide the color wheel into six basic colors – red, orange, yellow, green, blue, and purple – each individual color can have an almost infinite number of shades or variations in hue. The fabrics here are all green, but you can see the enormous variety of shades, from acid lime-green to a dark olive green.

of color schemes that would suit them. However, it is possible that you don't have any ideas about color and are starting from scratch; in this case, you can have great fun working out your color scheme.

Certain colors go together naturally, especially when they have a similar underlying color. For instance, blues that tend toward green rather than purple move toward yellow in the color wheel; green-blues tend to look harmonious with yellows and creams. In the same way, purple-blues go well with pinks because they both move toward red in the color wheel. Other colors create a vibrant reaction and set each other off in different ways; this is especially true of the complementary colors,

◀ **Light and dark**
All colors range from dark – very dark in some cases – to pale. The lightness or darkness of a color is known as its "value." Aim to have fabrics of several different values in your block; otherwise it may look bland and lacking in contrast.

COLOR WHEEL

Even a simple color wheel like this can help you to understand how colors relate to one another. Colors close together, such as the blues and purples, harmonize because they are the same family. The colors shown far right are the complementaries, which are opposite one another on the color wheel. These set up strong contrasts, so use them sparingly unless you want a particularly vibrant, dramatic effect.

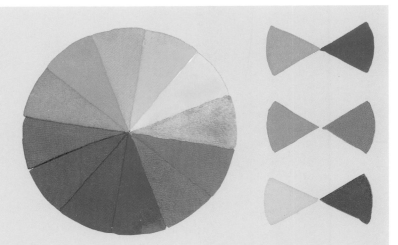

which are directly opposite each other on the color wheel – green and red, purple and yellow, orange and blue. Colors which are quite close to each other in the color wheel can create dramatic clashes – for example, red and puce, purple and turquoise, blue and lime-green.

If you're starting your color scheme from scratch, visit a fabric store or department which has a wide choice of cotton fabrics and pick two or three which please your eye when they are put together. Stand back to check the overall effect. If one is "killed" by the others, discard it and choose another. Continue until you are completely satisfied with your selection. In the end, it's your decision: if you like it, use it.

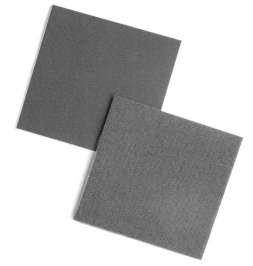

◀ **Vibrant colors**
Red and green, the strongest pair of complementary colors, create strong contrasts which can be effective on a small scale. You can play down the contrast by varying the proportions of the colors or by introducing some neutrals.

◀ **Clashing colors**
Some colors set up a discordant effect which can be dramatic. The lime green and dark turquoise are not natural partners, but such colors can be used successfully if separated by another color such as peachy-orange.

◀ **Harmonious colors**
Here, pink and mauve-pink is combined with a gentle slate gray. The effect is harmonious, with all the fabrics blending well with each other. Colors like these would give a gentle "country" feel to a bed quilt.

◀ **Adding neutrals**
Neutral colors are those which don't appear as pure color mixes in the color wheel: black, white, cream, brown, beige, dark gray, muddy green etc. All neutral colors can be used to great effect in patchwork, especially in backgrounds and to set off other colors.

33

Some fabrics, such as gingham and damask, have patterns woven into them, but this process tends to alter the characteristics of the fabric, especially the texture. Generally, when you want to use a mixture of solid and patterned fabrics in patchwork, fabrics which have patterns printed on them are best. The patterns may be small or large, seemingly random or printed in a very regular design; some

Small prints look good alternated with solid blocks and create a homely feel.

Prints and solids

patterned fabrics have individual motifs which can be picked out and placed in specific arrangements in your work.

Patchwork patterns can look very bold worked entirely in solid fabrics, but adding a print or two will often give an extra lift to the design and keep it from looking stark. It is possible to use more than one print in your patchwork; in fact, you can piece it entirely from print fabrics if you choose them carefully. The main rule of thumb is not to choose strong patterns that fight visually with each other, or which obliterate the lines of the piecing itself.

Striped fabrics can be very striking and lend themselves to special effects, but avoid striped designs which are not printed along the straight grain of the fabric – they can deceive the eye into believing that the patches are cut crookedly. If the pattern isn't straight, cut with it rather than with the fabric grain.

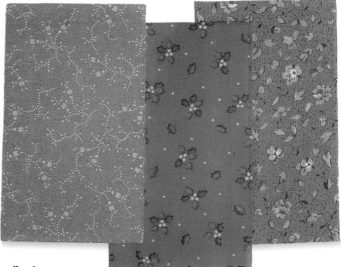

▲ Small prints
Small all-over prints are particularly suitable for patchwork; they provide texture without distracting the eye.

Large blocks of solid color create impact and have an immediate effect.

◄ Large prints
Large all-over prints can be very effective if used carefully, but if you use several large patterns together, you may lose the lines of the patchwork shapes themselves.

◄ Striped fabrics
Striped fabrics can have simple or complex patterns, ranging from a straightforward two-color stripe to a multicolored design in a random color sequence.

USING INDIVIDUAL MOTIFS OR AREAS

You may want to use just one part of a printed fabric – perhaps a particular motif or section of a design. In this case, you will need a transparent template, so that you can be sure that you have positioned it exactly where you want it on the fabric. This technique is rather wasteful of fabric, but it does allow you to produce some very dramatic effects.

35

Buying fabrics for a quilt can be a costly business, so you want to be sure that you've chosen fabrics that will work well together before you invest in large amounts of them. Coloring in a sample block will give you a good idea whether your chosen color scheme works well, but once you have a basic idea in mind, you need to start working with real fabrics. One of the best ways is to lay out a sample

Working it out

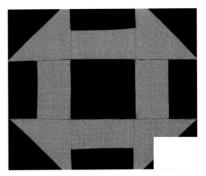

Making a shape come forward
When you want to emphasize a particular motif or part of a design, work the motif in the lighter fabric and set it on a dark background.

Individual motifs
This floral print has been carefully cut so that a flower appears in the center of each triangle, and in the center of the middle patch. Use a clear template when you want to position individual motifs accurately in this way.

block using scraps of fabric cut to shape. If you have a good collection of fabrics, you may have enough to try this out without buying anything; if not, most stores will sell short lengths or small patches of fabric. Move the shapes around until you have a good balance of color and intensity. If one fabric doesn't seem right, replace it with another one until you are satisfied with the result.

You may need to buy one fabric to blend in with several others you already have; if so, making a color fan may be useful. Glue long thin strips of your existing fabrics on thin cardboard, making sure that you don't leave a border of cardboard around the fabric – this way, you can lay your fabric right up against fabrics on the bolt and see how they look side by side. Secure all the strips together in one corner with a safety pin, or punch holes and put a ring through them; then you will be able to fan them out as necessary so you can see different combinations of fabric together.

Here you can see how some of the ideas in this section work in practice. All of the nine-patch blocks shown here have been made in the same design – the Churn Dash – and the same size. You can see, though, that each block looks different from the others, because of the fabrics that we have chosen and the ways that the fabrics have been arranged.

▼ *This color fan has been made with strips of fabric glued to cardboard; the strips have then been hooked together in one corner. The strips can be fanned out in different combinations so that they can be laid against new fabrics in the shop to assess their effect together.*

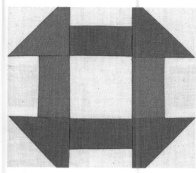

Making a shape recede
A dark shape placed on a light background seems to move away from you. Use this effect to reduce the emphasis of a very dramatic fabric.

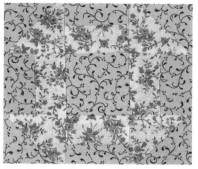

Fabrics too close in shade
Although the patterns on these two print fabrics are quite different when you look carefully, they are so close in shade that they merge together, losing the lines of the block design.

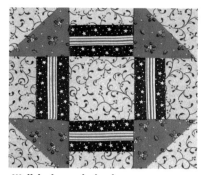

Well-balanced shades
This block has a background fabric similar to the previous one, but stronger fabrics have been chosen for the other patches, so that the lines of the block design can be seen clearly.

Asymmetric arrangements
In this block, the shades fade from light to dark diagonally. This can look very dramatic if you join several blocks made in the same way, so that the shading alters in a regular pattern.

Bright and bold fabrics
This block uses bright, acid solids and bold, brightly colored prints, giving a very modern look to the block. The asymmetrical arrangement of the fabrics add to the jazzy effect.

Exotic fabrics
Although cotton is the traditional choice for patchwork, you can use many other fabrics. This block has been made in subtle shades of silk, hand-dyed to give a soft and delicate appearance.

MAKING TRIAL GRIDS

If you draw your patchwork pattern (see page 40, Drawing designs) and photocopy it several times, you can use these grids to try out different color schemes and arrangements. Use colored pencils or felt-tip pens, depending on the intensity of color that you want in your finished patchwork.

37

When you are planning your quilt, you need to decide how the different elements will go together. If you are using several blocks, will they look best joined directly to one another, or separated? For the edges of the quilt, do you want a decorative border, or will you simply bind the edges?

When blocks are joined side by side, they can produce intriguing secondary designs (see

Sashing can be used in many ways to create different visual effects. The quilt above uses sashing at angles with a half-fan motif to give a feel and look of shells or scales. The quilt right uses sashing across the block motifs to create "quarter" blocks which are then echoed in the border.

QUILTING BASICS

Putting it together

opposite and page 146). You may decide, though, that you want each block to be seen on its own, and the best way of doing this is by adding sashing, or setting strips. Sashing is particularly important if you have made blocks in several different designs or techniques, such as for our sampler quilt; blocks in very different patterns rarely look good joined directly without sashing. Sashing should be made from a fabric that will show off the more decorative blocks to their best advantage; you might want to choose a neutral color, or one of the solid fabrics from your patchwork. Sashing can be in a patterned fabric, but since it is intended as a frame for the stronger patterns, it is best to use a small all-over print that doesn't distract the eye too much from the blocks.

Borders go around the whole quilt top and add extra visual interest; they are also a good way of increasing the size, for instance, if you want to extend a double-bed size to fit a king-size bed. A pieced quilt really calls for a pieced border, which will look most effective if it uses elements from the quilt itself – stars or diamonds for star quilts, borders with curved elements for Drunkard's Patch or Grandmother's Fan designs, squares and triangles for quilt designs made up from these basic shapes. Use the same fabrics as you used for piecing the blocks; plan the design on graph paper, and work the corners out carefully so that they carry the design around well.

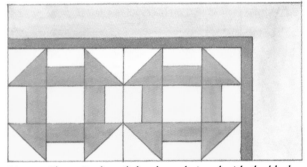

Here, a Churn Dash quilt has been designed with the blocks joining directly and edged with a narrow plain border.

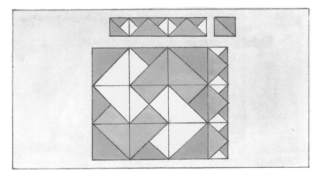

This border for a quilt made from Card Trick blocks uses smaller versions of the shapes in the blocks.

This pieced border for the same Churn Dash design uses one third of the basic block in reversed colors, with a corner made from a square divided into two triangles. The whole quilt top is then edged with a narrow border.

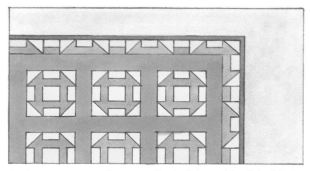

In this variation, sashing one third of the width of the block has been added between the blocks and around the edges. Because of the extra width produced by the sashing, a new element has been added to the patchwork border, repeating the rectangular shapes.

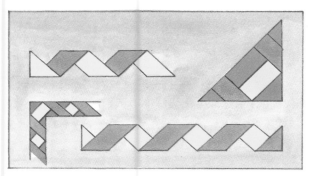

These examples show two variations of a pieced border known as Twisted Ribbon.

These pieced borders look very attractive around simple pieced quilts. Here they border Shoo Fly and Jack-in-the-Box blocks.

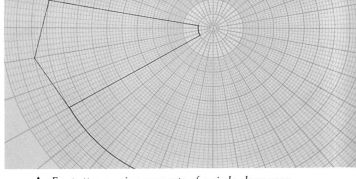

Many patchwork quilts are constructed from square blocks which are then joined, with or without separating strips of fabric (sashing, or setting strips – see page 38), to make the quilt top. Other designs are based on equilateral triangles, or circles divided into different segments, or other arrangements of shapes. Whatever basic design you choose, it is important to know how to draw accurate

Drawing designs

▲ *For patterns using segments of a circle, draw your design onto polar coordinate graph paper at the correct size, dividing the circle into the number of segments that you need. Mark the pieces you need for templates in the same way. If the graph paper is too small for a full pattern, use it to draw the correct angles in the center of the circle and simply extend the petal shapes out as far as needed.*

patterns at the right size so that you can calculate how much fabric you need and make perfect templates from your drawings. Once you have learned the basic principles, it is then very easy to change the size of a pattern or to change the design by altering a line or two.

Good-quality graph paper is essential for drafting patterns. It is available from stationery shops and art suppliers, and from quilting supply outlets, in both standard and metric measurements. A transparent plastic ruler is a great help, along with soft-to-medium pencils, a good pencil sharpener, and an eraser.

Graph paper makes it unnecessary to measure many of the angles, such as the angles of the triangles in a nine-patch design, but you will find polar coordinate graph paper or a compass and protractor (see page 27) useful for patterns such as Dresden Plate, which are formed from segments of a circle. Isometric graph paper (see page 26) is divided into equilateral triangles and is useful for patterns based on 60° angles and their multiples.

Once you have a full-size pattern, use it to cut pattern pieces for templates, or photocopy it and color in different versions to try out different color schemes and examine the effect of several blocks joined side by side.

ENLARGING AND REDUCING

When you are working with irregular patterns such as appliqué shapes you may want to enlarge or reduce them. To do this draw a grid of squares across the original pattern. Draw another grid containing the same number of squares, but making them larger or smaller depending on whether you want to enlarge or reduce. Now copy the main lines of the shape onto your grid; the squares will help you to see where the lines go.

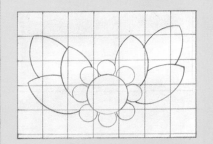

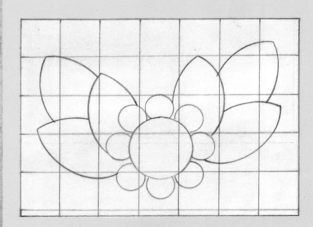

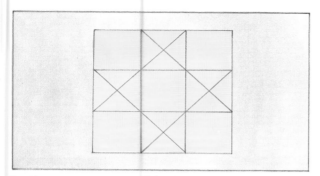

1 *Choose your pattern, and decide on the size of the block that you need. Your chosen size will depend on the kind of block you have chosen (see above), the number of blocks you need in your project, and the size of your finished project. For this example, we will use a 12 in. block and draw the Ohio Star design.*

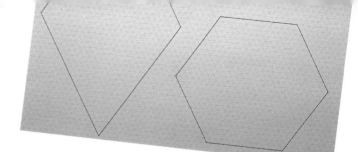

▲ *For patterns using 60° angles and their multiples, draw your design on isometric graph paper at the correct size and mark the pieces you need for templates in the same way.*

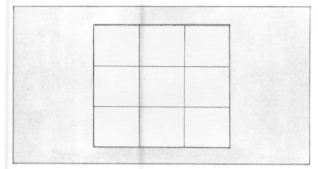

2 *Draw a 12 in. square on graph paper, and divide it into 9 equal squares, each measuring 4×4 in.*

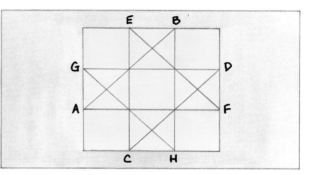

3 *Draw in the diagonals. In this example, they run from A-B, C-D, E-F and G-H. Draw each of the diagonals in one line for accuracy, even when they go across several squares.*

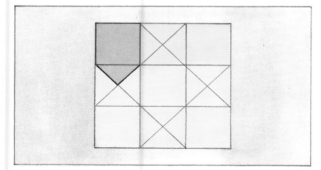

4 *Now work out how many individual template pieces you will need. If you look carefully at this block, you will see that although it is pieced from 21 different pieces of fabric, only two shapes are used – the 3 in. square, and the right-angled triangle which makes up a quarter of it.*

5 *Use a craft knife to cut out one example of each piece needed. If you don't want to spoil your full-size drawing make careful copies of the pieces needed on a separate piece of graph paper and cut them out. You now have accurate guides which you can use for making templates.*

Commercial templates are available for most patchwork designs, but it's far more satisfying and of course cheaper to make your own. Also, if you know the principles of making templates, you will be able to copy designs that you see, such as those in antique quilts.

If you only intend to use a particular template a few times, thin cardboard is adequate. After about 20 tracings cardboard tem-

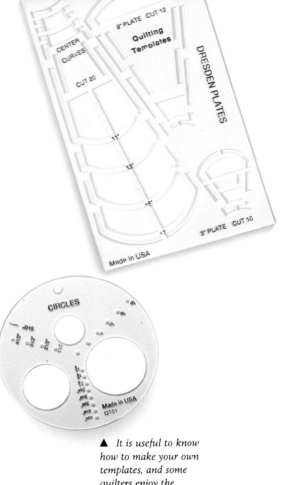

Making templates

plates start to become worn and are therefore inaccurate. The most durable materials are metal and plastic; for home use, plastic is better as it can be cut much more easily. Special template plastic, which is transparent and easy to cut and mark, is readily available from art, craft, and quilting suppliers.

If you are making templates for hand-pieced work (see page 46, Piecing), you should make them the exact size of the finished piece – i.e., without seam allowances. However, if you are making templates for machine piecing, you should include the seam allowances on your final template.

▲ *It is useful to know how to make your own templates, and some quilters enjoy the challenge. Nowadays, however, ready made templates are available in a wide range of shapes and sizes.*

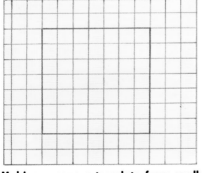

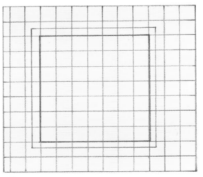

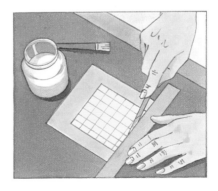

Making a square template from cardboard

1 *Draw a square of the required size on graph paper. Use a very sharp pencil so that the shape isn't distorted.*

2 *If you are sewing by hand, cut along the marked lines. If you are sewing by machine, add ¼ in. all around and cut along the outer line.*

3 *Glue the paper square face up on a piece of cardboard, then cut the card around the edges of the paper, using a steel ruler and craft knife for accuracy.*

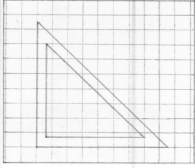
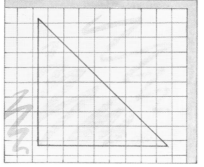
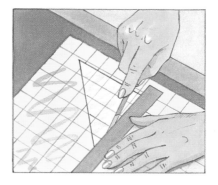

Making a triangular template using template plastic

1 *Draw a triangle of the required size on graph paper. Add seam allowances if necessary.*

2 *Place the plastic over the graph paper and trace the shape. If you have a specialized ruler for cutting triangles (see page 26, Equipment), you can draw onto the plastic.*

3 *Using a craft knife and a steel ruler, cut out the template. Keep your fingers away from the cutting edge.*

Making appliqué templates

1 *Draw or trace the shape onto paper, cardboard, or template plastic. If you are using a shape that isn't the right size, follow the instructions on page 40 for enlarging or reducing.*

2 *Add ¼ in. seam allowance around all the edges of the shape.*

3 *If you are using paper, glue it on cardboard, then cut around the outside line; if you are using template plastic, simply cut around the outside line.*

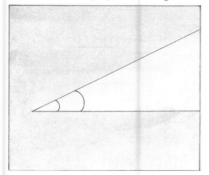
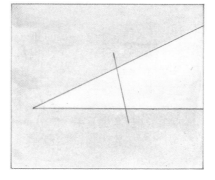
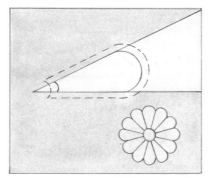

Making a Dresden Plate template

1 *Draw two straight lines at an angle to each other. The angle will be 360° divided by the number of petals that you want; a 12-petal design needs an angle of 30° (360÷12).*

2 *From the point, measure out the same distance along both lines. The distance will be half the diameter of the design, so for an 8 in. plate, measure 4 in. from the corner.*

3 *Join the two marks with a faint line, then draw in a point or a curve depending on the shape you want. Draw an inner curve a short way in from the angle. Add ¼ in. seam allowance, and cut the shape out.*

43

The most important thing to remember when you are cutting your fabric into pieces for patchwork is *accuracy*. If your patches aren't cut accurately, they won't fit together properly. The finished piecing may be too large or too small if you have cut the pieces with too much or too little seam allowance.

Make sure that your templates are very precise, checking them against your full-size

Cutting fabrics

pattern. Always use a very sharp pencil for marking your fabric, pressing it tightly against the template so that your line is accurate. A small piece of sandpaper glued to the back of your template will stop it from moving out of position while you are marking – this is also a useful trick if you are using a rotary cutter. Cut exactly on the line you have drawn, not either outside it or inside it.

Before you do any cutting, make sure that you have prepared your fabric by washing, pressing, and straightening any raw edges, and cutting off the selvages (this is because the selvage is more tightly woven than other areas and therefore pulls the fabric slightly). If you are a beginner, you may prefer to mark and cut one piece of fabric at a time, but experienced quilters cut several layers at once if they are using scissors, and up to eight thicknesses of fabric using a rotary cutter.

If you prefer to use scissors, choose a very sharp pair of dressmaking scissors and keep them only for cutting fabric. Never cut paper or cardboard with them; the fibers lie in numerous different directions and blunt the blades very quickly. If you are using a rotary cutter, you will also need a cutting mat and a quilter's transparent ruler (see page 26). Always sheath the blade of a rotary cutter after use; the blade is very sharp.

ESTIMATING YARDAGES

For an accurate estimate, make a chart with a column for each of your chosen fabrics as the example shown here. Down the left-hand side, list each piece needed for the patchwork, sashing, borders, and backing. Now draw each of these requirements on graph paper (you don't need to draw all 96, of course; just draw two or four and then multiply). Add up all your requirements for each fabric, and you will have exact yardage requirements. It is, however, worth adding a little extra as a safety margin in case you cut some pieces wrong.

Pieces Required	Fabric 1	Fabric 2	Fabric 3	Fabric 4	Fabric 5	Fabric 6
Border 82" x 4" 180 x 10cm		2				
Border 62" x 4" 150 x 10cm		2				
Sashing 82" x 2" 180 x 5cm			3			
Sashing 2" x 12" 5 x 30cm			20			
Square 4" 10cm	24					
Rectangle 2" x 4" 5 x 10cm	96			96		
Triangle 4" 10cm	96				96	
Backing 62" x 90" 150 x 228cm						1

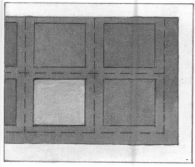

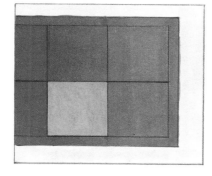

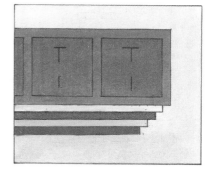

Cutting with scissors

1 *For hand piecing, position your template on the fabric and draw around it. Mark a ¼ in. seam allowance for each piece and re-position the template.*

2 *For machine piecing, butt the edges of the templates right up to each other and cut along the solid lines, as the seam allowances are included in the templates.*

3 *If you want to cut more than one layer at a time, mark one layer and stack it on top of two or three other pieces. Pin, then cut through all the layers together.*

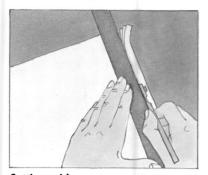

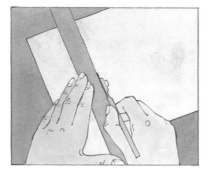

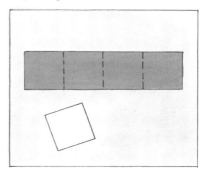

Cutting with a rotary cutter

1 *To minimize the number of cuts needed, the fabric is first cut into strips. Fold in half lengthwise twice. With a transparent ruler held at right angles to the fold, trim the raw edges.*

2 *Turn the fabric around so that the layers are to the right of the ruler (reverse if you are left-handed). Line up the ruler along the width needed for your strips and cut along the edge.*

3 *Now use your templates or special cutting rulers to cut the strips into squares, rectangles, triangles, or parallelograms, as needed.*

GENERAL CUTTING PRINCIPLES

Always mark, or allow for, the largest pieces on your fabric first. So, for instance, mark borders, sashing, and large pattern pieces on your fabric before cutting lots of small elements – otherwise, you may find that the areas you have left are not the right shape for your larger pieces. Make sure that the grain lines of your fabric are square, and position your templates so that the grain line arrow is straight along the grain. Always mark on the back of your fabrics.

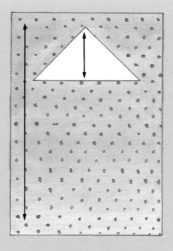

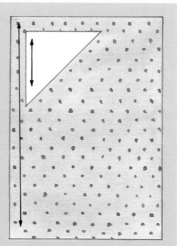

Once you have chosen the fabrics for each part of your patchwork, you need to decide how you are going to join the patches. Piecing may be done by hand or machine, and there are advantages to both methods.

If you decide to stitch by hand, you will be able to carry your work with you wherever you go. It will be slower, but you will often find a few moments when you can sew a few patches

Piecing

together. It is also easier to "fudge" a slightly inaccurate seam by hand and make seams meet where they should.

Much more accuracy is needed when you are stitching by machine, but of course it is much faster. More and more quilters are using their machines for piecing – not to mention quilting (see page 56) and embroidery embellishment. In fact, machine piecing has been used for quilts for about 100 years. A design with lots of small pieces is sometimes easier to piece by hand, but the choice is yours entirely.

Before using your machine for piecing, it is a good idea to use a spare piece of fabric to practice stitching an accurate $\frac{1}{4}$ in. seam. Make several parallel rows, using the pressure foot as a guide for spacing them. Or, place a length of masking tape on the throat plate of your machine exactly $\frac{1}{4}$ in. from the needle and use this as your guide.

Each seam should be pressed after it is stitched. The general rule is to press the seam allowance toward the darker fabric; this will stop the extra fabric from showing through lighter patches. With complex patterns where several seams join in one place, you may end up with the bulk of several seam allowances all pressed toward the same piece of fabric; if this happens, you can trim away some of the fabric, or press one seam in a different direction.

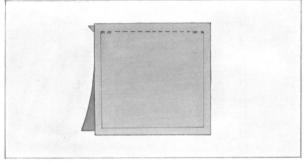

Pieced quilt with Flying Geese borders

Piecing by hand
Your pieces will have been cut with the stitching lines marked (see page 42). Pin the two pieces right sides together and sew with small running stitches along the stitching lines, beginning and ending with a few backstitches for extra strength.

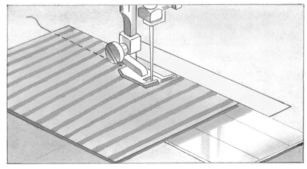

Piecing by machine
Your patches will have been cut with the seam allowance added and with no stitching lines marked. Pin the two pieces right sides together and sew $\frac{1}{4}$ in. away from the edge.

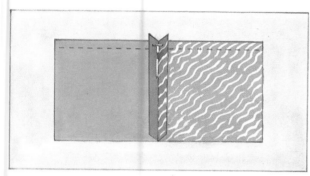

Matching seams

When you need to match the seams of two composite patches, put the fabrics together and then pin across the seam allowances. If you're careful, you should be able to sew across the pin while it is still in place.

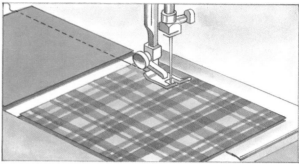

Assembly-line method

To save time when you are sewing several sets of patches, put them together in pairs, then stitch them on the machine one after another, without breaking the thread between each pair. When all the seams have been stitched, cut between the pairs.

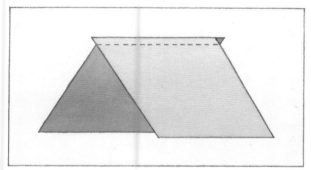

Offset seams

If a seam is between two angled pieces, position them right sides together so that the ends of the seam allowances, rather than the ends of the patches themselves, are aligned.

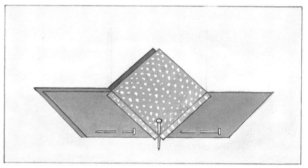

Joining multiple seams

To get an exact alignment, put a pin through one patch where the seams join, then push it through the seam in the other patch, right sides together. Pin the two patches across the seam allowances, then remove the first pin.

PIECING CURVED SEAMS

Mark the center of each seam with a pin or a notch. Match the pins or the notches at the center, right sides together, and pin in position, then pin the ends of the seams. Ease the seam allowances together evenly, pinning at right angles as you go.

Stitch along the seam line by hand or machine, then remove the pins and press the seam allowance toward the darker side. If the seam allowance doesn't lie flat, clip it slightly so that it can be pressed into position.

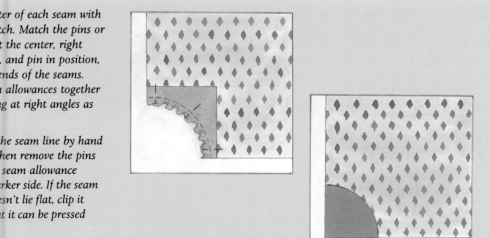

There are several basic ways of marking quilting patterns. Each method has its pros and cons, and some are more suitable for certain fabrics or for certain tasks than others; experiment with the methods shown here and see which ones you find most comfortable.

For making the actual marks on your fabric you can use several different tools. An ordinary medium-hard pencil, sharpened to a

Marking quilting patterns

good point, will make clear marks, but won't necessarily wash out, so only use this method if you are confident that your stitching will cover all of the pencil marks – for instance, if you are quilting a particular area with chain stitch. Pens with water-soluble ink, which produce strong marks that disappear when wetted, can be extremely useful. Pens with fading ink also produce strong marks which fade sometimes within a few hours, so don't mark a large area at one time! Fading-ink pens are useful if you don't want to have to wet the finished item. Colored pencils are often ideal for marking solid fabrics; choose a shade just slightly darker than your fabric and sharpen it to a good point. You will find that the marks are unnoticeable when the quilting is complete. Iron-on transfers and transfer pencils make a strong mark that doesn't usually wash out, so again make sure that your stitching will cover the line – some quilting patterns use a silver-gray transfer line, which is less noticeable. For marking patterns on stretched plain quilt tops, some people like to use a blunt needle or a silverpoint pencil; these make fine indented lines which, again, are unnoticeable when the quilting is complete.

▼ **A marked quilt pattern**
This is a pattern for a wholecloth pillow cover, marked on the fabric with water-soluble ink to produce a strong line.

Tracing around templates
If you are quilting a pattern without any internal lines, or if you have a template with the internal lines cut out, you can simply trace around the shape using pencil or colored pencil, soluble or fading ink, or a blunt needle or silverpoint pencil.

Tracing through fabric

When your fabric is very pale or very fine, you may be able to trace through it. Lay your pattern face-up on a flat surface, place your fabric, right side up, on top, and trace the pattern using pencil or colored pencil, or soluble or fading ink (see page 29).

Lightbox

If you have access to a designer's lightbox, it can be used to make a medium-shade fabric more transparent so that you can trace through it. Lay the pattern on the lightbox with the fabric right side up on top, and trace the pattern.

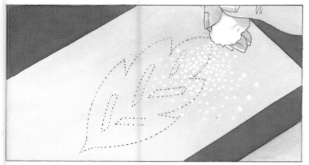

Prick and pounce

This method is useful for dark fabrics. Perforate your pattern along all the lines with a pin or machine stitching, lay it on top of your fabric and dust chalk, or talcum powder through the holes with a cotton ball.

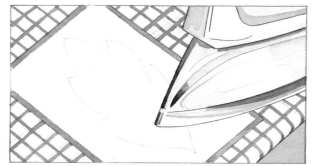

Iron-on transfers

Iron-on transfers are available for some patterns, and you can also buy transfer pencils for drawing your own design on paper. Lay the transfer face down on the right side of the fabric, then press with a warm iron. Remember that the design will be reversed.

Dressmaker's carbon paper

This is available in several different colors, so you can choose a color that will work well with your fabric. Lay the carbon paper face down on the right side of your fabric and place your pattern on top; run a dressmaker's tracing wheel over all the lines of the pattern.

Blunt needle or silverpoint

This method works best on solid-colored fabrics that have already been stretched taut on a frame. Lay your template down on the right side of your fabric and trace around all the lines with the blunt needle or silverpoint, which will make an indented line on the fabric.

Quilted border designs add interest to a quilt top. They can be added to plain sashings and fabric borders (see page 152), or stitched around the edges of wholecloth projects (see page 100) to provide visual contrast and interest. In many ways working a border design is similar to working with other quilted designs such as individual medallions or background textures; they are marked onto the fabric using

Adding quilted borders

A simple but effective example of a quilted border

the same methods (see page 48), and stitched in the same way by hand or machine (see page 56). However, quilted border designs present some extra challenges to the quilter, and you need to plan your border pattern carefully, watching out for some of the common pitfalls.

The first task is to choose your border pattern; you may decide to pick out some elements from your pieced or quilted center design, such as flower shapes or diamonds, and make a border using those, or you may choose a pattern that contrasts. Most border patterns are made of repeating shapes, and you need to choose a pattern that will fill your border area with whole repeats. If the measurement doesn't quite work out, you may find that you can adjust it by enlarging or reducing the border pattern slightly.

Continuing the border pattern around the corners of the quilt can be a little tricky. Some commercial quilting patterns for borders also include extra templates for corners. If you are making up your own border, you may need to make some sketches first to experiment with different ways of carrying the pattern around the corner. If it proves too difficult, you can finish the edges of the border neatly on each side of the corner and fill the corner itself with a complementary motif or medallion.

The notch method

1 *This method will help you to mark even borders for twisted designs such as cables, using just one small template. Draw your chosen pattern full-size very accurately onto paper; draw several repeats of the basic shape so that you can see exactly where each repeat begins and ends.*

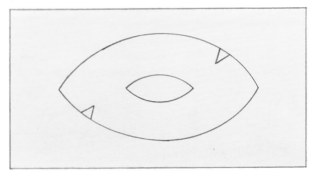

2 *Using either template plastic or sturdy cardboard (see page 42) so that you have a durable surface for marking against, cut the basic template for one repeat of your chosen pattern. Cut or mark a notch on each side of the shape where the next repeat begins.*

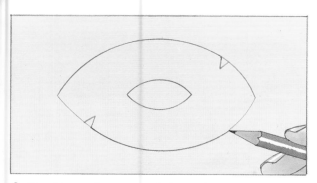

3 *Use this template as a guide for marking your fabric. Mark around the long outside edges between the tips of the template and the notches. Mark the inside edge all around.*

4 *Move the template along so that the tips and notches align with the previous marks, and mark the next pattern repeat in the same way. Continue this process until the border is as long as you need it.*

Working with corners

1 *If you have a matching corner template, mark it first in one corner and then work outward along each side to the other three corners.*

2 *If you don't want to take the border around the corner, finish off the border pattern neatly on each side of the corner and fill the space with a complementary motif.*

Working with one-way patterns

1 *If you are working with a pattern which moves in one direction, for instance a feathered design or a twisted cable, you may want the pattern going in the same direction all the way around the quilt border.*

2 *If you prefer the quilt design to be symmetrical, work a motif or medallion in the center of the side of the quilt and mark the border design outward from this, reversing the template so that each section goes in a different direction. Do the same on the other sides of the quilt.*

Before a block, or a whole quilt top, is quilted, a "sandwich" is made of the top fabric, a padded filling known as batting, and a backing fabric. Batting comes in several thicknesses and is made from several different fibers. Polyester is the most popular. It is light, easy to stitch, and has the great advantage of being washable. It comes in several different thicknesses, which are usually described by weight. The most

Batting and backing

▲ *These examples show the effects of different weights of batting; the same design has been quilted on the same fabric using 2 oz., 4 oz. and 6 oz. batting.*

common weights are 2 oz. (thin), 4 oz. (medium), 6 oz. (thick) and 8 oz. (extra-thick). If you want something that doesn't quite fall into any of these categories it is possible to combine two weights, or to separate the layers of batting. Dark-colored polyester batting can be used behind dark fabrics.

In the past, the type of batting used generally depended on what material was most readily available in that particular region; so, for example, North American quilters generally used cotton whereas British quilters tended to use wool. In both countries, silk batting was expensive, and kept for very special items. These older types of batting are becoming popular again for specialized projects; some quilters choose cotton or wool batting when they want a more compact filling for a quilted item, or use a silk batting to line a silk garment. When you are making a quilted garment, you don't want a lot of bulk, so flatter batting such as flannelette can be useful. Check the washing instructions on the batting before you use it, as many silk, cotton and wool battings can't be machine-washed.

If you don't want your quilting stitches to show on the back of the quilt, use a piece of cheesecloth or a similar fabric as an inner backing while you are quilting, and then attach the final backing fabric.

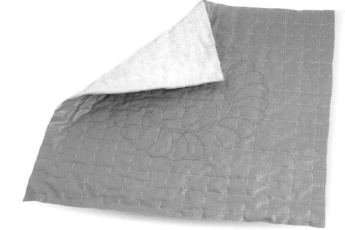

▲ *This is a wholecloth pillow ready for quilting; the fabric has been marked with the quilting pattern and then sandwiched together with batting and cheesecloth.*

The quilts below show how different backing fabrics work. The one on the left clearly shows the outlines of the quilting

patterns, while the backing fabric on the right almost camouflages the stitching.

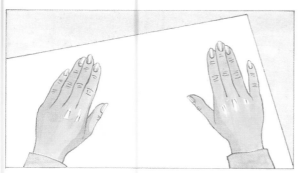

1 *To prepare a piece of fabric for quilting, place the ironed backing fabric right side down on a flat surface and smooth it out. If you are quilting a particularly large item, you may need to work on the floor.*

2 *Place the batting on top of the backing fabric and smooth out any creases. Place the fabric to be quilted right side up on top of the batting.*

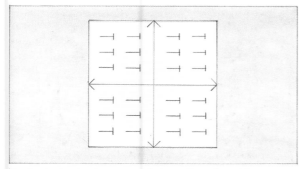

3 *Beginning in the center of the quilt and working out to the edges, pin through all three layers in rows spaced approximately 3 in. apart.*

4 *Baste through all three layers in parallel horizontal rows, about 2 in. apart. Then baste even rows of stitches vertically, forming a regular grid of basting across the sandwich of fabrics. This will keep the layers from moving around while you are quilting. Remove the pins.*

SAFETY-PIN METHOD

Stitching an even grid of basting can be time-consuming, and some quilters prefer quicker ways of securing their work. If you are in a hurry, try this method: make the sandwich of backing, batting, and top fabric as above, then secure the three layers together with large safety pins at regular intervals.

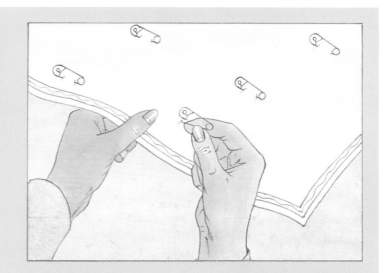

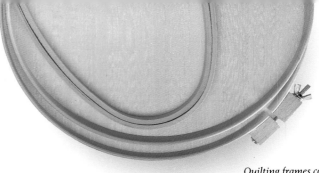

When you are quilting by hand or machine, each quilting stitch introduces tension into the work because you are pulling three layers together – the quilt top, the batting, and the backing. This process produces the slightly gathered effect which gives quilting its attractive texture, but the tension can cause the quilt top to become distorted. To prevent this problem from occurring, handwork is stretched

Quilting frames come in a variety of shapes and sizes

Using a quilting frame

fairly taut while it is being quilted; if your project is small, you may not need to stretch it, but if it is medium-sized or large, you will need some kind of frame.

Hand-held frames don't have any extra means of support and are used for stretching small areas of a quilt at a time. Hand-held frames can be circular or oval; they look like large embroidery frames and are used in the same way, catching the fabric sandwich between an inner and an outer ring.

Floor-standing frames are similar to hand-held frames, but you don't need to support them in your lap or on the edge of a table; they come with their own stands.

Full-size frames are large, free-standing frames which are used for stretching the entire quilt at once. Many quilting groups in the past used flat frames, which made the whole quilt top accessible so that it could be worked on by many quilters simultaneously. These days, few people have sufficient space, so they use a rolling frame, an adaptation of the same principle. The quilt top is attached to two rollers, and the bulk of the quilt is rolled up onto them, leaving an area exposed for quilting.

When you are quilting by machine, it is difficult to stretch your quilt top in the same way, since few frames will fit under the arm of the machine. If you have an oval frame, it may be useful for stretching machine quilting; if not, use your hands to spread the fabric evenly.

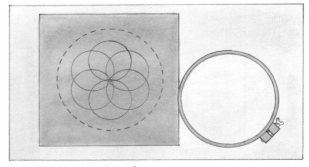

How to use a quilting hoop
1 *Separate the inner and outer hoops of a hand-held or floor-standing frame, and lay your basted quilt top smoothly across the top of the inner hoop.*

2 *Lay the outer hoop over the top layer of fabric so that it catches the quilt top between the two hoops; tighten the tension screw at the side so that the fabric is held firmly between the two rings.*

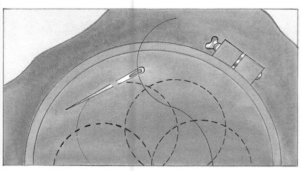

3 Quilt the area within the hoop, then move the hoop to the adjoining part of the quilt; continue in this way until you have completed the quilting.

4 If you find it difficult to quilt the corner, baste some extra fabric to the edges so that you can stretch it in the frame. When the quilting is complete, remove the extra fabric.

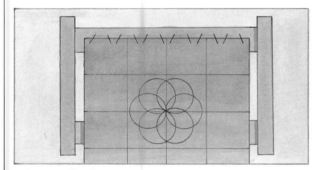

Using a roller frame
1 Lay your quilt top right side up over the frame so that the longer sides are parallel with the flat stretchers at the sides of the frame. Baste the shorter sides of the quilt to the tapes on the rollers.

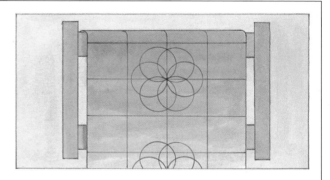

2 Turn the roller at one end so that it takes up the bulk of the quilt, leaving one end of the quilt top stretched across the frame. Secure the rollers to maintain an even tension.

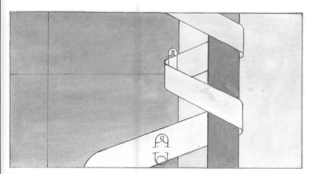

3 Stretch the sides of the quilt top by winding tape around the stretchers and pinning it in place on the quilt top with large safety pins.

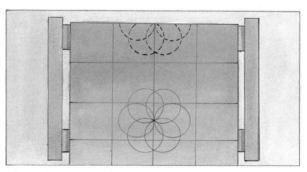

4 Quilt the exposed area of quilt top, then unpin the tape and loosen the rollers. Rewind the rollers until a fresh piece of quilt top appears for stitching, then secure and quilt it in the same way.

Quilting is the stitching you work through the layers of quilt top, batting, and backing fabric. The quilting is functional in that it holds the three layers together, but it is also decorative; as you stitch, you form a textured pattern on the quilt top which enhances your design.

It is possible to work quilting by hand or by machine. Many traditionalists always quilt their quilt tops by hand even if they have pieced

Quilting

them by machine, but there is no reason at all why you shouldn't quilt by machine if you want to. Your stitching will show more, but that isn't necessarily a disadvantage; also, quilting by machine is quicker. Don't worry about how many stitches there are to an inch, but practice working stitches of uniform size and tension and you will produce good results. If you are working a long chain or cable design by hand, you may find it useful to work your way along each portion of the pattern using a separate needle and thread for each line, rather than stitching one whole line first and then coming back to do the next one; this helps to keep the tension even.

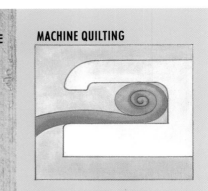

TIP

MACHINE QUILTING

For large items, roll the quilt so that it will fit into the space under the machine's arm. Some quilters use bicycle clips to hold the roll.

HAND QUILTING

Use a thimble or thumble (see page 26) on your stitching hand, and wind a piece of masking tape around whichever finger you use under the quilt; this will help you to guide the needle tip back up without pricking your finger.

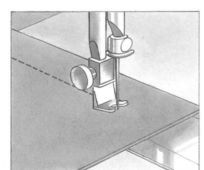

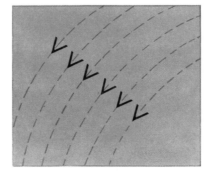

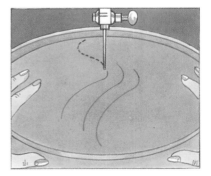

Quilting by machine

1 *Set your machine for a fairly long straight stitch, and stitch along the stitching line. To change direction, stop with the needle down, then lift the foot and pivot the fabric.*

2 *If you are quilting long parallel lines, stitch each row in the same direction; otherwise, the fabric may show slight puckering marks.*

3 *For quilting intricate designs, attach a darning or embroidery foot and lower the feed dog. Use either an embroidery frame or your hands to keep the fabric stretched, and move it freely around.*

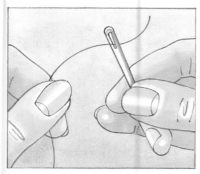
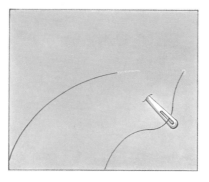
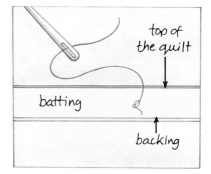

Quilting by hand

1 Cut a length of thread about 18 in. long, and thread one end through the eye of your quilting needle. Tie a small knot at the longer end of your thread.

2 Put the needle into the fabric, on the right side, about 1 in. away from the beginning of your quilting line.

3 Bring your needle up at the beginning of the stitching line and pull gently. The knot at the end of the thread will pop down under the surface fabric and remain hidden from view.

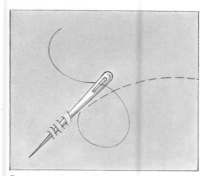
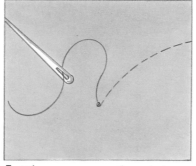
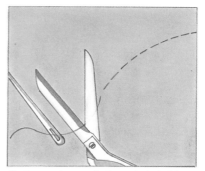

4 Sew with small, even running stitches, making sure that you go through all the layers of the quilt. Take several stitches at a time on your needle before you pull it through.

5 When you are near the end of your thread, wind it around the needle twice and draw the knot close to the fabric.

6 Insert the needle into the stitching line, making sure that you draw the knot down into the batting. Then pull the needle back through the fabric about 1 in. from the end of the stitching and cut the thread.

PROS AND CONS

Machine quilting

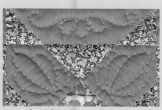

Hand quilting

Machine quilting: pros
It is very quick, so your project takes shape rapidly. It is useful for large, regular patterns. Specialized accessories such as quilting guides make the stitching very accurate. The stitching is always even.

Machine quilting: cons
You can't carry your work with you. It is harder to keep layers wrinkle-free. The stitching shows more on the right side. Large quilts are difficult to manipulate under the arm of the machine.

Hand quilting: pros
It is attractive because the stitching shows less. It is easier to "fudge" difficult areas of a design. It creates a soothing rhythm. You can carry small pieces with you to stitch.

Hand quilting: cons
It is very time-consuming. It requires short lengths (18 inches) of thread, so you are constantly rethreading needles. Long sessions lead to sore hands, pricked fingers, and tired eyes.

57

If you are quilting patchwork or appliqué designs, you can often use the patchwork or appliqué patterns themselves as starting points for your quilting design. The seam lines on pieced work, and the edges of appliqué pieces, can be followed or echoed by your lines of stitching. Or, if you prefer, you can quilt a traditional or modern design over the top of the pieced work, ignoring the lines made by the

Different ways of quilting blocks

fabric patches, or combine the two techniques, perhaps by quilting small motifs inside some of the patches. Here you can see several ways of quilting the same pieced block, the Churn Dash; all of these methods can be done by hand or by machine.

On this quilt, the shapes of the fabric patches have been used to suggest shapes for quilted patterns and spirals. Along the border, triangles and points have been built up with rows of quilting stitches at different angles.

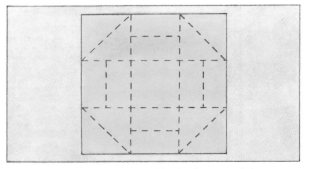

Quilting "in the ditch" is probably the fastest and the simplest method of quilting patchwork: stitch just next to the seam, on the side away from the seam allowance.

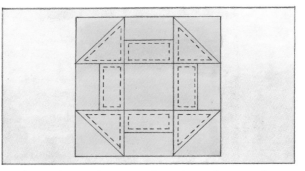

Outline quilting is done on each patch: stitch a row of quilting stitches ¹/₄ in. inside each patch, being careful to avoid the seam allowance.

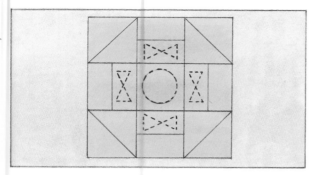

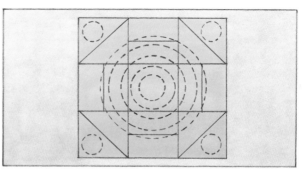

On this block, small individual motifs have been quilted inside some of the patches. This method can be combined very effectively with quilting in the ditch.

Here, the lines of the patchwork design have been ignored completely, and the whole block has been quilted over with concentric circles, adding tiny circles in the corners.

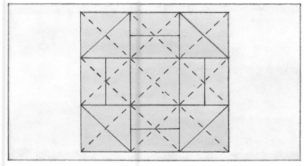

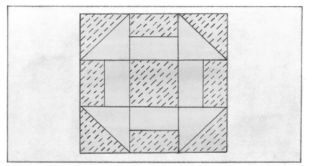

Here, the corners of the patchwork pieces have been used as guides for straight lines of quilting intersecting at the centers of the pieces.

This design uses straight lines of quilting stitched diagonally across the outside and central fabric pieces and keeping the same direction each time.

QUILTING APPLIQUE BLOCKS

Hawaiian quilts often use a method known as "echo quilting," where rows of quilting $\frac{1}{4}$ in. apart follow the outlines of the appliquéd design, filling in the spaces with flowing lines.

Background textures are popular for adding visual interest to appliqué blocks and quilt tops. The first line of quilting is worked close to the edge of the appliqué design or $\frac{1}{4}$ in. outside it; then the background fabric is quilted with a design to throw the appliqué into relief.

Once your quilt top has been quilted, the edges must be finished, and usually some kind of binding is used. For bed quilts, which will be subjected to quite a bit of wear, a good straight binding in a hard-wearing fabric is acceptable, but the ideal edging is bias binding – even better, a double thickness of bias binding. The first part of a quilt to show wear is usually the edge. If a straight binding is used,

Finishing quilts

the single thread at the outside edge can disintegrate, making it necessary to replace the binding. Bias edges are composed of many threads criss-crossing around the whole perimeter of the quilt, so they are far less likely to wear out quickly. A bias binding is also quite elastic and can be coaxed along curves and around corners.

The fabric you choose for your binding should coordinate with the fabrics in the quilt, and although bias binding can be bought in several widths, it is usually better to make your own. Cutting bias strips takes a great deal of fabric, and you will need to allow for this when you are buying the fabrics for a quilt. If you are binding a large quilt, sheeting is strong and comes in very wide widths, so it is useful for straight and bias bindings. A pieced binding can be made using all the fabrics from the quilt; this is particularly effective if your quilt top has a wide plain border or sashing.

Many quilters bind their quilts by using either the backing or the quilt top to cover the raw edges. If you decide to do this, remember to make the backing or the quilt top about 1 in. wider all around than the finished size of the quilt. The edges of the quilt are then pressed under, turned to the front or back of the quilt as appropriate, and stitched down. An even simpler way of finishing a quilt top is to trim away about ¼ in. of the batting, turn in the edges of the quilt front and back, and stitch them together close to the edge.

A well-made quilt is a work of art to be proud of, so you might think about finishing it off with your name or initials, as artists do. Or, if it's intended as a gift, embroider the name of the recipient. This is a "friendship quilt," with the names commemorating two women's shared experiences.

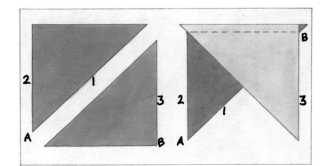

Making a continuous bias strip

1 *Take 1¼ yd. of 45 in. wide fabric. Remove the selvages and press the fabric. Fold the square across the diagonal and cut; you now have two large triangles. With the right sides together, place two of the short edges together as shown and stitch a ¼ in. seam by machine.*

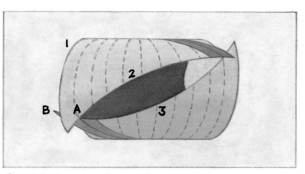

2 *Open out the piece and press the seam open; you now have a parallelogram. Mark the desired width of your strips, allowing for turning under the edges.*

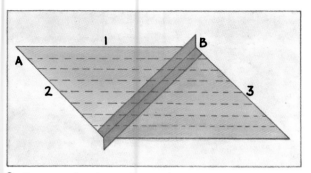

3 *With the right sides together, join side 2 to side 3, matching points A and B. Stitch a ¼ in. seam to form a tube; the end of side 3 will extend slightly at the end of the tube.*

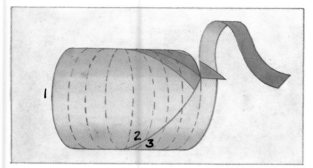

4 *Using the lines as a guide, cut around the tube until you reach the end. You will now have a long length of bias binding.*

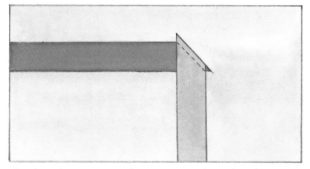

5 *If you have to join a bias strip, put the right sides together as shown and stitch a narrow seam either by hand or by machine.*

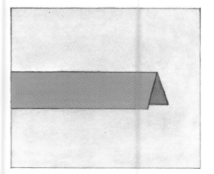

Making a straight binding

1 *Cut two strips 2½ in. wide by the length of the quilt, and two strips 2½ in. wide by the width of the quilt plus 1 in. Fold the strips in half lengthwise and press the fold.*

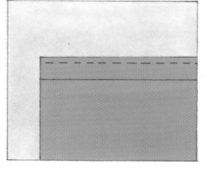

2 *Lay the longer strips face down along the longer edges of the quilt top; pin and sew them in position about ¼ in. from the edges.*

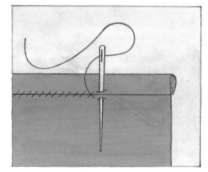

3 *Turn the strips over to the back of the quilt and turn under the raw edges; stitch into position by hand. Finish the other edges of the quilt the same way.*

3

The sampler quilt

Now that you are familiar with the basic principles of making a quilt, it's time to put your knowledge into practice. This section will take you through all the steps necessary for making a sampler quilt, from cutting and piecing to binding the edges of your finished quilt. As you work your way through each lesson, you will be increasing your practical understanding of the piecing, quilting, and

Introduction to the sampler quilt

▼ *These are swatches of the fabrics used in the sampler quilt. To make it easier to identify which fabric is being used in each part, every one has been given a letter. We have also given a brief description of the fabrics, all of which are medium-weight 100% cotton.*

finishing techniques. We have chosen traditional blocks and quilting designs so that once you have finished the sampler quilt, you will have mastered most of the basic techniques needed for producing a wide variety of other traditional quilt designs.

In each lesson, you will find cross-references to the relevant pages in the Pattern Library in case you want to substitute one design for another. Remember that yardages of the different fabrics may need to be adjusted if you decide to alter the blocks or borders significantly.

All of the quilting on the sampler quilt can be done by hand or by machine, so you can choose the method which suits you best – or use a mixture of the two methods.

To complement the traditional design of the sampler quilt, we have chosen a traditional color scheme of pinky reds, gray greens, and creams. You may decide to choose a totally different color scheme. If so, choose fabrics that have similar values (see page 32) to the ones shown here (so, for instance, your new fabric A would be dark, while your new fabric B would be a lighter version of the same color). Simply substitute the appropriate fabric each time the relevant letter is mentioned.

Before you start the quilt, wash your fabrics (see page 30) to check that they are color-fast and to pre-shrink them. If necessary, pull the fabrics to straighten the grain; then press them so that they are ready to be cut.

Fabric A
Dark pink background with a small, light green flower-sprig pattern.

Fabric B
Light pink background with a small all-over pattern in white.

Fabric C
Solid dark green.

Fabric D
Light green background with small flower-sprig design in pink.

Fabric E
Solid medium green.

Fabric F
Solid light-to-medium pink.

Fabric G
Unbleached muslin.

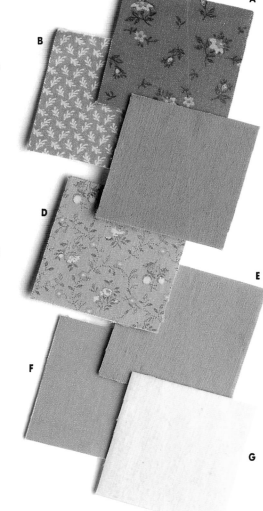

The nine blocks of the sampler quilt have been numbered for ease of reference and to correspond with the templates on pages 66-71.

1 *The Four-patch block (see page 72)*

9 *The Reverse Appliqué block (see page 88)*

3 *The Sugar Bowl block (see page 76)*

Sashing (see 10; page 90)

Pieced border (see 11; page 92)

Binding (see 14; page 98)

7 *The Star block (see page 84)*

8 *The Flying Geese block (see page 86)*

4 *The Appliqué block (see page 78)*

6 *The Strip-pieced block (see page 82)*

5 *The Log Cabin block (see page 80)*

Backing

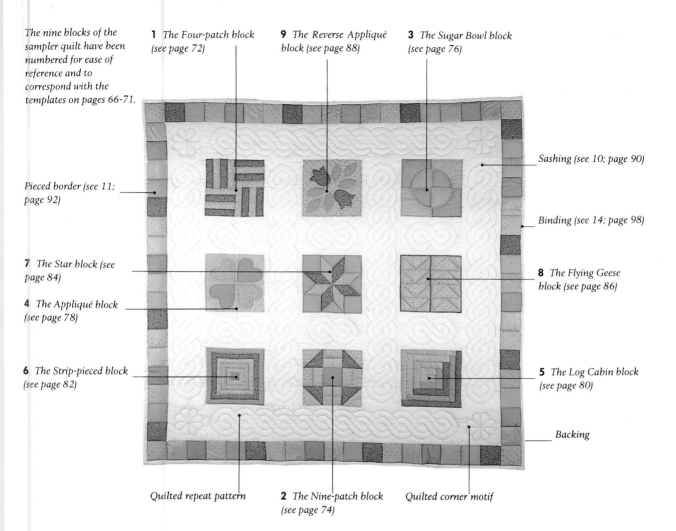

Quilted repeat pattern

2 *The Nine-patch block (see page 74)*

Quilted corner motif

MATERIALS REQUIRED

To make the sampler quilt, you will need the amounts given; all of the fabrics are 60 in. wide. The yardages given here should give you slightly more than you need, to allow for occasional accidents while marking or cutting; if you have large pieces left over, you could always make a pillow cover or two to go with the quilt.

Fabric A: $^3/_4$ yard

Fabric B: $^3/_4$ yard

Fabric C: $^3/_4$ yard

Fabric D: $^3/_4$ yard

Fabric E: $^3/_4$ yard

Fabric F: $^3/_4$ yard

Fabric G: 8 yards

You will also need:

2 spools of ordinary sewing thread in ecru

1 piece of medium-weight batting 78×78 in

Quilting thread in green, pink and ecru if you are quilting by hand, or sewing thread in your chosen colors if you are quilting by machine

1 water-soluble marking pen

Quilting needle if you are quilting by hand

A rotary cutter and cutting board

See pages 26-29 for general equipment for making templates, cutting, and sewing

On these and the following pages you will find all the templates that you will need for the pieced blocks and the quilting patterns that make up the sampler quilt. All of the templates are full-size, so copy each of them carefully onto paper, cardboard, or template plastic (see page 42) and use them as cutting guides. All the seam allowances are included and are ¼ in. unless indicated otherwise. The arrows on

Sampler quilt templates

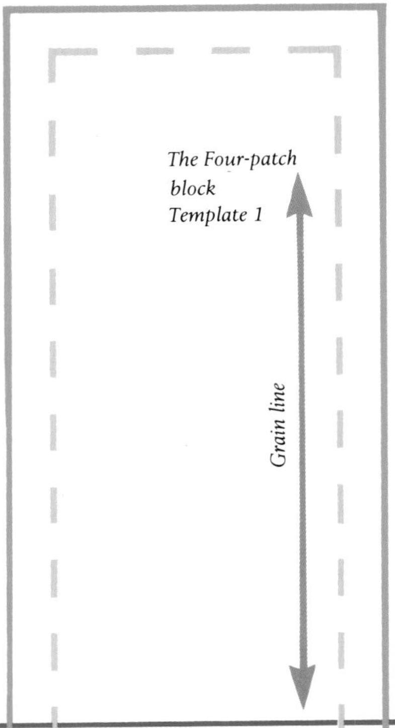

SAMPLER QUILT

some templates mark the straight grain of the fabric; the arrows should be lined up with either the warp or the weft threads on your fabrics. The blocks which don't require templates have full instructions in the appropriate lesson.

The Four-patch block Template 1

Grain line

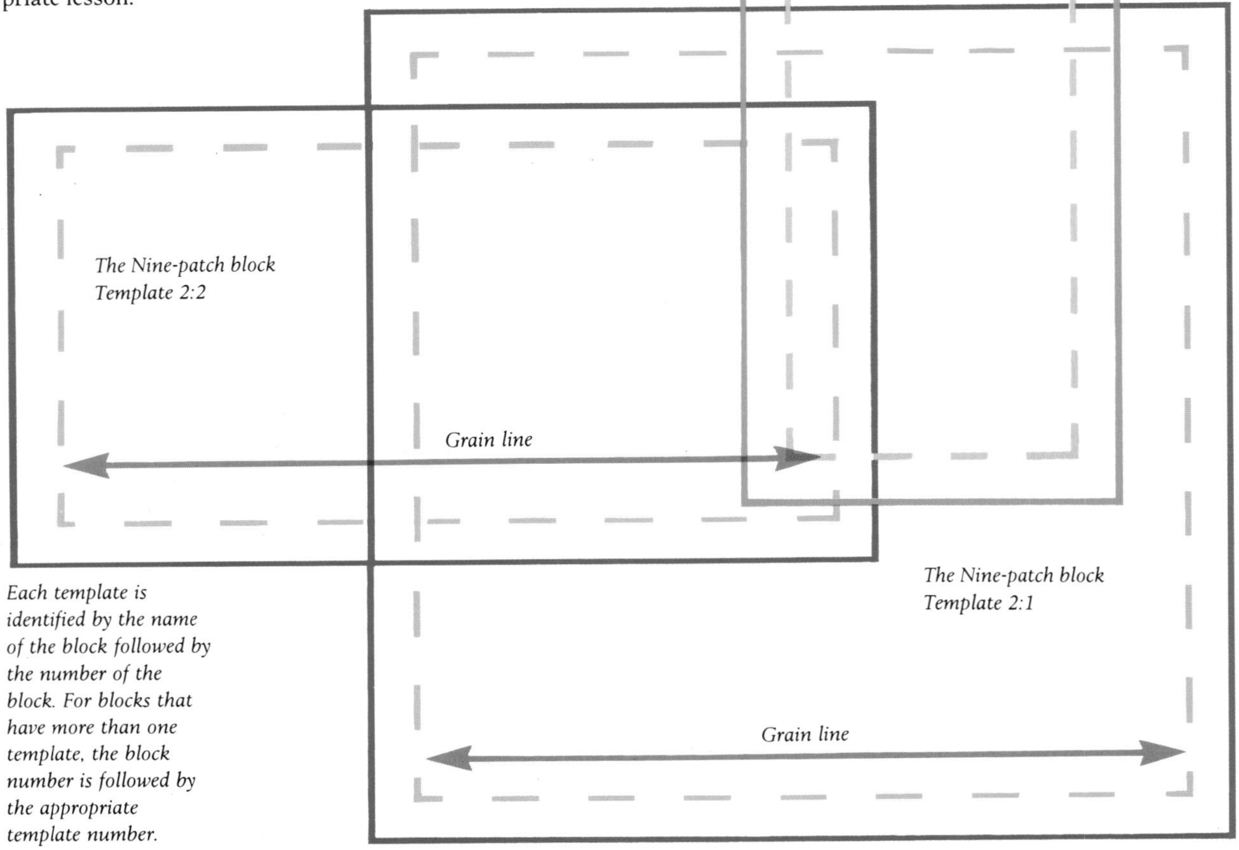

The Nine-patch block Template 2:2

Grain line

The Nine-patch block Template 2:1

Grain line

Each template is identified by the name of the block followed by the number of the block. For blocks that have more than one template, the block number is followed by the appropriate template number.

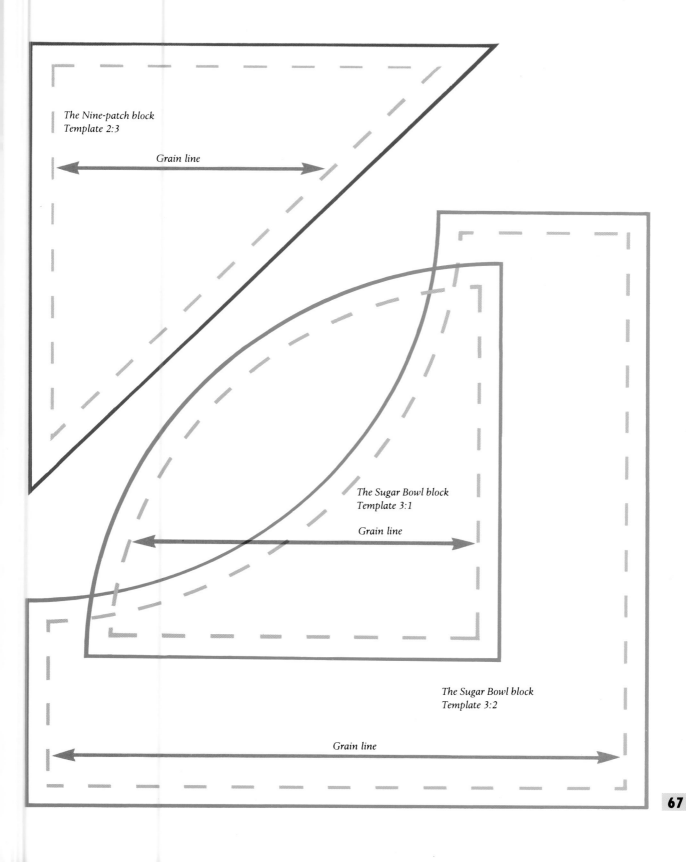

The Nine-patch block
Template 2:3

Grain line

The Sugar Bowl block
Template 3:1

Grain line

The Sugar Bowl block
Template 3:2

Grain line

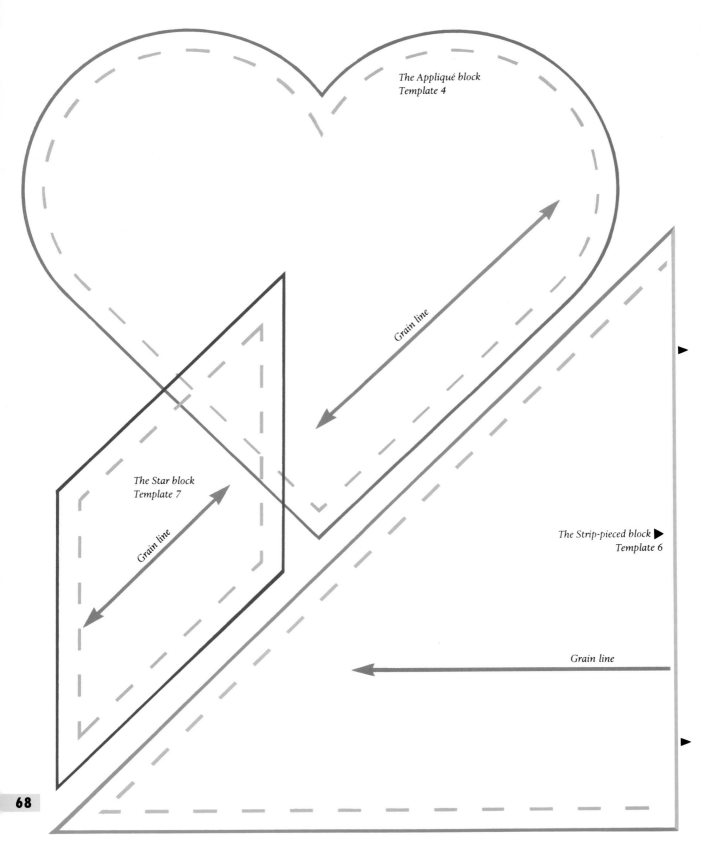

The Appliqué block
Template 4

Grain line

The Star block
Template 7

Grain line

The Strip-pieced block ▶
Template 6

Grain line

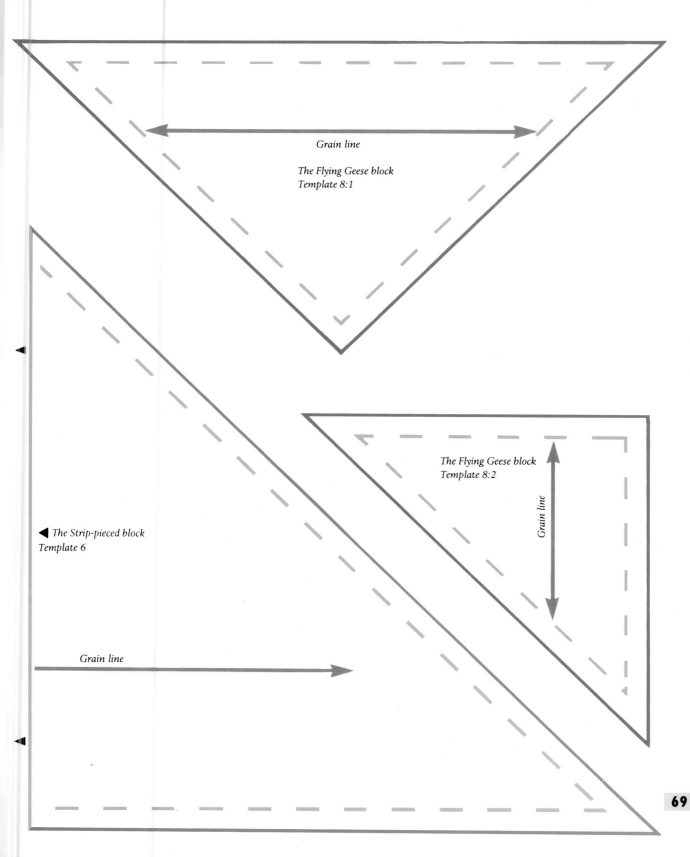

Grain line

The Flying Geese block
Template 8:1

The Flying Geese block
Template 8:2

Grain line

◀ The Strip-pieced block
Template 6

Grain line

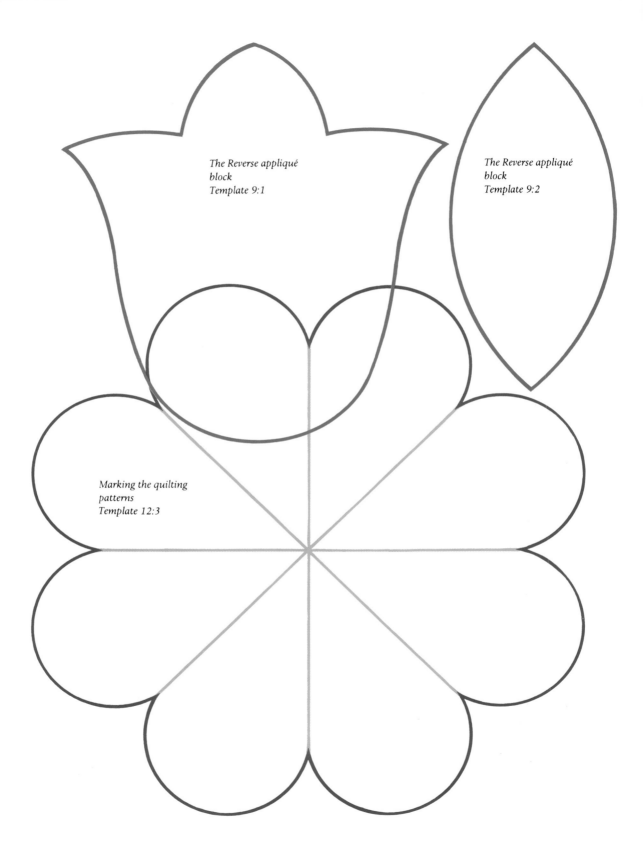

*The Reverse appliqué
block
Template 9:1*

*The Reverse appliqué
block
Template 9:2*

*Marking the quilting
patterns
Template 12:3*

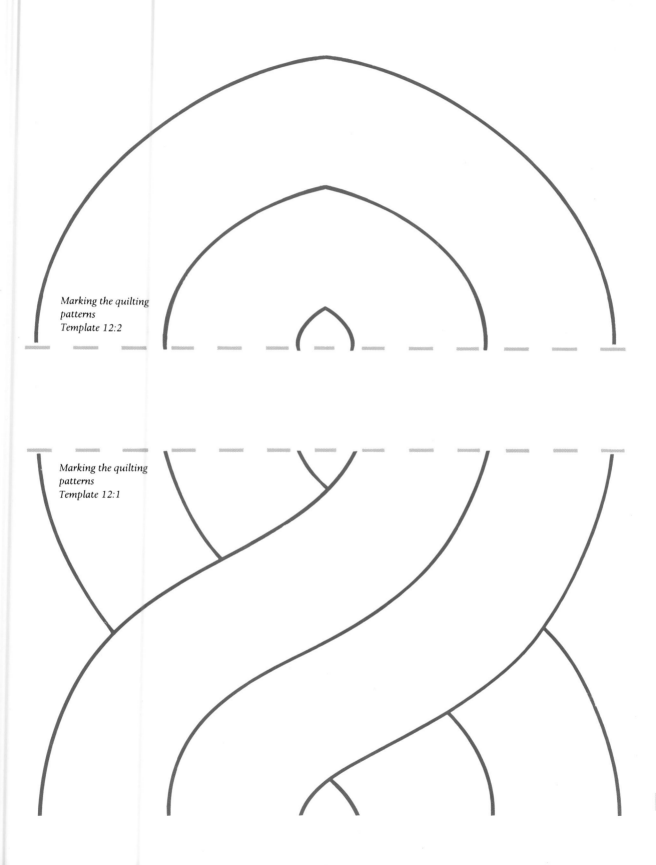

*Marking the quilting
patterns
Template 12:2*

*Marking the quilting
patterns
Template 12:1*

What exactly is a four-patch block? As its name suggests, it is a square design that is divisible into four separate basic patches, or units, which are constructed one at a time before being stitched together to form the complete block. There are many variations of four-patch blocks, and a selection is shown in the Pattern Library (page 122). In this lesson you'll learn how to construct the block called Rail

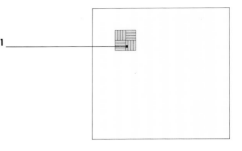

1 The Four-patch block

Fence, which is a simple four-patch design. Only two fabrics are used in this, and only one template, but the way that the fabrics are alternated, with two of the patches turned on their sides, makes an attractive block design.

▲ *The alternating colors produce a dramatic effect from a very simple pattern.*

IDENTIFYING A FOUR-PATCH BLOCK

This might seem self-evident, but some designs which seem to divide neatly into quarters are actually more complex. A design is a standard four-patch block if you can divide it into four quarters without cutting into any of the shaped pieces.

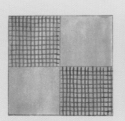

This is a four-patch design.

This is a four-patch design.

This is not a four-patch design.

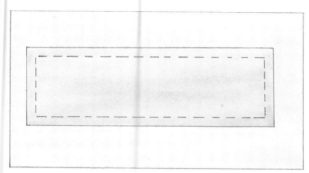

1 *Trace template 1 on page 66 full-size onto a piece of thin cardboard, and cut it out very accurately (see page 40, Making templates). Also mark the seam allowance lines and the grain line.*

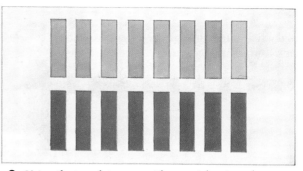

2 *Using the template as a guide, cut eight pieces from fabric A and eight pieces from fabric D. Make sure that you position the template each time so that the marked grain line lies either horizontally or vertically along the straight grain of the fabric.*

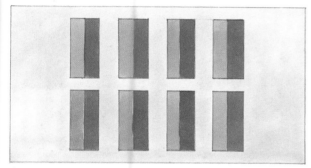

3 *Take one piece of fabric A and one piece of fabric D, and place them right sides together. Stitch a ¼ in. seam along one of the long edges by hand or machine (see page 46, Piecing), and press the seam toward the darker fabric. Repeat with the seven remaining pairs of pieces.*

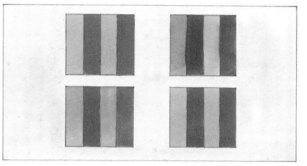

4 *Take two pairs of patches and place them right sides together so that the edge of fabric A on one piece is against the edge of fabric D on the other. Join this seam and press it to the darker side to form one of the four basic patches for the block. Repeat three times to make the other patches.*

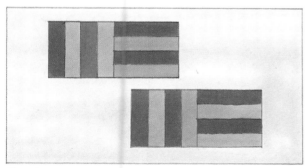

5 *Take one patch and turn it 90° so that the strips are horizontal. Right sides together, join it in the same way to the side of another patch turned so the strips are vertical. Press the seam open. Repeat for the other patches.*

6 *Join the two halves together as shown to complete the blocks, and press the seam open. You now have a complete Rail Fence block.*

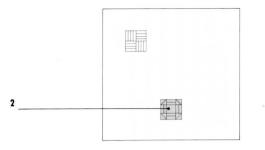

As the name implies, nine-patch blocks are divided into nine sections, which are joined first in rows of three; then three rows are joined to form the whole block. Nine-patch blocks are exciting to work with because the larger number of patches offers more variety in the designs. Nine-patch block designs often have a blank square in the center, which can be a focal point for a splash of color or some form

2 The Nine-patch block

of fancy quilted embellishment. We have chosen the Churn Dash block for the second block of our sampler quilt. It is based on an even grid of nine squares, it needs only three templates, and it will give you practice in stitching diagonal seams.

As with many other blocks, a nine-patch often has several names. Churn Dash and Hole in the Barn Door are sometimes called Wrench, and Jack in the Box is also known as Double Z. Some nine-patch designs, such as Bear's Paw and Hole in the Barn Door, have the block divided slightly differently from the basic nine-patch, in that the central section of the grid is narrower than the outer sections, but many nine-patch designs are based on a grid of nine equal squares.

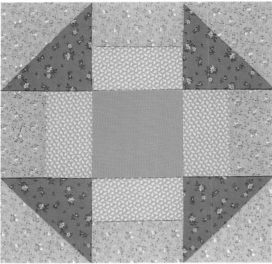

▲ *The finished block, showing an interesting interplay among the different fabrics.*

RECOGNIZING A NINE-PATCH BLOCK

The most regular nine-patch blocks are made up of nine equal squares a, so they are easy to recognize. However, more complex blocks may also be nine-patch designs. The test is whether you can construct them into three straight rows of three blocks, regardless of the widths of the blocks; designs b and c are both still nine-patch blocks, even though they look very different from traditional ones.

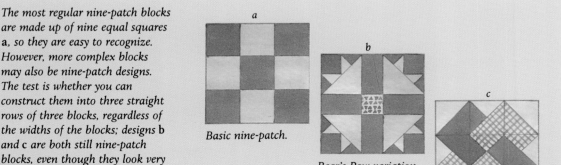

a

Basic nine-patch.

b

Bear's Paw variation.

c

Card Trick design.

74

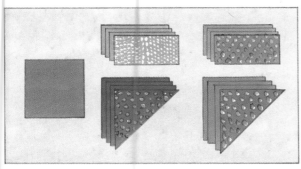

1 Make templates 2:1, 2:2, and 2:3 on page 66. Using template 2:1 cut one piece from fabric C (see page 44, Cutting fabrics). Using template 2:2, cut four pieces from fabric B and four from fabric D. Using template 2:3, cut four pieces from fabric A and four from fabric D.

2 Following the instructions on page 46 (Piecing), join the light green (Fabric D) triangles to the dark pink (Fabric A) triangles along the long edge, right sides together, taking care not to stretch the fabric as you stitch. This gives you four identical square patches, called unit **a**.

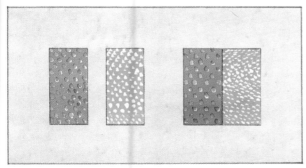

3 Right sides together join the light green (Fabric D) rectangles to the light pink (Fabric B) rectangles along one long edge. This will give you four more identical square patches, called unit **b**.

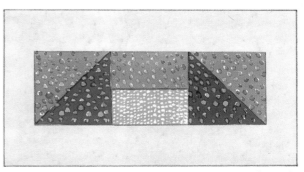

4 Join two unit **a** patches to the edges of one unit **b** patch. Position the patches so that the light green triangles and the light green rectangle are all at the top of the new design. Repeat to make two identical strips.

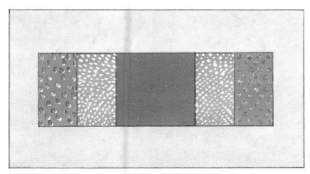

5 Join the two remaining unit **b** patches to the edges of the dark green (Fabric C) square, making sure that the light pink rectangles are next to the square on both sides. This makes the central row of the block.

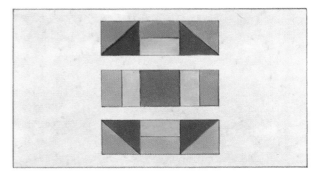

6 Join the three rows, making sure that the light pink rectangles of the top and bottom strips are next to the green central square. You now have a Churn Dash block.

Like the Rail Fence block (see page 72), this block is a four-patch design made in four even, square patches. This one, however, uses two templates and also introduces curved seams. Curved seams introduce exciting new dimensions into quilt patterns, because they take the eye away from the grid structure of the block and allow it to be drawn across the work to follow the curved lines. On page 146 you will

3 _____

On page 146 you will

3 The Sugar Bowl block

SAMPLER QUILT

find ways in which you can combine Sugar Bowl blocks to make more complex patterns such as Drunkard's Path where, as the name suggests, the curves weave to and fro across the quilt top. Here, though, we are making only one block; the light/dark contrast between the green and pink produces a strong design using just two different fabrics.

▼ *The finished block, showing a strong contrast between the two fabrics.*

CUTTING CURVED SEAMS

When you are cutting out your fabric it is very important to make sure that any curved edges are smooth. Cut them carefully with scissors, or use a rotary cutter against a strong template. It is important to have a strong template so that you don't cut into the template itself.

1 *Make templates 3:1 and 3:2 on page 67. Using template 3:1, cut two pieces from fabric B and two from fabric C. Using template 3:2, cut two pieces from fabric B and two from fabric C.*

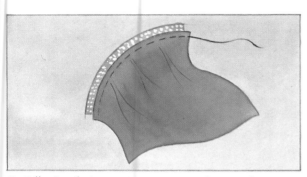

2 *Following the instructions on page 47 for curved seams, stitch the curved edges of the pink (Fabric B) quarter-circles inside the edges of the large green (Fabric C) pieces.*

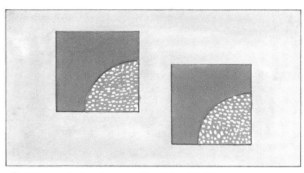

3 *Open out the pieces to the right side. You now have two identical patches, unit a.*

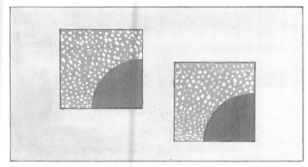

4 *Using the same method, stitch the green (Fabric C) quarter-circles to the curved edges of the large pink (Fabric B) pieces. You now have two more patches, unit b.*

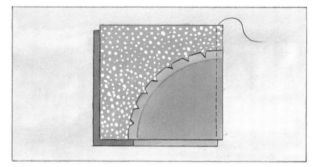

5 *Stitch one unit a to one unit b, matching the seams carefully so that you get a smooth half-circle.*

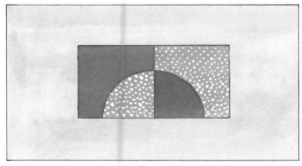

6 *Stitch the other two units a and b together to form an identical half-block.*

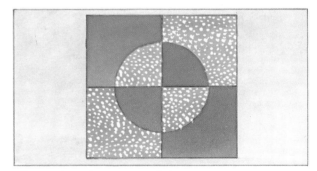

7 *Matching the seams carefully at the edges and in the center, stitch the two half-blocks together so that you have a complete circle in the center of the block.*

Appliqué can be worked by hand or machine. When you appliqué by machine, it is impossible to hide the stitching completely. You can achieve a low-key effect by turning under the edges of the shapes and applying them with a single line of machine straight stitch, or you can capitalize on the machine stitching and cover the raw edges by stitching around the edges of the shapes with satin stitch or a close

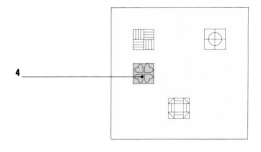

4 The Appliqué block

zigzag. When you stitch by hand, you can choose whether to make the stitching nearly invisible, or part of the decorative effect by using blanket, feather, or a variety of other embroidery stitches.

On this block we show you how to turn the edges under and baste them before you position the motifs. When you get more proficient, you may prefer to use the quicker turn-as-you-go method – the shapes are simply pinned in place, and you turn under the seam allowance as you stitch around the edges of the shape. Another method involves cutting the required shapes from freezer paper and sticking the edges under by pressing them to the tacky wax layer; the appliqué is stitched to the background fabric, then a slit is cut behind the appliqué to remove the paper.

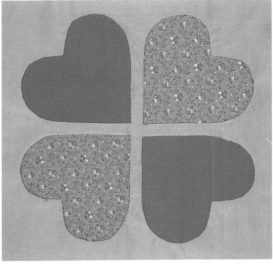

▲ The completed block, a simple design of hearts in green fabrics set off by the pink background.

TIP

When you are sewing by hand, your thread can easily become tangled and form small knots. There is nothing more irritating than this, but you can prevent it by running the thread across a lump of beeswax. The coating of wax must be quite light, however, or you may discolor the fabric.

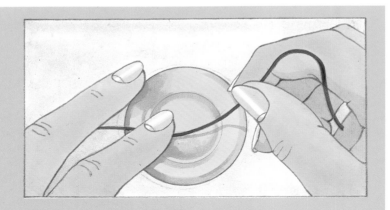

1 Trace template 4 on page 68, and cut a heart template for the appliqué pieces (see page 42, Making templates).

2 Using the template (see page 42, Making templates), cut two hearts from fabric C and two from fabric D (see page 44, Cutting fabrics).

3 Fold and baste under ¼ in. all around the edges of the heart shapes. Clip to the seam allowance at the top of each heart so that the fabric folds under smoothly. Keep the curves smooth around the edges of each shape.

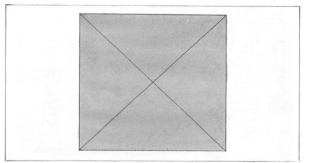

4 Cut a 12½ in. square from fabric F and fold it lightly across the diagonals, so that you have some guidelines for positioning your appliqué shapes.

5 Pin or baste the heart shapes in position on the background fabric so that there are even borders of the pink (Fabric F) square around the edges of the hearts and between them.

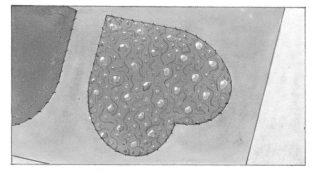

6 Using green sewing thread, blind-stitch the hearts to the background fabric by taking tiny hemstitches around the edges of the shapes. Remove the pins or basting threads. To reduce bulk you can cut away some of the background fabric behind the heart shapes.

L og Cabin is one of the most exciting and versatile of all patchwork designs. It can be made in two colors or fifty colors; any fabric can be used; the strips may be any width you choose; and once several blocks are completed, they can be arranged in many different ways to make an endless variety of designs. Even the ways in which the strips are attached can be varied. The Log Cabin designs in the Pattern

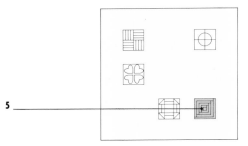

5

SAMPLER QUILT

5 The Log Cabin block

▼ *The finished Log Cabin block, half dark and half light to represent night and day.*

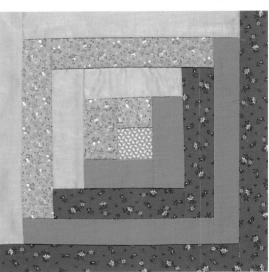

Library (pages 136-139) show you just a few of the myriad possibilities open to you.

To introduce you to the basic principle of Log Cabin, which is different from other methods of patchwork, we are using a standard block which makes use of five different fabrics.

To make the block, you will need strips of each fabric $1\frac{5}{6}$ in. wide; if you find this measurement difficult to achieve accurately, cut your strips 2 in. wide and take a fraction more than the standard $\frac{1}{4}$ in. for your seam allowance as you stitch each seam. The strips are best cut using a rotary cutter and board (see page 44, Cutting fabrics).

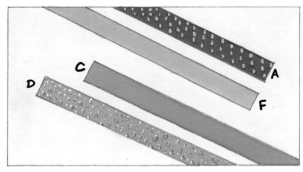

1 *From fabrics A and F, cut strips measuring $1\frac{5}{6}$ in. across; you will need a length of about 14 in. of each fabric, but this doesn't all need to be in one piece. From fabrics C and D, cut strips the same width and a total of 36 in. in length for each. Cut along the grain.*

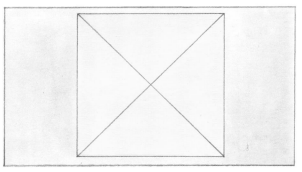

2 *From fabric G, cut a $12\frac{1}{2}$ in. square. Fold the square in half diagonally and then in half again, and press lightly; unfold it, and you will have your diagonals marked, which will help you to keep the strips straight.*

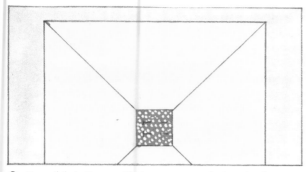

3 *From fabric B cut a 1⅝ in. square, and pin it in the exact center of the large fabric square, using the pressed lines as a guide for positioning it.*

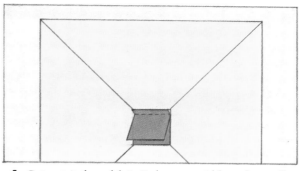

4 *Cut a strip from fabric D the same width as the small square and lay it face down over the square so that the two raw edges align. Stitch a ¼ in. seam by hand or machine.*

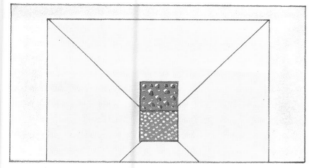

5 *Fold the fabric strip open so that the right side is up, and press the seam.*

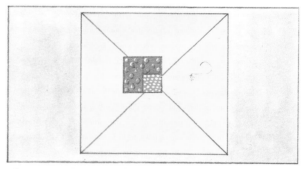

6 *Cut another strip of fabric D, this time long enough to go across the square and the edge of the first strip, and attach to the next edge around in the same way.*

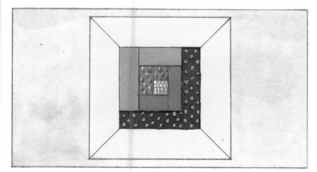

7 *Attach strips of fabric C to the remaining two sides in the same way. Continuing to work around the square in the same direction, add two strips of fabric F and then two strips of fabric A in the same way to make the next round. As you work your way outward on the block, you need longer and longer strips.*

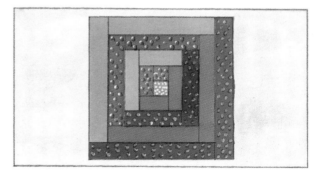

8 *Finish off the block with another round of strips D and C, and a final round of strips F and A. Make sure that you stitch around the block in the same order for every round.*

S trip piecing is a marvelous time-saver that enables you to produce very sophisticated results quickly.

In strip piecing, strips are cut from different fabrics, sometimes in varying widths, and joined together along their lengths before being cut into the required patches. If you don't have a sewing machine it is perfectly possible to do strip piecing by hand, but it is much

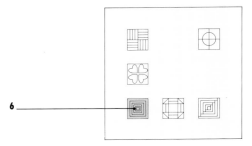

SAMPLER QUILT

6 The Strip-pieced block

faster to do the stitching by machine. Cutting the fabrics with a rotary cutter (see page 44, Cutting fabrics) is very quick and accurate, but if you prefer, the fabrics can be cut in the conventional way with scissors. This block uses even strips of six different fabrics.

If you cut your fabric strips to different widths before they are pieced and reassembled, the finished block has a more random effect.

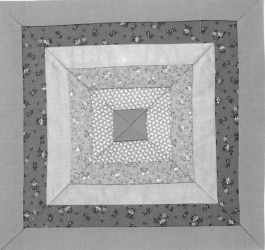

▲ *The finished block. Piecing the strips in this way gives the effect of several squares of fabric inside one another.*

VARIATIONS

String piecing

String piecing evolved as a way of using up long narrow pieces of fabric left over after cutting out garments. These "strings" are often irregularly shaped, but by trimming them into long triangles and sewing them together you can make a new fabric which can then be cut up and used for quilt patches or for garments. Stitch the strings onto a backing of thin fabric using the "face-down, fold-back" method shown on page 80 (the Log Cabin block.)

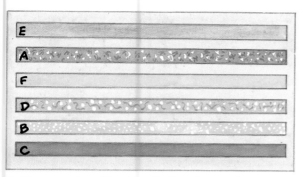

1 Cut two strips of fabric, each 28 in. long and 1½ in. wide, from each of fabrics A, B, C, D, E, and F.

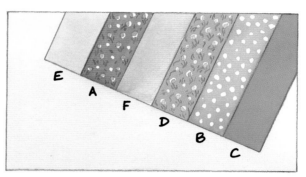

2 Following the method for piecing (see page 46), join one set of fabric strips along their long edges in the order E, A, F, D, B, C. Do the same with the other set of strips; you now have two identical lengths of strip-pieced fabric.

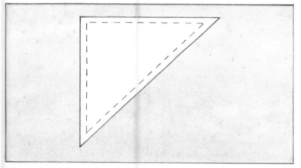

3 Make a template using template 6 on page 68 (see also page 42, Making templates).

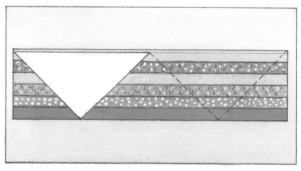

4 Use the template to cut two triangles from each length of strip-pieced fabric, laying the long edge of the triangle ¼ in. in from the raw edge of fabric E each time.

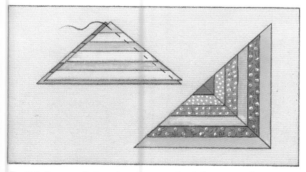

5 Stitch two of the triangles together along one short seam, matching the fabrics and making sure that the seam lines match exactly. Stitch the other two triangles together in the same way to form two identical half-blocks.

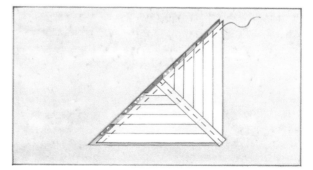

6 Stitch the two half-blocks together along their long edges, matching the fabrics and the seam lines exactly, to complete the block.

Diamonds can be used to produce wonderful star shapes simply by stitching them around in a circle. As you can see from the examples on page 132 (Non-block patterns), the stars can become quite spectacular; the Star of Bethlehem pattern is very dramatic and can be made large enough to cover a whole double quilt top. This star is a little more modest, to get you used to using diamonds in a star

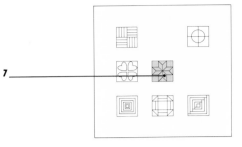

7

7 The Star block

SAMPLER QUILT

arrangement. When the basic star has been pieced, it is appliquéd by hand to the background fabric to make a block.

The number of points your star has is determined by the acute angle at the tip of the diamond; this star uses 45° diamonds, so the star has eight points (360° divided by 45°). The use of the two pink fabrics, one light and one dark, arranged in pairs, gives a three-dimensional look to the finished star. If you want to make stars with six points, then you need to use 60° diamonds (360°÷6). It is possible to create stars with even more points, but if the angle becomes too fine it is difficult to piece the diamonds accurately, so six-point and eight-point designs tend to be the most popular.

TIP *For the star to look effective, each point must be really sharp and crisp. It is easier to baste sharp points if you trim away some of the excess fabric. Cut across the top of the point and turn it down. Now turn down one side and then the other side.*

▼ *The finished block shows a good contrast between dark, light and middle values.*

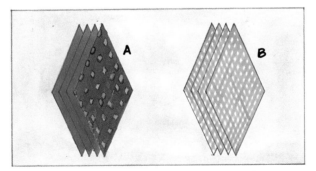

1 *Make template 7 on page 68 (see page 42, Making templates), and use it to cut four pieces from fabric A and four pieces from fabric B.*

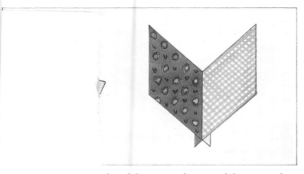

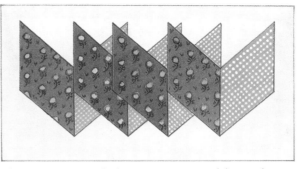

...d in fabric A and one in fabric B and put them right sides together. Following the instructions on page 46 (Piecing), stitch down one edge so that side **a** of the fabric A diamond is joined to side **b** of the fabric B diamond.

3 Do the same with the remaining pairs of diamonds so that you now have four identical V-shaped patches. On all the seams, leave the top open for the first ¹/₄ in.; this will make it easier to turn under the seam allowances later.

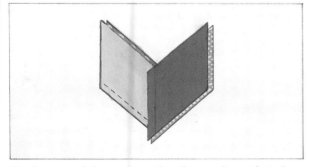

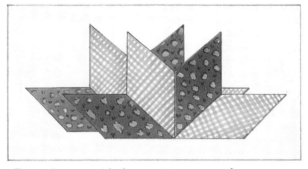

4 Place two of the patches right sides together and stitch down the right-hand lower edge to form a half-star. Once again, leave the top ¹/₄ in. of the seam open.

5 Do the same with the remaining two patches; you now have two identical half-stars.

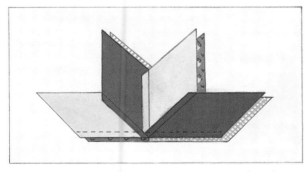

6 Place the two half-stars right sides together and stitch a straight seam across them; follow the suggestions in the Tip box on page 47 to make sure that all the points meet accurately. Leave this seam open for ¹/₄ in. at each end.

7 Tack under the ¹/₄ in. seam allowances on the edges of the star. Following the instructions on page 78 (Appliqué block), stitch the star by hand onto the center of a 12¹/₂ in. square of fabric E. You now have an eight-point star block for your quilt top.

This delicate block, made in two basic pieces, is a variation on the traditional pattern known as Flying Geese, which always features a pattern of right-angled triangles arranged in the same direction. The "geese" can be made to fly all around the block, or entirely in one direction across it, or around a border (see page 150, Pieced border patterns). Here, one gaggle flies south and the other gaggle north!

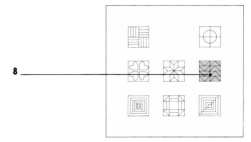

8 —————————

8 The Flying Geese block

▼ *The finished block, showing foursomes of "geese" flying in different directions.*

This is the most complex block for your sampler quilt, and you need to be very accurate when you are making the templates (see page 42) and cutting out the fabric (see page 44). A quilter's ruler for right-angled triangles will come in handy for cutting your shapes.

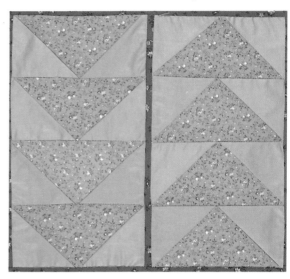

USING A QUILTER'S MAT

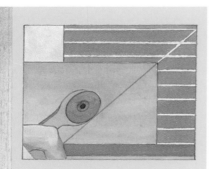

Cutting a strip of fabric will be much more accurate if you cut it with a rotary cutter and a quilter's ruler or a rotary cutter and a mat used for cutting triangles. Cut a strip of fabric the width of one of the perpendicular edges of the small triangles, then use the 45° angle guide to cut the triangles across it. Repeat for the larger triangles, using the larger template and a wider strip of fabric.

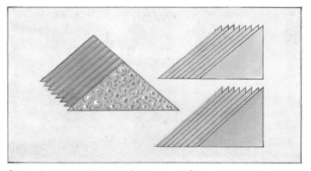

1 *Make triangular templates 8:1 and 8:2 on page 69. Using template 8:1, cut eight shapes from fabric D. Using template 8:2, cut 16 shapes from fabric F.*

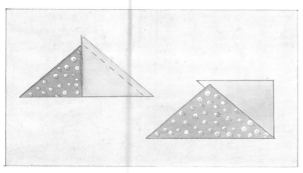

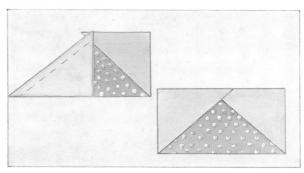

2 *Following the instructions for piecing on page 46, stitch the long side of one pink (Fabric F) triangle to the right-hand diagonal of one green (Fabric D) triangle. Repeat the procedure for the other green (Fabric D) triangles, and press all the seams.*

3 *Stitch the long side of one pink (Fabric F) triangle to the other diagonal of each green (Fabric D) triangle. You now have eight identical rectangles.*

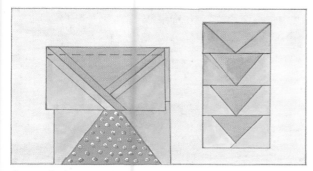

4 *Stitch the rectangles together in two groups of four, making sure that the green triangles point in the same direction in each group. Stitch the seams so that the point of one triangle just touches the base of the next.*

5 *From fabric A, cut three strips ¹/₄ in. wide and 12 in. long, and two strips ¹/₄ in. wide and 12¹/₂ in. long.*

6 *Stitch one of the shorter strips between the half-blocks, taking a ¹/₄ in. seam on each side and making sure that the green triangles point in different directions in each half. Stitch the other two short strips to the outside edges of the rectangles.*

7 *Stitch the longer strips to the top and bottom of the block, again taking ¹/₄ in. seams. You now have a complete Flying Geese block.*

This block introduces a new technique, reverse appliqué. Instead of stitching fabric shapes on top of a background fabric as you did for the appliqué block earlier, the second fabric is laid underneath the background, which is then cut away in shapes to reveal it.

Just as conventional appliqué gives a slightly puffed or three-dimensional look to the shapes applied onto the flat background fabric,

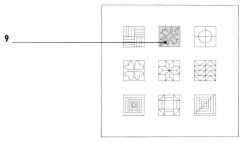

9 The Reverse appliqué block

this method gives a slightly puffed look to the top layer of fabric as it is turned and stitched over flat areas of fabric shapes.

There are many methods of reverse appliqué, and variations within the methods themselves, but this block uses one of the simplest. Use this method for virtually any conventional appliqué designs (see page 134, Appliqué motifs) to vary the final effect.

A well known form of reverse appliqué is that produced by the Indian women of Panama's San Blas Islands. Their traditional dress includes a sleeveless blouse called a mola, with reverse appliqué panels on both front and back. These colorful and intricate panels have semi-naturalistic designs based on plants, people, and creatures, or tales from local folklore. Several layers of different-colored fabrics are used; empty spaces are often filled with lines of plain stitching or embroidery.

▶ *The finished block: the red tulip shapes and dark green leaves produce a pretty pattern on the light green background.*

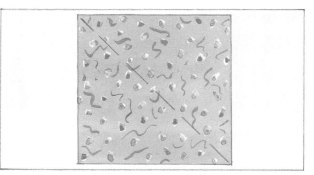

1 *Make templates 9:1 and 9:2 on page 70. From fabric D cut a 12½ in. square; this will be your background fabric. Make a soft diagonal fold across the square to divide it into two large triangles; this will help you position the templates accurately on both sides.*

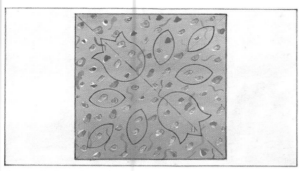

2 Mark the tulip and leaf shapes on the background square by drawing round with a soft pencil, positioning them so that each diagonal half is a mirror image of the other. Make sure that the shapes are at least ¹/₂ in. from the edges of the square.

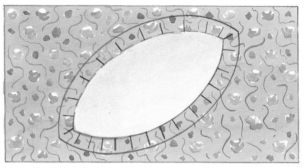

3 Using small, sharp scissors, cut ¹/₄ in. inside each of the pencil lines and carefully clip any curves; clip into the corners of the shapes also.

4 Using the tulip template as a rough guide, cut two shapes from fabric A that are at least ¹/₂ in. larger all around than the template.

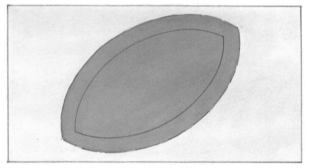

5 Using the leaf template as a rough guide, cut six shapes from fabric C that are at least ¹/₂ in. larger all around than the template.

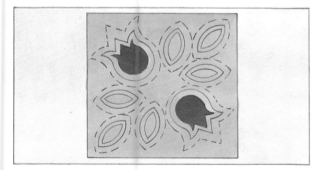

6 Baste the dark pink (Fabric A) pieces, face up, underneath the tulip-shaped holes in the background fabric. Baste the dark green (Fabric C) pieces behind the leaf-shaped holes in the same way.

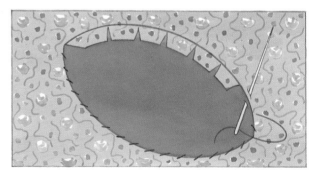

7 Roll under the raw edges of the background fabric until the pencil line is just hidden, and blind-stitch the background fabric to the colored shapes underneath. Keep the curves of the rolled fabric smooth so that each piece of reverse appliqué makes a pleasing shape.

You now have nine blocks for your sampler quilt, and it is time to put them together. This stage turns your work from a collection of blocks into a real quilt top, by adding sashing or setting strips between the blocks. Not all quilts made in blocks have sashing in between (see page 38), especially when the quilter wants to create a secondary design by arranging the blocks side by side, but the plain sashing in a

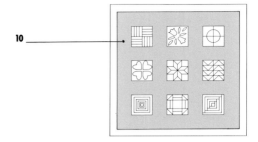

10 ____

10 Setting the blocks

SAMPLER QUILT

neutral color around the different designs of a sampler quilt sets all the blocks off very well and produces a sense of homogeneity.

The blocks are arranged in a pattern to give a pleasing balance of shades and colors across the quilt. If you have used different fabrics to make your blocks, lay them on the floor first to see whether you want to adjust the order of the blocks.

▲ The quilt top begins to take shape; sashing or setting strips of unbleached muslin divide the blocks.

VARIATIONS

Choosing the sashing

The kind of sashing you decide on depends on the overall effect you want to create. For a quilt with a large number of similar blocks, a narrow sashing could look effective, perhaps blending in with the colors used in the blocks.

If you used mainly solid colors for the blocks, the sashing could be patterned for contrast. Or it could be a much darker, lighter or brighter color to create the effect of a series of bars across the quilt.

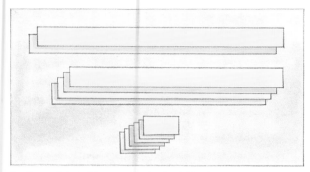

1 From Fabric G, cut strips in the following measurements:
six strips 8½ in. × 12½ in.
four strips 8½ in. × 52½ in.
two strips 8½ in. × 68½ in.

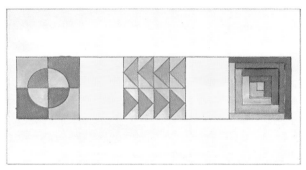

2 Taking ¼ in. seams each time, stitch one of the short strips between the Rail Fence block and the appliqué hearts block, and another between the appliqué hearts block and the strip-pieced block.

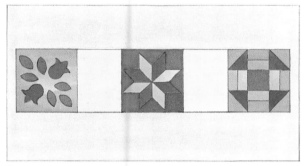

3 In the same way, make a second row with the reverse appliqué block left, the Diamond Star in the middle, and the Churn Dash block right.

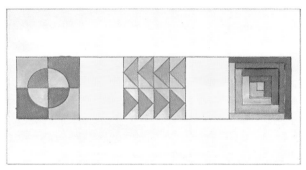

4 Make a third row in the same way with the Sugar Bowl block left, the Flying Geese in the middle and the Log Cabin block right. Make sure that the Flying Geese fly up and down, and that the dark edges of the Log Cabin are on the outside.

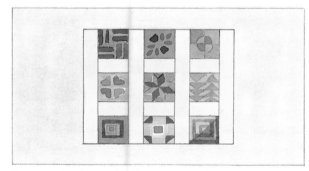

5 Stitch the four middle-length strips of muslin to join the rows of blocks and to finish the outside edges of the rows. Make sure that you join the strips in the correct order, so that the Diamond Star is in the center of the quilt top.

6 Add the two long strips of muslin to the top and bottom of the quilt top.

Adding a simple patchwork border to your quilt top is the final stage before you begin preparations for the quilting itself. This border uses a variation of the method that you used for the Strip-pieced block (see page 80), but on a much larger scale.

The squares in this border are 4 in. wide, so their seams should line up with your block edges. As you attach the border, make sure that

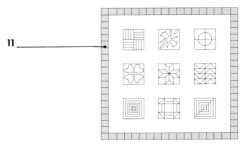

11 Adding a border

the seam lines match; this will make the quilt top look very neat. You will need 72 squares to go around the edge, so you should be able to use the same repeat of the six fabrics twelve times. Keep them in the same order around the quilt edges so that they don't distract the eye.

▶ *The completed quilt top: the patchwork border picks up the fabrics from the block designs.*

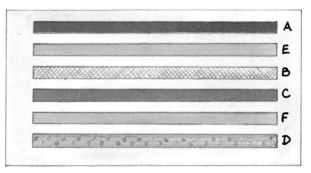

Detail of the sampler quilt border.

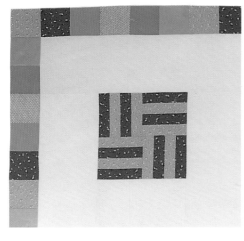

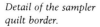

1 *From fabrics A, B, C, D, E, and F, cut strips 4½ in. wide. You will need a total length of about 60 in. for each fabric, but this doesn't all have to be in one strip; if it works better with the fabric you have, you could make two pieced strips of 30 in. each as you did for the strip-pieced block.*

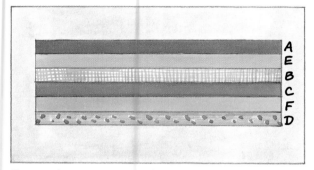

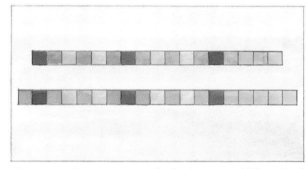

2 Use a ¼ in. seam to join the strips in the order A, E, B, C, F, D. This will give you a pieced strip (or two shorter ones) in which each individual strip is 4 in. wide.

3 Using a rotary cutter (see page 44, Cutting fabrics), cut strips 4½ in. wide across the width of the composite strip.

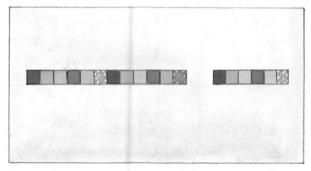

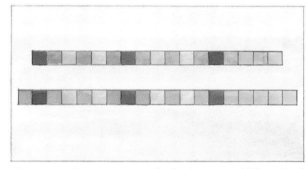

4 Join these new strips in groups of three to produce four strips containing 18 squares. Keep the squares in the same order each time.

5 Rip out the seam joining the final square (of fabric D) of two of the strips, and join the extra squares to the beginnings of the other two strips, next to fabric A. This gives you two strips of 17 squares and two of 19.

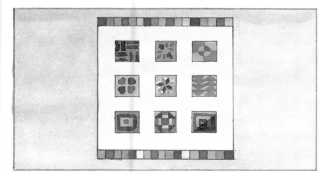

6 Join one of the shorter strips to the top edge of the quilt top, taking a ¼ in. seam. Join the other short strip to the bottom edge, making sure that the colors are running in the same order around the quilt.

7 Join the longer strips to the edges of the quilt, making sure that the colors still run in the same order around the quilt. You are now ready to prepare for quilting.

The piecing of your quilt top is now complete, and it is time to mark the quilting patterns onto the fabric. It is best to do this before you baste the quilt top to the batting; it is easier to make the marks accurately if you can rest the fabric on a hard surface. Once the batting is in place, the surface becomes spongy. Two traditional patterns have been selected to quilt the sashing; a twisting cable repeat pattern, and a

12 ——————

12 Marking the quilting patterns

corner flower motif. The cable pattern has a 4 in. repeat, so it fits in exactly three times along the edge of each block and exactly twice across the width of the sashing. The cable ends are finished off neatly by using the templates.

A checkerboard background texture has been chosen for the reverse appliqué block, so that you can practice stitching a texture of this kind. The checkering needs to be marked at this stage, too, but the other blocks don't need any marking as you will be using the seam lines as quilting guides.

There are many methods of marking quilt patterns (see page 48), but here we are using one of the easiest – tracing around a template with a water-soluble-ink pen. This gives you a good clear line to stitch on, and when you have finished, any visible marks can be gently sponged away with cold water.

There are, of course, many other designs which can be used on quilt tops; if you prefer to use alternative designs, there are plenty of ideas in the Pattern Libraries for quilted border patterns (see page 152), individual motifs (see page 134), and background textures (see page 154). Choose your design, scale it up or down to the appropriate size, then follow the instructions in this lesson for marking the designs onto the quilt top.

▲ *The marked quilt top: the lines made by the soluble-ink pen show up clearly on the fabrics.*

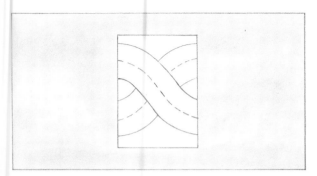

1 Make templates 12:1, 12:2, and 12:3 on page 71. Either use template plastic or cut them from paper and glue them on cardboard.

2 Start in the center of each side and, working outward, mark 11 repeats of template 12:1 down the centers of the sashing bands. Finish each end off neatly with template 12:2. Mark the two long pieces of sashing down the center of the quilt in the same way.

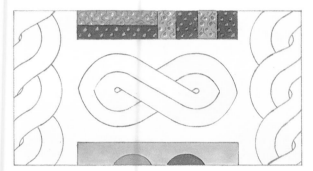

3 On each short section of sashing, mark template 12:1 once and template 12:2 twice to create six mini-cables.

4 At each corner of the sashing, use template 12:3 to mark a flower motif.

5 On the reverse appliqué block, draw the diagonals across the block using a water-soluble-ink pen.

6 Working outward from these lines in both directions, draw parallel lines 1 in. apart; a quilter's ruler (see page 86) is very useful for this task. Draw the lines outside the appliqué shapes.

Now you are ready for the final stage, turning your quilt top into a quilt. Your fabric is marked with the quilting patterns, and now needs to be put together with the batting and the backing fabric.

All of the quilting can be worked by hand or by machine (see page 56, Quilting). If you quilt by machine, remember to finish off the threads neatly, ideally by pulling the top thread

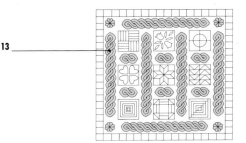

13 _____

13 Quilting the sampler quilt

through to the back of the quilt and knotting it with the bobbin thread. Or, if your sewing machine does a neat reverse stitch, you could work a few stitches in reverse at the end of each quilted line, but this shows on the right side unless you match the thread to the fabric color exactly. Whether you are quilting by hand or machine, choose the colors of thread that you want to use for the quilting either to blend in or to stand out; we have used green on the muslin, and pink and green on the blocks and border, but the patterns on the muslin would also look effective quilted in pink or ecru.

► *The quilt top with all the quilting complete.*

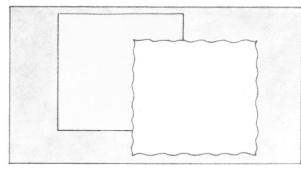

1 *If your batting is not already cut to the exact size, cut it to 78 in. square. Cut a piece of muslin the same size.*

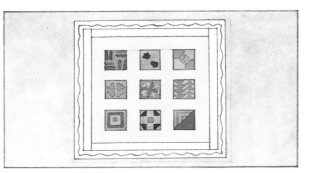

2 *Following the instructions on page 52, make a sandwich of the muslin, the batting, and the quilt top, and secure the layers together with a grid of basting threads. The muslin and batting should be ¼ in. larger than the quilt top all around.*

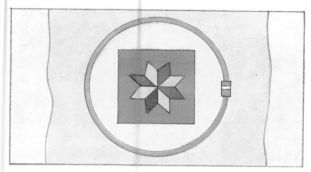

3 Secure the quilt to the frame as shown on page 54. Unless you are using a full-size frame, work on one area of the quilt at a time, quilting from the center out so that you minimize the risk of the fabric puckering. This applies to both hand and machine quilting.

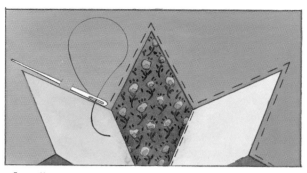

4 Following the instructions on page 58 for quilting in the ditch, quilt the Flying Geese, Rail Fence, Log Cabin, Diamond Star, Strip-pieced, and Churn Dash blocks. Quilt just outside the edges of the appliquéd Diamond Star shape.

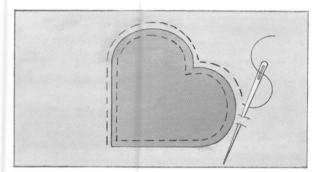

5 Following the instructions on page 58 for outline quilting, quilt the Sugar Bowl block. Stitch inside the appliqué hearts in the same way, and work a row of quilting stitches ¹/₄ in. outside the design as well.

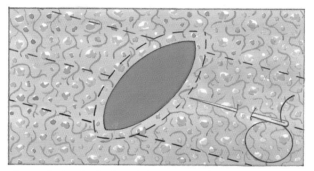

6 Quilt the checkerboard design around the reverse appliqué block, stitching a line ¹/₄ in. outside each leaf and flower and stopping each diagonal row on that line.

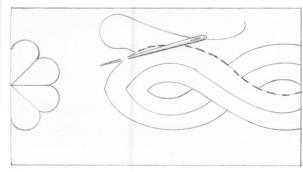

7 Quilt the cable designs first, and then the corner motifs on the sashing.

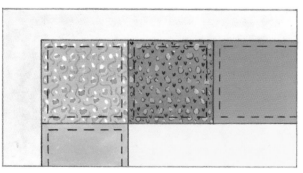

8 Quilt the border squares either "in the ditch" (see page 58) or ¹/₄ in. inside each patch. With a damp cloth, sponge away any blue marks remaining from the soluble-ink pen; your quilt is now almost finished.

You have now reached the final stage of your sampler quilt: binding the raw edges. There are many different ways of binding a quilt (see page 60), and the binding can be plain, patterned, or pieced. Plain quilts are sometimes finished with shaped edges, such as scallops or rows of triangle shapes. Piped edges or ruffles, either single or double, can also look effective for some quilts. In this case, though, the

14 Binding the sampler quilt

sampler quilt is quite ornate, and an elaborate binding might have detracted from it, so we have chosen a simple binding worked in the same fabric that you used for the sashing and the backing. This gives a neat but unobtrusive finish. The squared corners are easier to work than mitered ones, but if you prefer the effect of mitered corners, as many quilters do, follow the instructions below.

Be sure to add your name and date to the quilt for posterity. You might even include the reason for making the quilt, for example, to celebrate a wedding or to remember a friend of many years. Embroider the data on the quilt top in the sashing or inside a block. Or, if your sewing machine can form letters, sew the details into the backing fabric before it is joined to the quilt top and batting.

▲ The finished quilt, with all the raw edges neatly concealed inside a muslin binding.

MITERED CORNERS

To miter the corners of your binding, cut four strips 78½ in. long, and join them in a large circle by making seams at each end as shown left. The tip of the seam should be ¼ in. from the end of the strip, and the angle should be an exact right angle. Trim the seams down each side and cut away the tips, then press each length of binding in half lengthwise to mark the fold line. Attach the binding in the same way as for straight binding (see page 60), but machine stitch it all around the quilt edge before turning it to the back.

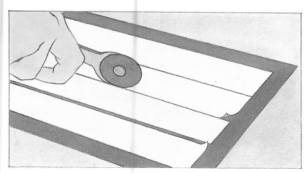

1 From the muslin (fabric G), cut four strips 79 in. × 2¹/₂ in. You will find it most accurate to use the rotary cutter and board for this; first cut a piece 79 in. × 10 in., then cut this wide strip into four narrow ones.

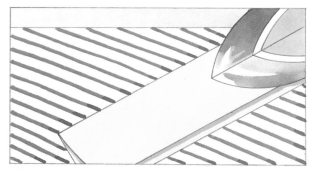

2 Fold each of the strips in half lengthwise and press; this will give you a good fold line when you turn the strips over the quilt edges.

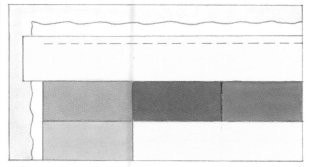

3 Open up one of the strips and place it face down on one side of the quilt, so that the raw edge aligns with the raw edge of the border (not the raw edge of the backing). Stitch a seam ¹/₄ in. from the edge, by hand or machine. Repeat along the opposite quilt edge.

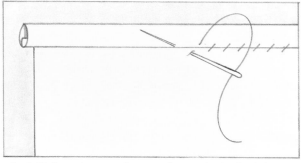

4 Fold the strips over the raw edges to the back of the quilt. Turn under ¹/₄ in. and hem by hand to the muslin backing to give a neat finish.

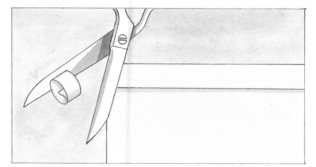

5 Trim the ends of the strips so that they align with the edges of the backing fabric.

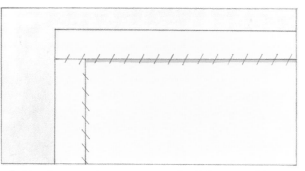

6 Use the remaining two strips to bind the top and bottom of the quilt in the same way, tucking the raw ends in at the corners and stitching them in place.

4

Extending your skills

Wholecloth quilting is worked on one body of fabric. No piecing is involved, and the decorative patterns are made entirely by the lines of quilting stitches rather than the patchwork designs.

Medallions are the main motifs used in wholecloth quilts. The medallion provides the main visual focus, usually forming a spectacular centerpiece. Some medallion designs have

Wholecloth pillow

histories and traditions. Heart shapes and lovers' knots, for instance, were traditionally stitched only on quilts meant for engaged or newlywed couples.

Many medallion designs were inspired by everyday objects – leaves, flowers, cords, fans, shells. Feather designs, in many different shapes, were especially popular. For this project, we have used a modern stylized flower shape which adds an attractive texture to the glazed cotton pillow top.

MATERIALS

- *Medium blue cotton: 1 circle, 20 in. diameter; 2 rectangles, each 20 in. × 14 in.*

- *Muslin or other backing fabric: 1 circle, 20 in. diameter*

- *Thin, lightweight (2 oz.) batting: 1 circle, 20 in. diameter*

- *Blue sewing thread (to match the cotton fabric)*

- *Blue quilting thread (darker than the cotton fabric)*

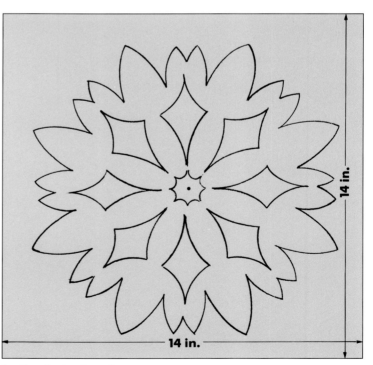

▲ *Chart for the Flower design.*

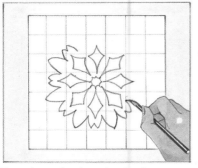

1 *Enlarge the chart for the flower to the correct size (see page 40). Remember to put in the center dot. This will help you to position the design in the center of the fabric.*

2 *Fold the blue circle in half, then in half again. Mark the center point on the right side with a dot, using a fading-ink pen (see page 29).*

3 *Transfer the flower design to the right side of the blue cotton circle (see page 48), aligning the dot on the chart with the dot in the center of the fabric.*

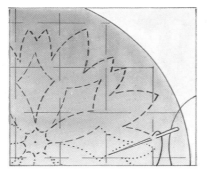

4 *Lay the muslin on a flat surface and put the circle of batting on top, then the marked fabric, right side up. Baste the layers together with a grid of horizontal and vertical stitches (see page 52).*

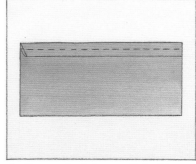

5 *Using the blue quilting thread, quilt the design (see page 56). Begin in the center and work out to prevent puckering. When your quilting is complete, remove the basting threads.*

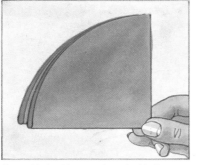

6 *Press and stitch a small double seam on one long edge of each rectangle.*

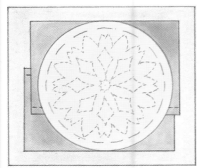

7 *Place the rectangles face up on a flat surface. Place the quilted medallion face down on top so that the seamed edges overlap and the sides are level with the edges of the circle. Baste around 1 in. from raw edges.*

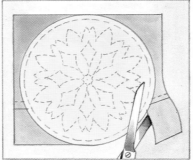

8 *Stitch around the edge twice by machine for strength. Remove the basting. Trim the seam to ¹/₄ in.; trim the excess fabric from the pillow back. Be careful not to cut through the stitching of the seam line. Clip seam.*

9 *Turn the pillow cover right side out and press the backs carefully. Don't press the quilted areas. If the front of the cover is creased, hold a hot steam iron a few inches above the quilting for a few seconds.*

The Amish people follow a simple and industrious way of life. Their stress on simplicity is noticeable in the plain, sometimes stark beauty of their quilts. Many Amish quilts are made from hand-dyed cottons in bright colors; black pieces are added, giving more intensity to the surrounding colors. The Amish sometimes use block patterns, but more usually a large central design is surrounded by one or two

Amish lap quilt

borders; quilting with contrasting threads shows off the exquisite patterns in the stitches. The colors used in the oldest Amish quilts, from Pennsylvania, are usually in the cool part of the spectrum. We have used these colors in this simple patchwork design called, among other things, Roman Stripes.

MATERIALS

- Cotton: ¼ yd. × 60 in. of each of 6 colors – pale pink, dark pink, mauve, purple, pale blue, dark blue

- Black cotton: 1½ yd. × 60 in.; 6 ft. 2 in. × 4 ft. 2 in.

- Thin batting: 6 ft. × 4 ft.

- Muslin: 6 ft. × 4 ft.

- Matching sewing thread

- Right-angle triangle template with shorter sides of 12 in.

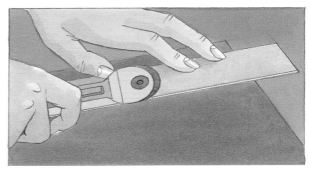

1 Use a rotary cutter to cut the colored cotton lengthwise into 2 in. strips (see page 44).

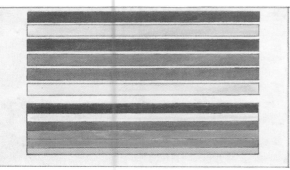

2 *Stitch the strips of fabric together along the long edges to make four wide strips. Work in this order each time – purple, light pink, dark blue, mauve, dark pink, light blue. Use ¹/₄ in. seam allowance.*

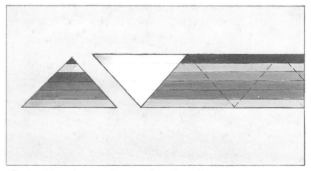

3 *Position the template so that the 90° point is on one edge of one wide strip and the long edge is along the other. Use a rotary cutter to cut a triangle from the strip-pieced fabric. Turn the template around and cut another triangle. Continue in this way until you have cut 24 triangles, 12 in each direction.*

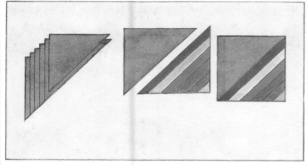

4 *Use the same template to cut 24 triangles from the black fabric. Place the short sides of the template along the grain. With right sides together, join the long edge of a black triangle to the long edge of a strip-pieced triangle. Repeat to form 24 blocks.*

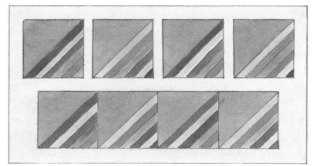

5 *If necessary, trim the blocks slightly to square them up. Follow the layout shown in the photograph to join the blocks in four rows of six, then join the rows together to form the quilt top.*

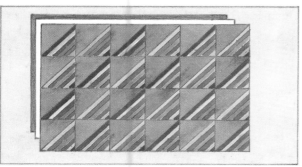

6 *Layer the muslin, the batting, and the quilt top (see page 52). Baste the layers together. Stitch by hand or machine along the seam lines between the blocks and between the triangles. Remove the basting threads.*

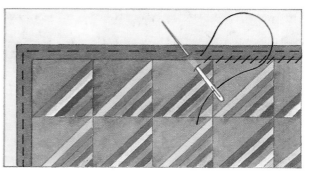

7 *Place the quilted patchwork on the backing fabric, wrong sides together. Turn over each edge of backing fabric ¹/₄ in., then ¹/₄ in. again. Baste backing over the edges of the patchwork; slipstitch into place. Remove basting threads.*

English patchwork is pieced work that is produced by stitching together pieces of fabric that have been basted onto paper shapes. It is very time-consuming, so is not the best method for traditional block patterns which can be stitched far more quickly by the conventional method. It is, however, very useful for shapes which cannot easily be joined with long straight seams, such as hexagons, diamond

English patchwork

stars, octagons, and patterns such as Tumbling Blocks or Baby's Blocks (see page 125).

To assemble the pieces for English patchwork, cut the paper shapes from paper such as typing paper, then cut corresponding fabric shapes, with a ¼ in. seam allowance all around. The fabric is then basted over the paper, turning the raw edges to the back, and the shapes are overcast together to build up the pattern. Here, the paper shapes are left in place to stiffen the decoration, but normally they are removed when the basting threads are taken out.

For an eye-catching variation, sew six hexagons instead of seven and make a wreath decoration by leaving out the middle shape.

- Cotton fabrics with Christmas motifs: 7 pieces, each no less than 6 in. square
- Thin card
- Sheet of typing paper
- Green or red sewing thread
- Ribbon or braid: 6 in. length
- Small amount of stuffing

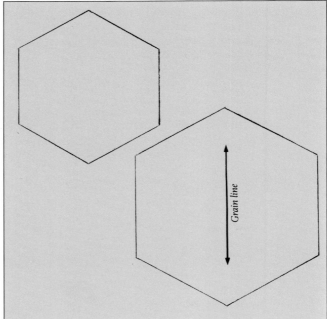

Grain line

▲ Template A for the paper shapes.

▲ Template B for the fabric shapes.

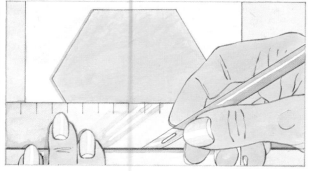

1 Trace the templates onto thin cardboard, and cut them out very accurately. Mark the grain line onto template B. Cut two shapes from each fabric using template B. Using template A, cut 14 paper shapes.

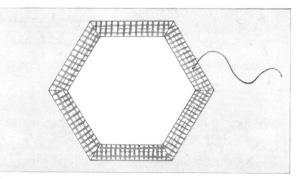

2 Baste each piece of fabric to a paper shape, stitching down the ¼ in. overlap all around. Tie a knot in the end of your basting thread and start stitching with the knot on the right side; this will make it easier to remove the basting.

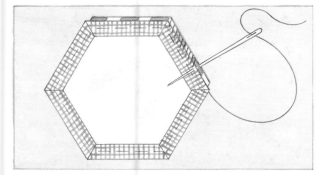

3 When all your shapes are basted, take two hexagons of different fabrics and place them right sides together. Stitch them together along one side, overcasting with close, firm stitches. Start and finish the thread securely.

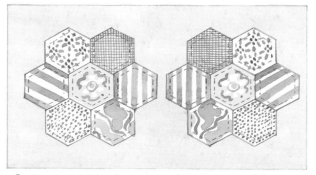

4 Continue joining hexagons to form a rosette of six different hexagons around a central one; make sure that all the seams between them are stitched. Join the other hexagons in the same way to form a mirror image rosette.

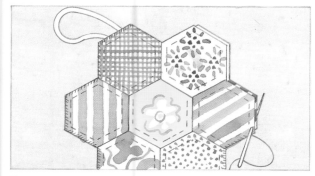

5 Place the rosettes, paper sides together, with the same fabric hexagons backing each other at the top, and blind stitch around the edges of the rosettes. Stitch the ends of the hanging loop into the seam at each side of the top hexagon, and leave two or three sides open for stuffing.

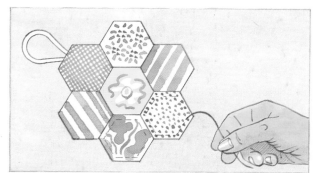

6 Pad the shape gently with a small amount of the stuffing, and close up the final edges of the rosette. Don't over-stuff, or the shape of the decoration will be distorted. Remove the basting threads.

This striking patchwork is a type of appliqué. The patches of fabric are laid onto a background, and the raw edges are covered with a length of binding. The final result resembles a stained glass window; the binding makes lines between the fabric pieces in the same way that leading separates panes of colored glass.

If all the lines in the patchwork design are straight, any kind of binding can be used for

Stained glass wallhanging

the "leading." If any of the lines are curved, you will need to use bias binding so that the tape can be shaped to follow the curves. You can use commercial bias binding or cut strips of fabric on the bias; the latter is useful when you want a particular color or size of bias binding.

This project uses the traditional black binding over bright, jewel-tone fabrics.

MATERIALS

- Pale green cotton: 30 in. square
- Muslin (or other backing fabric): 30 in. square
- Thin batting: 30 in. square
- Bright pink cotton: 18 in. square
- Bright purple cotton: 18 in. square
- Bright jade green cotton: 14 in. square
- Medium jade green cotton: 14 in. square
- 1 in. wide black bias binding: 16 yd.
- Black sewing thread

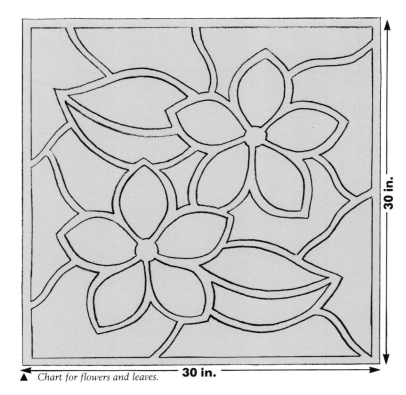

▲ *Chart for flowers and leaves.* **30 in.**

30 in.

1 Enlarge the chart to the correct size (see page 40). Go over it with dark felt-tip pen and trace it onto the right side of the pale green fabric. The lines will be covered by the bias binding.

2 Use the enlarged drawing to cut templates for the flower and leaf shapes. Cut one flower from each of the purple and pink fabrics and two half-leaves from the two green fabrics.

3 Lay out the fabric pieces in the correct position on the pale green fabric. Baste them into place.

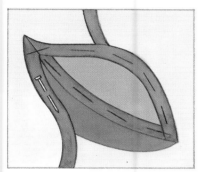

4 Pin and baste pieces of bias binding, with the edges folded under, along all the lines of the design. Make sure that raw ends are covered by the next piece of binding.

5 Lay the batting on top of the backing fabric, and the flower design, face up, on top. Baste the layers together with a grid of vertical and horizontal stitches (see page 52).

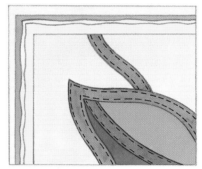

6 Machine stitch along both edges of each strip of bias binding. Stitch the inside edge of each curve first; this prevents the binding from stretching out of shape.

7 Remove basting threads. Add a small circle of black fabric to the center of the flower to cover the raw ends of bias binding. Turn under and hand stitch.

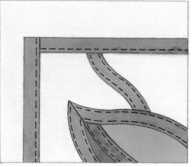

8 Bind the raw edges of the square with more black bias binding.

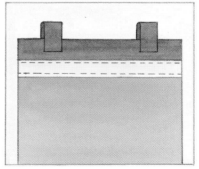

9 Attach tape loops or a casing made from bias binding to the back of the project for hanging.

Cathedral window patchwork is an unusual technique. It is neither pieced, appliquéd, nor quilted. It requires no batting, as the thickness comes from folding squares of fabric over on themselves. The finished result is rather three-dimensional in effect, with an overall design which is highly textured.

The base squares are usually made in plain colors, with the "windows" cut from prints.

EXTENDING YOUR SKILLS

Cathedral window

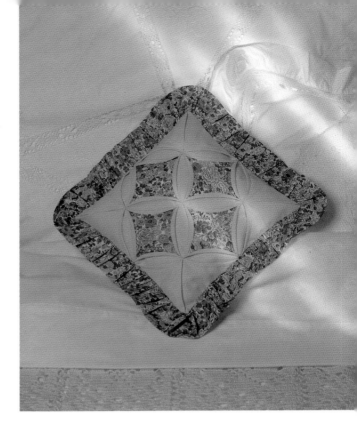

Interesting effects can be achieved by reversing this idea; use a small print for the frames and either a plain color, a large print, or a single motif in the windows. The shape and size of the panels lend themselves perfectly to this herb pillow design and provide an easy introduction to this technique. The potpourri or scented herbs will gradually release their fragrance into a room or drawer.

MATERIALS

- Pink cotton: 4 squares, each $10^1/_2$ in. × $10^1/_2$ in.
- Pink print cotton: $^1/_2$ yd.
- Pink sewing thread to match
- Potpourri or scented herbs to stuff pillow

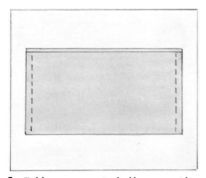

1 Fold one square in half, wrong sides together, and stitch a $^1/_4$ in. seam along both short edges. Repeat the process for the other squares.

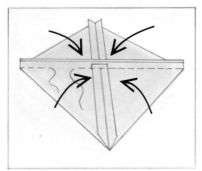

2 On each square, pin together the tops of the seams and then pin the remaining raw edges together along the top. Leaving an opening for turning, stitch a $^1/_4$ in. seam.

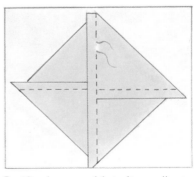

3 Clip the excess fabric diagonally at each of the corners. This will make the shapes lie flat after they are turned right side out.

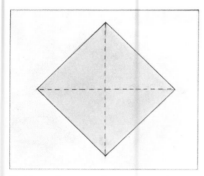

4 *Turn the seamed squares to the right side. Use the tip of a bodkin to push out the corners. Press into square shapes. The opening will be hidden when the pillow is finished.*

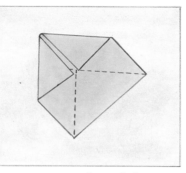

5 *Lay one square flat with the seams on top, then bring all four corners to the center. Press firmly. Repeat for the remaining squares.*

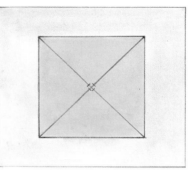

6 *Catch the corners of each square to the center with very small stitches through to the back.*

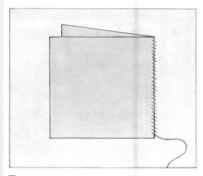

7 *Put two squares together so that the folded sides are facing each other; overcast down one side. Repeat for the other pair of squares, then stitch the pairs together in the same way.*

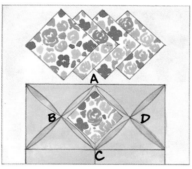

8 *Cut four squares of printed fabric a little smaller than the square made by points A, B, C, and D. Pin them inside the lines made by the folds on each side of the shape.*

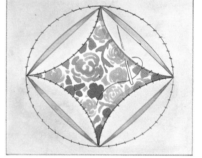

9 *Roll the edges of the "windows" over the edges of the print squares. Stitch the edges down, catching the corners together with two small stitches. Roll and catch the edges just outside the windows.*

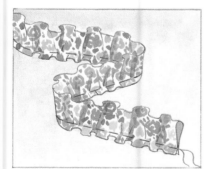

10 *From the print fabric, cut a length 3¼ in. × the complete width. Fold it lengthwise and press fold. Run a gathering thread along the bottom ¼ in. from the raw edges, and pull gently to make a folded ruffle.*

11 *Cut a square of print fabric the same size as your patchwork square plus ¼ in. all around. Pin the ruffle to the pillow top, right sides together. Stitch with a ¼ in. seam all around, then press ruffle out.*

12 *Place the patchwork square on the print backing square, wrong sides together. Slipstitch three edges, then stuff gently with potpourri. Slipstitch the final edge closed.*

Folded patchwork has several variations. The technique used here is also called Somerset patchwork and can be used for items like pillows, cards, and wallhangings. Folded patchwork of this kind is not suitable for bed quilts, however, as there are raw edges inside the folds which would tend to fray with frequent washing. Another folded technique, Prairie Points, is constructed so that the raw edges are

Folded star

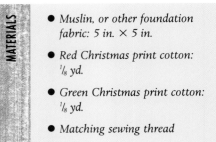

- Muslin, or other foundation fabric: 5 in. × 5 in.
- Red Christmas print cotton: 1/8 yd.
- Green Christmas print cotton: 1/8 yd.
- Matching sewing thread
- Glue
- White card or mat board with round opening approximately 3¾ in. diameter
- Red frame, approximately 4½ in. square

sealed; because of this extra protection, it is particularly recommended for items that have to be washed.

This project uses two print fabrics in Christmas colors. The circles are arranged so that a red star appears in the design. If you fold your fabric so that the same motif shows each time, you can create a secondary patern within the star. Use unusual fabrics to vary the design.

For appliqué shapes with extra dimension, use small pieces of folded patchwork to make trees or flowers; bind the edges and attach to a background. This patchwork is usually constructed from the center out, but for flowers and trees you can begin at the outside.

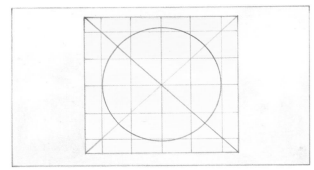

1 On the square of foundation fabric, draw in diagonals from corner to corner. From the center outward, draw a grid of 1 in. squares – a quilter's ruler (see page 84) is useful for drawing parallel lines. In the center of the grid, draw a circle the same size as the one on the card.

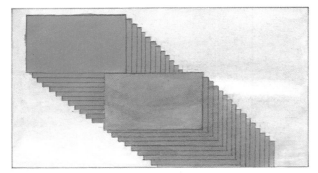

2 From the red fabric cut 12 rectangles each measuring 1½ in. × 2½ in. From the green fabric, cut 16 rectangles the same size. For accuracy and speed, use a rotary cutter (see page 45).

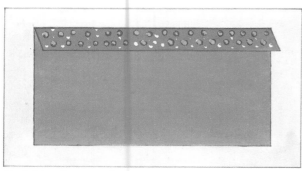

3 Fold and press under ¼ in. along one long edge of each one of the rectangles.

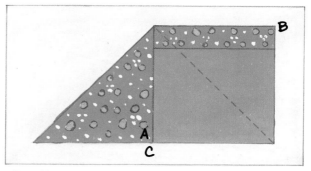

4 Fold and press points A and B to point C on all pieces, placing wrong sides together as shown. You now have 28 folded triangles; 12 red and 16 green. All show the right side of the fabric on both sides.

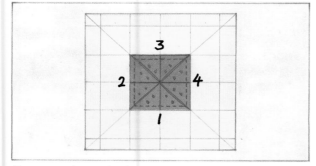

5 Lay 4 red triangles down on the center of the foundation square, folds up as shown. Use the guidelines to help you position them accurately. Secure each point with an invisible stitch; stitch to the foundation with running stitches around the edges.

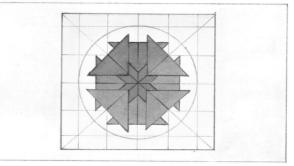

6 Lay 4 green triangles, points in, over the first 4 red ones. Overlap evenly all around, but position the green triangles further out than the red row. Use running stitch around the long edges as before. Work another row of 4 green triangles in the same way.

7 Now add a row of 8 red triangles, positioned in alternating layers as before. Finish off with a row of 8 green triangles to complete the star.

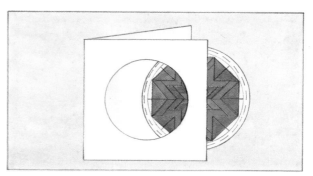

8 Baste, then stitch just outside the circle on the foundation fabric, and cut out the completed star and circle. Glue around the edges of the star shape. Place the star behind the opening in the card or mat, making sure that it is accurately centered. Place in frame.

Trapunto quilting, like conventional quilting, uses a layer of padding, but in trapunto only certain areas are padded rather than the whole of the item. The top layer of fabric is tacked to a firm backing layer, then the chosen areas are stitched to form hollow pockets. These are then lightly stuffed, producing an intriguing three-dimensional effect.

The project here uses a fabric-painted

Trapunto table mat

design, but you could just as easily use a printed fabric or one of the specially printed panels. Work the stitching by hand or by machine; machine stitching is much quicker if you have large areas to cover. If you stitch by hand, use a firm backstitch in a strong thread so that the stitching gives a definite outline to the pockets.

- *Pale yellow cotton: 18 in. square*
- *Muslin or other backing fabric: 2 squares, each 18 in. × 18 in.*
- *Fabric paints: medium and dark yellow; medium and dark orange; medium and dark moss green. (You can purchase colors separately or mix your own.)*
- *Brushes*
- *Yellow sewing thread (to match yellow fabric)*
- *Stuffing*

▲ *Actual size chart for the table mat design.*

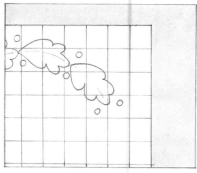

1 *Draw a circle 5½ in. in diameter and arrange leaf and berry shapes around it. Go over the design lines with black felt-tip pen.*

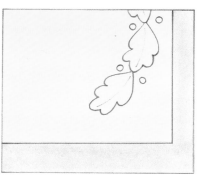

2 *Place the yellow fabric, right side up, over the design and trace the main lines using a matching crayon or silverpoint (see page 49).*

3 *Use the yellow, green, and orange fabric paints to color in the leaves and berries; alternate yellow leaves and green leaves.*

4 *With slightly darker shades of the same colors, add veins to the leaves and details to berries. When the paint is dry, set the colors according to the manufacturer's directions.*

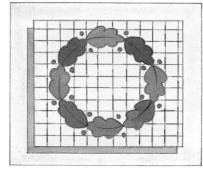

5 *Place the painted panel over one square of the backing fabric, wrong sides together, matching edges. Baste with a grid of horizontal and vertical stitches (see page 52).*

6 *Outline the leaves and berries with machine zigzag or straight stitch; use backstitch if stitching by hand.*

7 *Behind each pocket formed by the stitched outline, cut a small (½ in. – ¾ in. long) slit in the backing fabric. Be very careful not to cut through the top fabric.*

8 *Use a small amount of stuffing to pad each stitched pocket, checking your progress from the front. Don't overstuff or the fabric will distort. Close the slits in the backing fabric with small overcast stitch.*

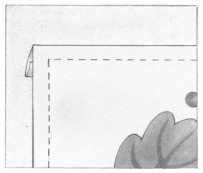

9 *Baste the second square of backing fabric to the back of the mat, wrong sides together. Fold raw edges to the inside; close with two rows of topstitching around outside edges.*

Italian, or corded, quilting involves stitching two layers of fabric together in a decorative pattern of lines and channels. When the stitching is complete, the channels are threaded with cord or thick wool. This raises the top fabric and produces a textured pattern. Italian quilting is excellent for strong linear designs like this Celtic knot, worked on silk for a skirt pocket. The stitching and quilting are completed

Corded pocket

before the pocket is attached to the garment. (For a ready-made garment, remove the pocket to embellish it, then stitch in place again.) This design is worked on a pocket for an evening skirt, but would also work smaller to decorate a shirt pocket.

MATERIALS

- Silk fabric: about 2 in. larger all around than pocket pattern piece

- Firmly woven silk for backing: same size as above

- Fine cotton cord: 2 yd.

- Cotton or silk thread to match silk fabric

- Large-eyed tapestry needle

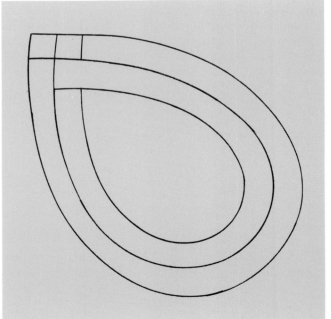

▲ One quarter of the Celtic Knot pattern, actual size for tracing.

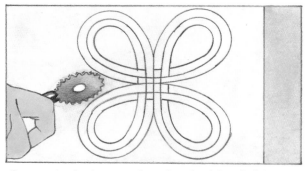

1 *Trace each quarter of the pattern (opposite below) on the same piece of paper. Turn the paper and reposition it carefully for each quarter.*

2 *Transfer the design to the right side of the silk fabric, using the tracing or prick and pounce method (see page 49). Allow at least 1 in. of plain fabric around the outside edge of the design.*

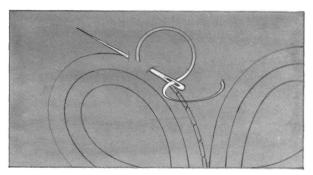

3 *Place the silk on top of the backing fabric, wrong sides together. Baste together with a grid of horizontal and vertical stitches (see page 53).*

4 *Using backstitch and three strands of cotton or silk thread, stitch along all the lines of the design to form channels. When the stitching is complete, press the design with a warm steam iron.*

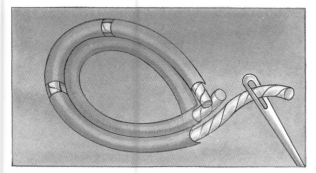

5 *Thread the tapestry needle with a length of cord. Take the needle through the backing fabric at the beginning of one channel. Thread all the channels with cord, taking the needle out of the backing fabric at the end of each channel. Along tight curves, you may need to take the needle in and out of backing fabric several times.*

6 *When the design is completely corded, lay it face down on a soft cloth and press it on the wrong side with a warm steam iron. Center the pocket pattern over the design, cut out, and continue making the garment.*

Sashiko quilting is a traditional Japanese technique. The stitching is worked in bold threads; the thickness depends on the thickness of the fabric. The stitches are longer than for ordinary quilting. Stitch length for sashiko is about twice as long on the front as on the back. The designs are usually geometric repeats. This silk evening bag illustrates the use of several different designs inside straight

Sashiko bag

outlines. Sashiko work can be flat or padded; this project is gently padded with a thin layer of batting to give it extra texture.

Because the stitches are designed to show, it is important to make them look as even and attractive as possible. On straight lines, pick up as many stitches as possible on your needle so that you get into an even rocking rhythm; on curves it will only be practical to pick up one or two stitches to keep the curve smooth. Try to sew the same number of stitches per inch throughout the design and make sure that they don't overlap.

MATERIALS

- Jade green silk: two pieces, 21½ in. × 7½ in. each; 3½ in. × 5 in. rectangle; 3 in. × 3 in. square
- Thin (2oz) polyester or silk batting: 21 in. × 7 in.
- Iron-on interfacing (light)
- Gold thread
- Small gold beads
- Green silk thread to match
- Green sewing thread to match
- Thin gold or jade cord
- Thick gold or jade cord for handle

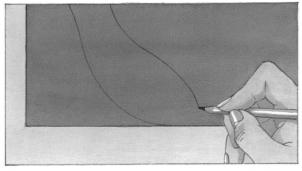

1 *Enlarge the chart to the correct size (see page 40). Using a crayon slightly darker than the silk, or a silverpoint (see page 49), transfer the design onto the right side of one of the large pieces of silk.*

118

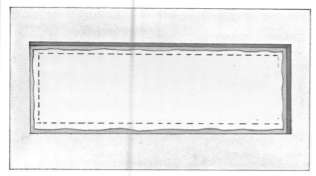

2 Place the silk pieces right sides together and pin the batting in the center of the top piece. Machine stitch around the rectangle, leaving one short side open for turning. Clip across the corners and remove the pins.

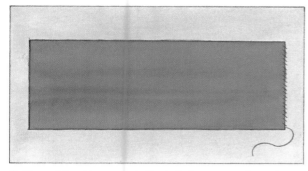

3 Turn right side out and slipstitch the open end, turning under ¹/₄ in. of each piece of fabric to make a rectangle 7 in. × 21 in.

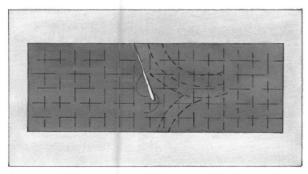

4 Baste the layers with a grid of horizontal and vertical stitches (see page 53). Using the gold thread, make sashiko running stitches along all the lines of the design. Begin each thread with a small knot pulled into the lining.

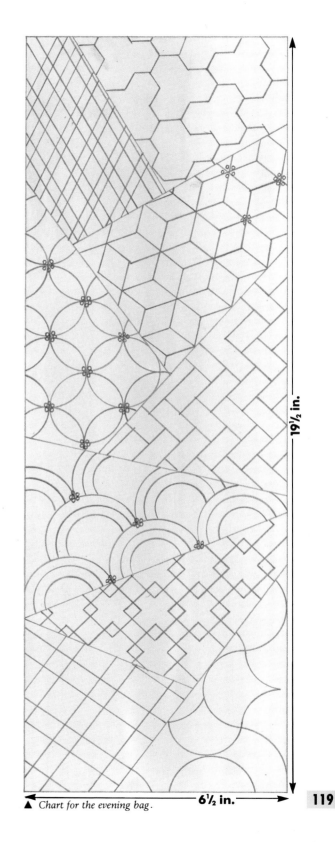

19¹/₂ in.

6¹/₂ in.

▲ Chart for the evening bag.

Back of sashiko evening bag.

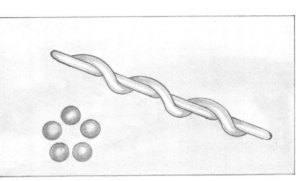

5 Using the gold thread, whip a line of stitches through the running stitches that divide each pattern block; this gives a solid gold line. Add several gold beads where indicated on the chart.

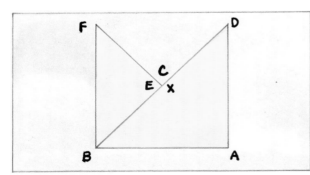

6 Lay the quilted rectangle face down; fold along line AB to make the shape shown.

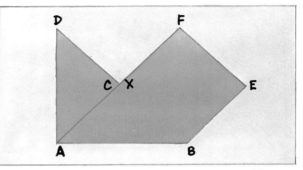

7 Fold corner C to point X; turn the piece over. Fold corner E to point X. Pin the edges together where they meet so that the bag keeps its shape.

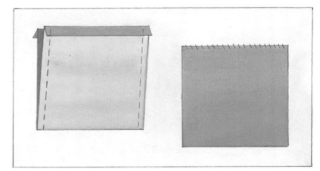

8 Turn the bag inside out and slipstitch from corner A to point CX and from corner B to point EX.

9 Add iron-on interfacing to back of two small green silk pieces. Fold the rectangular piece in half across its width, right sides together, and sew together with a ¼ in. seam allowance. Clip the corners and turn right side out. Slipstitch the open ends closed to make a 2 ½ in. square.

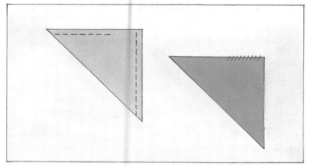

10 Fold the square of silk diagonally, right sides together, and stitch ¼ in. seams along two sides, leaving a small opening for turning. Clip corners, turn right side out and slipstitch the opening closed.

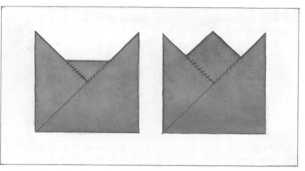

11 Slipstitch the triangular piece into the V shape at the front of the bag and the square piece into the V at the back, working the stitches neatly from the inside of the bag.

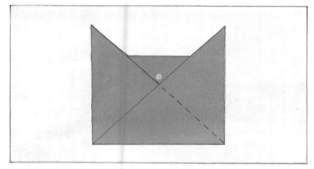

12 Fold the top half of the square over the front of the bag and add a snap or other closure underneath the flap.

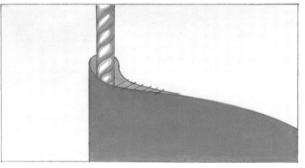

13 Cut a length of thick cord for the handle; stitch the raw ends invisibly to the points of the bag sides. If the cord is bulky, wrap the end in the point of the bag, then stitch the diagonal sides together to hide it.

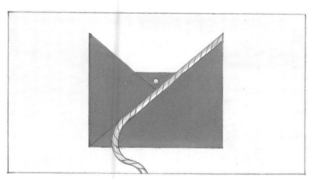

14 Add thin cord to the seam lines on the front and back of the bag, using invisible slipstitches.

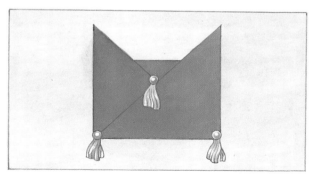

15 Make three tassels from the gold thread and the green thread; stitch them to the bottom corners of the bag and the tip of the front flap.

5

Pattern library

This section shows many popular piecing and quilting patterns, both traditional and modern. The Pattern Library is divided into types of patterns to make it easy to use. For example, nine-patch block designs are all together, as are Log Cabin designs, quilted motifs, pieced borders, block and sashing combinations, and so on.

You can use the patterns here in several ways. You might want to choose an alternative design for one of the sections in the sampler quilt. Or, incorporate the designs here into projects found elsewhere. Or, you can use the designs for your own projects. Mix and match the patterns to create your own unique designs.

Top: Fans variation block

Right: Strip-pieced quilt and border

Left: Sunflower Star

Bottom left: Star Blocks with Sawtooth border

Below: Tumbling Blocks with Baby Blocks

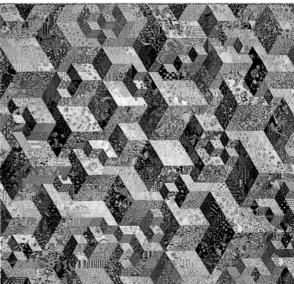

Four-patch blocks

Four-patch block designs range from very simple patterns to very complex ones. In some designs, such as **Flyfoot** *and* **Oh Susannah,** *all of the quarters in the block are identical; each quarter is stitched in the same relationship to the center of the block. Some designs, such as* **King's X,** *use quarters made as mirror images; others, such as* **Double Four Patch,** *use two quarters made up in one arrangement and two in another.*

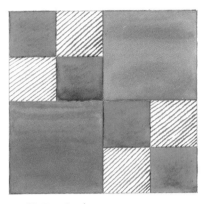

Simple Four Patch

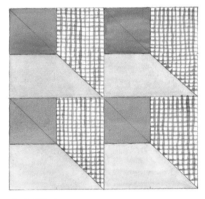

Double Four Patch

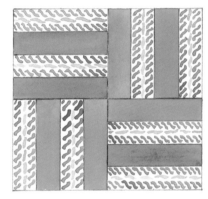

Rail Fence

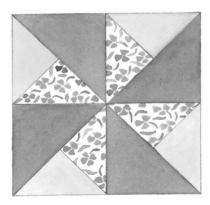

Attic Windows

Four-patch with pinwheels and wholecloth

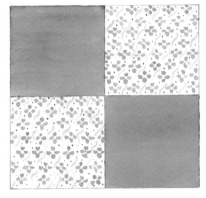

Pinwheel

Oh Susannah

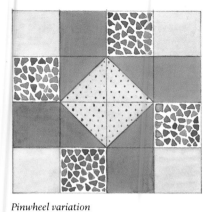

Pinwheel variation

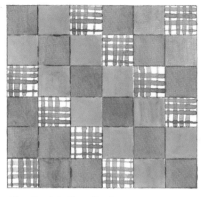

Nine Patch in Four Patch

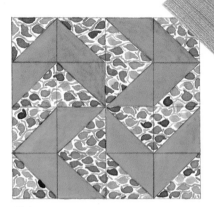

Flyfoot

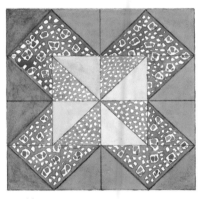

Double 2

Sawtoothed Square

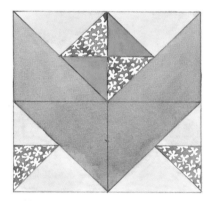

Ribbon

Star

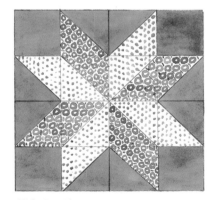

Eight Star Flower

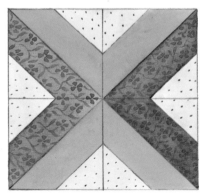

King's X

Nine-patch blocks

Because nine-patch blocks use more pieces, the possibilities for design variations are greater, and you can create some very complex effects. Nine-patch blocks are rarely made with each patch identical. In some designs, such as **Rolling Stone** *and* **Corner Nine Patch**, *the middle patch is a plain square of fabric. In the* **Nine-Patch Variation**, *the middle patch is pieced so that it provides a visual focus for the block. Many nine-patch designs build up a complex pattern across the patches, such as* **Jacob's Ladder**. **Maple Leaf** *is another example of a simple picture built from regular patches.*

Basic Nine Patch

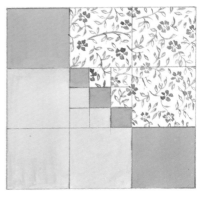

Nine Patch variation

Corner Nine Patch

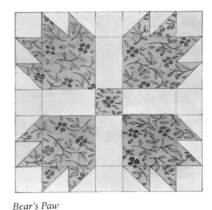

Bear's Paw

Double-patch blocks with wholecloth blocks

Ohio Star

Star variation

54- 40 or Fight

Jacob's Ladder

Cross and Crown

Maple Leaf

Card Trick

Churn Dash

Rolling Stone

Irregular blocks

Irregular blocks are less straightforward to piece. Some require curved seams or set-in seams, such as **Covered Bridge** *and* **Fruit Basket**. *In others, the piecing is all in straight seams, but the patches are quite complex; for example,* **Pine Tree, Pieced Tulip** *and* **School House**. *If you are making one of these blocks, look carefully at the piecing required. Break down the design into its component patches, and try to do most of the piecing in straight seams.*

Many of the irregular block designs use a combination of piecing and appliqué. **Grandmother's Fan, Dresden Plate,** *and their variations – some of the most popular block designs – are pieced first, then appliquéd onto a background square. The* **Carolina Lily** *design is pieced in patches, but the fine stems are then appliquéd onto the block (see page 78). These designs still make square blocks when they are finished, so they can be substituted for any of the blocks in the sampler quilt or any project that calls for a block design.*

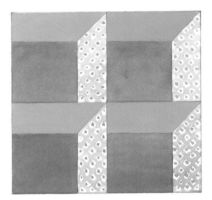

Attic Windows

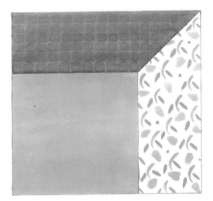

Attic Windows variation

Four Crown

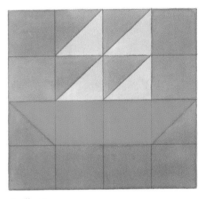

Sailboat

School House

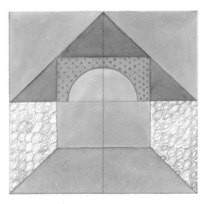

Covered Bridge

Pieced Tulip

Carolina Lily

Dresden Plate

Fruit Basket

Tree of Life

Pine Tree

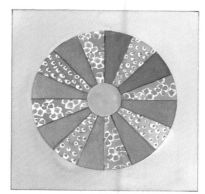

Grandmother's Fan

Grandmother's Fan detail

Milady's Fan

Non-block designs

The pieced designs on these pages create fascinating shapes which can be used for whole quilts or appliquéd to a plain background. Spectacular star shapes, such as **Lone Star** *and* **Broken Star** *can be built from the 45° diamond shapes shown. 60° diamonds can be used to piece hexagons. If you make partial star or hexagon motifs from triangles, the quilt can then be pieced in strips and the strips joined by machine, an easier approach than the traditional English patchwork method (see page 106). Triangles can also be used to build up large pieced areas.* **1000 Pyramids** *use 65° triangles.*

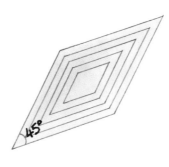

Template for Lone Star

Lone Star

Template for 1000 Pyramids

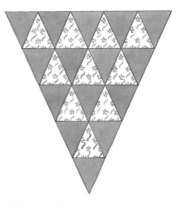

1000 Pyramids

Central non-block design with Flying Geese border

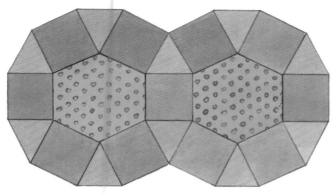

Hexagon Ferris Wheel

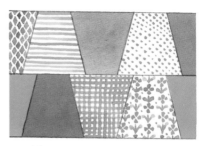

Tumbler

Tumbling Blocks

Star variation

Broken Star

Giant Dahlia

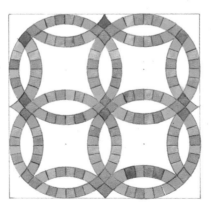

Complex Double Wedding Ring

Flying Geese

Appliqué designs

The shapes in appliqué are stitched onto the fabric and can be as simple or complex as you like. There are an unlimited number of designs that can be used for appliqué; these pages show some of the popular ones. If you are new to appliqué, try simple shapes first, such as leaves, flowers, and birds. Follow the guidelines on page 78 for turning under the raw edges and stitching the shapes to the background. Once you get more confident, you can begin to use more sophisticated designs. Try the **Rose of Sharon** patterns, **Crossed Tulip**, or **Radical Rose**. Appliqué shapes can be used on blocks (see Sampler quilt, page 78), or they can be arranged on a much larger background. Appliqué also works well on a background shape, such as a circle, heart, or trefoil.

Making your own appliqué designs is quite easy. Choose simple shapes or smooth out the lines of more complicated ones; avoid very sharp points and very fine lines. Draw your design full size, then follow the instructions on page 42 for producing templates.

Leaf

Dove

Flower

Shamrock

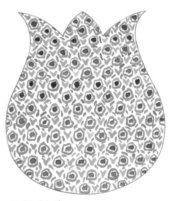

Rose wreath appliquéd quilt

Tulip detail

Bird

Tulip

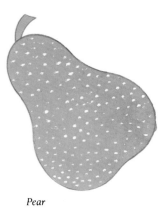

Pear

Radical Rose

Oak Leaf

Ohio Rose

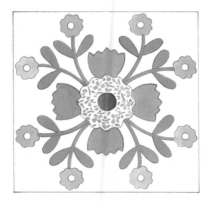

Rose of Sharon

Rose of Sharon variation

Crossed Tulip

Log Cabin blocks

The traditional **Log Cabin** block was used in the sampler quilt (see page 80), but the technique has many other variations. Two strips of fabric used in each layer produce a chevron design. **Court House Steps** applies the strips of fabric on opposite sides before completing the square with the remaining two strips. This design is often made with light and dark fabrics. The basic design can be varied further: make four smaller blocks to build up into a **Log Cabin** four-patch; make the fabrics different widths to produce an off-center design; stitch the strips at a slant; stitch the strips around a central rectangle rather than a square.

The **Log Cabin** technique can be used to build up blocks of different shapes, too. Work in the same way, but begin with a triangle or a diamond.

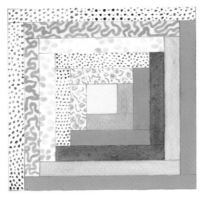

Basic Log Cabin

Log Cabin variation

White House Steps

Log Cabin four-patch

Log Cabin

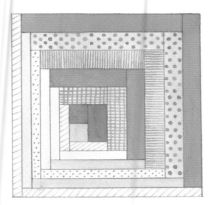

Thick and Thin Log Cabin

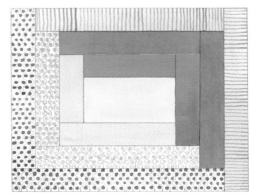

Rectangular Log Cabin

Log Cabin corner

Pineapple

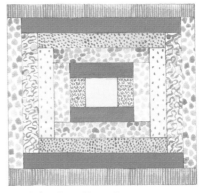

Log Cabin Court House Steps

Triangle Log Cabin

Diamond Log Cabin

Crazy Log Cabin

Log Cabin combinations

All of the designs on these pages are made from different types of **Log Cabin** *blocks. Using the traditional division of light and dark fabrics, several identical* **Log Cabin** *blocks can be stitched together to make secondary patterns, many of which have their own names, like* **Straight Furrows,** *and* **Barn Raising.** *The blocks can be combined so that the light or dark squares form pinwheels, using triangles, squares, rectangles, or parallelograms. Off-center* **Log Cabin** *blocks combine to make pretty star shapes, while several* **Pineapple** *blocks together create a design of secondary circles.*

Log Cabin Star

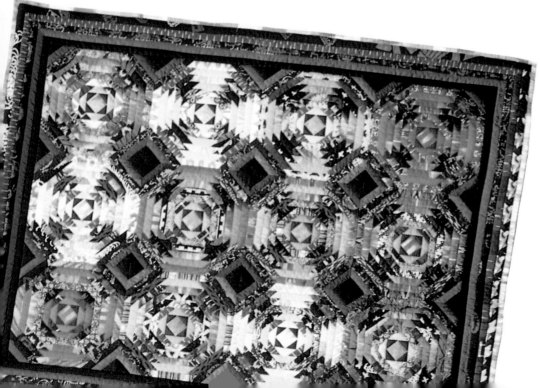

Pineapple Log Cabin design

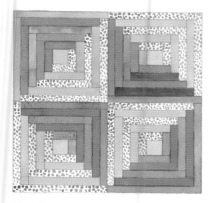

Block for Log Cabin Star

Off-center narrow logs block

Off-center narrow logs combination

Off-center wide logs

Log Cabin Cross

Pineapple

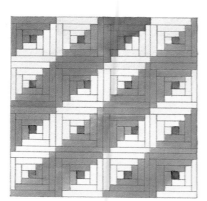

Straight Furrow

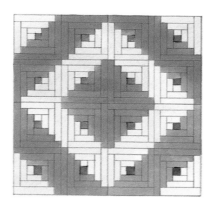

Barn Raising

Log Cabin variation

Strip-piecing patterns

The basic principle of strip-piecing involves joining strips of several fabrics, then cutting the new fabric into strips or other shapes and reassembling them to create a secondary pattern. This principle can be applied to create many different patterns, even using a basic combination of two fabric strips. Strips can be cut into diamonds or triangles and reassembled into stars and hexagons, which can in turn be built into larger patterns if you wish.

If you join many strips of fabric, you can create very complex designs like bargello patterns. **Irish Chain** *consists of strip-pieced blocks (each made up of five strips of five squares in alternating colors) alternated with plain blocks that have been appliquéd or strip-pieced with a contrasting square in each corner.*

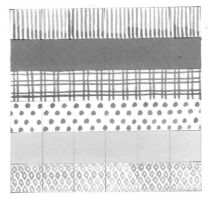

Sew together horizontal strips of even widths. Cut into vertical strips as indicated above.

Each new strip will contain several pieces of joined fabric.

Strip-pieced Irish Chain

Reassemble the new strips so that there are diagonal lines of identical fabrics.

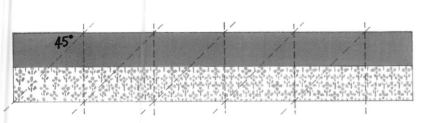

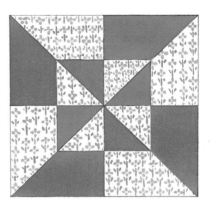

Sew together two strips of equal width. Cut the strip-pieced fabrics into different shapes. A 45° triangle (as shown above) will make patterns 1 and 2; 90° triangles will make pattern 3, and squares will make pattern 4.

Strip-piecing pattern 1

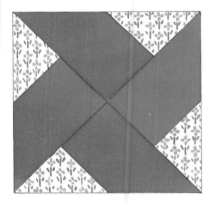

Strip-piecing pattern 2

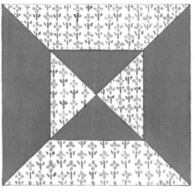

Strip-piecing pattern 3

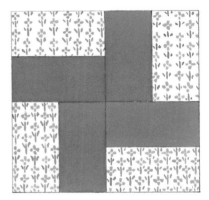

Strip-piecing pattern 4

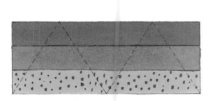

Sew together three strips of even widths and cut into 60° triangles. These triangles can be reassembled to create unusual hexagon designs.

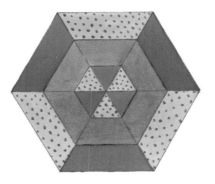

Hexagon

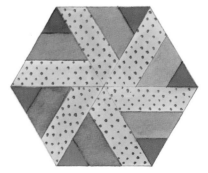

Hexagon variation

Seminole patterns

Seminole work is a variation of strip piecing, but is usually stitched to create long borders to be inserted into garments, purses, quilt borders, and such. Strips of fabric are joined in the normal way, then cut either straight or at an angle to form smaller strips. These smaller strips are then laid at an angle, or offset, or turned top to bottom, and joined once again. Any excess fabric is cut off. Using this method you can create chevrons, zigzags, diamonds, checkerboard designs, and many other variations.

Accuracy is very important in Seminole patchwork. A rotary cutter is excellent for this work. The original strips must be cut and joined accurately; cut any angled strips very carefully so that they are all at exactly the same angle. When rejoined, they need to be positioned against each other carefully so that each part is identical.

Sew together strips of various widths. Cut at an angle.

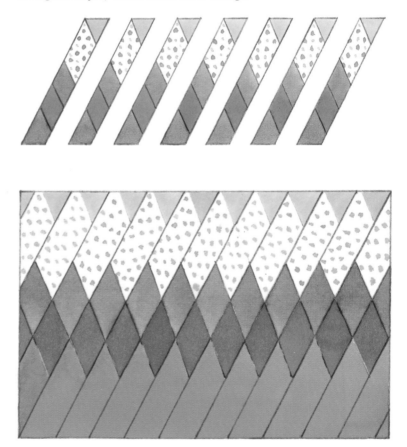

Reposition the cut strips at an opposite slant and reassemble to create different effects.

This sawtooth pattern is formed from diamond sections cut from two strip-pieced fabrics. The cut sections are turned and joined at an angle, then trimmed.

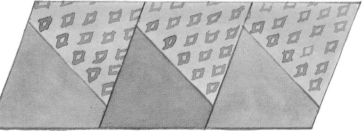

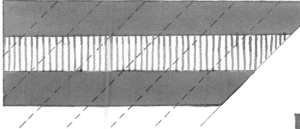

The two strip-pieced sections above and below are cut at opposite angles and joined to form a chevron pattern (right).

143

Block and sashing combinations

Blocks are separated with lines of sashing or setting strips (see page 38). These act as frames for the blocks, so that each design can be seen and appreciated in isolation as well as forming part of the whole design.

There are many different ways of setting blocks, and some of the methods are shown here. Blocks can be joined in shapes or in strips of several blocks, with each group then separated from the others by sashing. Amish quilters (see page 104) often set one or more blocks "on point" or as diamonds.

If the blocks are complex, sashing generally looks best in plain or lightly patterned fabrics. Some sashing designs use two different fabrics. Other designs look like criss-cross strips; the square where two strips intersect uses a different fabric, different color, or even a small pieced block.

Diamond blocks

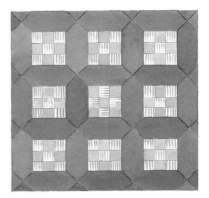

Nine-patch blocks

Star blocks

Plain sashing with double border

Maple Leaf blocks

Nine-patch variation

On point sashing

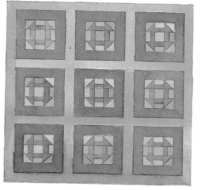

Churn Dash blocks

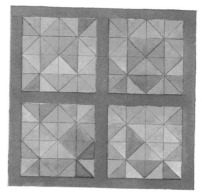

Plain sashing

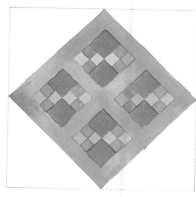

Cross sashing

Pieced-block sashing

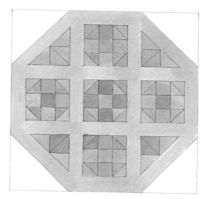

Octagonal design

Strip-pieced sashing

Churn Dash variation in border

Alternate blocks in border

Combining blocks

Quilters like to make use of the secondary patterns formed when blocks are sewn together without sashing. When certain block designs are placed edge to edge, the lines of one block carry visually into the next.

Some blocks can be used to create different patterns: **Sugar Bowl** (see page 76) can also make the meandering **Drunkard's Path** and the **Love Ring** flower. New outlines appear from parts of several blocks put together: each leaf of the **Ozark Maple Leaf** pattern is made from a large part of one block and small triangles on adjoining blocks. (Continued on page 148)

Sugar Bowl basic block 1

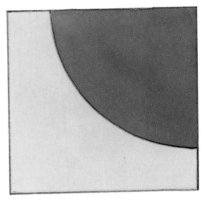

Sugar Bowl basic block 2

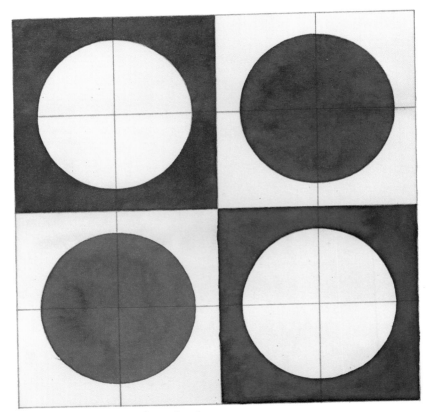

Sugar Bowl basic blocks 1 and 2 combined

Love Ring

Drunkard's Path

Maple Leaf basic block, light

Ozark Maple Leaf

Maple Leaf basic block, dark

Maple Leaf combined variation

◁ *Familiar block patterns can be adapted to form new patterns. The pattern at bottom right was created by alternating* **Rolling Stone** *blocks with an adaptation; the result is a new design.*

Snail Trail *makes a continuous pattern across the quilt by alternating pattern blocks of light or dark.*

Snail Trail component block

Snail Trail

Snail Trail component block

Snail Trail combined

Flyfoot

Flyfoot combined with reverse color blocks

Windmill block

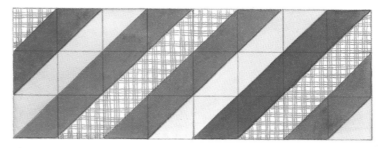

Windmill adapted and combined

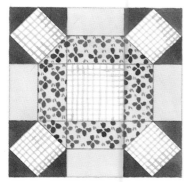

Rolling Stone block

Rolling Stone combined

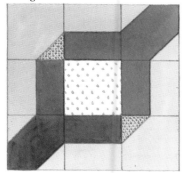

Rolling Stone adapted block

Pieced border patterns

When planning your border pattern, try to use a motif or an idea from your main quilt. If your central patchwork has a strong pattern of stars or squares, then choose a border pattern based on stars or squares. Sawtooth borders are good for blocks featuring many triangles, such as **Bear's Paw**, **Basket**, *and* **Tree of Life***; borders using curves are good for edging quilts with curved seams in the blocks, such as* **Drunkard's Path***. Strip-pieced borders with quarter-circle corners look just right on* **Dresden Plate** *or* **Grandmother's Fan** *quilts while diamond borders make spectacular edgings for complex star designs.*

Border made of squares

Diamond border

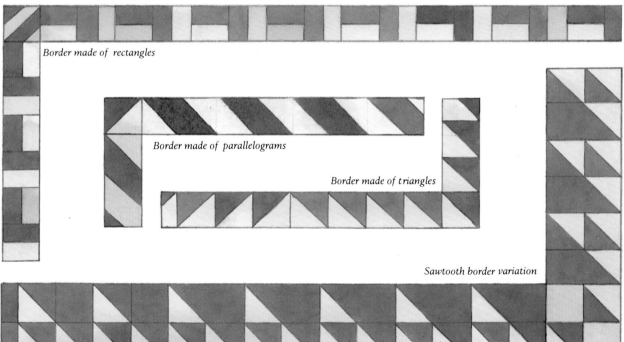

Border made of rectangles

Border made of parallelograms

Border made of triangles

Sawtooth border variation

Twisted Ribbon border

Flying Geese border

Twisted Ribbon variation

Strip-pieced border with
quarter-circle corner

Drunkard's Path border

Peaks border

Star border

Quilted border patterns

Border patterns for quilting are numerous and varied. Like the medallions, many of the traditional border patterns use everyday shapes such as flowers, stars, and feathers. Many designs have evolved using variations of braids (three or more strands), twisted cables, and waves. Complex border designs often combine several elements, such as a double cable twist of feathers with flower finials.

Choose your quilted border so that it complements the main design of your quilt. Select some of the same motifs and build a border out of flowers, fans, stars, or feathers, or incorporate a wine glass shape or spiral pattern to match a background texture. You can make an irregular border pattern, such as a waving cable or feather design, fit into a regular shape, such as a rectangle or circle, by filling in the background with one of the traditional textures like checkering or diagonal lines.

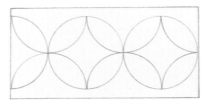

Cathedral Window

Crescent and Heart

Feather and Wave intertwined

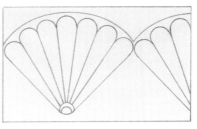

Fan

Crescent variation

Interlocked Diamonds

This quilted border pattern echoes the wavy binding

Braid

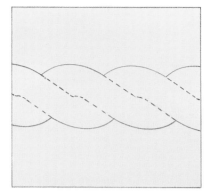

Cable

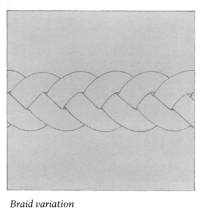

Braid variation

Braid corner

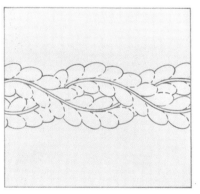

Intertwined Feathers

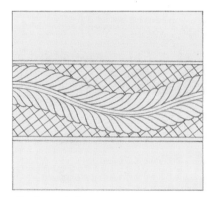

Feather variation

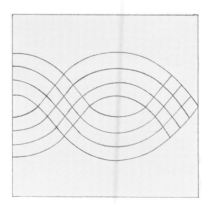

Wave variation

Heart and Flower

Spirals

Background textures

Background textures are used to set off the medallions and borders of quilted designs. Originally these were functional; background textures were added to keep the batting in position and prevent it from bunching. The textures also act as a visual contrast to the main motifs in the quilt.

Choose a pattern in keeping with the style and mood of your main motifs. For instance, if you have a large traditional flower medallion in the center of your quilt, a subtle checkerboard texture or regular diagonal lines will look better than modern asymmetric zigzags. Wineglass, clamshell, rainbow, and spiral designs can easily be marked onto fabric with a circular template if you position it carefully. This is quicker than enlarging a pattern and then tracing it on.

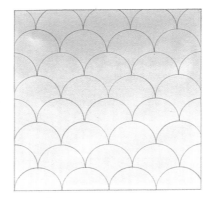

Clamshells

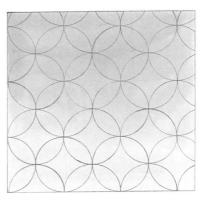

Wineglass

Rainbows

Tartan

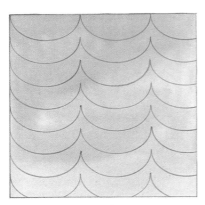

Drapes

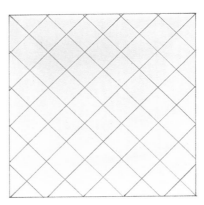

Diagonal lines

Diagonal lines variation

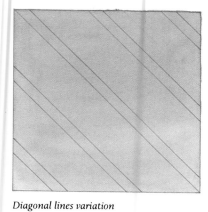

Diagonal lines variation

Diagonal lines variation

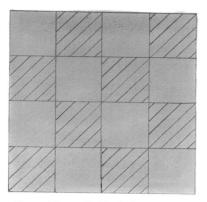

Diagonal lines with Checkerboard

Checkerboard

Checkerboard variation

Zigzag variation

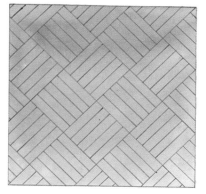

Diamonds

Diamond variation

Spirals

Binding and finishing patterns

The binding of your quilt deserves careful planning. Many complex quilts look best with a relatively plain binding. Bias binding (see page 60) can be used to round off corners or edge a scalloped shape; but binding, bias or straight, doesn't have to be plain. For more visual interest, you can bind a quilt with a patterned fabric from the piecing or make your own strip-pieced binding with straight strips (even or uneven), diamonds, or randomly pieced fabrics from the main body of the quilt.

If your project is made from a coarse-weave fabric, fringe the edges, then leave the fringe, or cut it into chevrons or scallops, or knot it. For delicate items like baby quilts, make a pretty ruffle. Finish off fine edges with shaped borders made from two layers of fabric seamed in the normal way or edged with hand or machine cutwork in scallops, waves or chevrons.

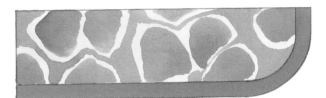

Curved binding

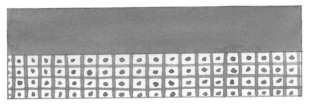

Straight binding with patterned fabric

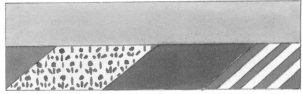

Strip-pieced variation

Strip-pieced variation

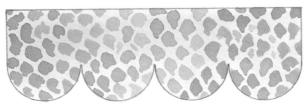

Scalloped edges

Random pieced binding

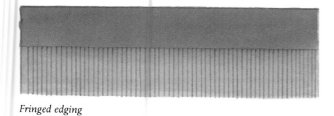

Fringed edging

Lace variation

Fringe variation

Lace edging

Knotted edging

Shaped binding

Plain ruffle

Cut-in diamonds

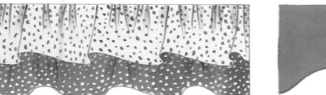

Double ruffles

Shaped variation

Wholecloth motifs

Many of the medallion designs, or wholecloth motifs, shown here are traditional patterns. These, and others, can be combined in an infinite number of patterns and arrangements to fit quilting projects of any size and shape. If you are making a large item, such as a bed quilt or wall hanging, you might want to add a quilted border design (see page 152) or a background texture (see page 154) to set off the main medallions, but the designs are also effective on their own.

Flowers are very common medallion motifs. As these examples show, the petals may be straight, feathered, overlapping, pointed or divided, and similar variations can be used on shell and fan shapes. Feathers are also common in quilting designs, and you can find or draw a feather design to fit virtually any shape. Emphasize the outline of your medallion with a double row of stitching around the main lines or by echo quilting just outside the edge of the design. Some motifs fit into right angles and are often used as corner designs on a rectangular quilt.

Flower with overlapping petals

Star with echo quilting

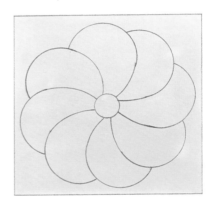

Flower variation

Wholecloth quilt with
feather motifs

Feather

Feather in heart shape

Flower with double stitching line

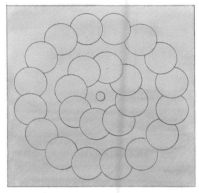

Ring circles

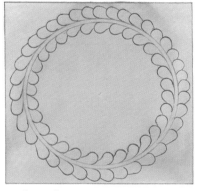

Feather circle

Corner feather

Flower variation

Flower and feather design

Feather circle variation

Amish patterns

Amish quilts are known for their bold use of color and you can give your Amish project extra authenticity by using a traditional design.

Many Amish quilts are built up from a single block set on point often an elaborately quilted diamond, surrounded by a series of colored and black borders, each stitched with its own intricate quilting design. Bars and split bars in vivid colors are favorites, again usually surrounded with single or multiple borders. Many Amish borders use a dark strip at the edge with a light square at the corner, or vice versa; the **Garden Maze** *design shown here is also popular. Amish block designs include the* **Double T, Bear's Paw, Pinwheel, Crown of Thorns, Basket,** *and* **Tree of Life. Friendship Star** *blocks form a pattern of interlocking stars when joined.* **Trip Around the World** *is a simple design which can be pieced in strips, then cut and reassembled into a stunning quilt top.*

Friendship Star

Water Wheel

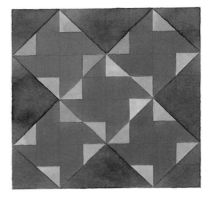

Water Wheel variation

Crown of Thorns

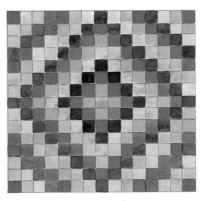

Trip Around The World

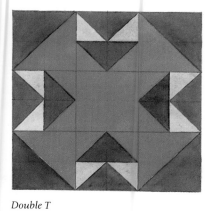

Double T

Bear's Paw

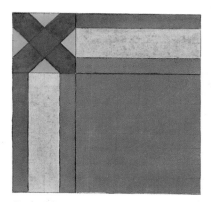

Garden Maze

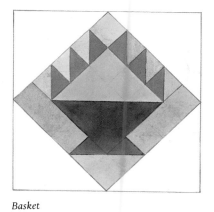

Basket

Basket variation

Tree of Life

Traditional Amish quilt

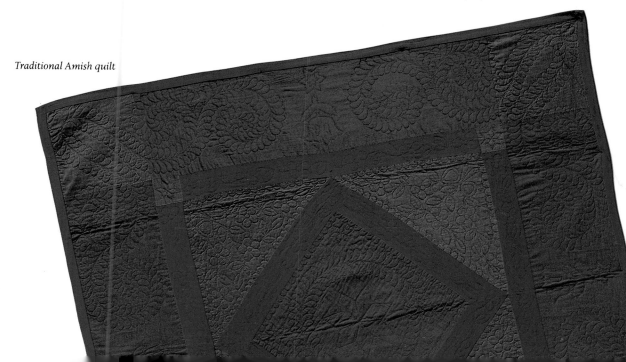

English patchwork patterns

Because English patchwork is pieced over paper and doesn't require straight machine seams, any mosaic pattern can be used; try and avoid inside angles (Vs) as they make the piecing considerably more difficult. Draw or trace the shapes very accurately, then use them as templates for cutting fabric and papers. Beautiful designs can be built up using simple squares.

To make the **Clamshell** *design, the outside curves of the fabric shapes are basted over the papers as usual, then pinned or basted in rows. The rows are appliquéd on top of each other, with the curved tops of one row concealing the raw edges of the row beneath.*

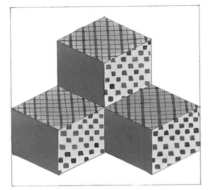

Tumbling Blocks

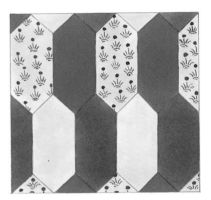

Mosaics

Mosaics variation

Checkerboard variation

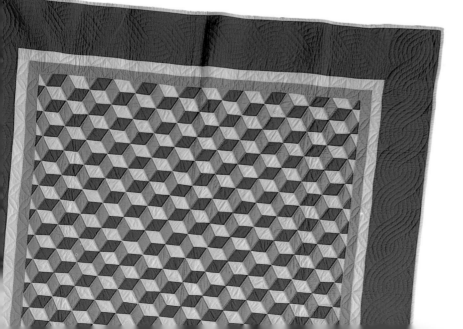

Tumbling Blocks pattern

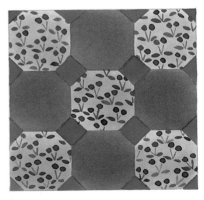

Octagons

Dark and light

Garden Path

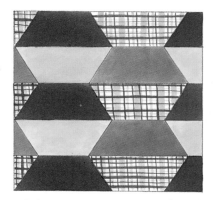

Split hexagons

Clamshells

Triangles

Diamond variation

Two-tone Diamonds

3-D Diamonds

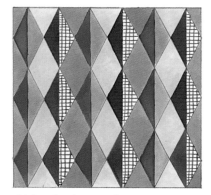

Multi-colored Diamonds

Sashiko patterns

Most Sashiko patterns are basic geometric shapes built into simple or complex repeat patterns. On quilted kimonos, Japanese designers often used many different patterns in asymmetric shapes (as we did for the evening bag on page 118). Some of these patterns are very straightforward and can be stitched using long straight or curving lines of stitching; others are more complex and have numerous corners or angles, but once you have marked your fabric clearly, the designs are all easy to stitch. If you use several patterns on a project, choose a variety of curves and straight lines, squares, circles and triangles, zigzags, and wavy lines.

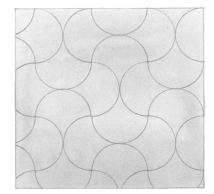

Curved lines

Interlocking lines

Squares and Corners

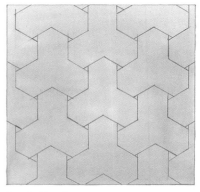

Interlocking shapes

Sashiko jacket quilted with several different patterns

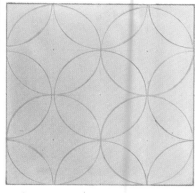

Circles within circles

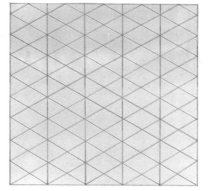

Diamonds

Arches

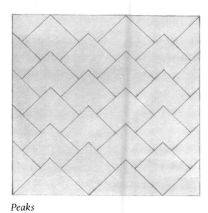

Peaks

Trellis pattern

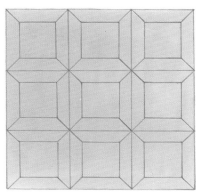

Clouds

Clamshells

Crosses and Squares

Corners

Every quilter dreams of browsing through the attic and discovering an immaculately stitched and perfectly preserved quilt. But the days of magical finds are generally over; most people are aware of the intrinsic value of such beautiful pieces and have rescued them from family storage to use or sell. The most likely way to acquire an old quilt today is to buy it.

Quilts in good condition command high

Restoring and caring for quilts

QUILT CARE

prices, especially if they are detailed. Before you begin any restoration efforts, remember that like any valuable antique, your quilt will depreciate in value if you alter it in any significant way, so you need to decide whether you have bought it as an investment or for your own use or pleasure. If you have bought it as an investment, it will be fine to clean it as long as you don't damage it in any way. If you plan to use it, you may want to restore it by repairing or even replacing damaged sections.

Cleaning old quilts is a very delicate matter; the cleaning process may damage them irreparably. The fabrics may not be colorfast or may not have been preshrunk. The battings may not be washable, and in any case, anything but the most gentle handwashing is likely to damage old fabrics. Always test any soap or cleaning substance on a tiny, unnoticeable area of the quilt in case of disasters. Use cold water, as this is less likely to make fabric colors run; always use the minimum amount of water.

If the fabrics are in good condition, you may want to try dry cleaning, though the quilt may not be robust enough to withstand it. If you know what fibers were used in the fabric and batting, the dry cleaner will be able to advise you better. If you aren't bothered about keeping the quilt exactly as it was, you can gently unpick a small area to check the batting and see if an inner backing fabric was used.

If you want to restore a quilt, you may have to replace worn fabrics or stitching. If a

seam has come apart, try to repair it with a ladder stitch so you can work from the right side but still produce an invisible join. If you have to replace pieces of fabric because they have worn through or have been damaged by moths or mold, try to find a fabric as much in keeping with the original as possible. Carefully cut the seams of the damaged pieces of fabric to separate them from the rest of the quilt, and use them as templates for cutting new pieces. Stitch as many of the seams as you can in the conventional way, then use ladder stitch to insert the new sections, requilting if necessary.

Old batting tends to flatten and bunch up. You may be able to fluff it up a little by holding a steam iron just an inch or so away from the quilt surface so the steam can penetrate the quilt. Be careful not to scorch the fabric. If the batting has bunched up beyond remedy but the pieced quilt top is still in good condition, you might consider removing the backing fabric and batting and requilting the quilt over new batting. If parts of the quilt are beyond redemption and the thought of cutting up an old quilt doesn't horrify you, cut out a good section and use it as a baby quilt, a pillow top, to decorate a piece of clothing, or mounted as a picture.

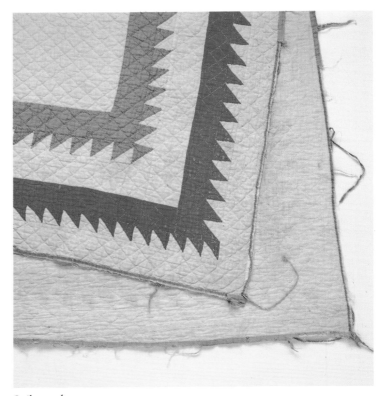

Quilts can become damaged very easily if not handled with care. Edging is particularly vulnerable to fraying through general wear and tear.

There are many ways of displaying quilts. Attach fabric casing or tape loops (see right and middle) to the back of the quilt along one edge. The quilt can now be hung from a rod.

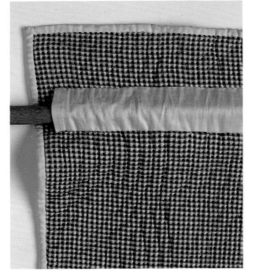

Although many gallery and museum quilts are constantly on display, protective measures are taken to insure they don't fade or gather dirt. When displaying a quilt at home, avoid strong light and excessive moisture, and try to keep it in a constant temperature.

Sew Velcro strips (right) to fabric and attach the fabric to the back of the quilt. Sew the Velcro loops to a fabric-covered frame or other surface. The quilt can now be stretched and hung using the Velcro fastenings.

Glossary

ALBUM QUILT
A quilt made up of different appliqué blocks, sometimes all the same but often with different designs in each block; also called a Baltimore quilt.

AMISH QUILT
A distinctive style of quilting of the Amish, a religious group known for their simple lifestyle.

APPLIQUÉ
A decorative technique which involves stitching one piece of fabric on top of another.

BACKING FABRIC
A piece of fabric, often plain, used to back a quilt or other item.

BACKSTITCH
An embroidery stitch used to create a firm line or outline.

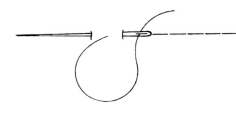

BASTING STITCH
A long, running stitch used to hold fabrics in place temporarily.

BATTING
A layer of padding for quilted work made of natural or synthetic fibers and available in several thicknesses.

BIAS BINDING
A narrow strip of fabric, cut diagonally across the grain; used for binding seams and edges, especially curves.

BINDING
The edging of a quilt which covers and holds all raw edges. Bindings may be plain or decorative.

BLOCK
A small section of patchwork, usually square; most quilts are made from a number of pieced blocks joined together.

BODKIN
A large needle with a large eye used for pulling cord, thick yarn, elastic, etc., through a casing or channel.

BORDER
A decorative pattern which runs around the edges of a quilt top. Borders may be straight, curved, flowing, swagged, and may be pieced or quilted or both.

BRODERIE ANGLAISE
An embroidered lace, white eyelet on white cotton, available as fabric or edging.

BRODERIE PERSE
An appliqué technique using motifs cut from printed fabric.

CASING
A channel of fabric or tape stitched to the back of a quilt through which a rod is inserted.

CATHEDRAL WINDOW PATCHWORK
Patchwork which involves folding squares of fabric into "frames"; the "windows" are filled with contrasting fabric. Sometimes called Mayflower patchwork.

CHARM QUILT
A pieced quilt in which every piece is the same shape, but cut from a different fabric.

CORDED QUILTING
Another name for Italian quilting.

CRAZY QUILT

Quilt made from random sizes and shapes of fancy fabrics such as velvets and silks; the patchwork is embellished with ornate embroidery along seam lines.

CUTTING MAT

A vinyl mat used under a rotary cutter.

DRESSMAKER'S CARBON PAPER

Colored carbon paper used for transferring designs or patterns onto fabric.

ECHO QUILTING

Concentric lines of quilting stitches worked around an outline at regular intervals.

ENGLISH PATCHWORK

A patchwork technique in which the fabric patches are basted over paper templates, then joined before the templates are removed.

FABRIC PAINT

Craft paint formulated for use on fabric; may be specific to particular fibers such as silk. Many fabric paints require heat to be set permanently.

FADING INK PEN

A pen used for marking quilting patterns on fabric; ink fades naturally in light over time.

FOLDED PATCHWORK

Pieced work made from fabric folded into points; typically assembled in star patterns.

FOUR-PATCH BLOCK

A patchwork design made from four rectangular pieces; individual squares can be pieced designs as well.

FRAME

A device used for stretching fabric flat. Quilting frames may be fairly small or large enough for an entire quilt top.

GRAIN

The straight warp or weft of a fabric. The direction of the grain is very important when cutting patchwork pieces or pattern designs.

GRAPH PAPER

Paper marked into small squares and used for drawing templates and patterns; also used to reduce and enlarge designs.

HEM

A finished edge, usually made by folding a raw edge over twice and stitching it down.

HOOP

A circular or oval quilting frame.

ITALIAN QUILTING

A decorative method of threading cord or yarn through channels stitched onto a double layer of fabric.

KAPA LAU

Hawaiian appliqué quilting; large, complex designs are appliquéd onto a background fabric and enhanced with echo quilting.

LADDER STITCH

Used for making an invisible seam from the right side.

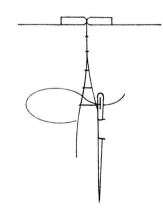

LIGHT BOX

A box with light inside and opaque glass on top; used in quilting for tracing patterns onto fabric or paper.

MEDALLION QUILT

A quilt design featuring one large central pattern or motif.

METALLICS

Fabrics or threads which have a metallic appearance.

MITERED CORNERS

Corners of a binding which are joined with a diagonal (45°) seam rather than with a straight one.

MUSLIN

Inexpensive plain weave cotton fabric often used as a backing fabric or a layer under batting.

NINE-PATCH BLOCK

A square block design made from nine square patches, three across and three down. Individual squares may be pieced designs in themselves.

ON POINT

Mounting a square block at an angle in a quilt top so that it appears as a diamond.

PATCHWORK

Joining one or more fabric shapes to make a pattern.

PIECING

Another name for patchwork.

PRICK AND POUNCE

Transferring designs to fabric by making holes along the main lines of the paper patterns and dusting chalk or other powder through the holes onto the fabric.

QUILTER'S QUARTER

A rectangular plastic rod used for adding $\frac{1}{4}$ in seam allowances to straight edges of fabrics or templates.

QUILTING

Stitching a decorative pattern through three layers, usually quilt top, batting, and backing.

QUILTING BEE

A group of people working together on the same quilt.

QUILTING IN THE DITCH

Quilting in which the stitching lines run next to the seam lines.

QUILTING NEEDLE

A short, fine needle helpful for making tiny quilting stitches.

QUILTING THREAD

A strong thread, often waxed, made specifically for quilting; available in many colors.

ROLLING FRAME

A large frame to hold a whole quilt; most of the quilt is scrolled onto the end rollers, leaving one section exposed for quilting.

ROTARY CUTTER

A circular blade used for cutting several layers of fabric simultaneously.

RUFFLE

A gathered edging of fabric or lace.

RUNNING STITCH

A straight stitch, used for most hand quilting.

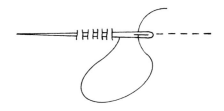

SATIN STITCH

A stitch with a very short length; each stitch touches the next.

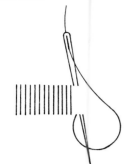

SASHIKO

A Japanese style of quilting, worked with long stitches in repetitive, often geometric, patterns.

SASHING

Strips of fabric used to separate blocks on a quilt top.

SILVERPOINT

Pencil-shaped metal implement used for marking quilting designs onto fabric.

SOMERSET PATCHWORK

One type of folded patchwork.

STAINED GLASS PATCHWORK

Patchwork method where the seams between fabrics are covered with strips of bias to simulate "leading."

STRAIGHT BINDING

A method of binding the edges of a quilt with straight pieces of fabric cut exactly along the grain.

STRAIGHT STITCH

The standard sewing stitch; has length, but no width.

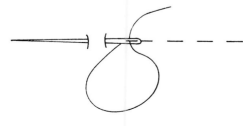

STUFFING

Soft fibers used for filling the pockets in trapunto quilting.

TEMPLATE

An accurate, full-size design used as a tracing and cutting guide; may be made from plastic, metal, paper, or cardboard.

TEMPLATE PLASTIC

A transparent or translucent plastic sheet ideal for making templates.

TONE

The shade of a particular color.

TRAPUNTO

A quilting technique which adds extra stuffing to small pockets stitched into a double layer of fabric.

VALUE

The lightness or darkness of a color.

VELCRO

A fastening material in which one layer of small plastic hooks adheres to another layer of small loops.

WALKING FOOT

A sewing machine foot to enable top and bottom fabric layers to feed at same speed.

WATER-SOLUBLE INK PEN

A pen used for marking quilting patterns on fabric; ink fades when sponged with water.

WHOLECLOTH QUILTING

A quilting method where the top layer is a single large piece of fabric; the design is made with quilting stitches rather than patchwork.

ZIGZAG

A basic machine sewing back-and-forth stitch; has width as well as length.

Index

Page references in

italics refer to pictures.

Acknowledgments

The publishers would like to acknowledge and thank the following for their help in the production of this book, especially the quilters whose work is featured.

page 1	Jenny Rees
page 2/3	Janice Gunner
page 4/5	Janine Whiteson
page 8/9	Jenny Rees
page 10/11	Janice Gunner
page 12/13	BEAMISH, The North of England Open Air Museum, County Durham
page 14/15	Crane Gallery, London
page 16/17	Crane Gallery, London
page 19	Alison Findlay/National Patchwork Championships
page 21	Shelburne Museum, Shelburne, Vermont
(top)	Shipley Art Gallery, Tyne and Wear Museums
(bottom)	Marilyn Garrow
page 22/23	Janine Whiteson
page 24/25	Judith Hammersla
page 34 (top)	Rose Hunneyball/National Patchwork Championships
(bottom)	Janice Gunner
page 38/39 (left)	Rosalie Rakow/National Patchwork Championships
(right)	Louise Bell
page 40	templates Chattels, London
page 46	Crane Gallery, London
page 50	Crane Gallery, London
page 57	Jenny Rees
page 57	Janice Gunner
page 60	Crane Gallery, London
page 62/63	Gail Lawther
page 100/101	Jenny Rees
page 102	Gail Lawther
page 104	Gail Lawther
page 105	Gail Lawther
page 106	Gail Lawther

Special thanks to the Quilt Room, 20 West Street, Dorking, Surrey RH4 1BL, England, whose equipment is featured throughout this book.

page 108	Gail Lawther
page 110	Gail Lawther
page 112	Angela Besley
page 114	Gail Lawther
page 116	Gail Lawther
page 118	Margaret Blakeley
page 122/123	Jenny Rees
page 124 (top)	Jenny Rees
(bottom)	Shelburne Museum, Shelburne, Vermont
page 125 (top)	Shelburne Museum, Shelburne, Vermont
(bottom left)	Crane Gallery, London
(botton right)	Deirdre Amsden
page 126	Crane Gallery, London
page 128	Shelburne Museum, Shelburne, Vermont
page 132	Crane Gallery, London
page 134	Crane Gallery, London
page 136	Gill Turley
page 138	Pamela Cross
page 140	Crane Gallery, London
page 144	Jenny Rees
page 152	Shelburne Museum, Shelburne, Vermont
page 158	BEAMISH, The North of England Open Air Museum, County Durham
page 160	Shelburne Museum, Shelburne, Vermont
page 164	Sashiko jacket, Margaret Blakeley
page 168	Shelburne Museum, Shelburne, Vermont
page 169	Shelburne Museum, Shelburne, Vermont
page 171	Crane Gallery, London.

THE Men'sHealth
BIG
BOOK
OF EXERCISES

RODALE.

RODALE
wellness

Live happy. Be healthy. Get inspired.

Sign up today to get exclusive access to our authors, exclusive bonuses,
and the most authoritative, useful, and cutting-edge information on health,
wellness, fitness, and living your life to the fullest.

Visit us online at RodaleWellness.com
Join us at RodaleWellness.com/Join

© 2009, 2016 by Rodale Inc.

First published as direct online edition in August 2009.

All rights reserved. No part of this publication may be reproduced or transmitted in any form or by any means, electronic or mechanical,
including photocopying, recording, or any other information storage and retrieval system, without the written permission of the publisher.

Rodale books may be purchased for business or promotional use or for special sales. For information, please write to:
Special Markets Department, Rodale Inc., 733 Third Avenue, New York, NY 10017

Men's Health is a registered trademark of Rodale Inc.

Printed in China
Rodale Inc. makes every effort to use acid-free ♾, recycled paper ♻.

Book design by George Karabotsos with John Seeger Gilman
Cover design by Joe Heroun

Photo editor: Mark Haddad

All photography by Beth Bischoff except Chapter 12 by Mitch Mandel/Rodale Images
Cover makeup artist: Lynn Lamorte at Vivian Artists
Cover hairstylist: Tomo Nakajima at Vivian Artists
Exercise footwear and apparel provided by Nike, Adidas, and Under Armour
Anatomy illustrations by bartleby.com, except Gluteus Maximus illustration by Kurt Walters

Library of Congress Cataloging-in-Publication Data is on file with the publisher.

ISBN-13   978-1-62336-841-8   paperback

Distributed to the book trade by Macmillan

4   6   8   10   9   7   5   paperback

RODALE.

We inspire health, healing, happiness, and love in the world.
Starting with you.

Contents

Acknowledgments

I could never properly thank all of the people who have contributed in some way to *The Men's Health Big Book of Exercises*. But I'm particularly grateful to Maria Rodale and the Rodale family, to whom I extend my deepest appreciation for this great opportunity. In addition, I would like to acknowledge the following:

The *Men's Health* team: I'm honored to contribute to your brand.

The talented and tireless George Karabotsos, who instantly shared my vision and enthusiasm for what this book should look like.

All of the designers: John Seeger Gilman, Laura White, Elizabeth Neal, Holland Utley, Mark Michaelson, and Joanna Williams. Your efforts were heroic.

Joe Heroun: The cover is outstanding.

Gail Gonzales, Kathy Zaborowski, Jennifer Levesque, Mark Weinstein, Karen Rinaldi, Chris Krogermeier, Marilyn Hauptly, Sean Sabo, Amy Ninos, Brooke Myers, and Jennifer Giandomenico, along with everyone else in Rodale Books who worked so hard to make this project happen.

Beth Bischoff, Michael Tedesco, Danelle Manthey, Mitch Mandel, and Troy Schnyder. The photography is terrific, from front to back.

Debbie McHugh and Mark Haddad: You went above and beyond.

Bill Phillips, Peter Moore, Matt Marion, Bill Stump, Bill Stieg, Kevin Donahue, Matt Goulding, Jeff Csatari, Lou Schuler, and Tom McGrath: You have influenced and inspired me beyond measure.

B.J. Gaddour: I'm extremely grateful for your many contributions—not only to this book, but also to my fitness I.Q.

Bill Hartman: Your knowledge of training and anatomy is unsurpassed. I can't thank you enough for lending me your expertise.

Rachel Cosgrove: Thanks for all the coaching on exercise technique. This book is far better because of you.

Alwyn Cosgrove: I become smarter every time I talk to you.

My friends and mentors: David Jack, Craig Ballantyne, Michael Mejia, Robert dos Remedios, Joe Dowdell, Valerie Waters, Mike Boyle, Galina Denzel, Mike Wunsch, Craig Rasmussen, Alan Aragon, Stuart McGill, Ph.D., and Jeff Volek, Ph.D. Thanks for all the advice—I'm indebted to each of you.

Very special thanks to Jen Ator, Jill Fanslau, Michael Easter, Maria Masters, Kyle Western, Carolyn Kylstra, Allison Falkenberry, Mary Rinfret, Alice Mudge, Roy Levenson, and Jaclyn Colletti. There wouldn't be a book without your behind-the-scenes work.

And to my wife, Jess, and my daughter, London: You are my favorites. I love you.   —A.C.

Introduction:
Your New Body Starts Here

This book isn't about exercises.

It's about empowerment.
And experimentation.
And finding out what works for you.

A nd ultimately, it's about getting the results you want. The exercises are simply your tools. And there are a lot of them. In fact, I added 114 for the updated version of this book alone, for a grand total of 733. Chances are, you'll have a love/hate relationship with more than a few. I won't take it personally. But they are all at your disposal. As are the workouts. With scores of premade plans and guides for how to create your own, there are literally thousands of routines you can try.

So the results you want are truly yours for the taking. Everything you need is in this book. For instance, say you want to lose your gut. Using the World's Greatest 4-Week Diet and Exercise Plan (page 22), you can expect to drop 2 to 3 pounds of pure fat a week. That's an inch of belly blubber every 14 days. Those size-38 jeans? You're just a month away from a pair of 36s.

Now, these numbers aren't just made up. They're based on scientific research from the University of Connecticut that shows you can lose up to 10 pounds of fat per month, without feeling hungry or deprived. In the study, the scientists discovered what's truly possible when you combine the right kind of diet with the right kind of exercise. These very same principles, in fact, are what all the nutrition and exercise plans in this book are based on.

The benefits don't end with fat loss, though. The researchers found that people following the program reduced their risk for heart disease and diabetes, too. Results vary, of course, but the upshot is that the diet and workout plans in this book are powerful tools. Together, they make every second of every exercise you do count a little more than it ever has before. The cumulative effect of which is the fastest results of your life.

Perhaps it's not convincing you need, though; maybe you're just short on time. After all, the busy lives most of us lead leave little room for long workouts. Well, that's covered, too. You can do each of the workouts in this book in under an hour, and most take just 30 to 40 minutes. You'll also find a section that has 10 routines that can each be completed in just 15 minutes a day, 3 days a week. These aren't the kind of 15-minute workouts that are half as good as a 30-minute session. They're scientifically designed to be as effective as they are efficient. So you'll achieve the best results possible in the least amount of time. Instead of working out longer, you'll simply be working out smarter.

You'll probably be surprised at what you can accomplish in 15 minutes. University of Kansas researchers found that these short routines can double a beginner's strength. And they may be just as beneficial for your psyche: Unlike the average person, who quits a weight-training program within a month, 96 percent of the subjects stuck with the plan for the entire 6-month study. What's more, the approach also boosted participants' flab-fighting efforts beyond their workout. That's because their bodies burned more fat for the other 23 hours and 45 minutes a day—even while they were sleeping.

But these 15-minute workouts are just the start. To make this book even more useful, the world's top trainers have provided dozens of cutting-edge plans, for just about every goal, lifestyle, and experience level. All of them can help you achieve the fast results you want.

For example, if you've never even picked up a weight, you'll want to try the Get-Back-in-Shape Workout (page 444) from Joe Dowdell, CSCS. Joe makes his living training celebrities, cover models, and professional athletes. And the strategies he uses when designing workouts for his high-profile clientele are the same ones he employs to help you burn fat, build muscle, and improve your overall fitness.

In the Big Bench Press Workout (page 482), world-class powerlifter Dave Tate shows you how to boost your bench by up to 50 pounds in just 8 weeks, using the strategies that helped him lift a personal best of 610 pounds.

If your goal is to look get lean and chiseled, or you just love fast-paced workouts that make you sweat, you'll find what you're after in Chapter 16. This is an all-new section that I created with B.J. Gaddour—one of the top fitness experts on the planet—for this updated version of the book. There, you'll find more than 40 fat-burning workouts that you can do in 30 minutes or less. But even better, Gaddour shows you how to put together your own routines using your favorite exercises. You'll decide how long you perform each exercise, and how long you rest between sets. Plus, you'll be able to customize any workout to fit into the time you have—whether that's 5 minutes, 10 minutes, 20 minutes, or more. That way, you get an expert-approved workout built the way you like it. And that can make a serious difference.

But wait, there's more! You'll also find the Scrawny-to-Brawny Workout (page 476), the Vertical-Jump Workout (page 474), the Wedding Workout (page 470), the Beach-Ready Workout (page 464), the Best Three-Exercise Workouts (page 481), the Best Workouts for a Crowded Gym (page 450), and the Best Body-Weight Workouts (page 490)—so you can burn fat and build muscle anywhere, anytime.

You might call *The Men's Health Big Book of Exercises* the book that keeps on giving. Giving results, that is.

Chapter 1:
The Genius of Weights

20 WAYS LIFTING HELPS YOU LOOK GREAT, STAY HEALTHY, AND LIVE LONGER

"You don't look like you lift weights."

I've heard this phrase more than once in my life, and it's always delivered by a burly guy in a sleeveless shirt who most certainly *does* look like he lifts weights. And who's no doubt basing his observation on the standards of a typical musclehead.

That's just it, though: I've never aspired to be a musclehead. Or a powerlifter. Or a strongman competitor. (All of which are fine pursuits, for sure.) So do I look like any of those? Of course not.

But do I look like I lift weights? Absolutely. I'm lean and fit, and my muscles are well-defined, even if they're not busting out of my shirt.

You see, lifting weights isn't just about building 20-inch biceps. In fact, for some of us, it may not be about that at all. That's because the benefits of resistance training extend far beyond a larger arm circumference and into nearly every aspect of your health and well-being. So much so that after nearly 12 years of research and reporting in the field of health and fitness, I've come to one rock-solid conclusion: You'd have to be crazy not to lift weights—even if you don't give a damn about your biceps.

Lifting Weights Gives You an Edge

Over belly fat.
Over stress.
Over heart disease, diabetes, and cancer. Lifting even makes you smarter and happier.

How can the simple act of picking up a weight, putting it down, and repeating a few times bestow such a bevy of benefits? It all starts at the microscopic level of a muscle fiber.

A quick primer: When you lift weights, you cause tiny tears in your muscle fibers. This accelerates a process called muscle-protein synthesis that uses amino acids to repair and reinforce the fibers, making them resistant to future damage. So when a muscle fiber is exposed to a frequent challenge—as it is when you regularly lift weights—it makes structural adaptations in order to better handle that challenge. For example, your muscles adapt by getting bigger and stronger, or by becoming more resistant to fatigue.

These adaptations occur to reduce stress on your body, which is why you can perform everyday functions—such as walking up stairs or picking up a light object—with little effort. It's also why if you routinely lift weights, you'll find that even the hardest physical tasks become easier. In scientific circles, this is known as the training effect. Turns out, this training effect improves not only your muscles but

your entire life, too. It is, in fact, what gives you the edge.

Want some proof? Here are 20 reasons you shouldn't live another day without lifting.

1. You'll Lose 40 Percent More Fat

This might be the biggest secret in fat loss. While you've no doubt been told that aerobic exercise is the key to losing your gut, weight training is actually far more valuable.

Case in point: Penn State University researchers put overweight people on a reduced-calorie diet and divided them into three groups. One group didn't exercise, another performed aerobic exercise 3 days a week, and a third did both aerobic exercise and weight training 3 days a week. Each of the groups lost nearly the same amount of weight— around 21 pounds. But the lifters shed about 6 more pounds of fat than did those who didn't pump iron. Why? Because the lifters' weight loss was almost pure fat, while the other two groups lost just 15 pounds of lard, along with several pounds of muscle. Do the math and you'll see that weights led to 40 percent greater fat loss.

This isn't a one-time finding. Research on non-lifting dieters shows that, on average, 75 percent of their weight loss is from fat, and 25 percent is from muscle. That 25 percent may reduce your scale weight, but it doesn't do a lot for your reflection in the mirror. It also makes you more likely to gain back the flab you lost. However, if you weight train as you diet, you'll protect your hard-earned muscle and burn more fat instead.

Think of it in terms of liposuction: The whole point is to simply remove unattractive flab, right? That's exactly what you should demand from your workout.

2. You'll Burn More Calories

Lifting increases the number of calories you burn while you're sitting on the couch. One reason: Your muscles need energy to repair and upgrade your muscle fibers after each resistance-training workout. For instance, a University of Wisconsin study found that when people performed a total-body workout comprised of just three big-muscle exercises, their metabolisms were elevated for 39 hours afterward. The exercisers also burned a greater percentage of calories from fat during this time, compared with those who didn't lift.

But what about during your workout? After all, many experts say jogging burns more calories than weight training. Turns out, when scientists at the University of Southern Maine used an advanced method to estimate energy expenditure, they found that lifting burns as many as 71 percent more calories than originally thought. The researchers calculated that performing just one circuit of eight exercises—which takes about 8 minutes—can expend 159 to 231 calories. That's about the same number burned by running at a 6-minute–mile pace for the same duration.

3. Your Clothes Will Fit Better

If you don't lift weights, you can say goodbye to your biceps. Research shows that between the ages of 30 and 50, you're likely to lose 10 percent of the total muscle on your body. And that percentage will double by the time you're 60.

Worse yet, it's likely that lost muscle is replaced by fat over time, according to a study in the *American Journal of Clinical Nutrition*. The scientists found that even people who maintained their body weights for up to 38 years lost 3 pounds of muscle and added 3 pounds of fat every decade. Not only does that make you look flabby, it increases your waist size. That's because 1 pound of fat takes up 18 percent more space on your body than 1 pound of muscle. Thankfully, regular resistance training can prevent this fate.

4. You'll Keep Your Body Young

It's not just the quantity of the muscle you lose that's important, it's the quality. Research shows that your fast-twitch muscle fibers are reduced by up to 50 percent as you age, while slow-twitch fibers decrease by less than 25 percent. That's important because your fast-twitch fibers are the muscles largely responsible for generating power, a combined measure of strength and speed. While this attribute is key to peak sports performance, it's also the reason you can rise from your living room chair. Ever notice how the elderly often have trouble standing up? Blame fast-twitch muscles that are underused and wasting away.

The secret to turning back the clock? Pumping iron, of course. Heavy strength training is especially effective, as is lifting light weights really fast. (Hint: Any exercise in this book with the word *explosive* or *jump* in its name is ideal for working your fast-twitch muscle fibers.)

5. You'll Build Stronger Bones

You lose bone mass as you age, which increases the likelihood that you'll one day suffer a debilitating fracture in your hips or vertebrae. That's even worse than it sounds, since Mayo Clinic researchers found that among men who break a hip, 30 percent die within 1 year of the injury. In addition, significant bone loss in your spine can result in the dreaded "dowager's hump," or hunch-back. The good news: A study in the *Journal of Applied Physiology* found that 16 weeks of resistance training increased hip bone density and elevated blood levels of osteocalcin—a marker of bone growth—by 19 percent.

6. You'll Be More Flexible

Over time, your flexibility can decrease by up to 50 percent. This makes it harder to squat down, bend over, and reach behind you. But in a study published in the *International Journal of Sports Medicine*, scientists found that three full-body workouts a week for 16 weeks increased flexibility of the hips and shoulders, while improving sit-and-reach

test scores by 11 percent. Not convinced that weight training won't leave you "muscle-bound"? Research shows that Olympic weight lifters rate second only to gymnasts in overall flexibility.

7. Your Heart Will Be Healthier

Pumping iron really does get your blood flowing. Researchers at the University of Michigan found that people who performed three total-body weight workouts per week for 2 months decreased diastolic blood pressure (the bottom number) by an average of eight points. That's enough to reduce the risk of a stroke by 40 percent, and the risk of a heart attack by 15 percent.

8. You'll Derail Diabetes

Call it muscle medication. In a 4-month study, Austrian scientists found that people with type-2 diabetes who started strength training significantly lowered their blood sugar levels, improving their condition. Just as important, lifting may be one of the best ways to prevent diabetes in the first place. That's because it not only fights the fat that puts you at an increased risk for the disease but also improves your sensitivity to the hormone insulin. This helps keep your blood sugar under control, reducing the likelihood that you'll develop diabetes.

9. You'll Cut Your Cancer Risk

Don't settle for an ounce of prevention; weights may offer it by the pound. A

University of Florida study found that people who performed three resistance-training workouts a week for 6 months experienced significantly less oxidative cell damage than non-lifters. That's important since damaged cells can lead to cancer and other diseases. And in a study published in *Medicine and Science in Sports and Exercise*, scientists discovered that resistance training speeds the rate at which food is moved through your large intestine by up to 56 percent, an effect that's thought to reduce the risk for colon cancer.

10. Your Diet Will Improve

Lifting weights provides a double dose of weight-loss fuel: On top of burning calories, exercise helps your brain stick to a diet. University of Pittsburgh researchers studied 169 overweight adults for 2 years and found that the participants who didn't follow a 3-hour-a-week training plan ate more than their allotted 1,500 calories per day. The reverse was also true—sneaking snacks sabotaged their workouts. The study authors say it's likely that both actions are a reminder to stay on track, reinforcing your weight-loss goal and drive.

11. You'll Handle Stress Better

Break a sweat in the weight room and you'll stay cool under pressure. Texas A&M University scientists determined that the fittest people exhibited lower levels of stress hormones than those who were the least fit. And a Medical

College of Georgia study found that the blood pressure levels of the people with the most muscle returned to normal the fastest after a stressful situation, compared to those who had the least muscle.

12. You'll Shrug Off Jet Lag

Next time you travel overseas, hit the hotel gym before you unpack. When researchers at Northwestern University and the University of California at San Francisco studied muscle biopsies from people who had performed resistance exercise, they discovered changes in the proteins that regulate circadian rhythms. The researchers' conclusion? Strength training helps your body adjust faster to a change in time zones or work shifts.

13. You'll Be Happier

Yoga isn't the only exercise that's soothing. Researchers at the University of Alabama at Birmingham discovered that people who performed three weight workouts a week for 6 months significantly improved their scores on measures of anger and overall mood.

14. You'll Sleep Better

Lifting hard helps you rest easier. Australian researchers observed that patients who performed three total-body weight workouts a week for 8 weeks experienced a 23 percent improvement in sleep quality. In fact, the study participants were able to fall asleep faster and slept longer than before they started lifting weights.

15. You'll Get in Shape Faster

The term *cardio* shouldn't just describe aerobic exercise. A study at the University of Hawaii found that circuit training with weights raises your heart rate 15 beats per minute higher than does running at 60 to 70 percent of your maximum heart rate. According to the researchers, this approach not only strengthens your muscles, it provides cardiovascular benefits similar to those of aerobic exercise. So you save time without sacrificing results.

16. You'll Fight Depression

Squats may be the new Prozac. Scientists at the University of Sydney found that regularly lifting weights significantly reduces symptoms of major depression. In fact, the researchers report that a meaningful improvement was seen in 60 percent of clinically diagnosed patients, similar to the response rate from antidepressants—but without the negative side effects.

17. You'll Be More Productive

Invest in dumbbells—it could help you land a raise. UK researchers found that workers were 15 percent more productive on the days they made time to exercise compared to days they skipped their workouts. Now consider for a moment what these numbers mean to you: On days when you exercise, you can—theoretically, at least—accomplish in an 8-hour day what normally would take you 9 hours and 12 minutes. Or you'd still work 9 hours but get more done, leaving you feeling less stressed and happier with your job—another perk that the workers reported on the days they exercised.

18. You'll Add Years to Your Life

Get strong to live long. University of South Carolina researchers determined that total-body strength was linked to lower risks of death from cardiovascular disease, cancer, and all causes. Similarly, University of Hawaii scientists found that being strong at middle age was associated with "exceptional survival," defined as living until 85 years of age without developing a major disease.

19. You'll Stay Sharp

Never forget how important it is to pump iron. University of Virginia scientists discovered that men and women who lifted weights three times a week for 6 months significantly decreased their blood levels of homocysteine, a protein that's linked to the development of dementia and Alzheimer's disease.

20. You'll Even Be Smarter

Talk about a mind-muscle connection: Brazilian researchers found that 6 months of resistance training enhanced lifters' cognitive function. In fact, the workouts resulted in better short- and long-term memory, improved verbal reasoning, and a longer attention span.

Chapter 2:
All Your Lifting Questions...
Answered

THE KNOW-HOW YOU NEED TO BUILD THE BODY YOU WANT

Learn enough about fitness, and you'll probably decide that the answer to just about every workout question should start with the same two words: *It depends*. After all, every person and situation is unique, and there's more than one way to achieve most goals. That's why this chapter provides you with basic principles and general guidelines, not unbreakable commandments. I've simply tackled the questions I'm asked most frequently and given you my take based on what I've learned over the years. Think of it as the CliffsNotes for my version of Training 101. The best part: I only use the word *caveat* once.

"How Many Repetitions Should I Do?"

When it comes to your workout, this is always the first question you should ask. Why? Because it forces you to decide what your main goal is. For instance, do you want lose fat faster or build more muscle? The answer will determine the number of reps you do. Just make your choice, then use the guidelines that follow to find the rep range you need.

You Want to Lose Fat Faster

This one's easy: All the top trainers I know have found that doing 8 to 15 repetitions works the best for fat loss. And perhaps it's no wonder, since research shows that performing sets in that same range stimulates the greatest increase in fat-burning hormones, compared with doing a greater or fewer number of repetitions. Of course, 8 to 15 reps is a fairly broad recommendation. So you'll need to break it down further. A good approach: Use three smaller rep ranges to vary your workouts, while staying between 8 and 15 repetitions. Examples:

12 TO 15 REPS
10 TO 12 REPS
8 TO 10 REPS

All of these rep ranges are effective for burning fat. So choose one—12 to 15 reps is a great place to start, especially for beginners—and then switch to another every 2 to 4 weeks.

You Want to Build More Muscle

There's a popular gym notion that doing 8 to 12 reps is the best way to build muscle. However, the origin of this recommendation might surprise you: It's from an English surgeon and competitive bodybuilder named Ian MacQueen, MD, who published a scientific paper in which he recommended a moderately high number of reps for muscle growth. The year? 1954. Now, this approach most certainly works. But we've learned a lot about muscle science in the past half-century. And it makes more sense that using a variety of repetition ranges—low, medium, and high—will lead to even better muscle growth. (To understand why, see "There's No Such Thing as a Bad Rep" on page 14.) For the best results, you can switch up your rep ranges every 2 to 4 weeks, or even every workout.

I like this 3-day-a-week, total-body scheme from strength coach Alwyn Cosgrove, CSCS, a longtime fitness advisor to *Men's Health:*

MONDAY: 5 REPS
WEDNESDAY: 15 REPS
FRIDAY: 10 REPS

This simple approach is supported by 21st century science. Case in point: Arizona State University researchers discovered that people who alternated their rep ranges in each of three weekly training sessions—a technique called undulating periodization—gained twice as much strength as those who did the same number of reps every workout.

"How Much Weight Should I Use?"

This question pops up a lot in my e-mail. I used to reply, "How should I know? I can't tell how strong you are over the Internet!" But I've come up with a much better answer: Choose the heaviest weight that allows you to complete all of the prescribed repetitions. That is, the lower the number of repetitions, the heavier the weight you should use. And vice versa. For instance, if you can lift a weight 15 times, it's not going to do your muscles much good to lift it only 5 times. And if you select a weight that's difficult to lift 5 times, there's no way you can pump out 15 repetitions.

So how do you figure out the right amount? Trial and error. You just have to make an educated guess and experiment. This is second nature for experienced lifters, but if you're new to training, don't stress over it; you'll catch on fast. The key is to get in there and start lifting. If you choose a weight that's too heavy or too light, just adjust it accordingly in your next set.

Of course, you'll realize pretty quickly if you're using a weight that's too heavy for your rep range. After all, you won't be able to complete all the reps. But gauging if a weight is too light is a little trickier. One simple way: Note the point at which you start to struggle.

Let's say you're doing 10 repetitions. If all 10 seem easy, then the weight you're using is too light. However, if you start to struggle on your 10th rep, you've chosen the correct poundage. What does "start to struggle" mean? It's when the speed at which you lift the weight slows significantly. Although you can push on for another rep or two, the struggle indicates that your muscles have just about had it. This is also the point when most people start to "cheat" by changing their body posture to help them lift the weight.

Remember, the goal is to complete all the repetitions in each set with perfect form while challenging your muscles to work as hard as they can. Using the start-to-struggle approach will help you do this. Go hard, and when you start to struggle, you've completed the set. This is also a great strategy to use when you're directed to do as many repetitions as possible on bodyweight exercises such as pushups, chinups, and hip raises. (You'll find this instruction in many of the workouts in Chapter 14.)

"How Many Sets of an Exercise Should I Do?"

A good rule of thumb: Do as many sets as you need to complete at least 25 repetitions for a muscle group. So if you're planning to do 5 reps of an exercise, you'd do five sets of that movement. If you're doing 15 reps, you'd only need to do two sets. The more reps of an exercise you do, the fewer sets you need to perform. And vice versa. This helps keep your muscles under tension for an appropriate amount of time no matter what rep range you're using.

THERE'S NO SUCH THING AS A BAD REP

Trainers don't just randomly choose the number of repetitions a person does. Well, at least the good ones don't. That's because the rep range you use dictates how your muscles adapt to your routine. In fact, by knowing the benefits of three key rep ranges, you can choose the strategy that's best for the results you want. Keep in mind that these rep ranges don't work like an on-off button; they're more like a dimmer switch. As you move up and down in reps, you're simply dialing back the benefits of one and emphasizing those of another. Here's a primer on each.

1. Low repetitions (1 to 5): This rep range allows you to use the heaviest weights, which puts your muscles under the highest amounts of tension. This increases the number of *myofibrils* in your muscle fibers. What the heck is a *myofibril*? It's the part of your muscle fiber that contains the contractile proteins. Think of it this way: When there are more of these proteins to contract, your muscles can generate greater force. That's why 1 to 5 is an ideal rep range for building strength. And, of

(continues on opposite page)

If you're in good-enough shape, you can certainly do more than 25 reps per muscle group, but cap your output at 50. For example, a common recommendation is to do three sets of 10 of three or four different exercises for one muscle group. That's as many as 120 total reps for the working muscles. Trouble is, if you can perform even close to 100 reps for any muscle group, you're not working hard enough. Think of it this way: The harder you train, the less time you'll be able to sustain that level of effort. Many people can run for an hour if they jog slowly, but you'd be hard-pressed to find anyone who could do high-intensity sprints—without a major decrease in performance—for that period of time. And once performance starts to decline, you've achieved most of the benefits you can for that muscle group.

"How Long Should My Workout Last?"

Only as long as it needs to, of course. The best way to gauge this is by the total number of sets you do. I first learned this years ago from famed Australian strength coach Ian King, and I find it still holds true today. The advice: Do 12 to 25 sets per workout. That is, when you add up the sets you perform for every exercise, the total should fall within this range (not including your warmup). So if you're using lengthy rest periods, your workout will take longer; and if you're using shorter rest periods, you'll finish faster. Beginners will probably find that 12

sets are plenty, while experienced lifters may be able to handle the upper end of the range. This total-set rule isn't set in stone, of course, but it works very well for building muscle and losing fat. For most people, doing more work than this in a single workout results in rapidly diminishing returns on their time investment. It also increases the time your muscles need to recover between your bouts of exercise. If you ignore this important factor, you can wind up overstressing your body, which slows your results. (One exception: fast-paced fat loss workouts, where you use light loads and very short rest periods.)

"How Long Should I Rest between Sets?"

Probably not long enough to chit-chat at the water fountain. The amount of rest between sets is a crucial but often overlooked factor in most workouts. To understand why, you'll need a quick lesson in exercise science: The lower your reps—and heavier the weights—the longer you need to rest between sets; the higher your repetitions—and lighter the weights—the shorter your rest. Why? When you lift heavy weights, you're recruiting fast-twitch muscle fibers, the fibers that generate the most force but also fatigue the fastest and take the longest to recover. So giving them ample time to rest helps ensure you train them fully each set. When you use lighter weights and do more reps, you're mainly hitting your slow-twitch muscle fibers. These are not only more resistant to fatigue than fast-twitch fibers but they recover much more quickly, too. The upshot is that, even after a challenging high-rep set, they're ready for a repeat performance in a short period of time.

What does this mean in regard to your stopwatch? I use these basic guidelines:

1 TO 3 REPS: REST FOR 3 TO 5 MINUTES
4 TO 7 REPS: REST FOR 2 TO 3 MINUTES
8 TO 12 REPS: REST FOR 1 TO 2 MINUTES
13 REPS OR MORE: REST FOR 1 MINUTE

But here's the real secret: These numbers simply describe the amount of time you rest before working a muscle group again. That is, if you think strategically, you can work other muscle groups instead of waiting around while the clock ticks. The two methods I like best for this are alternating sets and circuits. They slash minutes from your workout time, without sacrificing results. That's because one muscle group rests while the other works. Here's a description of each, but you'll find them used frequently in Chapter 14.

Alternating sets: Do one set of an exercise, rest, then do a set of an exercise that works the opposite muscle group. (You can also pair an upper-body exercise with a lower-body exercise.) Rest again, and repeat until you've completed the prescribed number of sets. For instance, if you do

6 reps of the bench press, you might rest for just 1 minute, instead of 2 minutes. Then you'd do a dumbbell row, and rest for 1 minute. Including the time it takes you to complete the dumbbell row, you've now rested for more than 2 minutes before repeating the bench press. The bottom line: Your rest periods can easily be cut in half.

Circuits: Do 3 or more (could be 4, 5, or even 10) exercises in succession without resting between sets. The most common approach here is to alternate between upper- and lower-body exercises. As an example, you might do the following exercises, one after another: squat, bench press, hip raise, dumbbell row, and so on. This way, your upper body rests while your lower body works. You can also add rest in between each set .

Ready to try these techniques? Use this chart to guide you.

PAIR THIS . . .	WITH THAT . . .
QUADRICEPS	GLUTES & HAMSTRINGS
CHEST	UPPER BACK
SHOULDERS	LATS
BICEPS	TRICEPS
UPPER BODY	LOWER BODY
UPPER BODY	CORE
LOWER BODY	CORE

course, more myofibrils increase the size of your fibers, making your muscles bigger. (Muscle trivia #1: This type of muscle growth is known as *myofibrillar hypertrophy*.)

2. High repetitions (11 or more): When you use higher reps, your muscles have to contract for long periods of time. This increases the number of mitochondria in your muscle fibers. Your mitochondria are energy-producing structures that not only burn fat (the more, the better!) but also lead to greater muscle endurance and cardiovascular fitness. What's more, these structural changes boost the fluid volume in your fibers, adding size to your muscles. (Muscle trivia #2: This type of muscle growth is called *sarcoplasmic hypertrophy*.)

3. Medium repetitions (6 to 10): With this approach, your muscles are under medium tension for a medium amount of time. Consider this just what it is: A mix of low- and high-rep lifting. So it helps you improve both muscle strength and muscle endurance. You might say it strikes a good balance between the two. However, if you use this rep range all the time, you'll miss out on the greater tension levels that come with lower reps and the longer tension time achieved by higher reps. Use them all.

"How Many Days a Week Should I Lift?"

At least 2. This number has been shown to provide many of the health benefits attributed to resistance training. So consider that the minimum. Ideally, though, you'll want to hit the weights 3 or 4 days a week, with either total-body workouts or an upper-lower split approach. I'll explain each.

Total-body workouts are just what they sound like. You work your entire body each workout. Then you rest a day, and repeat. There's a scientific rationale for this. In multiple studies, researchers at the University of Texas Medical Branch, in Galveston, have reported that muscle protein synthesis—a marker of muscle repair—is elevated for up to 48 hours after resistance training. So if you work out on Monday at 7 p.m., your body is in muscle-growth mode until Wednesday at 7 p.m. After 48 hours, though, the biological stimulus for your body to build new muscle returns to normal. That means it's time for another workout.

Turns out, this 48-hour period is also similar to the length of time your metabolism is elevated after you lift weights. As a result, total-body training is highly effective whether you're trying to build muscle or lose fat. In fact, I'm convinced it's the single best mode of exercise for burning blubber. That's because the more muscle you work, the more calories you burn—both during and after your workout.

The other strategy that works well is an upper-lower split. This is mainly used for adding muscle size and strength and for improving sports performance. In this method, you work your upper body and lower body on separate days. The reason: It allows you to train the muscle groups of both halves harder than you could in a total-body routine. However, it also means that you need to give your muscles a little extra time to fully recover. For instance, you might do a 4-day-a-week plan in which you complete a lower-body workout on Monday, an upper-body workout on Tuesday, and then rest for a day or two before repeating (on Thursday and Friday perhaps). That would give you 2 or 3 full days of rest between each type of workout. Or you could alternate between lower-body and upper-body workouts every other day, 3 days a week.

Keep in mind, there's no reason to use a split routine if you're gaining muscle and strength with total-body training. But if you reach a point when you can't fit all of the sets you want to do into a total-body workout, it's likely time to make the switch. Or you may simply want to experiment with different methods to determine what works best for your muscles and for your lifestyle. You'll find there are plenty of workouts in this book to keep you busy.

"How Many Exercises Should I Do per Muscle Group?"

One. It's an approach that's simple and effective. You actually obtain most of the benefits of weight lifting from the first exercise you do, when your muscles are fresh. For instance, let's say you complete three sets of each of the dumbbell bench press, the incline dumbbell bench press, and the dumbbell fly. By the time you reach the last exercise, the amount of weight you can handle is far lower than had you done that movement first. See for yourself by trying the routine in reverse order: You'll find that for the dumbbell bench press, you'll be able to lift far less than when you do it first—and have to use a weight you'd normally consider too light. So the benefit to your muscles will have diminished. That's why, most of the time, sticking with one exercise per muscle group makes the most sense, especially if you have a limited amount of time to work out.

Now it's okay to break the one-exercise rule if there's a good reason to do so. For example, if a muscle group has been lagging, you may want to work it a little harder for a 4-week period by doubling the total number of sets you do for that area. This is called prioritizing a muscle group. So instead of doing all of your sets with one exercise, you might use two or three different exercises, as in the example of the dumbbell bench press, incline dumbbell bench press, and dumbbell fly. (See "Build the Perfect Chest" in Chapter 4 for a ready-made plan.) While you won't be able to use as much weight in the second two exercises as you would if you had done them when your muscles were fresh, you will increase the total amount of work the muscle group has to perform.

This can help you break through plateaus and spark new muscle growth.

One *caveat*: If you try this method and find you're getting weaker, the workload is too high for you. Dial it back so that your muscles can better recover between workouts. What's more, prioritizing one muscle group may mean you have to cut back a little on other muscle groups. That's because the total-set-per-workout recommendation still applies. (See "How Long Should My Workout Last?" on page 14.)

"How Fast Should I Lift?"

Do this: Lower slowly, lift fast. Research shows that taking longer to lower the weight helps you build strength faster, and quickly lifting the weight activates the greatest number of muscle fibers. For most exercises, take 2 or 3 seconds to lower the weight, pause for a second in the "down" position, and then lift the weight as quickly as you can while maintaining control over it at all times. One big exception: If an exercise is to be performed explosively, perform the entire lift quickly, from start to finish.

Keep in mind that on some exercises, like the lat pulldown, it will seem like the lowering portion is the part of the lift in which your muscles are contracting. But realize that as you pull the bar down, the weight stack is actually rising.

"Do I Need a Spotter?"

The politically correct answer is yes. After all, a barbell might fall on your neck. This is no joke, because this very kind of accident happens every year. It kills people. But there's a bigger lesson here: Don't try to lift a weight that's too heavy for you, especially if that weight is attached to a bar. For instance, like many people, I work out by myself at home. So a spotter isn't an option. However, there's zero chance that I'll be pinned helplessly underneath a barbell. That's because I do my heavy pressing with dumbbells, which I can just drop to the floor if needed.

I also use the start-to-struggle strategy with every exercise. (See "How Much Weight Should I Use?" on page 13.) If I choose a weight that's too heavy for 6 reps, I'll know it before I ever reach the point of complete failure and I'll be able to simply end the set before trouble starts. How then, do I figure out my 1-rep max? I don't. It's not really important to me. But if it is to you, my advice is simple: Anytime you test your limits, make sure you have a spotter.

"What Equipment Do I Need?"

You already have enough to get started: your body. In fact, check out The Best Body-Weight Workouts in Chapter 14 for a workout you can do today. But if you want to build your own home gym, here's a rundown of everything worth having—from the essentials to the extras.

The Essentials

Dumbbells. If I could have only one training tool, the dumbbell would be my pick. It's simple, versatile, and durable. If you have the space, any type of dumbbell will do. The least expensive kind is a basic cast-iron hex dumbbell. (At the time of this printing, 1 dollar a pound was a competitive price.) Shop around; you may be able to find a special on an entire set. If you're strapped for space, consider buying a pair of PowerBlocks (powerblock.com). This all-in-one dumbbell set allows you to change the weight you want to use quickly, and it requires little storage room.

Bench. A basic flat bench is fairly inexpensive, but if you're going to invest the money, consider an adjustable bench so that you can perform exercises on both an incline and a decline. (The Web site performbetter.com has several options.) This can instantly give you dozens of more exercise variations.

Chinup bar. If you're handy, you can create and install your own using a piece of 1-inch-diameter pipe. Or you can purchase a premade joist-, wall-, or ceiling-mount chinup bar, like one of those at performbetter.com. You can also buy the kind that hangs on a door. Fair warning: These can be tough on your door frame, especially if you have an older house. But if you decide to purchase a power rack (see opposite page), you can get one that includes a chinup bar. Just make sure your ceiling is high enough so that your head can clear the bar each time you complete a repetition.

Swiss ball. This is also called a stability ball, a physio ball, and an exercise ball. (Why did I go with Swiss ball? Habit.) The Swiss ball is great for core exercises, as you'll see throughout Chapter 10: Core. You can pick up a basic Swiss ball just about anywhere—including Target and Wal-Mart—but heavier-duty balls are available at performbetter.com.

Barbell and weight plates. Two options here: a standard barbell or an Olympic barbell. A standard bar weighs 20 pounds and is less expensive, but the Olympic bar—which weighs about 45 pounds—is the kind you'll find in most gyms. The Olympic bar is also heavier duty. My advice: If you already have a standard bar, your muscles won't know the difference. But opt for a 7-foot Olympic barbell if you're starting your home gym or upgrading. Shop around and you can find an Olympic barbell with a 300-pound Olympic weight set for $300.

Power rack. You absolutely need a power or squat rack if you want to do barbell squats. But a good rack can also vastly expand your home gym. That's because you can buy one equipped with a chinup bar and even a high and low pulley systems for doing lat pulldowns, cable rows, and just about any other cable exercise. You can find options for high-quality power racks at elitefts.com, performbetter.com, and roguefitness.com.

The Extras

Cable station. This gives you hundreds more exercise variations. The most economical—in terms of both money and space—is a cable pulley system that's attached to a power rack. But if you have the space and the cash, the Free Motion EXT Dual Cable Cross is state of the art. The arms swivel into dozens of different positions, allowing you to work every muscle from every conceivable angle. See for yourself at freemotionfitness.com.

EZ-curl bar. When you do curls, this angled bar is easier on your wrists than a straight bar. It's also shorter than a barbell, making it easier to move to an open spot in the gym.

Kettlebells. These Russian imports—which look like bowling balls with handles—have been around for years but only recently have become a mainstay in gyms and exercise routines across the United States. You can use kettlebells for any number of exercises, but you'll find that they're the far superior choice when performing movements like the kettlebell swing (page 394). That's because the implement's shape makes it ideal for swinging back and forth. Its design also makes it a particularly great option for doing goblet squats, deadlifts, overhead presses, and Turkish getups. Practically speaking, you can substitute a kettlebell for almost any movement in this book that requires a dumbbell.

Medicine ball. Some equipment never goes out of style. Use medicine balls for core exercises, sports-specific training, and even as a way to make pushups harder (place each hand on a ball). Dynamax medicine balls (medicineballs.com) are one of the most popular choices among trainers. These nonbouncing balls are large and soft and absorb impact, making them easier and safer to catch and throw. (It's a great choice for exercises like wall ball, on page 377.) You can also buy a ball that bounces—such as a First Place Elite Medicine Ball—at performbetter.com.

Valslides. These foam-topped plastic sliders transform hard floors and carpets into ice rinks, intensifying old standbys like lunges by decreasing your stability and keeping your muscles under tension for the entire movement. What's more, Valslides are perhaps most useful for core exercises, because they provide an all-new way to work your abs, as you'll see in Chapter 10. Find them at valslide.com.

TRX Suspension Trainer. This set of nylon straps allows you take your workout anywhere. You can lock these lightweight straps onto any elevated fixture—a pullup bar, door, or tree branch—and you'll instantly be equipped to do hundreds of lower-body, upper-body, and core exercises that can be adjusted for any fitness level. (An accompanying DVD provides the complete instructions for different goals.) So it's perfect for anyone who travels or wants to add an effective new training tool to their workout arsenal. The fitness industry is plagued with plenty of gimmicky products, but TRX fully delivers on its promises. Check it out at trxtraining.com.

Step or box. You can do stepups on a bench, but a box or step works better because you can adjust the height. A Reebok step or generic aerobic step with risers will do the trick, but I really like the box squat box at elitefts.com. It provides a stable, no-slip surface to lift from, and you can quickly raise and lower the height of this box for stepups, single-leg squats, box lunges, split squats, depth jumps, and elevated pushups.

Continuous loop resistance bands. These are oversize rubber bands that allow you to perform assisted chinups without a special machine, and also work as subsitute for weights For a complete set that comes with handles, I like the Starter Fitness Package at resistancebandtraining.com.

Mini bands. These small elastic bands (available at performbetter.com) are especially useful for working your glutes and your inner thighs. You'll find that they're utilized throughout this book in exercises such as band walks, band hip abduction, and body-weight squats with knee press-out.

BOSU ball. BOSU stands for "both sides utilized." This training tool allows you to make pushups and hip raises more difficult. You can find it at just about any fitness outlet, or order it online at any number of Internet fitness stores.

Sandbag. The sand shifts as you lift the bag, changing your center of gravity. This forces your core to work harder to keep you from falling over. You might say these bags are awkward, but in a way that's great for your body. Plus, a sandbag is odd-sized compared to a barbell or dumbbell, so it more closely mimics the objects—such as a baby carrier, TV, or suitcase—that you have to pick up in real life. One problem: The sand leaks out of the bags you buy at Home Depot or Lowe's. But you can solve that problem with an Ultimate Sandbag (ultimatesandbagtraining .com), which houses the sand in a rugged shell and a sealable filler bag. Plus, you can buy water filler bags there as well. This allows you to convert your sandbag into—you guessed it—a "water bag." It won't be as heavy, but the water will move around even more than the sand, creating a whole different challenge. Suggestion: Don't worry too much about the weight when you first start. The sandbag (or water bag) will be significantly harder than holding the same load with dumbbells. So even what you might consider a light weight for squats can provide a tough workout that you feel the next day.

Airex Balance Pad. Doing lower-body exercises while standing on this soft foam pad forces the muscles that stabilize your ankle, knee, and hip joints to work harder. So that's one use. But you'll also see that, in this book, I've used the pad in other ways—for example, as a pad to press your knees against in the hip raise with knee squeeze (Chapter 9). You can pick one up at performbetter.com.

Chapter 3:
The World's Greatest 4-Week Diet and Exercise Plan

THE FAST WAY TO A LEAN BODY

If you want fast

results, and you want to start today, there's no easier way than this 4-week diet and exercise plan. It's based on the scientific research of Jeff Volek, PhD, RD, one of the world's top nutrition scientists.

In a recent study at the University of Connecticut, Volek and his colleagues found that the combination of a low-carb diet, workout nutrition, and weight training is an incredibly potent formula for shedding fat and quickly improving health. Study participants lost up to 10 pounds of pure fat per month, as they simultaneously gained muscle. In fact, one guy actually packed on an average of nearly a pound of new muscle each week while melting away his belly. And more important, the study subjects slashed their risks of heart disease and diabetes—even more so than those who followed a low-fat diet. The low-carb lifters dropped their total cholesterol by 12 percent, reduced triglycerides by 32 percent, decreased insulin by 32 percent, and lowered C-reactive protein (CRP)—a marker of inflammation—by 21 percent. And they did all of this simply by following a diet and exercise plan like the one in this chapter.

Consider this your 4-week quick-start guide to losing your gut and getting healthy for life.

The Diet Plan

The way this diet works is simple: Cutting back on carbs reduces your calorie intake, causing weight loss. But it also triggers your body to use its fat stores—instead of sugar—as its primary source of energy. Research shows this helps people better control blood sugar, hunger, and cravings. So you'll eat less without feeling deprived. The end result is that you'll lose fat faster and more easily than ever before.

What to Eat

Eat any combination of the foods from the three categories listed in the chart on page 25, until you feel satisfied but not stuffed. It's likely that this simple approach will regulate your appetite. The upshot: You'll automatically eat less and lose fat—without having to count calories.

The Guidelines

Consume high-quality protein at every meal. Eating protein ensures that your body always has the raw material to build and maintain your muscle, even while you lose fat. It also helps you feel fuller, faster.

Go ahead, eat fat. Dietary fat is a crucial factor in helping you control the total number of calories your body craves. That's because it's very effective at keeping you feeling satisfied after you've eaten. So know this: As long as you're losing fat, you're not eating too much of it.

Indulge in vegetables. When researchers at SUNY Downstate Medical Center in New York City polled more than 2,000 low-carbohydrate dieters, they found that, on average, those who were most successful consumed at least four servings of low-starch vegetables each day.

Avoid foods that contain sugar and starch. These are the foods that are high in carbohydrates. The list includes bread, pasta, potatoes, rice, beans, candy, regular soda, and baked goods—as well any other foods that contain grains, flour, or sugar. An easy way to gauge: Read the ingredients label. If a food contains more than 5 grams of carbohydrate per serving, skip it. And don't obsess either. When ordering food at a restaurant, just worry about the main components of the meal. Sure, there could be hidden sugar or starch in a dish, but if the recommended foods are the major players, you'll be fine. Just use your best judgment.

Limit your fruit and milk intake. In the study, participants were told to avoid these two foods as well, in order to keep their total carbohydrate intake below 50 to 75 grams a day without having to count carbs. However, you can consume milk as well as low-calorie fruits, particularly berries and melons, if you don't overdo it and you monitor your overall carb consumption.

As a general rule, limit yourself to two total servings of fruit and milk combined. A serving of fruit is ½ cup; a serving of milk is 1 cup (8 ounces). Each contains about 10 grams of carbohydrate. So in a day, you might have ½ cup of berries and a cup of milk, or just 1 cup of berries.

A Meal-by-Meal Guide

Don't complicate your eating plan. Just think of it as a meat-and-vegetables diet. Here's a sampling of what you might eat throughout your day.

Breakfast: Any type of eggs, whether scrambled, fried, boiled, poached, or made into an omelet (with all the fixings). You can add cheese, of course, and serve with any type of meat—even bacon and sausage.

Snacks: Just about any type of cheese makes a great snack, as do nuts and seeds—almonds, peanuts, sunflower

About the Expert
Jeff Volek, PhD, RD, is an associate professor at the University of Connecticut and has published more than 185 scientific papers on diet and exercise. In 2007, Dr. Volek and I teamed up to write the *Men's Health TNT Diet*, a book that details all of the science behind the plan you see here, complete with step-by-step instructions, recipes, and even more workouts.

HIGH-QUALITY PROTEINS	LOW-STARCH VEGETABLES*		NATURAL FATS
BEEF	ARTICHOKES	MUSHROOMS	AVOCADOS
CHEESE	ASPARAGUS	ONIONS	BUTTER
EGGS	BROCCOLI	PEPPERS	COCONUT
FISH	BRUSSELS SPROUTS	SPINACH	CREAM
PORK	CAULIFLOWER	TOMATOES	NUTS AND SEEDS**
POULTRY	CELERY	TURNIPS	OLIVES, OLIVE OIL, AND CANOLA OIL
WHEY AND CASEIN PROTEINS	CUCUMBERS	ZUCCHINI	FULL-FAT SOUR CREAM AND SALAD DRESSINGS

* These are just a few common examples of low-starch vegetables, but you can consider any vegetable besides potatoes, peas, and corn to be fair game.

** Limit yourself to two servings a day (a serving is about a handful).

Workout A

EXERCISES	SETS	REPS	REST
1. Core (Chapter 10)	3	12	1 min
2A. Glutes and hamstrings (Chapter 9)	3	12	1 min
2B. Upper back (Chapter 5)	3	12	1 min
3A. Quadriceps (Chapter 8)	3	12	1 min
3B. Chest (Chapter 4)	3	12	1 min

- **Exercise 1: Core** Choose any core exercise (Chapter 10) from the section labeled "Stability Exercises" (page 278). The plank (page 278), side plank (page 284), mountain climber (page 288), and Swiss-ball jackknife (page 290) are all great choices. *Note:* If the exercise—such as a plank or side plank—is done for "time" instead of "reps," simply hold it for the amount of time suggested in the exercise instructions. That's one set.
- **Exercise 2A: Glutes and Hamstrings** Choose any glutes/hamstrings exercise (Chapter 9) in which you work one leg at a time. This might be a single-leg barbell straight-leg deadlift (page 254), a single-leg hip raise (page 240), or a dumbbell stepup (page 262).
- **Exercise 2B: Upper Back** Choose any back exercise (Chapter 5) from the section labeled "Upper Back" (pages 72 to 95). So that's any variation of the dumbbell row (pages 78 to 82), barbell row (pages 76 to 77), or cable row (pages 92 to 95).
- **Exercise 3A: Quadriceps** Choose any quadriceps exercise (Chapter 8) in which you work both legs at the same time. This will be a version of the squat, such as the dumbbell squat (page 203), goblet squat (page 204), or barbell front squat (page 199).
- **Exercise 3B. Chest** Choose any chest exercise (Chapter 4). For example, you might choose a variation of the pushup (pages 34 to 43), a dumbbell bench press (pages 52 to 53), or a Swiss-ball dumbbell chest press (pages 56 to 57).

CARDIO

- Choose any "Finishers" from "The Fastest Cardio Workouts of All Time" (Chapter 14) or any of the cardio workouts that accompany other routines in this chapter.

Workout B

EXERCISES	SETS	REPS	REST
1. Core (Chapter 10)	3	12	1 min
2A. Quadriceps (Chapter 8)	3	12	1 min
2B. Lats (Chapter 5)	3	12	1 min
3A. Glutes and Hamstrings (Chapter 9)	3	12	1 min
3B. Shoulders (Chapter 6)	3	12	1 min

- **Exercise 1: Core** Choose any core exercise (Chapter 10) from the section labeled "Stability Exercises" (page 278). The plank (page 278), side plank (page 284), mountain climber (page 288), and Swiss-ball jackknife (page 290) are all great choices. *Note:* If the exercise—such as a plank or side plank—is done for "time" instead of "reps," simply hold it for the amount of time suggested in the exercise instructions. That's one set.
- **Exercise 2A: Quadriceps** Choose any quadriceps exercise (Chapter 8) in which you work one leg at a time. This will be any version of the barbell or dumbbell lunge (pages 206 to 211), barbell or dumbbell split squat (pages 212 to 221), dumbbell lunge (pages 216 to 217), or a single-leg squat (pages 196 to 197).
- **Exercise 2B: Lats** Choose any back exercise (Chapter 5) from the section labeled "Lats" (pages 96 to 107). For example, you could choose any version of the chinup (pages 96 to 100), lat pulldown (pages 102 to 105), or pullover (pages 106 to 107).
- **Exercise 3A: Glutes and Hamstrings** Choose any glutes/hamstrings exercise (Chapter 9) in which you work both legs at the same time. This might be a barbell deadlift (page 248), a dumbbell straight-leg deadlift (page 256), or a Swiss-ball hip raise and leg curl (page 243).
- **Exercise 3B: Shoulders** Choose any shoulder exercise (Chapter 6), such as the dumbbell shoulder press (page 120), lateral raise (page 126), or scaption and shrug (page 143).

CARDIO

- Choose any "Finishers" from "The Fastest Cardio Workouts of All Time" (Chapter 14) or any of the cardio workouts that accompany other routines in this chapter.

Chapter 4: Chest

PUT UP A GREAT FRONT

Chest

A muscular chest is powerful. It increases your presence in the boardroom, wins her over in the bedroom, and intimidates on the playing field. So it's no surprise that guys have an affinity for exercises that build their chest. Your pecs, after all, are the most prominent muscle you see in your bathroom mirror. And who doesn't want to improve that image?

What's more, if you stop lifting weights, your chest is one of the first muscle groups that will atrophy. That's because you rarely stress these muscles in daily activities. Think about it: How often in real life do you have to push heavy weights away from your chest? Keep in mind that losing muscle slows your metabolism—which means regularly training your chest also helps you fight belly fat.

The Bonus Benefits of a Bigger Chest

More power: Stronger chest muscles make it easier to push off opponents in any contact sport, whether your game is football, basketball, martial arts, or hockey.

A stronger swing: Forehand strokes in tennis and sidearm throws in baseball rely on powerful chest muscles for velocity, in addition to your core musculature.

A knockout punch: The chest's primary objective is to move the arms forward, so developing pectoral strength helps you deliver more energy into your target.

Meet Your Muscles

Pectoralis Major

Your main chest muscle is the pectoralis major [1]. Its job: to pull your upper arms toward the middle of your body. Think about that in terms of a bench press. As you push the bar away from your torso, your upper arms move closer to your chest (as they straighten. This is because your pectoralis major attaches to the inside of your upper arm bone. So when your pectorals contract, the muscle fibers shorten, pulling your upper arms toward the muscles' origin, your mid-chest.

This is why exercises such as pushups and bench presses are the best way to make your pecs pop. By holding a weight in your hands when you do a bench press, for instance, you increase the weight of your upper arms, which forces your pectoral muscles to contract harder. The end result: a bigger, stronger chest.

The sternal portion of the muscle is collectively considered to be your lower chest.

The muscle fibers that make up the clavicular portion form what many call the upper chest.

The fibers of your pectoralis major originate at three places on your chest: your collar bone [2], your breast bone [3], and your ribs [4], just below your breast bone.

Pectoralis Minor

The pectoralis minor [5] is a thin, triangular muscle that lies beneath your pectoralis major. It starts at your third, fourth, and fifth ribs, and attaches near your shoulder joint. Although this muscle is technically a "chest muscle," its main duty is to assist in pulling your shoulders forward—an action that occurs in back exercises such as the dumbbell pullover.

Chest |

In this chapter, you'll find 64 exercises that target the muscles of your chest. Throughout, you'll notice that certain exercises have been designated as a Main Move. Master this basic version of a movement, and you'll be able to do all of its variations with flawless form.

PUSHUPS AND DIPS

These exercises target your pectoralis major. However, they also hit your front deltoids and triceps, since these muscles assist in just about every version of the movements. What's more, your rotator, trapezius, serratus anterior, and abdominals all contract to keep your shoulders, core, and hips stable as you perform the moves.

MAIN MOVE
Pushup

A

- Get down on all fours and place your hands on the floor so that they're slightly wider than and in line with your shoulders.

Squeeze your glutes and hold them that way for the entire movement. This helps keep your hips stable and in line with your upper body.

Your arms should be straight.

Your body should form a straight line from your ankles to your head.

Straighten your legs, with your weight on your toes.

Set your feet close together.

Brace your abdominals—as if you were about to be punched in the gut—and maintain that contraction for the duration of this exercise. This helps keep your body rigid, and doubles as core training.

75

Percent of your body weight you lift when you do a standard pushup, according to research by the National Strength and Conditioning Association.

B

- Lower your body until your chest nearly touches the floor.
- Pause at the bottom, and then push yourself back to the starting position as quickly as possible.
- If your hips sag at any point during the exercise, your form has broken down. When this happens, consider that your last repetition and end the set.

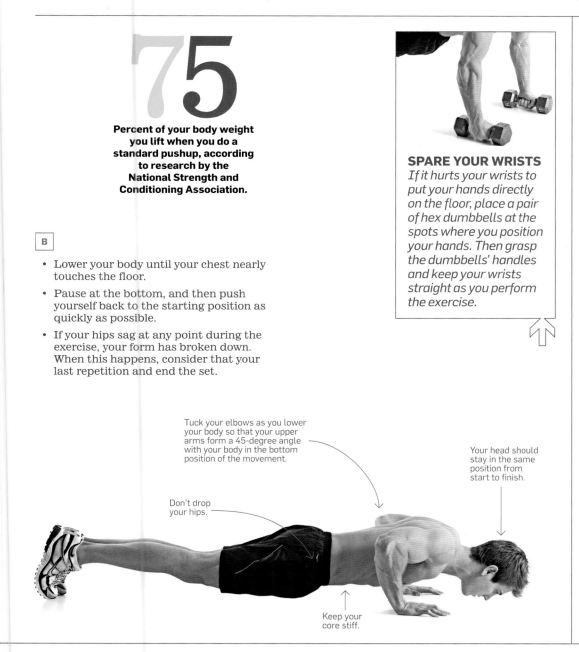

SPARE YOUR WRISTS
If it hurts your wrists to put your hands directly on the floor, place a pair of hex dumbbells at the spots where you position your hands. Then grasp the dumbbells' handles and keep your wrists straight as you perform the exercise.

Tuck your elbows as you lower your body so that your upper arms form a 45-degree angle with your body in the bottom position of the movement.

Don't drop your hips.

Your head should stay in the same position from start to finish.

Keep your core stiff.

MUSCLE MISTAKE
You Overwork Your Pecs

Or perhaps more accurately, you work your chest significantly harder than the muscles of your upper back. This can lead to muscle and joint imbalances that result in poor posture and an increased risk of injury. A good rule of thumb: Do a similar number of sets for your upper back as you do for your chest. And if you already have poor posture, devote an even greater proportion of your training time to your upper back muscles.

Chest | PUSHUPS

VARIATION #1
Incline Pushup
- Place your hands on a box, bench, or step instead of the floor. This reduces the amount of your body weight you have to lift, making the exercise easier.

The higher the surface and the more upright your body, the easier the exercise is.

You can do this exercise on a staircase, moving to a lower step as your strength improves.

VARIATION #2
Modified Pushup
- Instead of performing the exercise with your legs straight, bend your knees and cross your ankles behind you. This is another way to make the classic pushup easier.

65

Percent of your body weight you lift when you do a modified pushup.

Your body should form a straight line from your head to your knees.

Don't let your hips sag.

VARIATION #3
Decline Pushup
- Place your feet on a box or bench as you perform a pushup. This increases the amount of your body weight you have to lift, making the exercise harder.

STRENGTHEN YOUR SHOULDERS
Researchers in Texas found that the decline pushup works the muscles that stabilize your shoulders better than a traditional pushup.

VARIATION #4
Single-Leg Decline Pushup
- Place one foot on a box or bench and hold the other in the air.

PUSH AWAY FAT
The pushup is a good indicator of whether or not you're exercising enough now to avoid fat later, according to a Canadian study. The researchers found that people who perform poorly in a pushup test are 78 percent more likely to gain 20 pounds of flab over the next two decades.

If you feel strain on your lower back, you're not keeping your core tight.

VARIATION #5
Pushup with Feet on Swiss Ball

A

- Perform the movement with your feet placed on Swiss ball.

B

- Lower your body as far as you can, without allowing your hips to sag.

The instability of the ball forces your core to work harder, increasing the difficulty of the exercise.

VARIATION #6
Stacked-Feet Pushup
- Place one foot on top of the other so that only the lower one supports your body.

VARIATION #7
Weighted Pushup
- Have a workout partner place a weight plate on your back, at the level of your shoulder blades.

You can also increase the amount you're lifting by wearing a weighted vest or placing a heavy chain on your back.

The Pushup Spectrum

HARDEST

- 9. SWISS-BALL PUSHUP
- 8. BOSU PUSHUP
- 7. SINGLE-LEG DECLINE PUSHUP
- 6. PUSHUP WITH FEET ON SWISS BALL
- 5. DECLINE PUSHUP
- 4. STACKED-FEET PUSHUP
- 3. PUSHUP
- 2. INCLINE PUSHUP
- 1. MODIFIED PUSHUP

EASIEST

Chest | PUSHUPS

VARIATION #8
Triple-Stop Pushup

A

• Do a standard pushup, but pause for 2 seconds at the positions shown.

B

Pause at the halfway point on both your way down and your way up.

C

Pause when your chest is just off the floor.

D

As you push yourself back to the starting position, pause just before the point you straighten your arms.

MAKE TIME FOR THIS MOVE
Pausing briefly at each point increases strength at that joint angle and 10 degrees in either direction. So this method eliminates any weak point you might have. It also increases the time your muscles are under tension, stimulating growth.

VARIATION #9
Wide-Hands Pushup
• Place your hands about twice shoulder-width apart.

Setting your hands wide puts a greater emphasis on your chest. The downside: It also increases the stress on your shoulders.

VARIATION #10
Close-Hands Pushup
• Place your hands directly under your shoulders.

Placing your hands closer together works your triceps harder.

Keep your elbows tucked close to your sides as you lower your body.

VARIATION #11
Diamond Pushup

- Place your hands close enough together to make a triangle with your thumbs and forefingers.

Placing your hands closer together works your triceps harder.

VARIATION #12
Staggered-Hands Pushup

- Place one hand in standard pushup position and your other hand a few inches farther forward.

Staggering your hands increases the challenge to your core and shoulder muscles.

Alternate which hand is placed forward each set.

VARIATION #13
Spiderman Pushup

A

- Assume the standard pushup position.

B

- As you lower your body toward the floor, lift your right foot off the floor, swing your right leg out sideways, and try to touch your knee to your elbow.

- Reverse the movement, then push your body back to the starting position. Repeat, but on your next repetition, touch your left knee to your left elbow. Continue to alternate back and forth.

Chest | PUSHUPS

VARIATION #14
Swiss-Ball Pushup
- Place your hands on a Swiss ball instead of the floor.

TARGET YOUR TRICEPS
This exercise trains your triceps 30 percent harder than a standard pushup. The reason: The Swiss ball forces your triceps to stabilize your elbow and shoulder joints, which results in the recruitment of more muscle fibers.

Keep your core braced.

Squeeze the ball with your hands, almost like you're trying to grab onto it.

Your chest should nearly touch the ball.

VARIATION #15
Medicine-Ball Pushup
- Place both hands on a medicine ball.

CHISEL YOUR ABS
When you place your hands on a Swiss ball or a medicine ball, the instability causes your core muscles to work 20 percent harder than when you do pushups on the floor, report New Zealand researchers.

VARIATION #16
Single-Arm Medicine-Ball Pushup
- Place one hand on a medicine ball.

Do an equal number of sets with each hand on the ball.

If you don't have a medicine ball, you can use a basketball in its place.

VARIATION #17
Two-Arm Medicine-Ball Pushup
- Place each hand on a medicine ball.

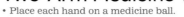

Don't let your hips sag.

VARIATION #18
T-Pushup

A

- Place a pair of hex dumbbells at the spot where you position your hands.
- Grasp the dumbbell handles and set yourself in pushup position.

Set your feet hip-width apart.

The dumbbells should be set slightly wider than shoulder-width apart.

B

- Lower your body to the floor.

C

- As you push yourself back up, rotate the right side of your body upward as you bend your right arm and pull the right dumbbell to your torso. Then straighten your arm so that the dumbbell is above your right shoulder.
- Lower the dumbbell back down, and repeat, this time performing the move to your left.

Raise the dumbbell and rotate your body in one fluid motion.

As you rotate your body, pivot on your toes and then lower your heels to the floor.

Your arms should form a T with your body.

VARIATION #19
Judo Pushup

A

- Begin in standard pushup position, but move your feet forward and raise your hips so your body almost forms an upside-down "V."

B

- Keeping your hips elevated, lower your body until your chin nearly touches the floor.

C

- Lower your hips until they almost touch the floor, as you simultaneously raise your head and shoulders toward the ceiling. Reverse the movement back to the starting position and repeat.

Pump Up Your Pushups

To boost the number of pushups you can do, try this simple ladder routine. Time how long it takes you to do as many push-ups (you can use any variation) as you can. Then rest for the same time period, and repeat the process two to four times. So if you do 20 push-ups in 25 seconds, you'll rest 25 seconds, and repeat. Let's say on your next round you complete 12 pushups in 16 seconds. You'd then rest for 16 seconds before your third set. Use this method two days a week to quickly raise your score.

Chest | PUSHUPS

VARIATION #20
Explosive Pushup

A

- Assume a pushup position.

B

- Bend your elbows and lower your body.

Your chest should nearly touch the floor.

C

- Press yourself up so forcefully that your hands leave the floor.

VARIATION #21
Iso-Explosive Pushup

- Do this movement just like the explosive pushup, but first pause 5 seconds in the down position. This pause technique eliminates all the elasticity in your muscles, which allows you to activate a maximum number of fast-twitch muscle fibers. These are the muscle fibers with greatest potential for size and strength gains.

VARIATION #22
Explosive Crossover Pushup

A

- Place your left hand on the floor and your right hand on the smooth side of a weight plate.

B

- Lower your body to the floor.

C

- Explosively push up and to the right so your hands leave the floor.

D

- Land with your left hand on the plate and your right hand on the floor.

E

- Then lower and repeat, alternating back and forth each repetition.

The crossover portion of this movement forces your upper arms toward the center of your body, which is the main function of the pectoralis major, your largest chest muscle.

VARIATION #23
Bosu Pushup

- Turn a Bosu ball over, so that the half-ball portion is on floor, and position your hands on the sides of the platform.

Brace your core and glutes.

Your chest should nearly touch the surface of the Bosu.

VARIATION #24
Suspended Pushup

- Attach a pair of straps with handles to a secure bar, so that the handles are a foot or so off the floor.
- Lower your body until your upper arms dip below your elbows.

Keep your body in a straight line from your ankles to your head.

One option for suspended pushups: Blast Straps, which can be found at elitefts.com

VARIATION #25
Pushup and Row

A
- Place a pair of hex dumbbells at the spot where you position your hands.
- Grasp the dumbbell handles and set yourself in pushup position.

B
- Lower your body to the floor, pause, then push yourself back up.

C
- Once you're back in the starting position, row the dumbbell in your right hand to the side of your chest, by pulling it upward and bending your arm.
- Pause, then lower the dumbbell back down, and repeat the same movement with your left arm. That's one repetition.

The dumbbells should be set slightly wider than shoulder-width apart.

THE ALL-IN-ONE UPPER BODY EXERCISE
The pushup and row works your middle and upper back as hard as it does your chest.

Your torso should not rotate as you row.

Hang On for More Muscle

Performing pushups while suspended from straps increases muscle activation in your abs and upper back, according to a study by Canadian researchers. One caution: This exercise can also place more stress on your lower back. To protect your spine, make sure to keep your core and glutes tight, as you should when you do any variation of the pushup. Simply brace your abs forcefully and squeeze your glutes, and hold those contractions as you lower and raise your body.

Chest | DIPS

MAIN MOVE
Dip

A

- Grasp the bars
  of a dip station
  and lift yourself so
  your arms are
  completely straight.

Keep your
wrists straight.

Cross your
ankles
behind you.

B

- Slowly lower yourself
  by bending your elbows
  until your upper arms
  dip just below your elbows.

- Pause, then push back
  up to the starting position.

Keep your
elbows
tucked
close to
your body.

Brace
your
core.

Your torso
should be upright.

VARIATION #1
Incline Dip

Don't round your lower back.

Your thighs should be parallel to the floor.

Your knees should be bent 90 degrees.

SAVE YOUR SHOULDERS
This version of the dip redistributes your weight so that your torso leans forward as you lower your body, placing more of the stress on your chest instead of your shoulders. It's particularly useful if you find the standard dip causes shoulder pain, but since it places less strain on your shoulder joint regardless, most guys would be better off sticking with this variation all the time.

Your upper arms should dip below your elbows.

VARIATION #2
Weighted Dip

• Perform the exercise with a dipping belt attached to your waist.

Allow your torso to lean forward.

Don't drop your legs as you lower your body.

A

• Raise your hips and thighs and hold them that way for the entire movement.

B

• Lower your body until your upper arms are just below parallel to the floor.

45

Chest | PRESSES

These exercises target your pectoralis major, the largest muscle of your chest. Most of the movements also hit your front deltoids and triceps, since these muscles assist in just about every version of the exercise. Your rotator cuff and trapezius also contract to help keep your shoulders stable as you perform the moves.

TRAINER'S TIP
Imagine that you're pushing your body away from the bar, instead of pushing the bar away from your body. This simple mind trick automatically encourages your body to use good form.

MAIN MOVE
Barbell Bench Press

A

• Grasp a barbell with an overhand grip that's just wider than shoulder-width, and hold it above your sternum with arms completely straight.

As you push the bar off your chest, squeeze and press the bar outward, as if you were trying to tear it apart. This forces more muscle fibers into play.

Hold the bar above your sternum.

Your wrists should be straight.

Squeeze your shoulder blades down and together and hold them as tight as you can during each set. This creates a stronger foundation for you to press from, which allows you to generate greater force.

Push your heels into the floor.

WHY FORM MATTERS
Pay closer attention to your exercise technique and you may notice something: People who review proper lifting form before bench-pressing may increase barbell velocity by 183 percent, report researchers at Barry University. The benefit: Faster bar speed helps you blast through sticking points, allowing you to lift heavier loads.

B

- Lower the bar straight down, pause, then press the bar in a straight line back up to the starting position.
- Keep your elbows tucked in, so that your upper arms form a 45-degree angle with your body in the down position. This reduces stress on your shoulder joints.

Make sure the bar is directly above your elbows at all times.

Lower the bar to your sternum.

Drive your head, upper back, and shoulders into the bench.

Don't allow your butt or hips to raise up off the bench.

Pull your elbows toward your sides.

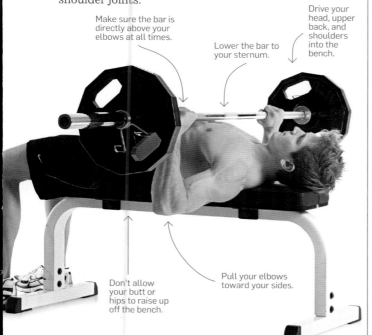

VARIATION #1
Close-Grip Barbell Bench Press
- Use an overhand grip that's shoulder-width apart.

MORE TRICEPS!
Using a close grip forces your triceps to work harder. In fact, the close-grip bench press is one of the best exercises for building size and strength in your triceps.

Keep your wrists straight.

Your shoulder blades should be pulled down and together.

Keep your elbows as close to your sides as you can.

Chest | PRESSES

VARIATION #2
Reverse-Grip Barbell Bench Press
• Use an underhand grip that's about shoulder-width apart.

BUILD YOUR UPPER CHEST
Canadian researchers found that the reverse-grip bench press activates your upper-chest muscles better than other versions of the flat bench press.

Your palms should be facing behind you.

Your arms should be completely straight.

Tuck your elbows close to your sides as you lower the bar.

VARIATION #3
Barbell Towel Press
• Roll a towel and place it long ways in the middle of your chest. Now perform a bench press, lowering the bar to the towel instead of to your chest.

Use a thick towel for this exercise.

Rest the bar on the towel momentarily before you push it back to the starting position.

Lowering the bar to the towel helps you overload the middle portion of the lift, where most people hit their sticking point. So this exercise helps you strengthen this common weak spot, enabling you to lift more on the traditional bench press.

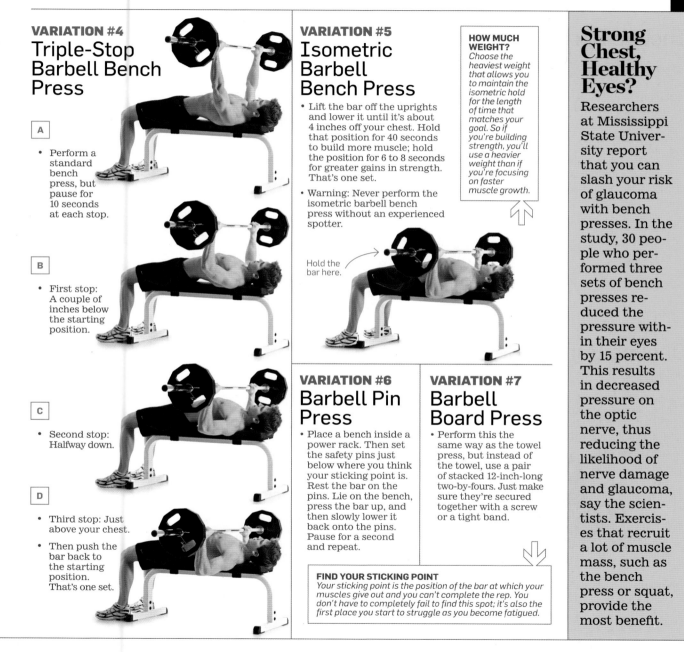

VARIATION #4
Triple-Stop Barbell Bench Press

A

- Perform a standard bench press, but pause for 10 seconds at each stop.

B

- First stop: A couple of inches below the starting position.

C

- Second stop: Halfway down.

D

- Third stop: Just above your chest.
- Then push the bar back to the starting position. That's one set.

VARIATION #5
Isometric Barbell Bench Press

- Lift the bar off the uprights and lower it until it's about 4 inches off your chest. Hold that position for 40 seconds to build more muscle; hold the position for 6 to 8 seconds for greater gains in strength. That's one set.

- Warning: Never perform the isometric barbell bench press without an experienced spotter.

Hold the bar here.

HOW MUCH WEIGHT?
Choose the heaviest weight that allows you to maintain the isometric hold for the length of time that matches your goal. So if you're building strength, you'll use a heavier weight than if you're focusing on faster muscle growth.

VARIATION #6
Barbell Pin Press

- Place a bench inside a power rack. Then set the safety pins just below where you think your sticking point is. Rest the bar on the pins. Lie on the bench, press the bar up, and then slowly lower it back onto the pins. Pause for a second and repeat.

VARIATION #7
Barbell Board Press

- Perform this the same way as the towel press, but instead of the towel, use a pair of stacked 12-inch-long two-by-fours. Just make sure they're secured together with a screw or a tight band.

FIND YOUR STICKING POINT
Your sticking point is the position of the bar at which your muscles give out and you can't complete the rep. You don't have to completely fail to find this spot; it's also the first place you start to struggle as you become fatigued.

Strong Chest, Healthy Eyes?

Researchers at Mississippi State University report that you can slash your risk of glaucoma with bench presses. In the study, 30 people who performed three sets of bench presses reduced the pressure within their eyes by 15 percent. This results in decreased pressure on the optic nerve, thus reducing the likelihood of nerve damage and glaucoma, say the scientists. Exercises that recruit a lot of muscle mass, such as the bench press or squat, provide the most benefit.

Chest | PRESSES

Incline Barbell Bench Press

A

- Set an adjustable bench to its lowest incline, about 15 to 30 degrees.
- Lie faceup on the bench and grab the barbell with an overhand grip that's slightly beyond shoulder width.

B

- Lower the bar to your upper chest.
- Pause, and then push the bar back to the starting position.

Hold the bar above your shoulders.

Your arms should be completely straight.

Keep your wrists straight.

Your feet should be flat on the floor.

Decline Barbell Bench Press

A

- Lie faceup on a decline bench and grab the barbell with an overhand grip that's slightly beyond shoulder width.
- Hold the bar above your chest with your arms straight.

B

- Lower the bar to your lower chest.
- Pause, and then push the bar back to the starting position.

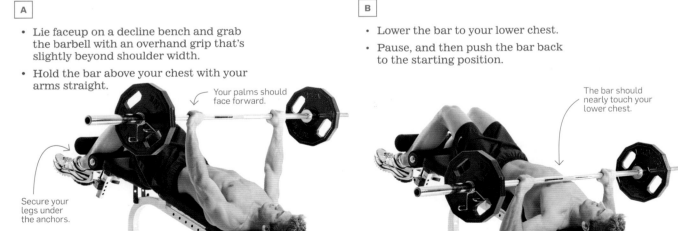

Your palms should face forward.

The bar should nearly touch your lower chest.

Secure your legs under the anchors.

Barbell Floor Press

A

- Lie on the floor instead of on a bench and hold a barbell with an overhand grip.

Your knees should be bent.

Your hands should be slightly beyond shoulder-width apart.

B

- Lower the barbell until your upper arms touch the floor.
- Keep your elbows pulled in toward your sides as you lower the bar.
- Pause, then push the bar back to the starting position.

Your upper arms should form a 45-degree angle with the sides of your torso.

Your feet should be flat on the floor.

MORE ON THE FLOOR!
The floor keeps your upper arms from descending below parallel, which limits your range of motion and concentrates the work on the muscles used during the last (and toughest) part of the bench press.

The Secret of Your Soreness

All of the chest exercises in this chapter work your entire pectoralis major. But you'll notice that when you perform an incline bench press, the upper portion of your chest is the area that's the most sore the next day. For decline bench presses, it's the lower portion. That's because changing the angle of your body puts more tension on a specific segment of your pecs. This causes a greater amount of muscle damage to those fibers, resulting in greater soreness.

Chest | PRESSES

MAIN MOVE
Dumbbell Bench Press

A

- Grab a pair of dumbbells and lie on your back on a flat bench, holding the dumbbells over your chest so that they're nearly touching.
- Your palms should be facing out, but turned slightly inward.
- Before you begin, pull your shoulder blades down and together, and hold them as tight as you can throughout the entire exercise.

B

- Without changing the angle of your hands, lower the dumbbells to the sides of your chest.
- Pause, then press the weights back up to the starting position as quickly as you can.
- Straighten your arms completely at the top of each repetition.

Turn your palms slightly toward each other.

Don't let the dumbbells clang together. (It's annoying.)

Keeping your shoulder blades tight stabilizes your shoulder joints, reducing your risk of injury and helping you lift heavier weights.

Your wrists should be straight.

In the down position, both your upper arms and the dumbbells should form a 45-degree angle to your body.

LIFT MORE—TODAY!
UK researchers found that people bench-press 12 percent more weight when they psych themselves up before a lift than when they're distracted. In the study, the scientists gave experienced weight lifters 20 seconds to mentally prepare. The take-home message: Before you approach the bench, skip the small talk and focus on the task at hand.

Keep your feet flat on the floor at all times.

STAY GROUNDED
Canadian researchers found that raising your feet off the ground while benching shifts as much as 30 percent of the load off your upper body and onto an overmatched core, significantly weakening your lift.

52

VARIATION #1
Alternating Dumbbell Bench Press

- Instead of pressing both dumbbells up at once, lift them one at a time, in an alternating fashion.

As you lower one dumbbell, press the other up.

VARIATION #2
Alternating Neutral-Grip Dumbbell Bench Press

The dumbbells should almost touch.

- Instead of pressing both dumbbells up at once, lift them one at a time, in an alternating fashion. So as you lower one dumbbell, press the other one up.

Your palms should face each other.

Alternating dumbbell presses increase your core activation because you're continually changing the weight distribution on each side of your body.

VARIATION #3
Neutral-Grip Dumbbell Bench Press

- Hold the dumbbells so that your palms face each other.

HIT YOUR CHEST HIGHER
Like the incline press, the neutral-grip bench press puts more of the emphasis on your upper chest. So if you don't have an adjustable bench, it's an effective way to target that part of your pectoralis major.

Tuck your elbows close to your sides as you lower the weights.

VARIATION #4
Single-Arm Dumbbell Bench Press

Place your free hand on your abs.

- For this exercise, simply use the same form as for a dumbbell chest press but complete the prescribed number of repetitions with one arm before immediately doing the same number with your other arm.

BENCH FOR ABS
Doing any exercise with one dumbbell at a time forces your core to work harder.

Chest | PRESSES

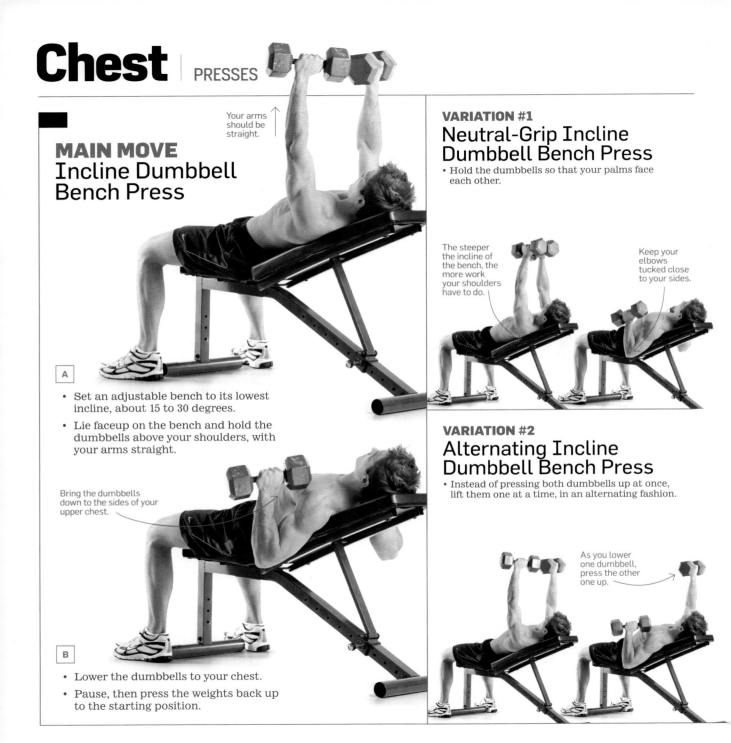

MAIN MOVE
Incline Dumbbell Bench Press

Your arms should be straight.

A

- Set an adjustable bench to its lowest incline, about 15 to 30 degrees.
- Lie faceup on the bench and hold the dumbbells above your shoulders, with your arms straight.

Bring the dumbbells down to the sides of your upper chest.

B

- Lower the dumbbells to your chest.
- Pause, then press the weights back up to the starting position.

VARIATION #1
Neutral-Grip Incline Dumbbell Bench Press
- Hold the dumbbells so that your palms face each other.

The steeper the incline of the bench, the more work your shoulders have to do.

Keep your elbows tucked close to your sides.

VARIATION #2
Alternating Incline Dumbbell Bench Press
- Instead of pressing both dumbbells up at once, lift them one at a time, in an alternating fashion.

As you lower one dumbbell, press the other one up.

Decline Dumbbell Bench Press

A

- Grab a pair of dumbbells and lie faceup on a decline bench.
- Hold the dumbbells above your chest.

Your arms should be straight.

B

- Lower the dumbbells to the sides of your lower chest.
- Pause, then press the weights back up to the starting position.

Your palms should face slightly inward.

Dumbbell Floor Press

A

- Grab a pair of dumbbells and lie faceup on the floor.
- Hold the dumbbells above your chest with your arms straight.

Your knees should be bent.

B

- Lower the dumbbells until your upper arms touch the floor.
- Pause, then press the weights back up to the starting position.

Your upper arms should form a 45-degree angle with the sides of your torso.

Keep your feet flat on the floor.

Chest | PRESSES

MAIN MOVE
Swiss-Ball Dumbbell Chest Press

The weights should form a 45-degree angle with your body.

Brace your core.

Your upper and middle back should be placed firmly on the ball.

A

- Grab a pair of dumbbells and lie on your back on a Swiss ball.
- Raise your hips so that your body forms a straight line from your knees to your shoulders.
- Your palms should be facing out, but turned slightly inward.

Keep your wrists as straight as you can.

Don't drop your hips.

Your feet should be flat on the floor at all times.

B

- Without changing the angle of your hands, lower the dumbbells to the sides of your chest.
- Pause, then press the weights back up to the starting position as quickly as you can.
- Straighten your arms completely at the top of each repetition.

A HARD CORE CHEST EXERCISE
Performing the chest press on a Swiss ball makes your core work 54 percent harder than when you do the exercise on a bench, according to an Australian study. However, it also reduces the amount of weight you can press, decreasing the demand on your chest muscles.

VARIATION
Alternating Swiss-Ball Dumbbell Chest Press

A

- Grab a pair of dumbbells and lie on your back on a Swiss ball.

Keep your body in a straight line from your knees to your shoulders.

B

- Instead of pressing both dumbbells up at once, lift them one at a time, in an alternating fashion.

As you lower one dumbbell, press the other one up.

MAIN MOVE
Incline Swiss-Ball Dumbbell Chest Press

A

- Position yourself on your back on a Swiss ball so your torso is at a 45-degree angle to the floor.
- Hold the dumbbells straight above your chin, with your arms straight.

Keep your core braced.

Your feet should be flat on the floor.

B

- Lower the dumbbells so that they end up just outside your upper chest.
- Pause, then press the weights back up to the starting position.

Don't let your hips drop.

Chest | PRESSES

Single-Arm Cable Chest Press

A

- With your right hand, grab the high-pulley handle of a cable station and face away from the weight stack.

- Stagger your feet and hold the handle at shoulder height, with your right arm bent and parallel to the floor.

B

- Push the handle forward and straighten your right arm in front of you.

- Then slowly bend your right elbow to return to the starting position.

- Complete the prescribed number of reps with your right arm, then switch hands and do the same number with your left.

Bend your right arm and pull it back.

Hold your left arm straight in front of you.

Keep your arm parallel to the floor.

As you push your right arm forward, pull your left arm back toward your shoulder.

Do not move your torso or drop your elbow.

20

Percent harder your core works when performing a standing cable chest press than during a standard barbell bench press.

Medicine-Ball Chest Pass

A

- Grab a medicine ball and stand about 3 feet in front of a concrete wall.
- Hold the ball with both hands next to your chest.
- Set your feet shoulder-width apart.

B

- Throw the ball at the wall with both hands, as if you were throwing a chest pass in basketball.
- Catch the ball as it rebounds off the wall, and repeat.

Straighten your arms forcefully and completely as you throw the ball.

Your knees should be slightly bent.

PLAY BALL, BUILD MUSCLE
You can also perform the medicine-ball chest press with a partner, instead of solo against the wall. Simply play catch back and forth. If you don't have a wall or a partner, you can bend over at the hips—until your torso is nearly parallel to the floor—and throw the ball toward the floor.

Chest | FLYS

These exercises target your pectoralis major. Your front deltoids assist in the movements.

Bend your elbows slightly.

MAIN MOVE
Dumbbell Fly

A

- Grab a pair of dumbbells and lie faceup on a flat bench.
- Hold the dumbbells over your chest with your elbows slightly bent and your palms facing out.

B

- Without changing the bend in your elbows, slowly lower the dumbbells down and slightly back until your upper arms are parallel to the floor.
- Pause, then lift the dumbbells back to the starting position.

In the down position, the dumbbells should be in line with your ears.

A PECKING ORDER FOR PEC EXERCISES
The chest fly is best placed at the end of your workout. Researchers at Truman State University found that pectoral muscles are activated for 23 percent less time during the chest fly than during the bench press. As a result, the scientists say that dumbbell and barbell chest presses can be used interchangeably but that the fly shouldn't be your primary lift for working your chest.

VARIATION #1
Incline Dumbbell Fly
• Lie faceup on a bench set to a low incline.

Your palms should face forward.

The dumbbells should nearly touch.

Lower the dumbbells down and slightly back.

VARIATION #2
Incline Dumbbell Fly to Press
• This exercise combines the incline fly with an incline press. Start by doing the incline fly, performing as many repetitions as you can until you start to struggle. Then immediately switch to incline dumbbell presses and complete as many repetitions as you can with perfect form.

VARIATION #3
Decline Dumbbell Fly
• Lie faceup on a decline bench.

VARIATION #4
Swiss-Ball Dumbbell Fly
• Lie with your middle and upper back placed firmly on a Swiss ball.

Your body should form a straight line from your knees to your shoulders.

MUSCLE MISTAKE
You Still Use the Chest Fly Machine
The chest fly machine, also known as the pec deck, can overstretch the front of your shoulder and cause the muscles around the rear of your shoulder to stiffen. The result is a higher risk for a painful injury called shoulder impingement syndrome. So skip the fly machine, and stick with the exercises in this chapter instead. For any exercise, perform it only if you can complete it pain-free for the full range of motion.

Chest | FLYS

Standing Cable Fly

A

- Attach two stirrup handles to the high-pulley cables of a cable-crossover station.
- Grab a handle with each hand, and stand in a staggered stance in the middle of the station.

B

- Without changing the angle of your elbows, pull the handles down and together, until they cross in front of your body.
- Pause, then return to the starting position.

Your arms should be outstretched but slightly bent.

Lean forward slightly at your hips; don't round your back.

Bend your front knee.

Cross the handles in front of your body.

61

Percent likelihood that after missing one workout you will also skip an exercise session the following week, according to a UK study. Keep that in mind the next time you consider forgoing a trip to the gym.

Turn the page to see
THE BEST CHEST EXERCISE YOU'VE NEVER DONE

Chest

THE BEST CHEST EXERCISE YOU'VE NEVER DONE
Pushup Plus

Besides working your chest, this exercise is highly effective at engaging your serratus anterior, a small but important muscle that helps move your shoulder blades. Neglect this muscle, as most guys do, and it becomes weak. That puts you at high risk for shoulder impingement—a painful injury in which a muscle tendon becomes entrapped in your shoulder joint. What's more, serratus anterior weakness often causes your shoulder blades to tilt forward and down, resulting in rounded shoulders—giving you a permanent slump.

Now, the classic pushup does work your serratus anterior. But adding the "plus"—pushing your upper back toward the ceiling at the end of the movement—makes the exercise even more effective. In fact, University of Minnesota researchers found that the pushup plus activates your serratus anterior 38 percent more than the standard pushup does.

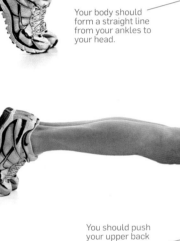

Your body should form a straight line from your ankles to your head.

Tuck your elbows as you lower your body, so that your upper arms form a 45-degree angle with your body in the bottom position of the movement.

Don't let your hips sag.

You should push your upper back toward the ceiling. Your shoulders will raise an inch or so past your starting position.

A

- Get down on all fours and place your hands on the floor so that they're slightly wider than and in line with your shoulders.
- Brace your abdominals—as if you were about to be punched in the gut—and hold them that way for the duration of this exercise.

B

- Lower your body until your chest nearly touches the floor.

C

- Pause, and then push yourself back to the starting position as quickly as possible.
- Once your arms are straight again, push your upper back toward the ceiling. The movement is very slight; it's hard to see, but you'll feel the difference.
- Pause for a count of one, then do another pushup and repeat.

BONUS EXERCISE!
Swiss-Ball Pushup Plus

A

- Place your hands directly under your shoulders and on the sides of a Swiss ball.

B

- Keeping your core tight, lower yourself until your chest grazes the ball, then push back up.

C

- Perform the "plus" by pushing your upper back away from the ball.

Chest

THE BEST STRETCH FOR YOUR CHEST
Doorway Stretch

Why it's good: This stretch loosens your pectoralis minor. When these muscles are stiff—as they are in almost anyone who works a desk job—they yank your shoulder blades forward, making you appear hunched instead of tall and straight.

Make the most of it: Hold this stretch for 30 seconds on each side, then repeat twice for a total of three sets. Do this routine daily, and up to three times a day if you're really tight.

Your arm should be at a 90-degree angle.

A

- Bend your right arm 90 degrees (the "high-five" position) and place your forearm against a door frame.
- Stand in staggered stance, your left foot in front of your right.

B

- Rotate your chest to your left until you feel a comfortable stretch in your chest and the front of your shoulder. Switch arms and legs and repeat for your other side.

You can also step forward with the same side leg as the side you're stretching, which will automatically put more tension on the muscle.

BUILD THE PERFECT CHEST

Pick your plan: Here are three routines for the results you want.

The Chest-Chiseling Complex

The premise behind this workout is simple: Don't allow your muscles time to fully recover and they'll learn to withstand fatigue better. As a result, over time you'll improve your ability to churn out more repetitions of any chest exercise. And that means more muscle.

What to do: Do eight dips and eight pushups without pausing between exercises. Continue alternating between moves, reducing the number of reps you do by one each time. So you'll do seven dips and seven pushups next, six and six, and so on, until you're down to one rep. Rest for 90 seconds, then try to repeat the complex. As your strength improves, add one rep to your starting number of reps. Do this workout once every 5 days, maximum.

The Super-Strength Workout

Research shows that people who vary their repetition ranges in a wavelike fashion—known by scientists as undulating periodization—gain twice as much strength as those who do the same routine every workout.

What to do: Do three workouts a week, resting for at least a day between sessions.

- On Monday (Workout 1), perform four sets of the barbell bench press, followed by four sets of the incline barbell bench press. Do four to six repetitions of each exercise, resting for 90 seconds between sets.

- On Wednesday (Workout 2), do three sets of the single-arm cable chest press, followed by three sets of the incline dumbbell bench press; perform 10 to 12 repetitions of each exercise, resting for 60 seconds between sets.

- On Friday (Workout 3), do two sets of dips followed by two sets of pushups. Perform 15 to 20 repetitions of each exercise, resting for 45 seconds between sets.

The Time-Saving Trifecta

Sure, performing three consecutive chest exercises without resting saves you time. But organizing your workout this way also keeps your muscles under tension longer, which is an effective means of stimulating growth.

What to do: Perform one set each of three different exercises in succession, without resting—a routine known as a triset. Mix and match movements as you like, choosing one from each of the exercise groups below (A, B, and C). Simply do four to six reps of Exercise A, 10 to 12 reps of Exercise B, and then 15 to 20 reps of Exercise C. Rest for 60 seconds, then repeat three times for a total of four rounds. Perform this workout 2 days a week, resting for at least 3 days between sessions.

EXERCISE GROUP A
Dumbbell bench press (page 52)
Alternating dumbbell bench press (page 53)
Neutral-grip dumbbell bench press (page 53)
Alternating neutral-grip dumbbell bench press (page 53)
Swiss-ball dumbbell chest press (page 56)
Alternating Swiss-ball dumbbell chest press (page 56)
Barbell bench press (page 46)

EXERCISE GROUP B
Incline dumbbell bench press (page 54)
Alternating incline dumbbell bench press (page 54)
Neutral-grip incline dumbbell bench press (page 54)
Incline Swiss-ball dumbbell chest press (page 57)
Reverse-grip barbell bench press (page 48)
Incline barbell bench press (page 50)

EXERCISE GROUP C
Any variation of the pushup or dip (pages 34–45)

Chapter 5: Back
THE SECRET TO A BETTER BODY

Back

Rarely do you hear someone say, "Wow! That guy has a great back!" After all, most men don't spend nearly as much time working their back muscles as they do the muscles on the fronts of their bodies. So even if a guy has a well-developed chest, it's quite likely that he's neglecting his back, by comparison. And that leads to a problem: poor posture. When your chest muscles are stronger than your back muscles, the resulting imbalance pulls your shoulders forward, leaving you with a hunched back.

The good news: By focusing more on your back, you can straighten your posture, and look as fit when you're walking away as you do on your approach.

Bonus Benefits

A bigger bench press! The muscles of your upper- and mid-back are key for stabilizing your shoulder joints. And strong, stable shoulders allow you lift heavier weights in just about every upper-body exercise, from the bench press to the arm curl.

Bulging biceps! Exercises that work your back are also great for targeting your arms. That's because any time that you have to bend your elbows to lift a weight, you're training your biceps—whether you're doing an arm curl, or a classic "back" exercise such as a row or chinup. Think about it: How would your *arms* know the difference?

A leaner midsection! Building your back can torch belly fat. It's metabolism 101: The more muscles you train, the more calories you burn.

Meet Your Muscles

Rear Deltoid

While your rear deltoid [1] is typically thought of as a shoulder muscle (and you'll learn more about it in Chapter 6), it's actually emphasized by many of the exercises that work your upper back. That's because its job is to pull your upper arm backward, a movement that you perform whenever you do a rowing exercise.

Teres Major

The teres major [2] starts on the outer edge of your shoulder blade, or scapula, and—like your lats—attaches to the inside of your upper arm. So it assists your lats in pulling your upper arm down to the side of your torso.

Latissimus Dorsi

Your latissimus dorsi [3] originates on the lower half of your back, along your spine and hip, and attaches to the inside of your upper arm. The primary job of your two lats is to pull your upper arms from a raised position down to the sides of your torso, as when you grab an object off a high shelf. That's why exercises that require this movement, such as chinups, pullups, lat pulldowns, and pullovers, are such popular back builders.

Trapezius

Your trapezius [4] is a long, triangle-shaped muscle located on the upper half of your back. Because of the way its muscle fibers are arranged, your traps have several jobs.

The upper portion of your traps [A] are responsible for lifting your shoulder blades. This allows you to shrug your shoulders. It's worth noting that the best movements for working these fibers—lateral raises, and shrugs—are classified as shoulder exercises and are found in Chapter 6.

The middle portion of your traps [B], with fibers running perpendicular to your spine, are responsible for pulling your shoulder blades closer together, toward the middle of your back. Rowing exercises emphasize these muscle fibers.

The lower portion of your traps [C], with fibers ascending to your shoulder blades, pull your shoulder blades down. Rowing movements work these fibers as well.

Rhomboids

Beneath your trapezius lie your rhomboids, specifically the rhomboid major [5] and rhomboid minor. [6] These are small muscles that start at your spine and attach to your shoulder blades. They assist your traps with pulling your shoulder blades together.

Upper Back | ROWS & RAISES

In this chapter, you'll find 103 exercises that target the muscles of your back. These exercises are divided into two major sections: Upper-Back Exercises and Lat Exercises. Within each section, you'll notice that certain exercises have been given the designation Main Move. Master this basic version of a movement, and you'll be able to do all of its variations with flawless form.

ROWS & RAISES

These exercises target your middle and lower traps, your rhomboid major, and your rhomboid minor. They also hit your upper traps, rear deltoids, and rotator cuff muscles, which assist in the rowing movement or act as stabilizers in every version of these exercises.

MAIN MOVE
Inverted Row

Hang with your arms completely straight and your hands positioned directly above your shoulders.

Your body should form a straight line from your ankles to your head.

A

- Grab the bar with an overhand, shoulder-width grip.

If your wrists start to "curl" as you perform the movement—that is, if you have trouble keeping them straight, it's a sign that your upper back and/or your biceps are weak.

THE REVERSE PUSHUP?
The inverted row is to your back as the pushup is to your chest. Not only is it great for working the muscles of your middle and upper back but it also challenges your core.

Try to keep your wrists straight.

Why Rows Matter

Rowing exercises train your trapezius and rhomboids, muscles that help keep your shoulder blades from moving as you lift a weight. That's important because unstable shoulders can limit your strength in exercises for your chest and arms. For instance, your chest muscles might be capable of bench-pressing 225 pounds, but if your shoulders can't support that weight, you won't be able to complete one rep. So boost your strength on rows to boost your strength all over.

B

Keep your body rigid for the entire movement.

- Initiate the movement by pulling your shoulder blades back, then continue the pull with your arms to lift your chest to the bar.
- Pause, then slowly lower your body back to the starting position.

Upper Back | ROWS & RAISES

VARIATION #1
Modified Inverted Row
- Instead of performing an inverted row with your legs straight, start with your knees bent 90 degrees.

Bending your knees reduces the amount of your body weight that you have to lift.

VARIATION #2
Underhand-Grip Inverted Row
- Use a shoulder-width, underhand grip.

An underhand grip forces your biceps to work harder.

VARIATION #3
Elevated-Feet Inverted Row
- Place your heels on a bench or box, instead of on the floor.

VARIATION #4
Inverted Row with Feet on Swiss Ball
- Instead of placing your heels on the floor, position them on a Swiss ball.

Elevating your feet increases the difficulty of the exercise by boosting the amount of your body weight you have to lift.

Because the ball is an unstable surface, your core has to work hard to keep your body rigid and balanced.

VARIATION #5
Weighted Inverted Row
- To make the inverted row even harder, perform the movement with a weight plate positioned on your chest.

VARIATION #6
Single-Arm Inverted Row
- Grab the bar overhand with your left hand, but keep your right hand free and hold it in the air, with your elbow bent 90 degrees.
- Pull your body up with your left arm, as you straighten your right arm and reach high with your right hand.
- Complete the prescribed number of repetitions with your left arm, then immediately switch arms, grabbing the bar with your right hand to do the same number of reps.

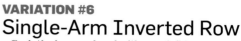

Keep your body rigid from your shoulders to your knees.

VARIATION #7
Suspended Inverted Row
- Attach a pair of straps with handles to a secure bar so that the handles are about 3 feet off the floor.

VARIATION #8
Towel-Grip Inverted Row
- Find your hand positions for an inverted row, then drape a towel over each of those spots on the bar.
- Grab the ends of each towel so that your palms are facing each other.
- Pull your chest as high as you can.

Unlike the bar, the straps aren't fixed, so your rotator cuff muscles have to work harder to keep your shoulders stable.

Grasping the towels increases the demand on your forearm muscles, helping improve grip strength as you build your back.

Upper Back | ROWS & RAISES

MAIN MOVE
Barbell Row

A

- Grab the barbell with an overhand grip that's just beyond shoulder width, and hold it at arm's length.

- Bend at your hips and knees and lower your torso until it's almost parallel to the floor.

Keep your lower back naturally arched.

Your knees should be slightly bent.

Let the bar hang straight down from your shoulders.

Set your feet shoulder-width apart.

Bend your elbows and raise your upper arms.

Squeeze your shoulder blades toward each other.

B

- Pull the bar to your upper abs.
- Pause, then slowly lower the bar back to the starting position.

Lift the bar without moving your torso.

MUSCLE MISTAKE
You Round Your Lower Back When You Row

This mistake can lead to injuries such as herniated disks. Here's how to avoid it: Pick up the weight and stand tall—with your lower back naturally arched. Keeping your upper body rigid, bend your knees slightly as you push your hips backward as far as possible. Then without changing the posture of your torso, lower your upper body until it's nearly parallel to the floor. Now check your form in the mirror.

Upper Back | ROWS & RAISES

Mix and match one of four grip positions—overhand, neutral, under-hand, elbows-out—with any of the eight versions of the dumbbell row that follow. All of the grips are interchangeable with each type of row, giving you 32 back-building options from this one classic move.

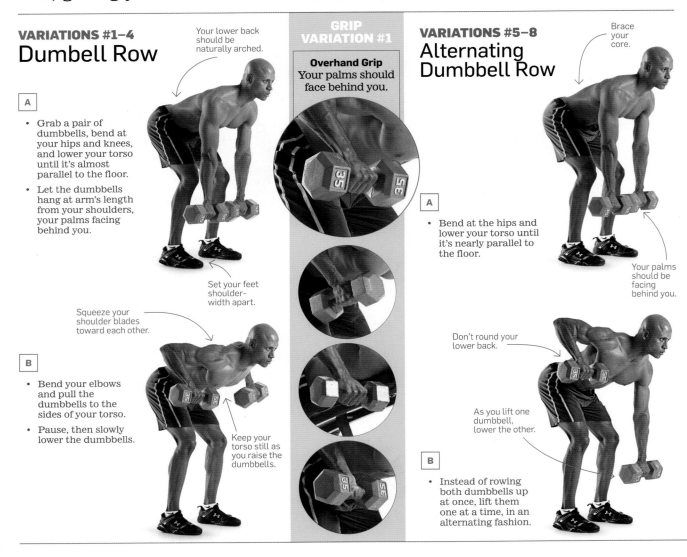

VARIATIONS #1–4
Dumbell Row

Your lower back should be naturally arched.

A

- Grab a pair of dumbbells, bend at your hips and knees, and lower your torso until it's almost parallel to the floor.
- Let the dumbbells hang at arm's length from your shoulders, your palms facing behind you.

Set your feet shoulder-width apart.

Squeeze your shoulder blades toward each other.

B

- Bend your elbows and pull the dumbbells to the sides of your torso.
- Pause, then slowly lower the dumbbells.

Keep your torso still as you raise the dumbbells.

GRIP VARIATION #1

Overhand Grip
Your palms should face behind you.

VARIATIONS #5–8
Alternating Dumbbell Row

Brace your core.

A

- Bend at the hips and lower your torso until it's nearly parallel to the floor.

Your palms should be facing behind you.

Don't round your lower back.

As you lift one dumbbell, lower the other.

B

- Instead of rowing both dumbbells up at once, lift them one at a time, in an alternating fashion.

78

VARIATIONS #9–12
Single-Leg Neutral-Grip Dumbbell Row

A

- Bend at the hips and lower your torso until it's nearly parallel to the floor.
- Raise one leg and hold it in the air.

Your lower back should be naturally arched.

Your palms should be facing each other.

B

- Row the dumbbells to the sides of your torso.
- Each set, switch the leg you balance on.

Tuck your elbows close to your sides.

Keep your leg elevated as your row.

GRIP VARIATION #2

Neutral Grip
Your palms should face each other. When you row the weight, keep your elbows close to your sides.

VARIATIONS #13–16
Single-Arm Neutral-Grip Dumbbell Row

Brace your core.

Place your free hand behind your back, palm facing up.

Use a neutral grip, so that your right palm is facing left.

A

- Grab a dumbbell in your right hand, bend at your hips and knees, and lower your torso until it's almost parallel to the floor.
- Let the dumbbell hang at arm's length from your shoulders.

The single-arm row allows you to work each side of your body separately, helping to shore up muscle imbalances while increasing the challenge to your core.

B

- Pull the dumbell to the side of your torso, keeping your elbow tucked close to your side.

Don't rotate or lift your torso as you row the weight.

Bend your knees slightly.

Upper Back | ROWS & RAISES

Lying Supported Elbows-Out Dumbbell Row

A

- Instead of standing, perform the exercise while lying chest down on a bench set to its lowest incline.
- Let the dumbbells hang at arm's length from your shoulders.

Your palms should be facing behind you.

B

- Keeping your elbows flared out, row the dumbbells toward the sides of your chest.

Your upper arms should be perpendicular to your body.

Keep your lower back naturally arched as you perform the movement, instead of allowing your upper body to "collapse" against the bench.

GRIP VARIATION #3

Elbows-Out Overhand Grip
Your palms should face behind you. As you row, keep your elbows flared so upper arm is perpendicular to your torso.

Kneeling Supported Elbows-Out Single-Arm Dumbbell Row

A

Don't round your lower back.

- Place your left hand and left knee on a flat bench.
- Your lower back should be naturally arched and your torso parallel to the floor.

Your palms should be facing behind you.

B

- Keeping your upper arm perpendicular to your body, row the weight toward the side of your chest.

Flare your elbow out to your side as you lift the dumbbell.

VARIATIONS #25–28
Single-Arm, Single-Leg Underhand-Grip Dumbbell Row

Your lower back should be naturally arched.

A
- Grab a dumbbell with your right hand using an underhand grip.
- Place your left hand on a bench in front of you and bend over at the hips.
- Raise your right leg in the air behind you.

Your palm should be facing forward.

Your raised leg should be in line with your upper body.

Bend your knee slightly.

B
- Tuck your elbow close to your side as you row the dumbbell to the side of your torso.

GRIP VARIATION #4

Underhand Grip
Your palms should face forward. Like the neutral grip, keep your elbows close to your sides as you row.

VARIATIONS #29–32
Standing Supported, Single-Arm Underhand-Grip Dumbbell Row

A
- Grab a dumbbell in your right hand.
- Place your left hand on a bench in front of you and bend over at the hips.
- Let the dumbbell hang at arm's length, your palm facing forward.

Your torso should be nearly parallel to the floor.

B
- Keep your elbow next to your side as you row the weight to the side of your torso.

Using an underhand grip increases the involvement of your biceps.

Upper Back | ROWS & RAISES

VARIATION #33
Dumbbell Face Pull with External Rotation

- Grab a pair of dumbbells and lie chest down on a bench set to a low incline.

- Let your arms hang straight down from your shoulders, with your palms facing each other.

- In one movement, bend your arms and pull the dumbbells toward the sides of your face as you simultaneously raise your upper arms as high as you can.

- Pause, then reverse the movement to the start.

In the up position, you'll look like you're flexing your biceps.

Squeeze your shoulder blades toward each other.

Your upper arms should be perpendicular to your torso.

VARIATION #34
Single-Arm, Neutral-Grip Dumbbell Row and Rotation

- Instead of using two dumbbells, work one arm at a time.

- As you row the dumbbell, rotate the same side of your torso upward.

- Pause, then lower your body and the weight back to the start.

- Complete the prescribed number of reps with one arm, then do the same number with your other arm.

VARIATION #35
Single-Leg, Single-Arm Rotational Dumbbell Row

Your lower back should be naturally arched.

Keep your elbow close to your side as you row the weight.

A

- Grab a dumbbell in your right hand and turn your palm so that it's facing right.

- Raise your right leg so that it's in line with your upper body.

B

- Pull the dumbbell up to your side, as you simultaneously rotate your palm inward so that it's facing your torso in the up position.

- Complete the prescribed number of reps with your right arm, then immediately do the same number with your left arm and leg.

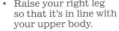

MAIN MOVE
Rear Lateral Raise

A

- Grab a pair of dumbbells and bend forward at your hips until your torso is nearly parallel to the floor.
- Let the dumbbells hang straight down from your shoulders, your palms facing each other.

B

- Without moving your torso, raise your arms straight out to your sides until they're in line with your body.
- Pause, then slowly return to the starting position.

Don't change the bend in your elbows.

Your back should be naturally arched.

Your arms should be slightly bent.

Keep your torso still as you lift the weights.

Set your feet shoulder-width apart.

The Most Surprising Back Exercise?

Most people think of the rear lateral raise as strictly a shoulder exercise, since it targets your rear deltoid. But consider: It's actually the same movement as a row, only you're not bending your elbows as you lift the weight. So it's also highly effective at working the muscles of your middle and upper back, which is why it's included in this chapter. For best results, focus on squeezing your shoulder blades together as you do the exercise.

Upper Back | ROWS & RAISES

VARIATION #1
Underhand-Grip Rear Lateral Raise

- Perform the movement with an underhand grip. Your palms should be facing forward, instead of facing each other.

Using an underhand grip increases the demand on your rotator cuff, a group of muscles that are key for healthy shoulders.

VARIATION #2
Overhand-Grip Rear Lateral Raise

- Perform the movement while holding the dumbbells with an overhand grip. Your palms should be facing behind you, instead of facing each other.

Using an overhand grip shifts more of the work to your rhomboids, upper-back muscles that help stabilize your shoulder blades.

VARIATION #3
Seated Rear Lateral Raise

- Grab a pair of dumbbells and sit at the end of a bench, instead of standing.

Keep your lower back naturally arched.

Raise your arms straight out to your sides.

Your palms should be facing each other.

VARIATION #4
Lying Dumbbell Raise

- Grab a dumbbell in your right hand and lie on your left side on a flat bench.
- Prop yourself up with your left elbow.
- Let your right arm hang straight down so that it's perpendicular to the floor, with your palm facing behind you and your elbow slightly bent.
- Without changing the bend in your elbow, raise your arm straight above your shoulder, while rotating your arm so that your palm is facing your head.
- Slowly return to the starting position.

84

VARIATION #5
Crossover Rear Lateral Raise

A

- Attach two stirrup handles to the low cables of a cable-crossover station.
- Grab the left handle with your right hand and the right handle with your left, and stand in the middle of the station.
- Bend at your hips and knees and lower your torso until it's nearly parallel to the floor.

B

- Without changing the bend in your elbows, raise your arms until they're parallel to the floor.
- Pause, then slowly return to the starting position.

Keep your torso still as you raise your arms.

Keep your back naturally arched.

Your arms should hang down from your shoulders.

Y-T-L-W-I RAISE

This is a fantastic, multi-part exercise that targets the muscles of your upper back that stabilize your shoulder blades—particularly your trapezius. It also strengthens your shoulder muscles in every direction, emphasizing your rotator cuff and deltoids.

You can perform all parts of the Y-T-L-W-I raise as a *complete* upper-back workout, with or without the dumbbells (depending on your ability). If you don't use weights, make sure your hands are positioned just as if you were holding the dumbbells. When using weights, you'll likely find that all you'll need is, at most, a very light pair of dumbbells. You can do the exercise while lying chest down on an incline bench or a Swiss ball. The ball makes the movements even harder, since it engages your core muscles to help you maintain your position. Three of the movements—Y-T-I—can also be effectively performed on the floor, which can come in handy in a hotel room.

Incline Y Raise

A

- Set an adjustable bench to a low incline and lie with your chest against the pad.

Let your arms hang straight down from your shoulders.

Turn your arms so that your palms are facing each other.

B

- Raise your arms at a 30-degree angle to your body (so that they form a Y) until they're in line with your body.

- Pause, then slowly lower back to the starting position.

The thumb sides of your hands should point up.

Floor Y Raise

A

- Lie facedown on the floor. Allow your arms to rest on the floor, completely straight and at a 30-degree angle to your body, your palms facing each other.

The thumb sides of your hands should point up.

Your arms should form a Y with your body.

B

- Raise your arms as high as you can.
- Pause, then slowly lower back to the starting position.

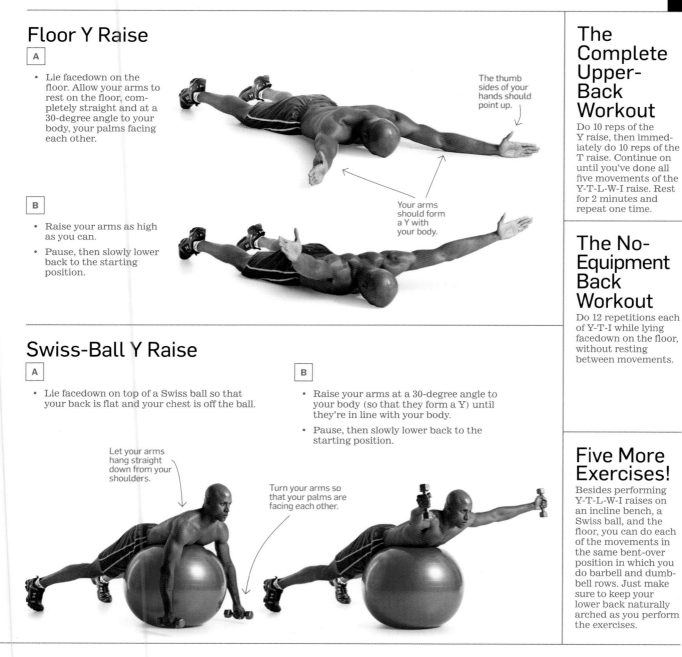

Swiss-Ball Y Raise

A

- Lie facedown on top of a Swiss ball so that your back is flat and your chest is off the ball.

Let your arms hang straight down from your shoulders.

Turn your arms so that your palms are facing each other.

B

- Raise your arms at a 30-degree angle to your body (so that they form a Y) until they're in line with your body.
- Pause, then slowly lower back to the starting position.

The Complete Upper-Back Workout

Do 10 reps of the Y raise, then immediately do 10 reps of the T raise. Continue on until you've done all five movements of the Y-T-L-W-I raise. Rest for 2 minutes and repeat one time.

The No-Equipment Back Workout

Do 12 repetitions each of Y-T-I while lying facedown on the floor, without resting between movements.

Five More Exercises!

Besides performing Y-T-L-W-I raises on an incline bench, a Swiss ball, and the floor, you can do each of the movements in the same bent-over position in which you do barbell and dumbbell rows. Just make sure to keep your lower back naturally arched as you perform the exercises.

Upper Back | ROWS & RAISES

Incline T Raise

Let your arms hang straight down from your shoulders.

- Grab a pair of dumbbells and lie chest down on an adjustable bench set to a low incline.

- Raise your arms straight out to your sides until they're in line with your body.

- Pause, then slowly lower back to the starting position.

Turn your arms so that your palms are facing out.

The thumb sides of your hands should point up.

Floor T Raise

- Move your arms so that they're out to your sides— perpendicular to your body with the thumb sides of your hands pointing up—and raise them as high as you comfortably can.

- Pause, then slowly lower back to the starting position.

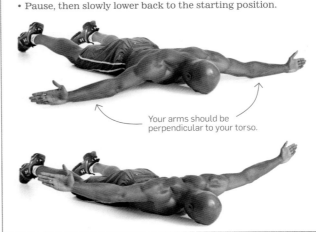

Your arms should be perpendicular to your torso.

Swiss Ball T Raise

A

- Lie facedown on top of a Swiss ball so that your back is flat and your chest is off the ball.

B

- Raise your arms straight out to your sides until they're in line with your body.

- Pause, then slowly lower back to the starting position.

Let your arms hang straight down from your shoulders.

Turn your arms so that your palms are facing out.

Incline L Raise

A

- Grab a pair of dumbbells and lie chest down on an adjustable bench set to a low incline.
- Let your arms hang straight down from your shoulders, your palms facing behind you.

B

- Keeping your elbows flared out, lift your upper arms as high as you can by bending your elbows and squeezing your shoulder blades together.

Your upper arms should be perpendicular to your torso.

C

- Without changing your elbow position, rotate your upper arms up and back as far as you can.
- Pause, then slowly lower back to the starting position.

Swiss-Ball L Raise

A

- Lie facedown on top of a Swiss ball so that your back is flat and your chest is off the ball.

Let your arms hang straight down from your shoulders, your palms facing behind you.

B

- Keeping your elbows flared out, lift your upper arms as high as you can by bending your elbows and squeezing your shoulder blades together.
- Your upper arms should be perpendicular to your torso at the top of the move.

C

- Without changing your elbow position, rotate your upper arms up and back as far as you can.
- Pause, then slowly lower back to the starting position.

Keep your chest up.

Upper Back | ROWS & RAISES

Incline W Raise

A

- Grab a pair of dumbbells and lie chest down on an adjustable bench set to a low incline.

- Bend your elbows more than 90 degrees and hold them close to your sides with your palms facing up, the thumb side of your hands pointing out.

B

- Without changing the bend in your elbows, squeeze your shoulder blades together as you raise your upper arms.

- At the top of the movement, your arms should form a W.

- Pause, then slowly lower back to the starting position.

Swiss-Ball W Raise

A

- Grab a pair of dumbbells and lie facedown on top of a Swiss ball so that your back is flat and your chest is off the ball.

- Bend your elbows more than 90 degrees with your palms facing up, the thumb side of your hands pointing out.

B

- Without changing the bend in your elbows, squeeze your shoulder blades together as you raise your upper arms.

- At the top of the movement, your arms should form a W.

- Pause, then slowly lower back to the starting position.

Keep your chest up.

Incline I Raise

- Grab a pair of dumbbells and lie chest down on an adjustable bench set to a low incline.
- Let your arms hang straight down from your shoulders, your palms facing each other.
- Raise your arms straight up, so that they're in line with your body and form an I.
- Pause, then slowly lower back to the starting position.

Floor I Raise

- Position your arms straight above your shoulders so your body forms a straight line from your feet to your fingertips.
- Raise your arms as high as you comfortably can.
- Pause, then slowly lower back to the starting position.

Your palms should be facing each other so that the thumb sides of your hands point up.

Swiss-Ball I Raise

A

- Grab a pair of dumbbells and lie facedown on top of a Swiss ball so that your back is flat and your chest is off the ball.

B

- Raise your arms straight up, so that they're in line with your body and form an I.
- Pause, then slowly lower back to the starting position.

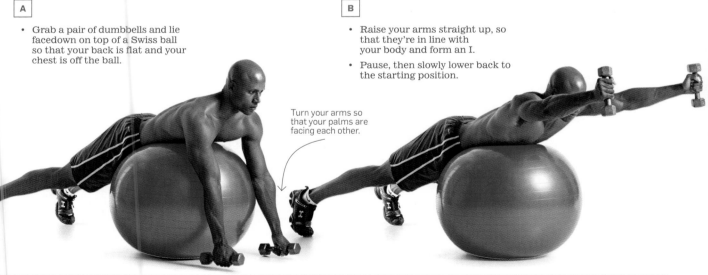

Turn your arms so that your palms are facing each other.

Upper Back |

MAIN MOVE
Cable Row

A

- Attach a straight bar to the cable and position yourself with your feet braced.
- Grab the bar with an overhand grip that's just beyond shoulder width.

Sit up straight and push your chest out and pull your shoulders down and back.

Your knees should be slightly bent.

B

- Without moving your torso, pull the bar to your upper abs.
- Pause, then slowly lower your body back to the starting position.

Your torso should remain upright and motionless throughout the movement. So don't lean forward and back to perform the exercise.

Keep your core braced.

2

Number of 20-minute weight-training sessions per week that resulted in people having fewer sick days from their jobs, according to an Oklahoma State University study of 79,000 workers.

MUSCLE MISTAKE
You Row with High Shoulders

When you do any type of row, start the movement by pulling your shoulders back and down. Why? Because otherwise, you'll tend to keep your shoulders elevated, which allows you to hyperextend them as you row your elbows back. This stresses both the front of your shoulder and a rotator cuff muscle called the *subscapularis*. Over time, this can cause your shoulder joint to become unstable, which often leads to injuries.

Upper Back | ROWS & RAISES

VARIATION #1
Wide-Grip Cable Row

- Position your hands about 1½ times shoulder-width apart, and pull the bar to your lower chest.

The wider grip increases the involvement of your rear deltoids.

VARIATION #2
Underhand-Grip Cable Row

- Grasp the bar with a shoulder-width, underhand grip and pull the bar to your lower abs.

The underhand grip allows your biceps to work harder.

VARIATION #3
Rope-Handle Cable Row

- Attach a rope handle to the cable, grab an end with each hand, and perform a cable row.

Pull toward your upper abs.

VARIATION #4
V-Grip Cable Row

- Attach a V-grip to the cable, grasp it with both hands, and pull it toward your midsection.

Keep your torso upright; don't lean forward or back.

VARIATION #5
Single-Arm Cable Row

- Attach a stirrup handle to the cable and perform the movement with one arm at a time. Without moving your torso, pull the handle to your side.

- Complete the prescribed number of repetitions to your right side, then immediately do the same number to your left side.

VARIATION #6
Single-Arm Cable Row and Rotation

- Attach a stirrup handle to the cable and grasp it with your right hand.

- Pull the handle toward your right side as you rotate your torso to the right.

- Pause, then reverse the movement back to the starting position.

Sit tall and keep your torso upright.

Keep your core tight as you perform this exercise.

VARIATION #7
Cable Row to Neck with External Rotation

- Attach a rope handle to the cable and position yourself in front of the machine.

- Pull the middle of the rope toward your face, as you squeeze your shoulder blades together and rotate your upper arms and forearms up and back.

- Pause, then slowly return to the starting position.

Grab the bottom of the rope with each hand, your palms facing each other.

Rotating your upper arms backward strengthens your rotator cuff, muscles that help stabilize your shoulder joints.

Sit up straight.

VARIATION #8
Standing Single-Arm Cable Row

- Attach a stirrup handle to the low pulley of a cable station, grab it with your right hand, and stand in a staggered stance.

- Pull the handle toward your right side as you rotate your torso to the right.

- Pause, then reverse the movement back to the starting position.

- Complete the prescribed number of repetitions to your right side, then immediately do the same number to your left side.

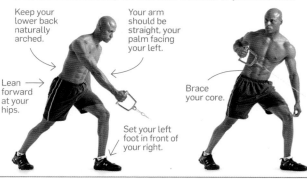

Keep your lower back naturally arched.

Your arm should be straight, your palm facing your left.

Lean forward at your hips.

Set your left foot in front of your right.

Brace your core.

Lats |

CHINUPS & PULLUPS
These exercises target your lats. They also hit your teres major and biceps. What's more, your core and middle and upper back muscles are involved, assisting in the movement or acting as stabilizers in most versions of this exercise.

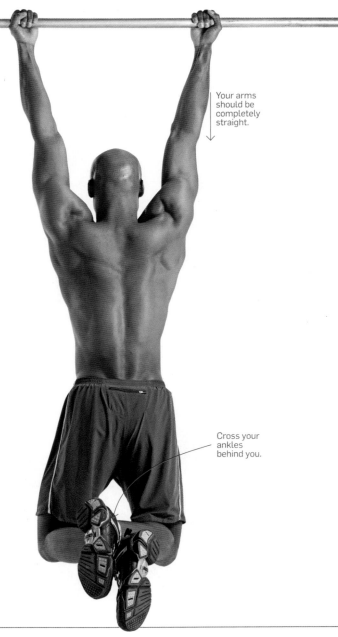

Your arms should be completely straight.

MAIN MOVE
Chinup

A

- Grab the chinup bar with a shoulder-width, underhand grip.

- Hang at arm's length. You should return to this position—known as a dead hang—each time you lower your body back down.

Cross your ankles behind you.

The Chinup vs the Pullup

In case you're wondering about the difference between a chinup and a pullup, it's simple: For a chinup, you use an underhand grip; for the pullup, you use an overhand grip. Of course, you'll quickly discover that the chinup is a little easier. (Or perhaps "less hard" would be more accurate.) This is because an underhand grip allows your biceps to be more involved with the exercise, providing more total muscle power to pull you up.

TRAINER'S TIP
Imagine that you're pulling the bar to your chest, instead of your chest to the bar.

Squeeze your shoulder blades together.

Pull your upper arms down forcefully.

B

- Pull your chest to the bar.
- Once the top of your chest touches the bar, pause, then slowly lower your body back to a dead hang.

LIFT YOURSELF HIGHER
Perhaps a better name for the chinup and pullup would be the chest-up. That's because to attain the most benefit from this exercise, you should actually pull your chest to the bar. This increases the range of motion for the exercise, engaging more of the muscles that surround your shoulder blades.

97

Lats | CHINUPS & PULLUPS

VARIATION #1
Negative Chinup

A

- Set a bench under a chinup bar, step up on the bench, and grasp the bar using a shoulder-width, underhand grip.

- From the bench, jump up so that your chest is next to your hands, then cross your ankles behind you.

B

- Try to take 5 seconds to lower your body until your arms are straight. If that's too hard, lower yourself as slowly as you can.

- Jump up to the starting position and repeat.

> Lower your body at the same rate of speed from the top position of the negative chinup to the bottom. If you notice that you speed up at a specific point, make a mental note. Then, on your next set, pause for a second or two just above that point as you lower your body. This will help you improve your performance faster. A good way to gauge your progress: Once you can complete a 30-second negative chinup, you can probably perform one full standard chinup.

VARIATION #2
Band-Assisted Chinup

A

- Loop one end of a large rubber band around a chinup bar and then pull it through the other end of the band, cinching the band tightly to the bar.

- Grab the bar with a shoulder-width, underhand grip, place your knees in the loop of the band, and hang at arm's length.

B

- Perform a chinup by pulling your chest to the bar.

- Once the top of your chest touches the bar, pause, then slowly lower your body back to a dead hang.

> The band-assisted method will allow you to do full chinups, and it more accurately mimics the movement than does the assisted-chinup machine you find in commercial gyms. Try a SuperBand (available at www.ihpfit.com) or a Jump Stretch Mini Flex Band (which you can find at www.elitefts.com).

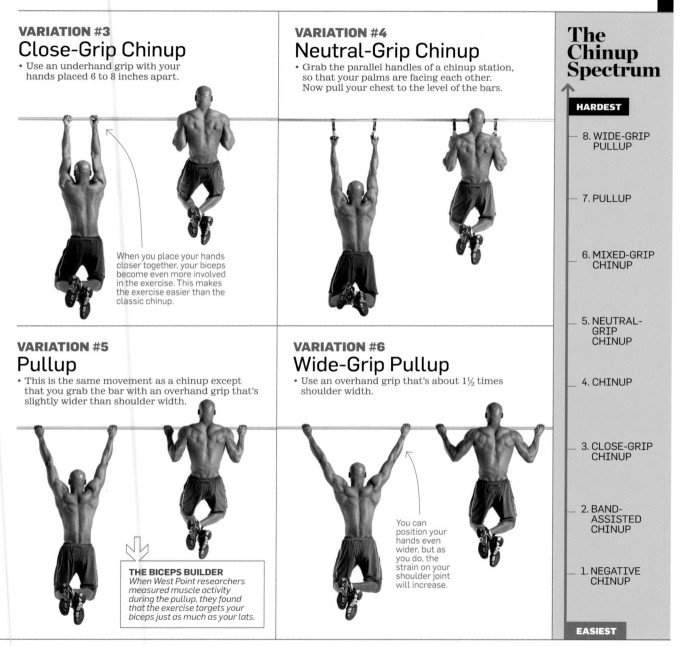

The Chinup Spectrum

HARDEST

- 8. WIDE-GRIP PULLUP
- 7. PULLUP
- 6. MIXED-GRIP CHINUP
- 5. NEUTRAL-GRIP CHINUP
- 4. CHINUP
- 3. CLOSE-GRIP CHINUP
- 2. BAND-ASSISTED CHINUP
- 1. NEGATIVE CHINUP

EASIEST

VARIATION #3
Close-Grip Chinup
- Use an underhand grip with your hands placed 6 to 8 inches apart.

When you place your hands closer together, your biceps become even more involved in the exercise. This makes the exercise easier than the classic chinup.

VARIATION #4
Neutral-Grip Chinup
- Grab the parallel handles of a chinup station, so that your palms are facing each other. Now pull your chest to the level of the bars.

VARIATION #5
Pullup
- This is the same movement as a chinup except that you grab the bar with an overhand grip that's slightly wider than shoulder width.

THE BICEPS BUILDER
When West Point researchers measured muscle activity during the pullup, they found that the exercise targets your biceps just as much as your lats.

VARIATION #6
Wide-Grip Pullup
- Use an overhand grip that's about 1½ times shoulder width.

You can position your hands even wider, but as you do, the strain on your shoulder joint will increase.

Lats | CHINUPS & PULLUPS

VARIATION #7
Mixed-Grip Chinup
- Placing your hands shoulder-width apart, use an underhand grip with one hand and an overhand grip with the other.

To prevent your torso from rotating as you perform the mixed-grip chinup, your back, shoulder, and core muscles have to work harder than in a conventional chinup or pullup.

VARIATION #8
Crossover Chinup
- Instead of pulling your chest straight to the bar, pull toward your right hand. Pause, then lower back to the start. On your next repetition, aim for your left hand. Alternate back and forth with each rep.

VARIATION #9
Suspended Chinup
- Attach a pair of straps with handles to a chinup bar, grasp the handles, and hang at arm's length. Then perform a chinup, allowing your arms to rotate naturally as you pull yourself up.

VARIATION #10
Towel Pullup
- Find your hand positions for a chinup, then drape a towel over each of those spots on the bar.
- Grab the ends of the towels so that your palms are facing each other, cross your ankles behind you, and hang at arm's length.
- Pull your chest as high as you can.
- Pause, then slowly lower your body back to a dead hang.

Grasping the towels engages more of your forearm muscles, improving grip strength and endurance.

Scapular Retraction

A

- Grab a chinup bar with an overhand grip and hang at arm's length.

B

- Without moving your arms, pull your shoulder blades down and together. Hold this position for 5 seconds, breathing steadily. That's one repetition.

TEST YOUR UPPER BACK
Try to hold the hanging scapular retraction for as long as you can. If you don't last at least 10 seconds, you have an upper back weakness, and this exercise should instantly become a part of your workout. This move also trains you to hold your shoulders down and back, which promotes good posture.

101

PULLDOWNS & PULLOVERS

These exercises target your lats. They also hit your teres major and biceps. What's more, your middle and upper back muscles are involved to varying degrees, assisting in the movement or acting as stabilizers in most versions of the exercises.

MAIN MOVE
Lat Pulldown

A

- Sit down in a lat pull-down station and grab the bar with an overhand grip that's just beyond shoulder width.

Your arms should be completely straight.

Your torso should be nearly upright.

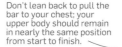

- Without moving your torso, pull the bar down to your chest as you continue to squeeze your shoulder blades.
- Pause, then slowly return to the starting position.

Initiate the movement by pulling your shoulders back and down.

Don't lean back to pull the bar to your chest; your upper body should remain in nearly the same position from start to finish.

THE CHINUP ALTERNATIVE
Walk into any gym and look around: Of all the exercises in this chapter, you'll find that the lat pulldown is probably the most popular. That's because it's the most logical substitute for a classic chinup (other than a negative chinup or a band-assisted chinup).

Lats | PULLDOWNS & PULLOVERS

Wide-Grip Lat Pulldown
• Use an overhand grip that's about 1½ times shoulder width.

Pull the bar to your upper chest.

Underhand-Grip Lat Pulldown
• Use a shoulder-width, underhand grip.

Keep your torso upright as you pull the bar down.

30-Degree Lat Pulldown

A

• Sit down in a lat pulldown machine and grab the bar with a shoulder-width, underhand grip.

• Lean back until your body forms a 30-degree angle with the floor.

• Hold this position for the entire exercise.

B

• Without moving your torso, pull the bar down to your chest.

• Pause, then slowly return to the starting position.

Leaning back increases the involvement of your middle and upper back muscles and decreases the demand on your lats.

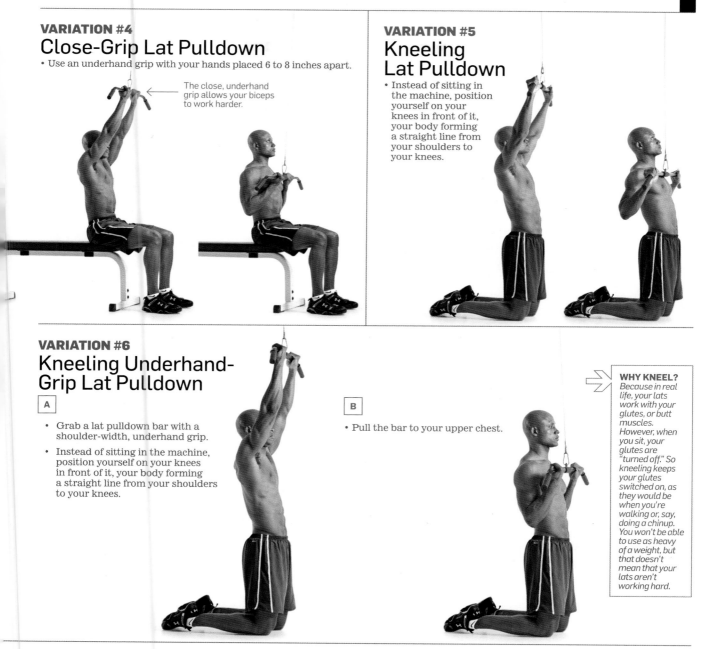

VARIATION #4
Close-Grip Lat Pulldown
• Use an underhand grip with your hands placed 6 to 8 inches apart.

The close, underhand grip allows your biceps to work harder.

VARIATION #5
Kneeling Lat Pulldown
• Instead of sitting in the machine, position yourself on your knees in front of it, your body forming a straight line from your shoulders to your knees.

VARIATION #6
Kneeling Underhand-Grip Lat Pulldown

A

• Grab a lat pulldown bar with a shoulder-width, underhand grip.

• Instead of sitting in the machine, position yourself on your knees in front of it, your body forming a straight line from your shoulders to your knees.

B

• Pull the bar to your upper chest.

WHY KNEEL?
Because in real life, your lats work with your glutes, or butt muscles. However, when you sit, your glutes are "turned off." So kneeling keeps your glutes switched on, as they would be when you're walking or, say, doing a chinup. You won't be able to use as heavy of a weight, but that doesn't mean that your lats aren't working hard.

Lats | PULLDOWNS & PULLOVERS

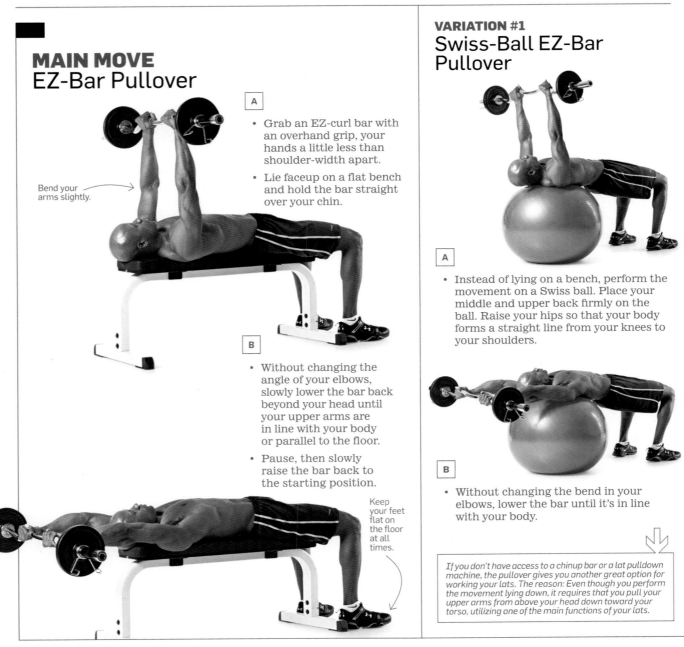

MAIN MOVE
EZ-Bar Pullover

A

- Grab an EZ-curl bar with an overhand grip, your hands a little less than shoulder-width apart.
- Lie faceup on a flat bench and hold the bar straight over your chin.

Bend your arms slightly.

B

- Without changing the angle of your elbows, slowly lower the bar back beyond your head until your upper arms are in line with your body or parallel to the floor.
- Pause, then slowly raise the bar back to the starting position.

Keep your feet flat on the floor at all times.

VARIATION #1
Swiss-Ball EZ-Bar Pullover

A

- Instead of lying on a bench, perform the movement on a Swiss ball. Place your middle and upper back firmly on the ball. Raise your hips so that your body forms a straight line from your knees to your shoulders.

B

- Without changing the bend in your elbows, lower the bar until it's in line with your body.

If you don't have access to a chinup bar or a lat pulldown machine, the pullover gives you another great option for working your lats. The reason: Even though you perform the movement lying down, it requires that you pull your upper arms from above your head down toward your torso, utilizing one of the main functions of your lats.

Standing Cable Pullover

A

- Stand in front of a lat pulldown machine and grab the bar with an overhand grip, your hands slightly beyond shoulder width apart.

Lean forward at your hips about 10 degrees.

B

- Keeping your back and arms straight, pull the bar down in an arcing motion until it touches your thighs.

- Pause, then slowly reverse the movement back to the starting position.

PULL FOR ABS!
The standing cable pullover works your abs harder than the classic crunch does, according to Finnish scientists.

107

Back

THE BEST BACK EXERCISE YOU'VE NEVER DONE
Cable Face Pull with External Rotation

This unique movement simultaneously targets your upper back's scapular muscles and the rotator cuff muscles of your shoulders. Collectively, these muscles, which tend to be a weak spot in most guys, are the key to stable, healthy shoulders. As a result, the face pull with external rotation will help you avoid injuries and improve your upper-body strength. In fact, according to a survey of top *Men's Health* fitness advisors, this exercise is one of the best you can do.

A

- Attach a rope to the high pulley of a cable station (or a lat pulldown) and grab an end with each hand.
- Back a few steps away from the weight stack until your arms are straight in front of you.

B

- Flare your elbows out, bend your arms, and pull the middle of the rope toward your eyes so your hands end up in line with your ears.
- Pause, then reverse back to the starting position.

Your palms face each other.

You should feel tension in the cable.

You should be positioned in the classic bodybuilder's "double-biceps pose."

BONUS EXERCISE!

Lying Cable Face Pull with External Rotation

- If you can't maintain an upright posture while performing the cable face pull, try it while lying faceup on a flat bench.

THE BEST STRETCH FOR YOUR BACK
Kneeling Swiss-Ball Lat Stretch

Why it's good: This stretch loosens your lats. When these muscles are tight, they rotate your upper arms inward, which contributes to poor posture.

Make the most of it: Hold this stretch for 30 seconds on each side, then repeat twice for a total of three sets. Perform this routine daily and up to three times a day if you're really tight.

A

- Kneel on the floor and place a Swiss ball about 2 feet in front of you. Place your hands on the ball, about 6 inches apart.

- Lean forward at your hips and press your shoulders toward the floor.

Don't round your lower back.

Your palms should face each other.

Back

THE ULTIMATE CHINUP WORKOUT

Whether you can't yet manage a single chinup or simply want to break out of your eight-rep rut, this training guide from Alwyn Cosgrove, CSCS, will provide the right plan for your body.

If you can't do more than one chinup . . .

EXERCISE 1: Band-Assisted Chinup
What to do: Do two sets of six repetitions, resting for 60 seconds between sets, before moving on to Exercise 2.

EXERCISE 2: Negative Chinup
What to do: Do two sets, resting for 60 seconds between them. Take as long as you can to lower your body—you should time yourself with a stopwatch—until your arms are straight. A key requirement: Try to lower yourself at the same rate from start to finish. When you're able to take 30 seconds to lower your body, or your combined lowering time for both sets is 45 seconds, add a third set. Complete all your sets, and then move on to Exercise 3.

EXERCISE 3: Explosive Kneeling Lat Pulldown
What to do:
• Choose the heaviest weight that allows you to complete four repetitions (but not five).
• Do 10 sets of two repetitions each, resting for 60 seconds between sets.
• Perform each repetition as quickly as possible.
• Each week, reduce each rest period by 15 seconds.
• In week 5, do one set of as many repetitions as you can.
• In week 6, start the process over again.

When you can do at least two chinups . . .

It's time to upgrade your routine. Your best option is a method called diminished-rest interval training. Instead of trying to do more repetitions, you'll focus on reducing your rest times between sets. Eventually, you'll eliminate the rest times altogether—and as a result, you'll be able to do more reps continuously.

What to do: Simply take the number of chinups you can complete with perfect form and divide that number in half. That's the number of repetitions you'll do in each set. So if you can do two chinups, you'll do one-rep sets. If you can do five chinups, you'll do three-rep sets. (Round up if the dividend isn't a whole number.) Once you've determined your repetition range, complete three sets with 60 seconds of rest after each. Do this workout twice a week, spacing the sessions at least 3 days apart. Each week, reduce each rest period by 15 seconds. Once each rest period is zero, do an additional set at each workout.

Once you can do 10 chinups . . .

You'll probably be tempted to stick with the status quo—three sets of 10 repetitions each workout, say. However, you won't improve very quickly that way. Instead, build pure strength by adding additional weight and doing fewer repetitions. You'll automatically increase the number of reps you can complete with just your body weight.

What to do: To perform this workout, you'll need a TKO dip belt (available at www.elitefts.com). This is a strap that goes around your waist and that allows you to attach a weight plate to it. Now do the workout below. For each set, use the heaviest weight that allows you to complete the prescribed number of repetitions. So as the number of reps you perform decreases, the amount of weight you use increases. Do each workout three times a week; rest for 60 seconds between sets.

	SET 1	SET 2	SET 3	SET 4	SET 5	SET 6
WEEK 1	8	6	4	8	6	4
WEEK 2	7	5	3	7	5	3
WEEK 3	6	4	2	6	4	2
WEEK 4	5	3	1	5	3	1

Once you reach week 5, start the process over, using the same number of sets and reps that you did in week 1 but adjusting the weight so that it corresponds to your current strength level. You should expect to use more weight for each set in weeks 5 through 8 than you did in the corresponding sets of weeks 1 through 4.

BUILD THE PERFECT BACK

Carve your torso into a perfect V with this 15-minute routine, courtesy of Craig Ballantyne, MS, CSCS, *Men's Health* fitness advisor and owner of TurbulenceTraining.com. It fully trains your lats but really zeroes in on the muscles of your middle and upper back. These are the common weak spots that lead to poor posture. Strengthening these muscles not only helps you stand tall but also improves the stability of your shoulders. The end result: You'll be able to lift more in nearly every upper-body exercise.

What to do: Choose one movement from each exercise group (A, B, C, and D). Then do one set of each exercise in succession, resting for 60 seconds between sets. So you'll do one set of Exercise A, rest for 60 seconds, do one set of Exercise B, rest for another 60 seconds, and so on. Once you've completed one set of all four exercises, rest for 2 minutes and repeat the entire circuit two more times. Perform this workout once or twice a week.

EXERCISE GROUP A
For any of the exercises except the negative chinup, do as many reps as you can up until the point at which you really start to struggle. On each rep, take 3 seconds to lower your body back to the starting position. For the negative chinup, do five reps in which you take 5 seconds to lower your body each time.

Negative chinup
  (page 98)

Band-assisted chinup
  (page 98)

Chinup (page 96)

Neutral-grip chinup
  (page 99)

Mixed-grip chinup
  (page 100)

Pullup (page 99)

EXERCISE GROUP B
Do as many repetitions as you can up until the point at which you really start to struggle. (This is usually about two repetitions short of failure.) On each repetition, take 2 seconds to lower your body back to the starting position.

Inverted row
  (page 72)

Modified inverted row
  (page 74)

Underhand-grip
  inverted row
  (page 74)

Elevated-feet inverted
  row (page 74)

Inverted row with feet
  on Swiss ball
  (page 74)

Towel-grip inverted
  row (page 75)

EXERCISE GROUP C
Do 12 repetitions of this exercise. On each repetition, take 2 seconds to lower the weights back to the starting repetition.

Rear lateral raise
  (page 83)

Overhand-grip rear
  lateral raise
  (page 84)

Underhand-grip rear
  lateral raise
  (page 84)

Crossover rear lateral
  raise (page 85)

EXERCISE GROUP D
Do 10 repetitions of this exercise. On each repetition, take 2 seconds to lower the weights back to the starting repetition.

Swiss-ball Y raise
  (page 86)

Incline Y raise
  (page 86)

Swiss-ball T raise
  (page 88)

Incline T raise
  (page 88)

Chapter 6: Shoulders
THE BOLDER, THE BETTER

Shoulders

A great set of shoulders can work magic: They make your waist look slimmer, your arms look bigger, and your back look broader. And even better, they're among the easiest muscles for you to define, since the shoulder region is one of the last places your body deposits fat.

Plus, without strong shoulders, you're not likely to reach your full potential for size and strength in any of your other upper-body muscles. That's because your shoulders assist in most exercises for your chest, back, triceps, and biceps. So you might say they're your muscle-building MVP.

Bonus Benefits

An injury-proof upper body! Shoring up weaknesses in the muscles that surround your shoulder joint reduces your risk of a painful dislocation or rotator cuff tear.

Extra power! Whenever you throw or swing, your arms rotate from the shoulder joints. Strong shoulder muscles make it easier to move your arms with more power.

You'll stand taller! Weakness in the rotator cuff, the network of muscles on the back side of the shoulder joint, allows muscles on the front side of the joint to pull your shoulders forward, causing a slumped posture. But you can shift this balance of power by building a strong rotator cuff—so that you once again stand tall and proud.

Meet Your Muscles

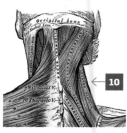

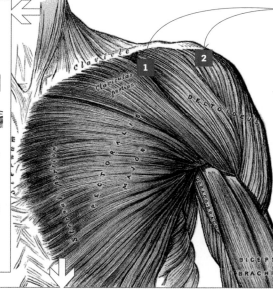

Deltoid
The roundish-looking muscle that caps the top of your upper arm is called your deltoid, and it's the shoulder muscle you're showing off when you wear a sleeveless shirt. It's made up of three distinct sections: your front deltoid [1], middle deltoid [2], and rear deltoid [3]. The best exercises for your front and middle delts are shoulder presses and shoulder raises. However, the top moves for working your rear deltoid are actually found in Chapter 5. That's because the same exercises that train the muscles of your middle and upper back are also the ones that work your rear delts.

Levator Scapula
Most guys would consider the levator scapula [10] to be a neck muscle. And indeed, this ropelike muscle runs down the back of your neck and attaches to the inside edge of your shoulder blade. However, it works with your upper trapezius to help shrug your shoulder, which is why you can strengthen it with the barbell and dumbbell shrugs.

Serratus Anterior
Your serratus anterior [9] starts next to the outer edge of your pectorals, on the surface of your upper eight ribs. It wraps around your rib cage until it connects to the undersurface of your shoulder blade, along the inner edge. This muscle's job is to help stabilize and rotate your shoulder blade. You can make it stronger with the serratus shrug and the serratus chair shrug.

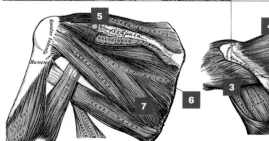

Rotator Cuff
Your rotator cuff muscles are a network of four muscles that attach your shoulder blade to your shoulder joint. They are the supraspinatus [5], the infraspinatus [6], the teres minor [7], and the subscapularis [8]. While these muscles are activated in just about every upper-body exercise—they contract to help stabilize your shoulder joint—they also need to be worked directly with shoulder rotation exercises.

Upper Trapezius
Although the trapezius as a whole is categorized as a back muscle, the upper portions of your traps [4] are best developed with exercises such as the lateral raise and the shoulder shrug, both of which are featured in this chapter.

MUSCLE MISTAKE

Your Shoulders Hurt, but You Lift Anyway

Think of it this way: When your car gets a flat tire, you don't risk driving on it, since that could permanently damage the rims. It's the same way with your shoulders. But just avoiding the offending exercise isn't good enough. After all, a flat tire doesn't fix itself if you simply park the car in your garage. You need to take action. If you notice recurring shoulder pain, see an orthopedist or a physical therapist.

Shoulders | PRESSES

In this chapter, you'll find 40 exercises that target the muscles of your shoulders. Throughout, you'll notice that certain exercises have been given the designation Main Move. Master this basic version of a movement, and you'll be able to do all of its variations with flawless form.

SHOULDER PRESSES

These exercises target your front deltoids, middle deltoids, and triceps. They also activate your upper traps, rotator cuff, and serratus anterior, which assist in the movement or act as stabilizers.

MAIN MOVE
Barbell Shoulder Press

A

- Grab a barbell with an overhand grip that's just beyond shoulder width, and hold it at shoulder level in front of your body.

- Stand with your feet shoulder-width apart.

Brace your core.

Your hands should be positioned just beyond shoulder-width apart.

Your knees should be slightly bent.

Set your feet shoulder-width apart.

The bar should be directly above your shoulders.

Your arms should be completely straight.

All of the movement should come from your arms and shoulders.

B

- Push the barbell straight overhead, leaning your head back slightly but keeping your torso upright.
- Pause, then slowly lower your body back to the starting position.

12

**Total number of sets
in a weight workout that made
previously tired people
feel energized, according to
University of Georgia researchers.**

What about the Back Rest?

People often do the shoulder press seated, with their backs braced against a back rest. This provides a stable surface from which to lift, allowing the use of heavier weights. However, greater loads also mean increased stress on the shoulder joint in the "at-risk position"—the point at which your elbows are bent 90 degrees with your palms facing forward. This is the portion of the lift in which you're most likely to suffer a shoulder injury. Avoid that fate by skipping the back rest.

Shoulders | PRESSES

VARIATION #1
Barbell Push Press

A
- Grab a barbell with an overhand grip that's just beyond shoulder-width, and hold it at shoulder level in front of your body.

B
- Dip your knees.

C
- Explosively push up with your legs as you press the barbell over your head.

Keep your core tight.

Push your hips forward.

Lock your elbows.

Straighten your knees.

MORE WEIGHT, LESS RISK
If you want to press heavier weights, try the push press. It doesn't carry the same injury risk as doing a shoulder press against a back rest (see "What about the Back Rest?" on the previous page). That's because your legs help you push through the at-risk position, reducing the strain on your shoulders.

VARIATION #2
Barbell Split Jerk

Hold the bar at shoulder level.

Straighten your arms completely.

Your front knee should be slightly bent.

A

- Grab a barbell with an overhand grip that's just beyond shoulder-width, and hold it at shoulder level in front of your body.

Your feet should be shoulder-width apart.

B

- Dip your knees.

C

- Explosively push up with your legs as you press the barbell over your head.
- As you press the barbell, split your legs apart so that you land in a staggered stance, one foot in front of the other.

VARIATION #3
Seated Barbell Shoulder Press

The barbell should be directly over your shoulders.

A

- Sit at the end of a bench with your torso upright.

Brace your abs.

Your feet should be flat on the floor.

B

- Press the barbell over your head.

Don't bend forward. Your torso should be completely upright.

Keep your lower back naturally arched as you perform the movement.

Shoulders | PRESSES

MAIN MOVE
Dumbbell Shoulder Press

Push the dumbbells directly above your shoulders.

Lock your elbows.

Keep your core braced.

A

- Stand holding a pair of dumbbells just outside your shoulders, with your arms bent and palms facing each other.
- Set your feet shoulder-width apart, and slightly bend your knees.

B

- Press the weights upward until your arms are completely straight.
- Slowly lower the dumbbells back to the starting position.

Your knees should be slightly bent.

TRAINER'S TIP
Make sure to push the dumbbells in a straight line, rather than pushing them up and toward each other as many people do—a habit that increases the risk for shoulder injuries.

VARIATION #1
Dumbbell Push Press

Stand tall
and straight.

A

- Hold the dumbbells next to your shoulders with your elbows bent.

B

- Dip your knees.

Bend your knees so that you can generate more power to press the dumbbell.

C

- Explosively push up with your legs as you press the dumbbells over your head.

VARIATION #2
Alternating Dumbbell Shoulder Press

A

- Hold the dumbbells next to your shoulders with your elbows bent.

Your palms should be facing each other.

Hold your core tight as you perform the exercise.

B

- Instead of pressing both dumbbells up at once, lift them one at a time, in an alternating fashion.

As you lower one dumbbell, press the other one up.

121

Shoulders | PRESSES

VARIATION #3
Seated Dumbbell Shoulder Press
• Sit at the end of a bench with your torso upright.

Your lower back should be naturally arched.

Press the dumbbells directly above your shoulders.

VARIATION #4
Swiss-Ball Dumbbell Shoulder Press
• Sit on a Swiss ball with your torso upright.

Your palms should be facing each other.

Brace your core.

Don't lean forward.

VARIATION #5
Alternating Swiss-Ball Dumbbell Shoulder Press
• Sit on a Swiss ball with your torso upright.

• Instead of pressing both dumbbells up at once, lift them one at a time, in an alternating fashion.

As you lower one dumbbell, press the other up.

VARIATION #6
Single-Arm Dumbbell Shoulder Press
• Perform a dumbbell shoulder press using only one dumbbell at a time.

• Complete the prescribed number of reps with your right arm, then immediately do the same number with your left arm.

Let your free hand hang to your side or place it on your hip.

Because using just one dumbbell causes uneven weight distribution across your body, this exercise increases the challenge to your core, making those muscles work harder to keep you balanced.

VARIATION #7
Dumbbell Alternating Shoulder Press and Twist

A

- Hold the dumbbells next to your shoulders with your elbows bent.

B

- Rotate your torso to the right as you press the dumbbell in your left hand at a slight angle above your shoulder.
- Reverse the movement back to the start, rotate to your left, and press the dumbbell in your right hand upward. Alternate back and forth.

Your palms should be facing each other.

Rotating your torso activates your obliques, core muscles that are often weak.

Press the dumbbell up diagonally.

Straighten your left arm completely.

Keep your abs braced as you rotate your torso. This will limit the amount your lower spine can twist, protecting you from injury.

Pivot your feet.

Floor Inverted Shoulder Press

- Assume a pushup position, but move your feet forward and raise your hips so that your torso is nearly perpendicular to the floor.
- Your hands should be slightly wider than your shoulders, and your arms should be straight.

- Without changing your body posture, lower your body until your head nearly touches the floor.
- Pause, then return to the starting position by pushing your body back up until your arms are straight.

Inverted Shoulder Press

- Assume a pushup position, but place your feet on a bench and push your hips up so that your torso is nearly perpendicular to the floor.

Your arms should be straight.

- Without changing your body posture, lower your body until your head nearly touches the floor.

Your hands should be slightly wider than shoulder width apart.

While the inverted shoulder press is technically a pushup, the tweak to your form shifts more of the workload to your shoulders and triceps, reducing the demand on your chest.

Shoulders | RAISES

SHOULDER RAISES

These exercises target your front and middle deltoids. However, the different variations shift the section of the muscle that works the hardest. What's more, shoulder raises work your rear deltoids, upper traps, rotator cuff, and serratus anterior, since these muscles assist in raising the weight or act as stabilizers on nearly every version of this exercise.

MAIN MOVE
Front Raise

A

- Grab a pair of dumbbells and let them hang at arm's length next to your sides, with your palms facing each other.

B

- Raise your arms straight in front of you until they're parallel to the floor and perpendicular to your torso.
- Pause, then slowly lower the dumbbells back to the starting position.

The hardest-working muscle during the front raise: your front deltoids.

The thumb sides of your hands should be facing up.

Bend your elbows slightly and hold them that way.

Lift the dumbbells to shoulder level.

Set your feet shoulder-width apart.

VARIATION #1
Weight-Plate Front Raise

A

- Instead of holding two dumbbells, grab the sides of a weight plate with both hands.

B

- Raise the weight to shoulder level.

17

Percent more reps per three sets people could do when they were well-hydrated, according to University of Connecticut researchers. Remember, your muscles are about 80 percent water.

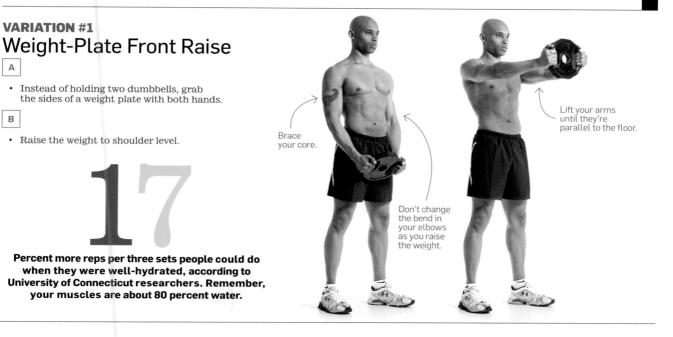

Brace your core.

Lift your arms until they're parallel to the floor.

Don't change the bend in your elbows as you raise the weight.

VARIATION #2
Cable Front Raise

A

- Attach a rope handle to the low pulley of a cable station, and stand facing away from the weight stack.
- Hold the handle with your right hand, your arm hanging next to your side and your palm facing your thigh.

B

- Without changing the bend in your elbow, raise your arm straight out in front of you until it's parallel to the floor.
- Pause, then slowly lower back to the starting position.
- Complete the prescribed number of repetitions with your right arm, then immediately switch hands and do the same number with your left arm.

The rope should be taut.

The thumb side of your hand should be facing up.

Let your free hand hang to your side or place it on your hip.

Shoulders | RAISES

MAIN MOVE
Lateral Raise

A

- Grab a pair of dumbbells and let them hang at arm's length next to your sides.
- Stand tall, with your feet shoulder-width apart.
- Turn your arms so that your palms are facing forward, and bend your elbows slightly.

B

- Without changing the bend in your elbows, raise your arms straight out to your sides until they're at shoulder level.
- Pause for 1 second at the top of the movement, then slowly lower the weights back to the starting position.

The hardest-working muscle during the lateral raise: your middle deltoid.

Stand as tall as you can.

Set your feet shoulder-width apart.

Your arms should be straight out to your sides, so that they form a T with your body.

Keep your core braced.

WHAT NOT TO DO!
Don't rotate your upper arms inward in the up position of the lift. (Picture the movement you make when pouring a pitcher of beer.) It can lead to shoulder impingement.

VARIATION #1
Alternating Lateral Raise with Static Hold

A

- Stand holding a pair of dumbbells straight out from your sides, as you would in the "up" position of a lateral raise.

B

- Lower and raise one arm, then lower and raise the other. That's one repetition.

Your arms should be at shoulder level.

Hold your left arm in the up position as you lower your right arm.

Your palm should be facing forward.

VARIATION #2
Leaning Lateral Raise

A

- Hold a dumbbell in your left hand, at arm's length next to your side.
- Stand with your right leg next to a sturdy object such as a power rack.
- Place your left foot next to your right.
- Grab the power rack with your right hand, and allow your right arm to straighten so that you're leaning to your left.

B

- Without changing the bend in your elbow, raise your left arm straight out to your side until it's at shoulder level.
- Lower and repeat.
- Complete the prescribed number of repetitions with your left arm, then immediately do the same number with your right arm.

Your body, arms, and legs will form a triangle with the rack.

The thumb side of your hand should face up.

Your palm should face forward.

Shoulders | RAISES

VARIATION #3
Bent-Arm Lateral Raise and External Rotation

A

- Grab a pair of dumbbells and hold them at arm's length with your palms turned toward each other.
- Bend your elbows 90 degrees.
- Without changing the bend in your elbows, raise your upper arms out to the sides until they're parallel to the floor.

B

- Rotate your upper arms up and back so that your forearms are pointing toward the ceiling.
- Pause, then reverse the movement and return to the starting position.

Rotate your forearms back as far as you can.

Keep your elbows bent 90 degrees.

Don't drop your upper arms.

Your feet should be shoulder-width apart.

VARIATION #4
Side-Lying Lateral Raise

A

- Grab a dumbbell in your right hand and lie on your left side on an incline bench that's set to 15 degrees.
- Hold the dumbbell next to your right side with your palm facing your thigh.

Your right elbow should be slightly bent.

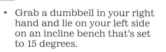

B

- Without changing the bend in your elbow, raise your arm until it's in line with your shoulder as you rotate your palm outward.
- Lower the weight and repeat.

Your palm should be facing forward.

Your arm should be perpendicular to your body.

Combo Shoulder Raise

Since the combo shoulder raise is a combination of the front raise and the lateral raise, it targets both your front and middle deltoids.

A

- Grab a pair of dumbbells and hold them at arm's length next to your thighs.
- Turn your left palm so that it's facing the side of your thigh, and your right palm so that it's facing forward.

Your right palm should be facing forward.

Your left palm should be facing your thigh.

B

- Simultaneously raise your right arm straight out to your side, as you would for a lateral raise, and lift your left arm straight out in front of you, as you would for a front raise.
- When both arms are at shoulder level, pause, and lower back to the starting position.
- On your next rep, rotate your arms so that you do a lateral raise with your left and a front raise with your right.

The thumb side of both hands should be facing up.

Scaption

A

- Standing with your feet shoulder-width apart, hold a pair of dumbbells at arm's length next to your sides.
- Your palms should be facing each other and your elbows slightly bent.

Stand as tall as you can.

B

- Without changing the bend in your elbows, raise your arms at a 30-degree angle to your body (so that they form a Y) until they're at shoulder level.
- Pause, then slowly lower the weights back to the starting position.

Your arms should form a horizontal Y shape.

The thumb sides of both hands should be facing up.

Shoulders | SHRUGS

SHOULDER SHRUGS

Most of these exercises target your upper traps and levator scapulae. You work these muscles anytime you shrug your shoulders toward your ears. However, the last two exercises in this section target your serratus anterior. In these movements, you perform a "reverse shrug," pushing your shoulders down as you raise the rest of your body upward.

MAIN MOVE
Barbell Shrug

A

- Grab a barbell with an overhand grip that's just beyond shoulder-width apart, and let the bar hang at arm's length in front of your waist.

- Keeping your back naturally arched, lean forward at your hips.

Lean forward about 10 degrees.

Bend your knees slightly.

Set your feet shoulder-width apart.

B

- Shrug your shoulders as high as you can.
- Pause, then reverse the movement back to the starting position.

Raise the tops of your shoulders toward your ears.

Your arms should be straight.

MUSCLE MISTAKE
You're Still Doing Upright Rows

Turns out, about two-thirds of men are at high risk for shoulder impingement when performing this popular upper-trap exercise. This is a painful condition in which the muscles or tendons of your rotator cuff become entrapped in your shoulder joint. Impingement most often occurs when your upper arms are simultaneously at shoulder level or higher and rotated inward—the exact position they're in at the top of the upright row.

2

Times more likely people are to stick to an exercise program when they perform shorter workouts—30 minutes or less—compared to longer sessions, according to a YMCA study.

Shoulders | SHRUGS

VARIATION #1
Wide-Grip Barbell Shrug

A

- Hold the barbell with an overhand grip that's about twice shoulder width.

Lean forward at your hips about 10 degrees.

B

- Shrug your shoulders as high as you can.

Using a wider grip increases the demand on your middle traps and rhomboids.

Keep your arms straight as you shrug.

VARIATION #2
Overhead Barbell Shrug

A

- Hold a barbell above your head with an underhand grip that's about twice shoulder width.
- Your arms should be completely straight.

Lock your elbows and keep them that way.

Your feet should be shoulder-width apart.

B

- Shrug your shoulders as high as you can.
- Pause, then reverse the movement back to the starting position.

SHRUG FOR BALANCE
Holding the weight above your head as you shrug works your upper traps while reducing the emphasis on your levator scapulae. (The levator scapulae are frequently overused compared to the upper traps.) For many guys, this can lead to better posture, since these muscles are often imbalanced.

Try to raise the tops of your shoulders as close to your ears as you can. The movement is slight; you'll feel it, but it's hard to see.

MAIN MOVE
Dumbbell Shrug

A

- Grab a pair of dumbbells and let them hang at arm's length next to your sides, your palms facing each other.

B

- Shrug your shoulders as high as you can.
- Pause in the up position, then slowly lower the dumbbells back to the start.

VARIATION
Overhead Dumbbell Shrug

A

- Hold a pair of dumbbells straight above your shoulders, with your arms completely straight and your palms facing out.

B

- Shrug your shoulders as high as you can.
- Pause, then reverse the movement back to the starting position.

To shrug, imagine that you're trying to touch your shoulders to your ears without moving any other parts of your body.

THE DUMBBELL ADVANTAGE? *Compared to the barbell shrug, the dumbbell shrug places less stress on your shoulder joints. That's because your shoulders don't have to rotate to hold the bar. This keeps them more stable as you perform the movement.*

Keep your arms straight.

Shoulders | SHRUGS

MAIN MOVE
Serratus Shrug

A

- Grab the bars of a dip station and lift yourself so your arms are fully extended.

- Bend your knees and cross your ankles behind you.

A MUSCLE YOU SHOULDN'T NEGLECT
As its name suggests, the serratus shrug targets your serratus anterior. Weakness in this muscle promotes poor posture and can also lead to shoulder impinge-ment during shoulder presses. Use this "shrug" to make your serratus strong.

Lock your elbows.

Let your torso sink between your shoulders.

Bend your knees.

Cross your ankles behind you.

B

- Without changing your arm position, press your shoulders down as you lift your upper body.

- Pause for 5 seconds, then return to the starting position and repeat. That's one rep. As you progress, try to hold each repetition for a longer period of time.

Imagine that you're "shrugging" your shoulders down instead of up.

Keep your torso upright.

VARIATION
Serratus Chair Shrug

A

- Sit upright on a chair or bench and place your hands flat on the sitting surface next to your hips.
- Completely straighten your arms.

B

- Press your shoulders down as you lift your upper body.
- Pause for 5 seconds, then lower your body back to the starting position. That's one rep.

WORK YOUR SERRATUS ANYWHERE! *You can do this version of the exercise at your desk or even on your couch while watching TV.*

Allow your shoulder and back muscles to relax, so your torso lowers between your shoulders.

Keep your lower back naturally arched.

Your hips should be just off the edge of the bench.

Your torso should rise between your shoulders.

Keep your arms straight.

Your feet should be flat on the floor.

Shoulders | ROTATIONS

SHOULDER ROTATIONS
These exercises target your rotator cuff muscles, particularly your infraspinatus and teres minor.

MAIN MOVE
Seated Dumbbell External Rotation

A

- Grab a dumbbell in your left hand and sit on a bench.
- Place your left foot on the bench with your knee bent.
- Bend your left elbow 90 degrees and place the inside portion of it on your left knee.

Your elbow should be bent 90 degrees.

Keep your wrist straight.

Your foot should be flat.

Position your free hand on the bench for support.

Embrace External Rotation

External rotation is when you rotate your upper arms outward (or "externally"). For a visual, raise your arm as if you're about to give someone a high-five. Notice how your upper arm rotated outward? That's external rotation. And it's important because it targets the three rotator cuff muscles—your supraspinatus, infraspinatus, and teres minor—that attach to the outside of your upper arm. This helps create balance with your lats and pecs, which attach to the *inside* of your upper arm. If these muscles overpower your rotator cuff, they can permanently rotate your arms inward, causing caveman-like posture. External rotation is your exercise weapon against that.

B

- Without changing the bend in your elbow, rotate your upper arm and forearm up and back as far as you can.
- Pause, then return to the starting position.
- Complete the prescribed number of repetitions with your left arm, then immediately do the same number with your right arm.

Keep your torso upright.

Keep your elbow fixed so that your forearm rotates in an arc around it.

Shoulders | ROTATIONS

VARIATION
Lying External Rotation

A

- Grab a dumbbell in your right hand and lie on your left side on an incline bench.
- Place a folded-up towel on the right side of your torso and then position your right elbow on the towel, with your arm bent 90 degrees.
- Let your forearm hang down in front of your abs.

Set the bench to a 15-degree incline.

B

- Rotate your upper arm up and back as far as you can, without allowing your elbow to lose contact with the towel.
- Pause, then slowly lower the weight back to the starting position.
- Complete the prescribed number of repetitions with your right arm, then immediately lie on your right side and do the same number of reps with your left arm.

Your arm should be bent 90 degrees.

Keep your elbow fixed as you rotate your arm.

Dumbbell Diagonal Raise

A

- Grab a dumbbell in your right hand and hold it next to the outside of your left hip, your palm facing your hip.
- Your elbow should be slightly bent.

Your right palm should be in front of your pocket.

B

- Without changing the bend in your elbow, raise the dumbbell up and across your body until your hand is above your head and your palm is facing forward.
- Reverse the movement to return to the starting position.
- Complete the prescribed number of repetitions with your right arm, then immediately do the same number with your left arm.

Keep your elbow slightly bent.

Let your free arm hang at arm's length or place it on your hip.

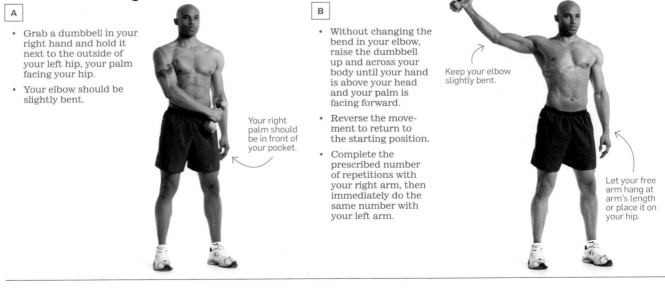

Cable Diagonal Raise

A

- Attach a stirrup handle to the low pulley of a cable station.
- Standing with your left side toward the weight stack, grab the handle with your right hand and position it in front of your left hip, with your elbow slightly bent.

B

- Without changing the bend in your elbow, pull the handle up and across your body until your hand is above your head.
- Lower the handle to the starting position.
- Complete the prescribed number of repetitions with your right arm, then immediately do the same number with your left arm.

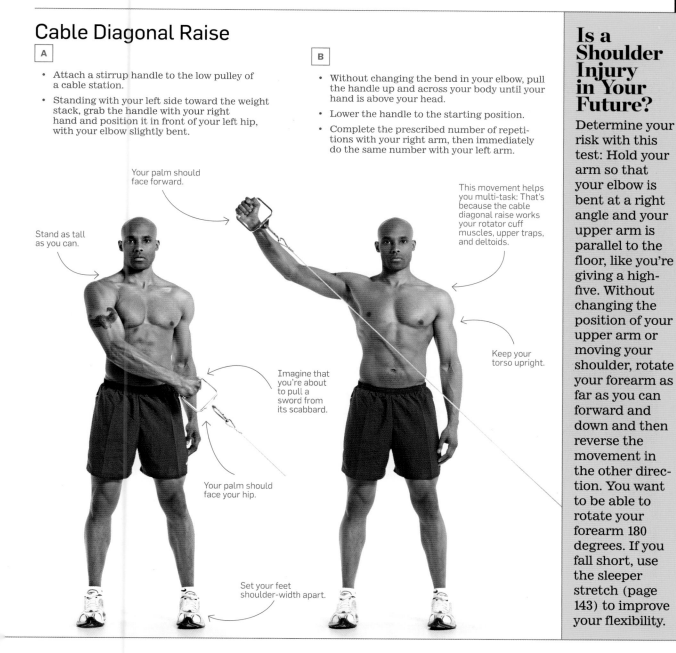

Your palm should face forward.

Stand as tall as you can.

This movement helps you multi-task: That's because the cable diagonal raise works your rotator cuff muscles, upper traps, and deltoids.

Imagine that you're about to pull a sword from its scabbard.

Keep your torso upright.

Your palm should face your hip.

Set your feet shoulder-width apart.

Is a Shoulder Injury in Your Future?

Determine your risk with this test: Hold your arm so that your elbow is bent at a right angle and your upper arm is parallel to the floor, like you're giving a high-five. Without changing the position of your upper arm or moving your shoulder, rotate your forearm as far as you can forward and down and then reverse the movement in the other direction. You want to be able to rotate your forearm 180 degrees. If you fall short, use the sleeper stretch (page 143) to improve your flexibility.

Shoulders | ROTATIONS

MAIN MOVE
Cable External Rotation

Your forearm should be touching your abs.

Your palm should be facing forward.

Keep your elbow in place.

A

- Attach a stirrup handle to the low pulley of a cable station, grab it with your right hand, and stand with your left side next to the weight stack.

- Bend your right elbow 90 degrees, and position your upper arm so that it's next to your side and perpendicular to the floor.

Set your feet shoulder-width apart.

B

- Rotate your forearm outward, as if it were a gate swinging open, with your upper arm acting as a hinge.

- Pause, then slowly return to the starting position.

- Complete the prescribed number of repetitions with your right arm, then immediately do the same number with your left arm.

VARIATION #1
45-Degree Cable External Rotation

A

- Stand at an angle to the weight stack.
- Hold your upper arm at a 45-degree angle to your body.

B

- Without changing the position of your upper arm, rotate your forearm up and back as far as you can.

Your upper arm should be at an angle between parallel to the floor and the side of your torso.

Don't raise or lower your elbow as you rotate your arm.

VARIATION #2
90-Degree Cable External Rotation

A

- Stand facing the weight stack.
- Hold your upper arm at a 90-degree angle to your body.

B

- Without changing the position of your upper arm, rotate your forearm up and back as far as you can.

Pull your shoulders down and hold them that way.

Keep your wrist straight.

Stand tall and straight.

Your palm should be facing behind you.

Your elbow should be bent 90 degrees.

Shoulders

THE BEST SHOULDER EXERCISE YOU'VE NEVER DONE
Scaption and Shrug

This movement is the exercise that keeps on giving. That's because when you raise the dumbbells to perform scaption, you target your front deltoids, rotator cuff, and serratus anterior. Then comes the shrug. Like an overhead shrug, this version of the movement emphasizes your upper traps over your levator scapulae. This helps better balance the muscles that rotate your shoulder blades. The end result: Healthier shoulders and better posture.

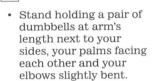

A

- Stand holding a pair of dumbbells at arm's length next to your sides, your palms facing each other and your elbows slightly bent.

B

- Without changing the bend in your elbows, raise your arms at a 30-degree angle to your body (so that they form a "Y") until they're at shoulder level.

C

- At the top of the movement, shrug your shoulders upward.
- Pause, then slowly lower the weight back to the starting position.

Stand as tall as you can.

Your arms should be parallel to the floor.

Raise the tops of your shoulders toward your ears.

Set your feet shoulder-width apart.

THE BEST STRETCH FOR YOUR SHOULDERS
Sleeper Stretch

Why it's good: It loosens your rotator cuff muscles. A stiff rotator cuff can lead to shoulder strain.

Make the most of it: Hold the stretch for 30 seconds, and repeat three times. Perform this routine two or three times a day to improve flexibility, or three times a week to maintain flexibility.

A

- Lie on the floor on your left side with your left upper arm on the floor and your elbow bent 90 degrees.

- Adjust your torso so that your right shoulder is slightly behind your left, not directly over it.

- Your fingers on your left hand should point toward the ceiling.

B

- Gently push your left hand toward the floor until you feel a comfortable stretch in the back of your left shoulder.

- Hold for the prescribed amount of time, then roll over and repeat the stretch for your right shoulder.

Your right shoulder should be slightly behind your left shoulder, not directly over it.

Your elbow should be placed just below the level of your shoulder.

You should feel this stretch here.

Shoulders

BUILD PERFECT SHOULDERS

This 4-week upper-body workout from Nick Tumminello, owner of Performance University in Baltimore, prioritizes your shoulders— to improve your posture and leave you looking great in a tank top.

What to do: Do this workout twice a week, resting your upper body for 3 or 4 days between sessions. Perform each pair (1A, 1B) or trio of exercises (2A, 2B, 2C) as a mini-circuit. That is, do one set of each exercise without resting. Then catch your breath, and repeat the circuit until you've finished all of the prescribed sets. Once you've done two or three sets (your choice), move on to the next group.

For a training plan that works your entire body, combine this "Build Perfect Shoulders" upper-body routine with the "Build the Perfect Backside" lower-body workout on page 272. Simply do the two routines on consecutive days.

EXERCISE	SETS	REPS
1A. Chinup (page 96)	2–3	AMAP*
1B. Inverted shoulder press (page 123)	2–3	AMAP*
2A. Barbell or dumbbell bench press (page 46 or 52)	2–3	8
2B. Seated dumbbell external rotation (page 136)	2–3	8
2C. Underhand-grip inverted row (page 74)	2–3	AMAP*
3A. Barbell push press (page 118)	2–3	6–8
3B. Overhead barbell shrug (page 132)	2–3	8–12
3C. Serratus shrug (page 134)	2–3	8–12
4A. Pushup plus (page 64)	2–3	15–25
4B. Hammer curl (page 161)	2–3	8–12

*As many as possible

Chapter 7: Arms
THE MUSCLES THAT GET YOU NOTICED

Arms

Your arms are like built-in publicists for all the hard work you do in the gym. That's because they're the only major muscles you can expose almost anywhere, anytime. If your biceps and triceps are well-defined, people will assume the rest of you is chiseled as well.

The best part is that a sculpted set of arms isn't as hard to achieve as you might think. The reason: Just about every upper-body exercise—whether it's for your chest, back, or shoulders—also involves your arms. After all, these exercises require that you use your arms to help move the weights. So work hard on your other upper-body muscles, and your arms will benefit by default. Then you can simply use the specific biceps, triceps, and forearm exercises in this chapter to give them a little extra love.

Bonus Benefits

Life is easier! Stronger biceps allow you to carry just about any object with less effort. So whether you're toting groceries or holding a baby, you'll notice the difference.

Damage control! Your triceps protect your elbow joints by acting as shock absorbers, lessening stress whenever your elbows are forced to flex suddenly, such as in breaking your fall in football or bracing yourself when mountain biking.

More muscle, everywhere! Your arms assist in exercises for all the muscles of your upper body. So if the smaller muscles of your arms give out too early, you'll be shortchanging the bigger muscles of your chest, back, and shoulders. Make sure your arms are strong, and you'll benefit all over.

Meet Your Muscles

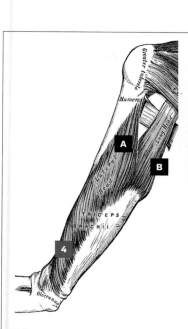

Biceps
The front of your upper arm owes its bulge to two muscle groups: your biceps brachii and your brachialis.

Your biceps brachii [1] originates at your shoulder and attaches to your forearm. Its duties are to bend your elbow and to rotate your forearm—a movement known as supination. Any type of arm curl works this muscle, as do chinups and rows.

Your brachialis [2] starts in the middle of your upper-arm bone and also attaches to your forearm. It assists your biceps brachii in bending your elbow.

The brachioradialis [3] originates on your upper-arm bone, near your elbow, and attaches close to your wrist. So it helps your biceps brachii bend your elbow and rotate your forearm, but it contributes little to the size of your biceps.

The biceps brachii is composed of two separate sections, or heads, that unite just before they attach to a forearm bone called the radius. The brachialis attaches to your ulna, the longer of the two forearm bones.

Triceps
The muscle on the back of your upper arm is called the triceps brachii [4]. When well-defined, it forms a horseshoe-like shape. Considering its name—triceps—it should be no surprise that the muscle is composed of three different sections, or heads. All three heads start on the back of either your upper arm or your shoulder blade, and then unite so that they attach together on your forearm. As a result, the primary job of your triceps is to straighten your arm. So this muscle is engaged in any exercise in which you straighten your arm against resistance: triceps extensions, triceps pressdowns and, of course, chest and shoulder presses.

The outer segment of your triceps is called the lateral head [A].

The middle segment of your triceps is called the medial head (not shown; hidden by the lateral head).

The inner segment of your triceps is called the long head [B].

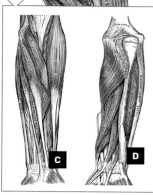

Forearms
Your wrist and finger flexors [C] are located on the inside of your forearm. They allow you to bend your wrist forward, and they can be trained with exercises such as wrist curls.

Your wrist extensors [D] are located on the outside, or "top," of your forearm. They allow you to bend your wrist backward, and they can be trained with exercises such as wrist extensions.

Biceps | ARM CURLS

In this chapter, you'll find 74 exercises that target the muscles of your arms. These exercises are divided among three major sections: Biceps, Triceps, and Forearms. Within each section, you'll notice that certain exercises have been given the designation Main Move. Master this basic version of a movement, and you'll be able to do all of its variations with flawless form.

ARM CURLS

These exercises target your biceps brachii, brachialis, and brachioradialis. Your upper-back and rear-shoulder muscles also come into play, since they keep your shoulders stable as you curl a weight in front of your body.

MAIN MOVE
EZ-Bar Curl

A

- Grab an EZ-curl bar with an underhand, shoulder-width grip.
- Your palms should angle inward.
- Let the bar hang at arm's length in front of your waist.

Imagine that you're trying to create as much space between your ears and shoulders as you can.

Pull your shoulders down and back and hold them that way.

Set your feet shoulder-width apart.

2.5

Times more strength lifters gained when lowering a weight slowly and lifting it fast compared to performing each rep at a slow speed from start to finish, according to a George Washington University study.

Keep your chest up.

Stand as tall as you can for the entire exercise.

B

- Without moving your upper arms, bend your elbows and curl the bar as close to your shoulders as you can.

- Pause, then slowly lower the weight back to the starting position.

- Each time you return to the starting position, completely straighten your arms.

HOW DO YOU MEASURE UP?

Finding the circumferences of your arms is an excellent way to gauge the effectiveness of your arm workout. For the most accurate results, take all your measurements at the same time of day, such as before breakfast. (Your arms may be slightly larger after a workout or meal, when blood rushes to your muscles.) Extend your arm straight in front of you and wrap a measuring tape around the largest portion of your upper arm. Record the circumference, then measure your other arm.

Biceps | ARM CURLS

VARIATION #1
Close-Grip EZ-Bar Curl

- Hold the bar with a narrow under-hand grip, your hands about 6 inches apart.

Set your feet shoulder-width apart.

VARIATION #2
Wide-Grip EZ-Bar Curl

- Hold the bar with an under-hand grip that's about 1½ times shoulder width.

Stand as tall as you can.

VARIATION #3
Swiss-Ball Preacher Curl

A

- Kneel over a Swiss ball and rest your upper arms on it.
- Hold the bar with a narrow underhand grip, your elbows bent about 5 degrees.

Your elbows should be slightly bent.

B

- Without moving your upper arms off the ball, curl the weight toward your shoulders.

Your lower back should be naturally arched.

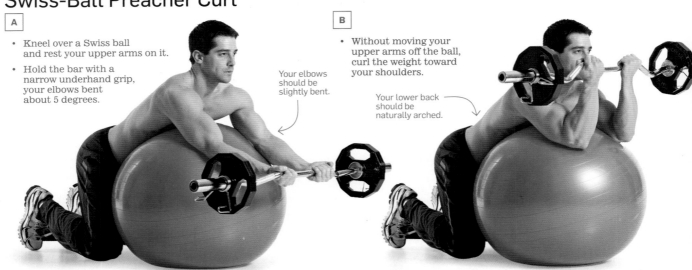

VARIATION #4
EZ-Bar Preacher Curl

- Rest your upper arms on the sloping pad of a preacher bench and hold the bar in front of you, your elbows bent about 5 degrees.

- Without moving your upper arms, bend your elbows and curl the bar toward your shoulders.

Your hands should be about 6 inches apart.

Keep your upper arms on the pad.

VARIATION #5
Reverse EZ-Bar Curl

- Hold the bar with an overhand, shoulder-width grip.

Your palms should be angled toward each other facing your thighs.

VARIATION #6
Telle Curl

Stand tall and straight.

Hold your upper and lower arms in place when you bend over.

Keep your lower back naturally arched.

Your elbows should be bent about 90 degrees.

A
- Grab an EZ-curl bar with an overhand, shoulder-width grip and let the bar hang at arm's length in front of your waist.

B
- Without moving your upper arms, bend your elbows and curl the bar as close to your shoulders as you can. Hold the bar in that position.

C
- Bend forward at your hips until your forearms are parallel to the floor.

D
- Raise your torso back to an upright position while keeping your forearms parallel to the floor. (Your arms will straighten slightly.)

Biceps | ARM CURLS

MAIN MOVE
Barbell Curl

Curl the bar as close to your shoulders as you can.

Keep your upper arms still.

Your arms should be completely straight.

Your palms should be facing forward.

A

- Grab a barbell with an underhand, shoulder-width grip, and let it hang at arm's length in front your hips.
- Stand tall with your feet shoulder-width apart.

B

- Without moving your upper arms, bend your elbows and curl the bar as high as you can.
- Pause, then slowly lower the weight back to the starting position.
- Each time you return to the starting position, completely straighten your arms.

VARIATION
Wide-Grip Barbell Curl

Keep your shoulders held down and back as you raise the weight.

Don't move your upper arms.

A
- Hold the bar with an underhand grip that's about 1½ times shoulder width.

Set your feet shoulder-width apart.

B
- Raise the bar toward your shoulders.

MUSCLE MISTAKE
You Rock Back and Forth when You Curl

This is better known as "cheating." While this approach can allow you to lift heavier weights, it doesn't benefit your biceps. Colorado State University researchers found that leaning back and forth to complete a barbell curl simply transfers more of the workload to your shoulders. What's more, wildly swinging the weights up and down can damage the muscles, joints, and ligaments of your back. So stick to strict form.

Biceps | ARM CURLS

MAIN MOVE
Standing Dumbbell Curl

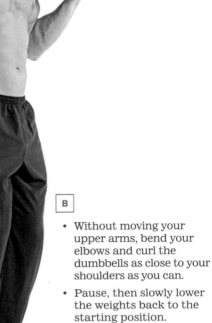

Keep your upper arms still.

Stand as tall as you can.

Your palms should face forward.

Set your feet shoulder-width apart.

A

- Grab a pair of dumbbells and let them hang at arm's length next to your sides.
- Turn your arms so that your palms face forward.

B

- Without moving your upper arms, bend your elbows and curl the dumbbells as close to your shoulders as you can.
- Pause, then slowly lower the weights back to the starting position.
- Each time you return to the starting position, completely straighten your arms.

VARIATION #1
Twisting Standing Dumbbell Curl

Besides using this method while standing, you also use the twisting technique with any of the other body positions listed on the next page.

Your arms should be straight.

Your palms should be facing your shoulders.

Keep your chest up.

Don't move your upper arms.

Your palms should be facing each other.

A
- Start with a hammer grip, your palms next to your thighs.

B
- As you curl the weights, rotate your palms so that you're using a standard grip in the top position.

More Ways to Curl!

Instead of curling both dumbbells at once, lift them one at a time, in an alternating fashion. Simply raise and lower one dumbbell, then repeat with the other. You may be able to do more reps this way since one arm rests each time the other curls the dumbbell. So your biceps won't fatigue as fast. Another approach for variety: Simultaneously raise one dumbbell as you lower the other. You can use these techniques with any of the body positions and grips listed on the next page, as well as just about any other curl.

Biceps | ARM CURLS

VARIATIONS #2-25

Mix and match any of five grips with any of five body positions for 25 different versions of this biceps exercise. Here, you'll see five examples of how the grips and body positions can be paired. But vary the combos frequently for best results.

BODY POSITION #1: INCLINE
Incline Offset-Thumb Dumbbell Curl

- Lie faceup on a bench that's set to a 45-degree incline.

- Lying on an incline causes your arms to hang behind your body, which emphasizes the long head of your biceps brachii to a greater degree.

Use an offset-thumb grip.

BODY POSITION #2: DECLINE
Decline Hammer Curl

- Lie with your chest against a bench that's set to a 45-degree incline.

- This position causes your arms to hang in front of your body, placing more emphasis on your brachialis.

Don't move your upper arms.

BODY POSITION #3: SEATED
Seated Reverse Dumbbell Curl

- Sit tall on a bench or Swiss ball.

- Performing the exercise in a seated position may make you less likely to rock your torso back and forth—or "cheat"—as you curl the weights.

Keep your chest up and your shoulder pulled down and back.

BODY POSITION #4: STANDING

Standing Dumbbell Curl

- Stand with your feet shoulder-width apart. (For complete instructions, see the standing dumbbell curl, also listed as the Main Move on page 156.)

- Anytime you're standing, you engage more core muscles than when you're sitting.

Stand tall and straight.

BODY POSITION #5: SPLIT STANCE

Split-Stance Offset-Pinky Dumbbell Curl

- Place one foot in front of you on a bench or step that's just higher than knee level.

- Putting one foot on a bench forces your hip and core muscles to work harder in order to keep your body stable.

Keep your torso upright.

Use an offset-pinky grip.

Standard Grip
Your palms face forward, and you grip the handle in the middle.
   This is the default dumbbell curl grip.

Offset-Pinky Grip
Your palms face forward, and each pinky finger touches the inside head of a dumbbell.
   This shifts the way the weight is distributed, providing more variety.

Offset-Thumb Grip
Your palms face forward, and each thumb touches the outside head of a dumbbell.
   This forces your biceps brachii to work harder to keep your forearm rotated outward as you curl the weight.

Hammer Grip
Your palms face each other.
   This causes your brachialis muscle to work harder for the entire movement.

Reverse Grip
Your palms face behind you.
   This exercise targets your brachioradialis but decreases the activity of your biceps brachii. You'll really feel it in your forearms.

Biceps | ARM CURLS

VARIATION #26
Standing Zottman Curl

Keep your upper arms still.

Turn your palms out.

Don't move your upper arms as you lower your forearms.

A
- Start with a standard grip.

Palms should face forward.

B
- Without moving your upper arms, curl the weights toward your shoulders.

C
- At the top of the curl, rotate your wrists outward so your palms face forward. Slowly lower them in that position.

D
- Slowly lower the weights back down.
- Rotate your wrists and dumbbells back to their starting position, and repeat.

VARIATION #27
Static Curl

- Grab a dumbbell with your right hand and stand behind a raised incline bench.
- Place the back of your upper arm across the top of the bench.
- Lower the dumbbell until your arm is bent about 20 degrees.
- Hold that position for 40 seconds to build more muscle, or hold for 6 to 8 seconds for greater gains in strength. Then repeat with your left arm. That's one set.

The mid-part of your upper arm should be the only part touching the bench.

PICK THE RIGHT WEIGHT
Choose the heaviest dumbbell that allows you to hold for the length of time that matches your goal. So if you're building strength, you'll use a heavier weight than if you're focusing on faster muscle growth.

VARIATION #28
Dumbbell Curl with Static Hold

Hold the position where your elbow is bent at 90 degrees.

A
- Grab a pair of dumbbells and let them hang at arm's length next to your sides, your palms facing forward.
- Raise your left forearm so your elbow is bent 90 degrees and hold it there.

B
- Perform a set of dumbbell curls with your right arm. After you've finished all your reps, switch arms, performing the static hold with your right arm and curling with your left.

VARIATION #29
Hammer Curl to Press

A
- Let the dumbbells hang at arm's length at your sides, your palms facing each other.

Stand as tall as you can.

B
- Curl the dumbbells toward your shoulders.

Keep your upper arms still.

C
- Press the dumbbells above your head until your arms are straight.

The dumbbells should be directly over your shoulders.

VARIATION #30
Split-Stance Hammer Curl to Press

A
- Stand tall, with one foot in front of you and placed on a bench or step that's just higher than knee level.
- Let the dumbbells hang at arm's length at your sides, your palms facing each other.

Brace your core.

B
- Curl the dumbbells toward your shoulders.

C
- Press the dumbbells above your head until your arms are straight.

Your torso should be upright.

Biceps | ARM CURLS

Cable Alternating Flex Curl

Bend your elbows slightly.

A

- Stand between the weight stacks of a cable crossover station and grab a high-pulley handle in each hand.
- Hold your arms out to the sides so they're parallel to the floor but slightly bent.

Keep your upper arm in the same position from start to finish.

Stand tall and straight.

Your knees should be slightly bent.

Set your feet shoulder-width apart.

B

- Without moving your right arm, curl your left hand toward your head.
- Slowly allow your left arm to straighten, then repeat the move with your right arm.

Cable Curl

A

- Attach a straight bar to the low pulley of a cable station.
- Grab the bar with a shoulder-width, underhand grip and hold it at arm's length.

B

- Without allowing your upper arms to move, curl the bar as close to your chest as you can.
- Pause, then lower back to the starting position.

Keep your upper arms tucked against your sides.

Stand tall with your feet shoulder-width apart.

Cable Hammer Curl

A

- Attach a rope to a low-pulley cable and stand 1 to 2 feet in front of the weight stack.
- Grab an end of the rope in each hand, your palms facing each other.

B

- With your elbows tucked at your sides, slowly curl your fists up toward your shoulders.
- Pause, then lower back to the starting position.

Pull your shoulders down and back and hold them that way.

ARM EXTENSIONS

These exercises target your triceps brachii. Your upper-back and rear-shoulder muscles come into play, too, since they keep your shoulders stable as you perform the movements.

MAIN MOVE
EZ-Bar Lying Triceps Extension

A

- Grab an EZ-curl bar with an overhand grip, your hands a little less than shoulder-width apart.

- Lie faceup on a flat bench and hold the bar with your straight arms over your forehead so that your arms are at an angle.

Your arms should be angled back slightly and completely straight.

Keep your feet flat on the floor.

You can also perform a lying triceps extension using a barbell.

Percentage increase in arm strength you'll develop by performing cardio after lifting weights instead of before, according to a study in the *Journal of Applied Physiology*.

19

B

- Without moving your upper arms, bend your elbows to lower the bar until your forearms are just past parallel to the floor.

- Pause, then lift the weight back to the starting position by straightening your arms.

Keep your upper arms still.

DON'T FORGET THIS MUSCLE!
Your triceps muscle makes up close to 60 percent of your upper arm. So giving your triceps as much attention as your biceps will help you increase your arm size faster than focusing only on the muscles in front.

VARIATION #1
Incline EZ-Bar Lying Triceps Extension

- Instead of lying on a flat bench, perform the movement on an incline bench. Set the backrest to a 30-degree angle.

Hold the bar above your forehead.

Don't move your upper arms.

VARIATION #2
Swiss-Ball EZ-Bar Lying Triceps Extension

- Instead of lying on a flat bench, perform the movement while lying with your middle and upper back placed firmly on a Swiss ball. Raise your hips so that your body forms a straight line from your knees to your shoulders.

Your forearms should be below parallel to the floor.

VARIATION #3
Static Lying Triceps Extension

- Lower the bar until your elbows are bent 90 degrees.

- Hold that position for 40 seconds to build more muscle, or hold for 6 to 8 seconds for greater gains in strength. That's one set.

Your elbows should be bent 90 degrees.

Your feet should be flat on the floor.

Hold the bar here for the prescribed time.

VARIATION #4
Lying Triceps Extension to Close-Grip Bench Press

- Start by doing an EZ-bar lying triceps extension, performing as many reps as you can until you start to struggle. Then, without changing the position of your hands, immediately switch to a bench press. Complete as many reps as you can with perfect form.

After you complete the lying triceps extension, lower the bar to your lower chest.

Press the bar straight up, and repeat.

165

Triceps | ARM EXTENSIONS

MAIN MOVE
Dumbbell Lying Triceps Extension

A

- Grab a pair of dumbbells and lie faceup on a flat bench.
- Hold the dumbbells over your head with straight arms, your palms facing each other.

Your arms should be angled back slightly.

Completely straighten your arms.

As you lower the weight, keep your upper arms still.

B

- Without moving your upper arms, bend your elbows to lower the dumbbells until your forearms are beyond parallel to the floor.
- Pause, then lift the weights back to the starting position by straightening your arms.

Keep your feet flat on the floor.

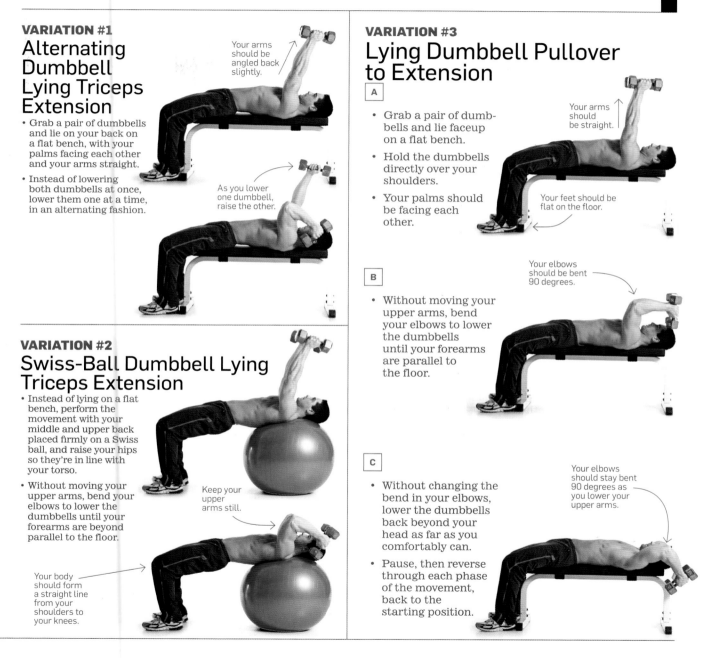

VARIATION #1
Alternating Dumbbell Lying Triceps Extension

- Grab a pair of dumbbells and lie on your back on a flat bench, with your palms facing each other and your arms straight.

- Instead of lowering both dumbbells at once, lower them one at a time, in an alternating fashion.

Your arms should be angled back slightly.

As you lower one dumbbell, raise the other.

VARIATION #2
Swiss-Ball Dumbbell Lying Triceps Extension

- Instead of lying on a flat bench, perform the movement with your middle and upper back placed firmly on a Swiss ball, and raise your hips so they're in line with your torso.

- Without moving your upper arms, bend your elbows to lower the dumbbells until your forearms are beyond parallel to the floor.

Keep your upper arms still.

Your body should form a straight line from your shoulders to your knees.

VARIATION #3
Lying Dumbbell Pullover to Extension

A

- Grab a pair of dumbbells and lie faceup on a flat bench.

- Hold the dumbbells directly over your shoulders.

- Your palms should be facing each other.

Your arms should be straight.

Your feet should be flat on the floor.

B

- Without moving your upper arms, bend your elbows to lower the dumbbells until your forearms are parallel to the floor.

Your elbows should be bent 90 degrees.

C

- Without changing the bend in your elbows, lower the dumbbells back beyond your head as far as you comfortably can.

- Pause, then reverse through each phase of the movement, back to the starting position.

Your elbows should stay bent 90 degrees as you lower your upper arms.

Triceps | ARM EXTENSIONS

Cable Overhead Triceps Extension

A

- Attach a rope handle to the high pulley of a cable station.
- Grab the rope and stand with your back to the weight stack.
- Stand in a staggered stance, one foot in front of the other.
- Bend at your hips until your torso is nearly parallel to the floor.
- Hold an end of the rope in each hand behind your head, with your elbows bent 90 degrees.

B

- Without moving your upper arms, push your forearms forward until your elbows are locked.
- Pause, then return to the starting position.

Keep your upper arms still.

Keep your back naturally arched.

Allow your palms to turn downward as you completely straighten your arms.

Your knees should be slightly bent.

MAIN MOVE
Triceps Pressdown

TRAINER'S TIP

If you use too much weight in the triceps pressdown, you'll involve your back and shoulder muscles, defeating the purpose. One strategy to avoid that mistake: Imagine you're wearing tight suspenders that hold your shoulders down as you do the exercise. Can't keep them down? You need to use a lighter weight.

Pull your shoulders down and back and hold them that way for the entire movement.

Allow your elbows to bend more than 90 degrees.

Don't lean forward or back as you perform the exercise.

A

- Attach a straight bar to the high pulley of a cable station.
- Bend your arms and grab the bar with an overhand grip, your hands shoulder-width part.
- Tuck your upper arms next to your sides.

B

- Without moving your upper arms, push the bar down until your elbows are locked.
- Slowly return to the starting position.

173

Triceps | ARM EXTENSIONS

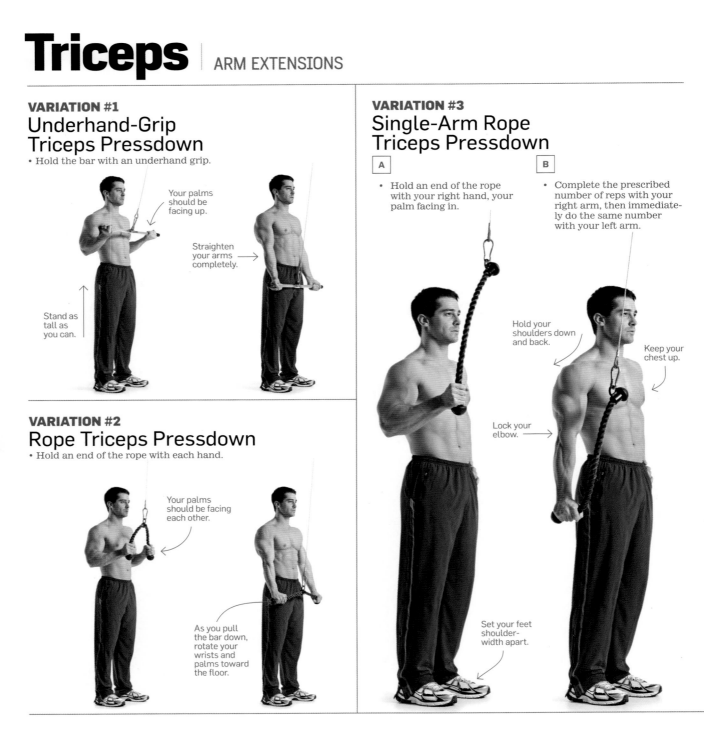

VARIATION #1
Underhand-Grip Triceps Pressdown
• Hold the bar with an underhand grip.

Your palms should be facing up.

Straighten your arms completely.

Stand as tall as you can.

VARIATION #2
Rope Triceps Pressdown
• Hold an end of the rope with each hand.

Your palms should be facing each other.

As you pull the bar down, rotate your wrists and palms toward the floor.

VARIATION #3
Single-Arm Rope Triceps Pressdown

A

• Hold an end of the rope with your right hand, your palm facing in.

B

• Complete the prescribed number of reps with your right arm, then immediately do the same number with your left arm.

Hold your shoulders down and back.

Keep your chest up.

Lock your elbow.

Set your feet shoulder-width apart.

Dumbbell Kickback

Don't round your lower back.

Your upper arm should be parallel to the floor.

Lock your elbow.

Keep your upper arm still.

A

- Place your left hand and left knee on a flat bench.
- Your lower back should be naturally arched and your torso parallel to the floor.
- Hold your right upper arm so that it's parallel to the floor, with your elbow bent.

B

- Without moving your right upper arm, raise your forearm until your arm is completely straight.
- Reverse the movement back to the starting position.

These exercises target either your wrist flexors or wrist extensors, forearm muscles that contribute to grip strength. The muscles of your hands, fingers, and thumbs, which are also important for a strong grip, are trained with many of the exercises as well.

Wrist Curl

A

- Grab a barbell with an underhand, shoulder-width grip.
- Kneel in front of a bench.
- Place your forearms on the bench so that your palms are facing up and your hands are hanging off the bench.
- Allow your wrists to bend backward from the weight of the barbell.

Your lower back should be naturally arched.

B

- Curl your wrists upward by raising your palms toward your body.
- Reverse the movement to return to the starting position.

The movement should only occur from your wrists.

Wrist Extension

A

- Grab a barbell with an over-hand, shoulder-width grip.
- Kneel in front of a bench.
- Place your forearms on the bench so that your palms are facing down and your hands are hanging off the bench.
- Allow your wrists to bend forward from the weight the barbell.

B

- Extend your wrists upward by raising the backs of your hands toward your body.
- Reverse the movement to return to the starting position.

Don't raise your forearms off the bench.

Bar Hold

- Set a barbell on a rack at the level of your hips, and load it with a heavy weight.
- Grab the bar with an overhand grip that's beyond shoulder-width. (The wider your grip, the harder the bar is to hold—in a good way.)
- Dip your knees to lift the bar off the rack, then hold it for the appropriate amount of time for your goal. For maximum strength, choose the heaviest weight you can hold for about 20 seconds. To build more muscle, choose the heaviest that you can hold for about 60 seconds.

Keep your chest up.

Stand as tall as you can.

A FAT BAR FOR YOUR FOREARMS
To better target the muscles of your forearms and hands, wrap a towel around each spot where you grasp a barbell or dumbbell. This increases the diameter of the bar, which forces you to work harder to grip it. You can use this strategy with just about any forearm exercise—wrist extensions, bar holds, farmer's walks—as well as with any other movement you can think of, from barbell rows to dumbbell curls.

Set your feet shoulder-width apart.

177

Forearms | WRIST AND HAND EXERCISES

Hex Dumbbell Hold

A

- Grab the top of a hex dumbbell with each hand. (You can also work each hand separately.) Hold the dumbbell for the appropriate amount of time for your goal.

- For maximum strength, choose the heaviest weight you can hold for about 20 seconds. To build more muscle, choose the heaviest that you can hold for about 60 seconds.

> To make the hex dumbbell hold harder, try to perform an arm curl while grasping the weight in this manner.

HOLD FOR MUSCLE
Simply holding barbells or dumbbells strengthens your wrists and forearms by as much as 25 percent and 16 percent, respectively, in 12 weeks, according to a study at Auburn University.

Keep your chest up.

Stand tall with your feet shoulder-width apart.

Farmer's Walk

A

- Grab a pair of heavy dumbbells and let them hang naturally, at arm's length, next to your sides.

- Walk forward for as long as you can while holding the dumbbells.

- If you can walk for longer than 60 seconds, use a heavier weight.

Let the dumbbells hang naturally, at arm's length.

Plate Pinch Curl

A

- Grab a pair of light weight plates in your left hand.

- Hold the two plates together with your fingers and thumb by pinching the plates. (If you have the option, you should pinch the smooth side of the plates.)

- Let the plates hang at arm's length next to your sides.

Pinch the plates together.

B

- Without moving your upper arms, bend your elbows and curl the weights as close to your shoulders as you can.

- Slowly lower the weights back to the starting position.

Keep your upper arm still.

19

Average number of points people were able to lower their systolic blood pressure after 8 weeks of doing exercises to improve grip strength, according to a study in the *European Journal of Applied Physiology*. Diastolic blood pressure decreased by 5 points.

Arms

THE BEST ARM EXERCISES YOU'VE NEVER DONE
Triple-Stop EZ-Bar Curl

What makes these moves so special? They require you to stop for 10 seconds at three different positions as you perform the movement. Pausing at each point increases strength at that joint angle and 10 degrees in either direction. So this helps eliminate any weak points you might have. It also keeps your muscles under tension for more than 30 seconds each set, a key for building muscle. You can apply the technique to nearly any variation of the arm curl or arm extension.

Stand tall with your chest up.

Keep your upper arms still.

A

- Do an EZ-bar curl, but as you lower the bar, pause for 10 seconds each at the three positions shown. One complete repetition is one set.

B

- First stop: You've lowered the bar about 2 inches.

C

- Second stop: Your elbows are bent 90 degrees.

D

- Third stop: A couple of inches before your arms are straight.

Triple-Stop Lying Dumbbell Triceps Extension

A

- Do a lying dumbbell triceps extension, but pause for 10 seconds each at the three positions shown. One complete repetition is one set.

B

- First stop: You've lowered the weights about 4 inches.

C

- Second stop: Your elbows are bent about 90 degrees.

D

- Lower the weights to the bottom position of the exercise.

181

Arms

BUILD PERFECT ARMS

The key to a great arm workout: Keep it simple. And in fact, the best approach is to save exercises that target your arms for the end of your workout. After all, your arms are involved in every upper-body exercise. So if they tire out early, you won't be able to work the muscles of your chest, back, and shoulders as hard. Try this total-arm workout from Charles Staley, author of *Escalating Density Training*. It's designed to give your arms the work they need to grow, without requiring that you ever increase the duration of your workout. Instead, you'll simply do more work in less time—a little-known secret for building your muscles fast.

What to do: Choose one exercise from the Biceps section of this chapter, and one exercise from the Triceps section. For each, select the heaviest weight that allows you to complete 10 repetitions. (Just ballpark it.) Then start your stopwatch, and do five reps of the decline hammer curl, followed by five reps of the triceps exercise. Rest for as little or as long as you want, and repeat. Continue to alternate back and forth in this manner for 10 minutes. At anytime, you can drop your reps as desired. So as you fatigue, you might just do a set of three reps or two reps—go by feel. However, make sure to keep track of the total reps you perform in the 10 minutes. Then, in your next workout, try to beat that number. Repeat this routine every 4 days.

BONUS WORKOUT: THE BICEPS BLASTER

Your biceps muscles are composed of both fast-twitch and slow-twitch muscle fibers. So the key to maximizing arm size is to make sure you work all of these fibers. Try this three-move routine twice a week for 4 weeks. It hits your fast-twitch fibers with heavy weights and low repetitions, a combination of your fast- and slow-twitch fibers with medium weights and repetitions, and your slow-twitch fibers with light weights and high repetitions. You'll perform the first exercise with your arms in front of your body, the second with your arms in line with your body, and the third with your arms behind your body, to help hit the entire complex of fibers that make up your biceps.

What to do: Do this workout as a circuit, performing one set of each exercise after the next, with no rest in between. After you've completed one set of each exercise, rest for 2 minutes, then repeat the routine one to two more times. Choose any exercise from the menu, but make sure that you don't use the same grip (standard, hammer, offset-pinky, offset-thumb) on any of the movements. And to keep your muscles growing, choose new exercises every 4 weeks. For even more variety, you can also switch the order of exercises. So you might place the Exercise 3 movement first in your workout, the Exercise 1 movement second, and the Exercise 2 movement last, and so forth.

EXERCISE 1

Choose any one of these movements, and do six repetitions.

Incline dumbbell curl (page 158)

Incline hammer curl (page 158)

Incline offset-pinky curl (page 158)

Incline offset-thumb curl (page 158)

EXERCISE 2

Choose any one of these movements, and do 12 repetitions.

Standing dumbbell curl (page 156)

Standing hammer curl (page 159)

Standing offset-pinky curl (page 159)

Standing offset-thumb curl (page 159)

EXERCISE 3

Choose any one of these movements, and do 25 repetitions.

Decline dumbbell curl (page 158)

Decline hammer curl (page 158)

Decline offset-pinky curl (page 158)

Decline offset-thumb curl (page 158)

Chapter 8:
Quadriceps & Calves
STRONG LEGS, STRONG BODY

Quads
& Calves

I can be tempting to skip exercises that work your quadriceps. No doubt this is because the movements that best train these muscles—squats and lunges—require a lot of effort. But, of course, that's exactly what makes them so worthwhile.

Take the squat, for example. It burns more calories per rep than almost any other exercise. And along with targeting your quadriceps, it hits all the other muscles in your lower body, too, including your hamstrings, glutes, and calves.

So sure, squats and lunges are hard, but embracing the quadriceps exercises in this chapter will reward you with strong, muscular legs and a leaner midsection. And for those who want to give their lower legs extra attention, this section also includes moves that focus *directly* on your calves.

Bonus Benefits

Great abs! Besides helping you burn belly flab, squats work the muscles of your core harder than many ab exercises do.

Stronger back! In a study of lifters who did both upper- and lower-body exercises, Norwegian scientists found that those who emphasized lower-body movements such as the squat and lunge gained the most upper-body strength.

Better balance! Conditioning your quads also strengthens the ligaments and tendons within your legs—helping make your knees more stable and less susceptible to injury.

Meet Your Muscles

Quadriceps

The main muscles on the front of your thigh are your quadriceps [1]. This muscle group has four distinct sections: the rectus femoris [A], vastus lateralis [B], vastus medialis [C], and vastus intermedius [not shown; hidden beneath the rectus femoris]. All of these segments come together at the quadriceps tendon [D] and attach just below your knee joint. As a whole, their main function is to straighten your knee. That's why squats and lunges are the best exercises for working your quadriceps: They require that you straighten your legs against a resistance, even if it's just your body weight.

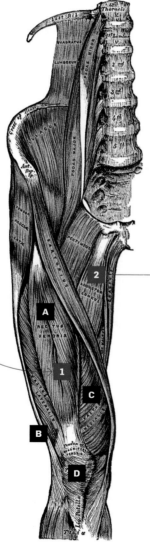

Gastrocnemius

Your calf consists of two separate muscles, both located on the back of your lower leg. The muscle closest to the surface of the skin is called the gastrocnemius [3]. It's composed of two sections—one on the inside of your leg, the other on the outside. These sections start just above your knee and come together at your Achilles tendon [4], which attaches to the back of your heel.

Hip Adductors

Your hip adductors [2] are the muscles on the inside of your thigh, or what's typically referred to as your groin. When your leg is straight out to the side, your hip adductors allow you to pull it back toward your body, a movement known as "hip adduction." (Creative name, huh?) These muscles are heavily involved in squats and lunges.

Soleus

Your other calf muscle, the soleus [5], lies underneath your gastrocnemius. It starts just below your knee and joins up with the gastrocnemius at your Achilles tendon. The primary duty of both calf muscles is to extend your ankle. Think of this as the action of raising your heel when your foot is flat on the floor. So besides calf raises, any exercise that features some level of ankle extension—such as the squats or jumping movements—also work your calf muscles.

Qu ds & C lve |

In this chapter, you'll find 99 exercises that target the muscles of your front thighs and lower legs. Throughout, you'll notice that certain exercises have been given the designation Main Move. Master this basic version of a movement, and you'll be able to do all of its variations with flawless form.

SQUATS

These exercises target your quadriceps. They also activate your core and just about every other muscle of your lower body, including your glutes, hamstrings, and calves. This makes the squat one of the best all-around exercises you can do.

Hold your arms straight out in front of your body at shoulder level.

Brace your core and hold it that way.

MAIN MOVE
Body-Weight Squat

Your lower back should be naturally arched.

A

- Stand as tall as you can with your feet spread shoulder-width apart.

1,250

Most weight, in pounds, ever squatted in competition.

SET YOUR STANCE
Jump as high as you can three times in a row. Then look down at your foot placement. This is roughly where you want to place your feet when you squat.

The Secret to a Perfect Squat

Hone your squat technique with this muscle-memory trick from Mel Siff, PhD, author of *Supertraining* and one of the all-time great minds in the field of exercise science. It's an easy way to help your body and brain learn the proper movement of the lift.

What to do: Prior to your first set of squats, sit tall on a bench with your back upright and naturally arched, your shoulders pulled back, and your lower legs perpendicular to the floor and at least shoulder-width apart. Hold your arms straight out in front of your body at shoulder level so that they're parallel to the floor. Bend forward at your hips—without changing the arch in your back—and move your feet back toward you just enough that you're able to stand up slowly, without having to rock backward or forward or change your body posture. Pay attention: That's the position you should be in when you squat. Once standing, reverse the movement and slowly lower your body to the seated position. Repeat several times.

Your arms should stay in the same position from start to finish.

Your torso should stay as upright as possible.

Don't let your lower back round.

Keep your core tight.

The tops of your thighs should be parallel to the floor or lower.

Keep your weight on your heels, not on your toes, for the entire movement. One gauge: If your weight is distributed correctly, you should be able to wiggle your toes at any moment during the lift.

B

- Lower your body as far as you can by pushing your hips back and bending your knees.

- Pause, then slowly push yourself back to the starting position.

Quads & Calves | SQUATS

VARIATION #1
Prisoner Squat

- Place your fingers on the back of your head (as if you had just been arrested).

Pull your elbows and shoulders back.

Stick your chest out.

Push your hips back.

VARIATION #2
Body-Weight Squat with Knee Press-Out

- Place both legs between a 20-inch mini-band and position the band just below your knees.

- As you squat, focus on pushing your knees outward.

If your knees fall inward when you squat, your hips have a glaring weakness. The good news: Pushing your knees outward against a resistance band can help better activate and strengthen these important muscles.

Your knees should stay over the centers of your feet as you squat.

VARIATION #3
Body-Weight Wall Squat

PAUSE FOR POWER
The pause technique helps eliminate weaknesses throughout the entire range of motion of the squat.

Hold each position for 5 to 10 seconds.

In the last position, your upper thighs should be parallel to the floor or lower.

| A | B | C | D | E |

- Lean back against a wall, with your feet about 2 feet away from it and shoulder-width apart.

- Keeping your back against the wall, bend your knees slightly so that your body descends a few inches. Now hold that position for 5 to 10 seconds.

- Continue to lower yourself a few inches at time, four more times.

- Once you've paused at all five positions, stand up and rest. That's one set.

VARIATION #4
Swiss-Ball Body-Weight Wall Squat

A

- Hold a Swiss ball behind you and stand so that the ball is pinned between your back and the wall.
- Place your feet about 2 feet in front of your body.

B

- Keeping your back in contact with the ball, lower your body until your upper thighs are at least parallel to the floor.

THE BEGINNER'S SQUAT

If you have trouble doing a standard body-weight squat, try the Swiss-ball version. It requires less core strength, which makes the exercise easier while helping you learn perfect form.

Hold your body in the down position for 1 to 2 seconds, and then return to the standing position.

The center of the ball should be against your lower back.

Your knees should be slightly bent.

The ball will roll with you as you squat.

193

Quads & Calves | SQUATS

VARIATION #5
Body-Weight Jump Squat

A

- Place your fingers on the back of your head and pull your elbows back so that they're in line with your body.

SQUAT FOR FAT LOSS
While the jump squat variation shown here is great for athletic performance, use a deeper squat when doing the exercise for fat loss. In fact, lower your body until your upper thighs are parallel to the floor (as shown in the iso-explosive body-weight jump squat below).

B

- Dip your knees in preparation to leap.

C

- Explosively jump as high as you can.
- When you land, immediately squat down and jump again.

JUMP HIGHER
Imagine that you're pushing the floor away from you as you leap.

VARIATION #6
Iso-Explosive Body-Weight Jump Squat

- Place your fingers on the back of your head and pull your elbows back so that they're in line with your body.
- Push your hips back, bend your knees, and lower until your upper thighs are parallel to the floor.
- Pause for 5 seconds in the down position.
- After your pause, jump as high as you can.
- Land and reset.

WORK YOUR LEGS ANYWHERE
The 5-second pause during this exercise eliminates all the elasticity in your muscles, which allows you to activate a maximum number of muscle fibers as you push yourself off the floor. This makes it a great exercise to use when you don't have access to weights.

VARIATION #7
Braced Squat

- Hold a weight plate in front of your chest with both hands, your arms completely straight.

BUILD YOUR BICEPS, TOO!
As you perform the braced squat, you can work your arms by doing a curl at the top of each repetition. With your arms outstretched, simply curl the plate toward your shoulders without moving your upper arms. Straighten your arms as you lower your body.

The braced squat overloads your core, helping to improve stability, strength, and performance. It's categorized as a body-weight exercise because the amount of weight you can use is limited due to shoulder fatigue from holding the plate in front of your body.

High Box Jump

A

- Stand in front of a sturdy, secure box that's high enough so that you have to jump with great effort in order to land on top of it.
- Your feet should be shoulder-width apart.
- Dip your knees.

B C

- Jump up onto the box with a soft landing.
- Step down and reset your feet.

If you can't "stick" the landing, the box is too high.

Set your feet shoulder-width apart.

Depth Jump

A

- Stand at the edge of a 12-inch box.

ADD INCHES TO YOUR VERTICAL
The depth jump is one of the best drills for improving your vertical leap. Try it twice a week, doing four or five sets of three repetitions at the beginning of your workout. Rest for 60 to 90 seconds between sets.

B

- Simply step off the box so that you land on both feet simultaneously (balls of feet first, followed by heels).

C

- When you make contact with the floor, jump as high as you can. That's one repetition.

Qu a ds & C alv s | SQUATS

MAIN MOVE
Single-Leg Squat

A

- Stand on your left leg on a bench or box that's about knee height.
- Hold your arms straight out in front of you.

Keep your torso as upright as possible.

Flex your right ankle so that your toes are higher than your heel.

B

- Balancing on your left foot, bend your left knee and slowly lower your body until your right heel lightly touches the floor.
- Pause, then push yourself up.
- Complete the prescribed number of reps with your left leg, then immediately do the same number with your right.
- If this exercise is too hard, try the partial single-leg squat or the single-leg bench getup.

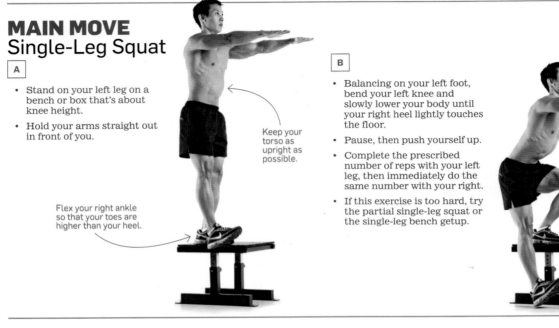

VARIATION #1
Single-Leg Bench Getup

A

- Sit tall on a bench with your back upright and naturally arched.
- Hold your arms straight out in front of your body at shoulder level, parallel to the floor.
- Raise your left foot off the floor.

Your lower back should be naturally arched.

B

- Without leaning foward, press your body to a standing position. (If you can't do this, try sliding your foot slightly back toward your body in the starting position.)
- Sit back down.

Push your hips forward.

Straighten your right knee.

VARIATION #2
Partial Single-Leg Squat

A

- Stand on your left leg on a bench or box that's about knee height.
- Hold your arms straight out in front of you.

Flex your right ankle so that your toes are higher than your heel.

B

- Lower your body to just above your breaking point (see "Find Your Breaking Point" at right).
- Pause for 2 seconds before you push yourself back to a standing position.

To return to the start, press your left heel into the step and forcefully drive your body upward.

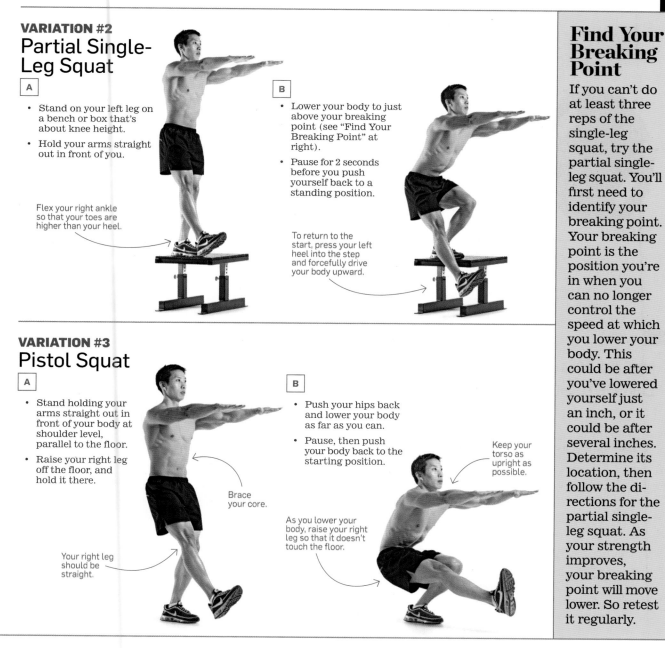

VARIATION #3
Pistol Squat

A

- Stand holding your arms straight out in front of your body at shoulder level, parallel to the floor.
- Raise your right leg off the floor, and hold it there.

Brace your core.

Your right leg should be straight.

B

- Push your hips back and lower your body as far as you can.
- Pause, then push your body back to the starting position.

Keep your torso as upright as possible.

As you lower your body, raise your right leg so that it doesn't touch the floor.

Find Your Breaking Point

If you can't do at least three reps of the single-leg squat, try the partial single-leg squat. You'll first need to identify your breaking point. Your breaking point is the position you're in when you can no longer control the speed at which you lower your body. This could be after you've lowered yourself just an inch, or it could be after several inches. Determine its location, then follow the directions for the partial single-leg squat. As your strength improves, your breaking point will move lower. So retest it regularly.

Pull your shoulders back so that the bar can rest comfortably on the shelf created by your shoulder blades.

FAST REPS FOR FAST RESULTS

A version of the barbell squat known as the speed squat *can help improve your strength and power by targeting your fast-twitch muscle fibers. Simply choose a weight that's about 50 to 70 percent of the most you can squat for one repetition. Then do repetitions of the squat as fast as you can from start to finish. Your goal: 1 second per rep.*

The tops of your thighs should be parallel to the floor or lower.

Your torso should stay as upright as possible.

Your lower back should be naturally arched.

Brace your core.

MAIN MOVE
Barbell Squat

A

- Hold the bar across your upper back with an overhand grip.

Set your feet shoulder-width apart.

B

- Keeping your lower back arched, lower your body as deep as you can.

- Initiate the movement by first pushing your hips back, then bend your knees.

- Pause, then reverse the movement back to the starting position.

Drive your heels into the floor when you push yourself back up.

VARIATION #1
Wide-Stance Barbell Squat

A

- Perform a squat with your feet set at twice shoulder width.

If your heels rise off the floor when you do a standard barbell squat, your hips are tight. But the wide-stance version of the exercise can help. Simply lower your body into the deepest position of the wide-stance squat that you can without allowing your heels to rise. Hold for 2 seconds. Try to lower your body a little farther with each workout. As your flexibility improves, narrow your stance and decrease the angle at which your toes point out.

WHY GO WIDE?
Using a wider stance forces your hip adductors to work harder, strengthening your groin.

Your feet should be pointing outward at a slight angle.

Make sure that your knees stay in line with your toes as you lower your body.

VARIATION #2
Barbell Front Squat

A

- Hold the bar with an overhand grip that's just beyond shoulder width.

- Raise your upper arms until they're parallel to the floor.

- Allow the bar to roll back so that it's resting on the fronts of your shoulders.

B

- Slowly lower your body until the tops of your thighs are *at least* parallel to the floor.

- Pause, then push your body back to the starting position.

Keep your upper arms parallel to the floor for the entire movement. This prevents the bar from rolling forward and also helps you maintain a more upright posture.

Set your feet shoulder-width apart.

STRAPS
If your wrists aren't flexible enough to perform the traditional version of the barbell front squat, use this trick: Loop a pair of wrist straps around the bar—spaced shoulder-width apart—and cinch them tight. Then grasp the straps instead of bending your wrists back and resting the bar on your fingers.

Quads & Calves | SQUATS

VARIATION #3
Crossed-Arm Barbell Front Squat

- Set a bar on a squat rack and cross your arms in front of you so that each hand is on top of the bar.

- Step under the bar so that it's resting on the tops of your shoulders, and raise your arms so that the bar can't roll off them.

- Step back and perform a squat, keeping your arms in the same position for the entire movement.

- Push yourself back to a standing position.

Don't let your arms drop.

VARIATION #4
Zercher Squat

- Hold the bar in the crooks of your arms—tightly against your chest—instead of across your back.

- Push yourself back to a standing position.

You can use a bar pad or a rolled-up towel for cushioning.

Keep your torso as upright as possible.

The Zercher squat not only strengthens your lower body but also works your biceps and front deltoids, muscles that have to stay contracted in order to hold the bar.

VARIATION #5
Barbell Siff Squat

- Before you squat, raise your heels as high as you can and hold them that way for the entire lift.

Keeping your heels raised forces your calves to work even harder.

VARIATION #6
Barbell Quarter Squat

- Lower your body only until your knees are bent about 60 degrees.

VARIATION #7
Barbell Squat with Heels Raised

A
- Position your heels on a pair of 25-pound weight plates.

Elevating your heels puts even more emphasis on your quadriceps.

B
- Push your hips back, bend your knees, and lower your body as far as you can.

VARIATION #8
Barbell Hack Squat

A
- Hold a barbell at arm's length behind your back, using an overhand grip. Place each heel on a 25-pound weight plate.

B
- Lower your body as far as you can.

Squat Heavier— Instantly!

While it's best to use a full range of motion most of the time—as you do in other versions of the squat—the quarter squat allows you to lift about 20 percent more weight than you can when you squat lower. This reduces the involvement of your glutes and hamstrings and helps you overload lagging quads. Use the technique in stints of just 4 weeks at a time, though, in order to prevent muscle imbalances that occur when your quads become so strong that they overpower your hamstrings.

Quads & Calves | SQUATS

VARIATION #9
Barbell Jump Squat

> **37 POUNDS**
> *Average greater increase in the amount of weight people could squat after adding jump squats to their intense lower-body workouts for 5 weeks, compared to those who did the same routine but skipped the explosive exercise, according to a study at the College of New Jersey.*

A
- Hold the barbell tightly against your upper back.

Set your feet about shoulder-width apart.

B
- Dip your knees in preparation to leap.

C
- Immediately change directions and push from your calves to straighten your body so explosively that your feet come off the floor.
- Land as softly as you can on your toes, then quickly shift your weight to your heels and repeat.

VARIATION #10
Overhead Barbell Squat

> **SCULPT YOUR ABS**
> *Holding a barbell over your head increases the challenge to your core and also tests your shoulder and hip flexibility.*

A
- Hold a barbell over your head with an overhand grip that's about twice shoulder width.

Your arms should be completely straight.

Brace your core.

Set your feet shoulder-width apart.

B
- Don't allow the bar to move forward as you lower your body.

Keep your lower back naturally arched.

Your arms should stay perpendicular to the floor for the entire lift.

Your upper thighs should be parallel to the floor or lower.

MAIN MOVE
Dumbbell Squat

A

- Hold a pair of dumbbells at arm's length next to your sides, your palms facing each other.

B

- Brace your abs, and lower your body as far as you can by pushing your hips back and bending your knees.

- Pause, then slowly push yourself back to the starting position.

> **KEEP YOUR HEAD UP**
> *Looking down when you squat puts you at greater risk of injury, say scientists at Miami University of Ohio. The researchers found that gazing down during the movement causes your body to lean forward 4 to 5 degrees. This increases the strain on your lower back. Looking at yourself in the mirror can also cause a forward lean. Your best approach: Before you descend, find a mark that's stable and just above eye level, and stay focused on it throughout the movement.*

Keep your torso as upright as you can for the entire movement, with your lower back naturally arched.

Stick your chest out.

The tops of your thighs should be parallel to the floor or lower.

Keep your weight on your heels, not on your toes, for the entire movement.

Quads & Calves | SQUATS

VARIATION #1
Goblet Squat

- Hold a dumbbell vertically next to your chest, with both hands cupping the dumbbell head. (Imagine that it's a heavy goblet.)

- Pause, then push yourself back to the starting position.

Don't be afraid to lower your body as deep as possible. Research shows that the most unstable knee angle during the squat is when your knees are bent 90 degrees—a few inches above the point where your upper thighs are parallel to the floor.

Your elbows should brush the insides of your knees; in fact, it's perfectly fine if they push your knees outward.

Your elbows should point down to the floor.

VARIATION #2
Wide-Stance Goblet Squat

- With both hands, hold a dumbbell vertically next to your chest.

Keep your torso as upright as possible.

Set your feet about twice shoulder-width apart, your toes pointing out at an angle.

VARIATION #3
Sumo Squat

- Grasp a head of a heavy dumbbell in each hand, and hold the weight at arm's length in front of your waist.

Keep your lower back naturally arched for the entire movement.

Set your feet at about twice shoulder width, your toes turned out slightly.

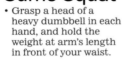

VARIATION #4
Dumbbell Front Squat

- Hold a pair of dumbbells so that your palms are facing each other, and rest one of the dumbbell heads on the meatiest part of each shoulder.

- Keep your body as upright as you can at all times.

- Don't allow your elbows to drop down as you squat.

Keeping your upper arms parallel to the floor helps to keep your torso from leaning forward excessively.

VARIATION #5
Dumbbell Jump Squat

A

- Hold a pair of dumbbells at arm's length next to your sides, your palms facing each other.
- Dip your knees in preparation to leap.

B

- Explosively jump as high as you can.
- When you land, reset quickly before jumping again.

Land as softly as you can on the balls of your feet, then lower your heels back to the floor.

> **JUMP HIGHER, RUN FASTER**
> *You can boost your vertical and improve your speed with a simple jump squat routine, according to an 8-week study in the Journal of Strength and Conditioning. In the study, subjects used a weight that was 30 percent of the amount they could squat one time. Try it yourself: Twice a week, do five sets of six reps, resting 3 minutes after each set.*

VARIATION #6
Overhead Dumbbell Squat

A

- Hold a pair of dumbbells straight over your shoulders, your arms completely straight.

B

- Lower your body until your upper thighs are at least parallel together.

Don't let the dumbbells fall forward as you squat.

Your lower back should stay naturally arched for the entire movement.

Keep your torso as upright as possible.

Brace your core.

Set your feet slightly wider than hip-width apart.

43

Percent reduction in knee pain after sufferers performed lower body exercises such as the squat for 4 months, according to a Tufts University study.

MUSCLE MISTAKE
You Think Smith Machine Squats Are Superior

While the Smith machine—a squat rack with a bar that runs on guides—may look like a foolproof way to squat, it has a major flaw. The bar must travel straight up and down instead of in an arc as it does in a barbell squat. This places more stress on your lower back. What's more, Canadian scientists found that free-weight squats activate the quads almost 50 percent more than Smith machine squats.

Pull your shoulders back so that the bar rests comfortably on the shelf created by your shoulder blades.

Brace your core.

Your front knee should be slightly bent.

MAIN MOVE
Barbell Split Squat

A

- Hold a bar across your upper back with an overhand grip.
- Stand in a staggered stance, your left foot in front of your right.

Stand on the ball of your back foot, with your heel raised.

Set your feet 2 to 3 feet apart.

167

Percentage increase in core activity during the squat when people were reminded to keep their abs braced—as if they were about to be punched in the gut—according to a Utah State University study. The scientists say that hearing instructions reminds you that you may not be stiffening your core as much as you think. What's more, applying this to your workout subconsciously may work even better. The study subjects needed only one reminder. Consider this yours.

B

- Slowly lower your body as far as you can.

- Pause, then push yourself back up to the starting position as quickly as you can.

- Complete the prescribed number of reps with your left leg forward, then do the same number with your right foot in front of your left.

Your lower back should be naturally arched.

Keep your torso as upright as possible.

Your rear knee should nearly touch the floor.

Quads & Calves | SQUATS

VARIATION #1
Elevated-Front-Foot Barbell Split Squat
• Place your front foot on a 6-inch step or box.

Lower your body as far as you can.

VARIATION #2
Elevated-Back-Foot Barbell Split Squat
• Place your back foot on a 6-inch step or box.

Elevating your foot increases your range of motion and the challenge.

VARIATION #3
Barbell Front Split Squat
• Hold the bar with an overhand grip that's just beyond shoulder width.
• Raise your upper arms until they're parallel to the floor.

Allow the bar to roll back so that it's resting on the fronts of your shoulders.

Keep your upper arms parallel to the floor for the entire movement.

VARIATION #4
Barbell Bulgarian Split Squat
• Place just the instep of your back foot on a bench.

When you're doing split squats, the higher your foot is elevated, the harder the exercise. In fact, the barbell Bulgarian split squat is one of the most challenging exercises you'll ever do.

BODY-WEIGHT SPLIT SQUAT
You can do just about any version of the split squat without holding weights of any kind. Simply cross your arms in front of your chest or place your hands behind your ears or on your hips. The body-weight versions are ideal warmup exercises and are also valuable if weighted variations are too hard or if you don't have weights available.

MAIN MOVE
Dumbbell Split Squat

A

- Hold a pair of dumbbells at arm's length next to your sides, your palms facing each other.
- Stand in a staggered stance, your left foot in front of your right.

TRAINER'S TIP
Just like in the two-legged version of the squat, be sure to brace your core as you perform this exercise.

B

- Slowly lower your body as far as you can.
- Pause, then push yourself back up to the starting position as quickly as you can.
- Complete the prescribed number of reps with your left foot forward, then do the same number with your right foot in front of your left.

Keep your torso upright for the entire movement.

Set your feet 2 to 3 feet apart.

Your rear knee should nearly touch the floor.

Quads & Calves | SQUATS

VARIATION #1
Elevated-Front-Foot Dumbbell Split Squat
• Place your front foot on a 6-inch step or box.

Your front knee will bend significantly more on this exercise than when you do the standard split squat.

Your back knee should nearly touch the floor.

VARIATION #2
Elevated-Back-Foot Dumbbell Split Squat
• Place your back foot on a 6-inch step or box.

Keep your torso as upright as you can.

Stand on the ball of your back foot, with your heel raised.

To push yourself back up, press your front heel into the floor.

VARIATION #3
Overhead Dumbbell Split Squat
• Hold a pair of dumbbells directly over your shoulders, with your arms completely straight.

The dumbbells should be directly over your shoulders.

Your arms should be completely straight.

Stiffen your core and hold it that way.

VARIATION #4
Dumbbell Bulgarian Split Squat
• Place just the instep of your back foot on a bench.

Pull your shoulders back.

Keep your chest up.

Lower your body as deeply as you can.

VARIATION #5
Dumbbell Split Jump

University of North Carolina scientists found that doing exercises like the split jump for 3 weeks can spike your vertical leap by up to 9 percent.

Keep your torso as upright as you can.

While in the air, scissor-kick your legs so you land with the opposite leg forward.

A
- From a standing position, lower your body into a split squat.

B
- Quickly switch directions and jump with enough force to propel both feet off the floor.

C
- Repeat, alternating back and forth with each repetition.

MUSCLE MISTAKE
You're Still Doing Leg Extensions

While the leg extension machine may seem like a safer alternative to squats and even lunges, it's actually quite the opposite. Case in point: Physiologists at the Mayo Clinic determined that leg extensions place significantly more stress on your knees than free-weight squats do. Why? Because the resistance is placed near your ankles, which leads to high amounts of torque being applied to your knee joint every time you lower the weight.

Qu ds & C lv s | LUNGES

These exercises target your quadriceps. However, they also work just about all of the other muscles of your lower body, including your glutes, hamstrings, and calves.

Pull your shoulders back.

Keep your lower back naturally arched.

Brace your core.

Stick your chest out.

Stand tall with your feet hip-width apart.

MAIN MOVE
Barbell Lunge

A

- Hold a bar across your upper back with an overhand grip.

212

1

Number of sets of an exercise needed to boost your levels of fat-burning hormones, according to a study at Ball State University.

TRAINER'S TIP
When doing the barbell lunge, visualize lowering your body straight down, not forward and down.

B

- Step forward with your left leg and slowly lower your body until your front knee is bent at least 90 degrees.

- Pause, then push yourself to the starting position as quickly as you can.

- Complete the prescribed number of repetitions with your left foot forward, then do the same number with your right foot in front of your left.

Keep your torso upright for the entire movement.

Your front lower leg should be nearly perpendicular to the floor.

Your rear knee should nearly touch the floor.

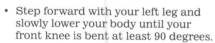

VARIATION #1
Alternating Barbell Lunge

- Instead of performing all of your reps with one leg before repeating with the other, alternate back and forth—doing one rep with your left, then one rep with your right.

VARIATION #2
Walking Barbell Lunge

- Instead of pushing your body backward to the starting position, raise up and bring your back foot forward so that you move forward (like you're walking) a step with every rep. Alternate the leg you step forward with each time.

VARIATION #3
Reverse Barbell Lunge

- Step backward with your right leg (instead of forward with your left). Then lower your body into a lunge. This looks the same in a photo as the barbell lunge. Do all your reps and repeat with your other leg. You can also use the alterating technique, stepping backward with a different leg each rep.

Quads & Calves | LUNGES

VARIATION #4
Barbell Box Lunge

- Place a 6-inch step or box about 2 feet in front of you.
- Step forward onto the box with your left leg, and then lower your body into a lunge.

Keep your torso upright.
↓

The upper thigh of your front leg should be well below parallel to the floor.

VARIATION #5
Reverse Barbell Box Lunge

- Stand on a 6-inch step or box.
- Step backward with your left leg into a lunge.

Your back knee should nearly touch the floor.

To push your body back up, drive your front heel into the box.

VARIATION #6
Barbell Stepover

A
- Place a 6-inch step or box about 2 feet in front of you, and stand with your feet hip-width apart.

B
- Step forward onto the step with your left foot as you lower your body into a lunge.

C
- Push yourself up so that you lift your right foot over the step and onto the floor in front of you.

D
- Lower yourself into a lunge.
- Reverse the movement to return to the starting position.

  Don't allow your momentum to cause you to bend your torso forward; you should remain upright.
  ↓

Drive your front heel into the box to push your body up.

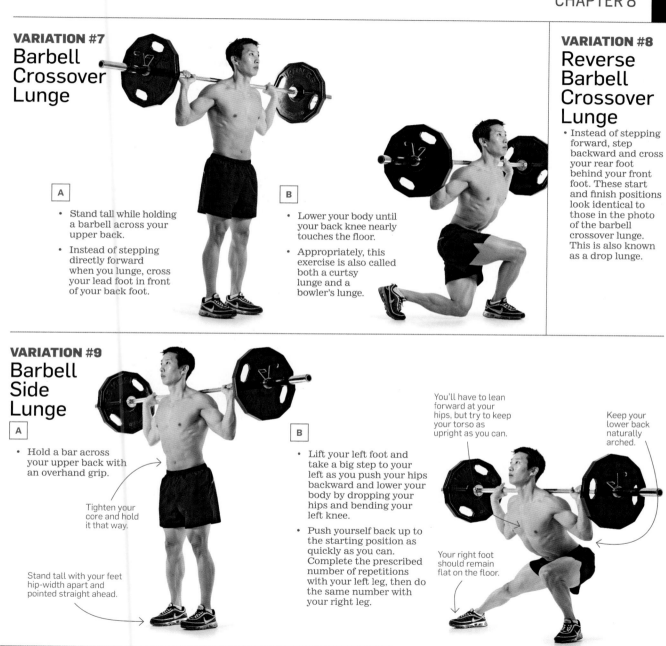

VARIATION #7
Barbell Crossover Lunge

A

- Stand tall while holding a barbell across your upper back.
- Instead of stepping directly forward when you lunge, cross your lead foot in front of your back foot.

B

- Lower your body until your back knee nearly touches the floor.
- Appropriately, this exercise is also called both a curtsy lunge and a bowler's lunge.

VARIATION #8
Reverse Barbell Crossover Lunge

- Instead of stepping forward, step backward and cross your rear foot behind your front foot. These start and finish positions look identical to those in the photo of the barbell crossover lunge. This is also known as a drop lunge.

VARIATION #9
Barbell Side Lunge

A

- Hold a bar across your upper back with an overhand grip.

Tighten your core and hold it that way.

Stand tall with your feet hip-width apart and pointed straight ahead.

B

- Lift your left foot and take a big step to your left as you push your hips backward and lower your body by dropping your hips and bending your left knee.
- Push yourself back up to the starting position as quickly as you can. Complete the prescribed number of repetitions with your left leg, then do the same number with your right leg.

You'll have to lean forward at your hips, but try to keep your torso as upright as you can.

Keep your lower back naturally arched.

Your right foot should remain flat on the floor.

Pull your shoulders back.

Lift your chest up.

Stand as tall as you can.

Brace your core and hold it that way for the entire exercise.

Stand tall with your feet hip-width apart.

MAIN MOVE
Dumbbell Lunge

A

• Grab a pair of dumbbells and hold them at arm's length next to your sides, your palms facing each other.

50

Percent less likely people were to die of heart disease when they first started working out in their 40s compared to those who never got off the couch, according to a German study.

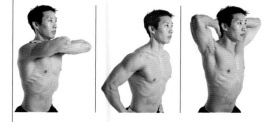

BODY-WEIGHT LUNGE
You can do just about any version of the lunge without holding weights of any kind. Simply cross your arms in front of your chest, or place your hands on your hips or behind your ears. These are ideal warmup exercises and are also valuable as great alternatives to the weighted variations.

VARIATION #1
Alternating Dumbbell Lunge
• Instead of performing all of your reps with one leg before repeating with the other, alternate back and forth—doing one rep with your left, then one rep with your right.

VARIATION #2
Walking Dumbbell Lunge
• Instead of pushing your body backward to the starting position, raise up and bring your back foot forward so that you move forward (like you're walking) a step with every rep. Alternate the leg you step forward with each time.

VARIATION #3
Reverse Dumbbell Lunge
• Step backward with your right leg. Then lower your body into a lunge. This looks the same in a photo as the dumbbell lunge. Do all your reps and repeat with your other leg. You can also use the alterating technique.

B

• Step forward with your left leg and slowly lower your body until your front knee is bent at least 90 degrees.

• Pause, then push yourself to the starting position as quickly as you can.

• Complete the prescribed number of repetitions with your left leg, then do the same number with your right leg.

Keep your torso upright for the entire movement.

Your front lower leg should be nearly perpendicular to the floor.

Your rear knee should nearly touch the floor.

217

Qu⌐ds & C⌐lv⌐s | LUNGES

VARIATION #4
Dumbbell Box Lunge

- Place a 6-inch step or box about 2 feet in front of you.
- Step forward onto the box with your left leg, and then lower your body into a lunge.

Stand as tall as you can.

Keep your torso upright and your lower back naturally arched.

VARIATION #5
Reverse Dumbbell Box Lunge

- Stand on a 6-inch step or box, and step backward with your left leg into a lunge.

Stick your chest out.

Lower your body as far as your flexibility allows.

Step backward.

VARIATION #6
Dumbbell Stepover

A
- Place a 6-inch step or box about 2 feet in front of you.

Set your feet hip-width apart.

B
- Step forward onto the step with your left foot as you lower your body into a lunge.

C
- Push yourself up so that you lift your right foot over the step and onto the floor in front of you.

D
- Lower yourself into a lunge.
- Reverse the movement to return to the starting position.

Drive your heel into the box to push your body up.

VARIATION #7
Reverse Dumbbell Box Lunge with Forward Reach

Hold the dumbbells so that your palms are facing each other.

Keep your lower back naturally arched.

Step backward.

- Stand on a 6-inch box or step, holding a pair of light dumbbells at your sides.
- Step backward into a lunge with your left leg as you lean forward at your hips and reach toward your feet. Reverse the movement to return to the starting position.

VARIATION #8
Dumbbell Crossover Lunge

- Instead of stepping directly forward when you lunge, cross your lead foot in front of your back foot, as if you were doing a curtsy.

Keep your torso as upright as possible.

VARIATION #9
Reverse Dumbbell Crossover Lunge

- Instead of stepping forward, step backward and cross your rear foot behind your front foot.

VARIATION #10
Dumbbell Lunge and Rotation

- Grab a dumbbell and hold it by the ends, just below your chin.
- Step forward into a lunge. As you lunge, rotate your upper body toward the same side as the leg you're using to step forward.

If you're stepping forward with your left leg, rotate your torso to your left side. If you're stepping with your right, rotate to your right.

Brace your core and hold it that way for the entire movement.

VARIATION #11
Overhead Dumbbell Lunge

- Hold a pair of dumbbells directly over your shoulders, with your arms completely straight.
- Step forward with your left leg into a lunge.

Don't allow the weight to carry you forward. Instead, think about dropping your hips straight down as you step forward. Keep your abs tight and your chest up.

VARIATION #12
Overhead Dumbbell Reverse Lunge

- This time, step backward with your right leg into a lunge.

Quads & Calves | LUNGES

VARIATION #13
Offset Dumbbell Lunge

- Hold a dumbbell in your right hand next to your shoulder, with your arm bent.
- Step forward into a lunge with your right foot.
- Complete the prescribed number of reps on that side, then switch arms and lunge with your left leg for the same number of reps.

STRENGTHEN YOUR CORE
Holding a weight on just one side of your body increases the demand placed on your core to keep your body stable.

Let your left hand hang next to your side.

Keep your torso upright at all times.

Step forward.

VARIATION #14
Offset Dumbbell Reverse Lunge

- Hold a dumbbell in your left hand next to your shoulder, with your arm bent.
- Step backward into a lunge with your right foot.
- Complete the prescribed number of reps on that side, then switch arms and lunge backward with your left leg for the same number of reps.

Step backward.

VARIATION #15
Dumbbell Rotational Lunge

A

- Hold a pair of dumbbells at arm's length next to your sides, your palms facing each other.
- Lift your left foot and step to the left and back, placing that foot so it's diagonal to your body and pointed toward 8 o'clock.

B

- Shift your weight onto your left leg, pivot on your right foot, and lower your body into a lunge as you simultaneously rotate your torso and the dumbbells to the left, over your front leg.
- Reverse the movement and push yourself back up to the start.
- Complete the prescribed number of reps with your left leg, then do the same number with your right leg. (Your right foot will point to 4 o'clock.)

Keep your core braced as you rotate your torso.

Stand tall with your feet hip-width apart, pointing ahead to 12 o'clock.

Your right foot should rotate to point in the same direction as your left foot.

Your left foot should point to 8 o'clock in relation to your starting position.

VARIATION #16
Dumbbell Side Lunge

- Hold a pair of dumbbells at arm's length next to your sides, your palms facing each other.
- Lift your left foot and take a big step to your left as you push your hips backward and lower your body by dropping your hips and bending your left knee.
- Pause, then quickly push yourself back to the starting position.

Your right foot should remain flat on the floor.

Your feet should be pointed straight ahead in both the up and the down positions.

VARIATION #17
Dumbbell Diagonal Lunge

- Instead of stepping straight forward, lunge diagonally at a 45-degree angle.
- Complete all your reps, then switch legs and repeat.

Lunge forward or back in this direction.

VARIATION #18
Reverse Dumbbell Diagonal Lunge

- You can also perform this exercise by lunging backward at a 45-degree angle.

VARIATION #19
Dumbbell Side Lunge and Touch

If you can't touch the floor without rounding your lower back, only lower as far as you can while keeping your back naturally arched.

You'll have to lean forward at your hips, but focus on keeping your head and chest up, instead of allowing your torso to slump forward.

Don't allow your right foot to raise up off the floor.

A
- Hold a pair of dumbbells at arm's length next to your sides.

B
- As you lower your body into a side lunge, bend forward at your hips and touch the dumbbells to the floor.

These exercises target your hip adductors, the muscles on the inside of your upper thigh.

MAIN MOVE
Standing Cable Hip Adduction

A

- Attach an ankle strap to the low pulley of a cable station, and then place the strap around your right ankle.
- Stand with your right side facing the weight stack.
- Take a big step away from the weight stack so that when you move your right leg toward the weight stack, the cable remains taut.
- Raise your right leg straight out to the side, toward the weight stack.

Place your hand on a sturdy object for support.

There should be tension on the cable.

Your left knee should be slightly bent.

B

- Without bending your knee, pull your right leg sideways so that it crosses in front of your left leg.
- Pause, then slowly return to the starting position. Complete the prescribed number of repetitions with your right leg, then do the same number with your left leg.

Valslide Hip Adduction

A

- Kneel on the floor and place each knee on a Valslide.

Your torso should be upright.

Your thighs should be close together.

B

- Push your knees out as far as you can.
- Pause, then pull your knees back together again.

From this position, slide your knees toward each other.

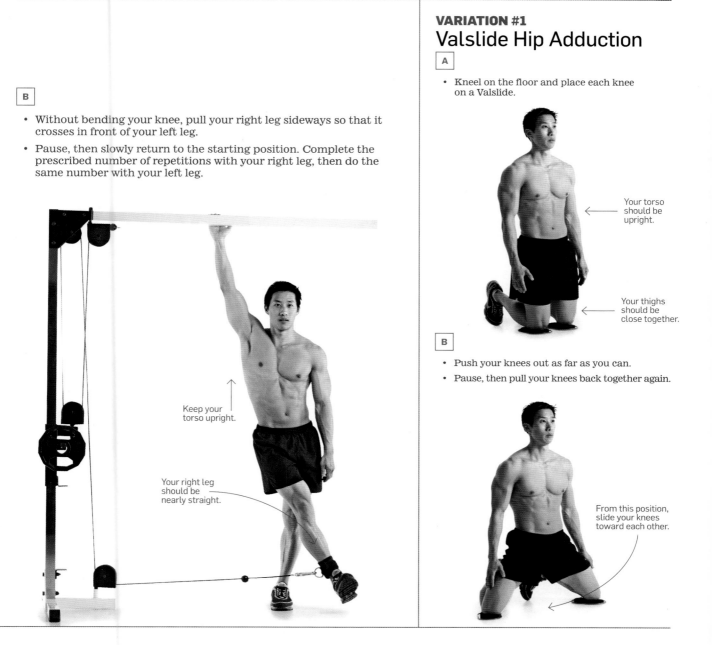

Keep your torso upright.

Your right leg should be nearly straight.

Quads & Calves | CALF RAISES

The targets for these exercises are your gastrocnemius and soleus muscles.

MAIN MOVE
Standing Barbell Calf Raise

A

- Grab a barbell with an overhand grip and place it so that it rests comfortably across your upper back.
- Place the ball of each foot on a 25-pound weight plate.

B

- Rise up on your toes as high as you can.
- Pause, then slowly lower back to the starting position.

↑ Keep your torso upright.

Stand as tall as you can.

Lift your heels as high as possible.

VARIATION #1
Single-Leg Standing Dumbbell Calf Raise

A

- Grab a dumbbell in your right hand and stand on a step, block, or 25-pound weight plate.
- Cross your left foot behind your right ankle, and balance yourself on the ball of your right foot, with your right heel on the floor or hanging off a step.

Put your left hand on something stable—a wall or weight stack, for instance.

B

- Lift your right heel as high as you can. Pause, then lower and repeat.
- Complete the prescribed number of reps with your right leg, then do the same number with your left (while holding the dumbbell in your left hand).

VARIATION #2
Single-Leg Bent-Knee Calf Raise

- Bend your knee, and hold it that way as you perform the exercise.

VARIATION #3
Single-Leg Donkey Calf Raise

- Keeping your back naturally arched, bend at your hips and lower your torso until your upper body is almost parallel to the floor.
- Complete the prescribed number of reps with your right leg, then do the same number with your left.

Don't round your lower back.

Place your hands on a sturdy object for support.

Raise your heel as high as you can.

Bend for More Muscle

Of the two muscles that make up your calf, your soleus is more involved in extending your ankle when your knee is bent. Your gastrocnemius takes on a greater workload when your knee is straight. As a result, bent-leg calf raises target your soleus best, while standing calf raises—performed with your knee straight—zero in on your gastrocnemius. That's why if your calves don't seem to be growing, many experts recommend doing both versions of the exercise.

225

THE BEST QUADRICEPS EXERCISE YOU'VE NEVER DONE
Wide-Grip Overhead Barbell Split Squat

This movement is known as a "big bang" exercise since it works so many muscles at once. While your legs are the obvious emphasis during the split-squat portion of the move, holding the weight over your head challenges your shoulders, arms, upper back, and core, too. So it's a great strength and muscle builder, but it also burns tons of calories. If you're intimidated by holding a barbell overhead, start by performing it with just a broomstick or a pole instead.

A

- Hold a barbell straight over your head with an overhand grip that's about twice shoulder width.
- Stand in a staggered stance with your feet 2 to 3 feet apart.

B

- Slowly lower your body as far as you can.
- Pause, then push yourself back up to the starting position as quickly as you can.
- Complete the prescribed number of repetitions with your left leg forward, then do the same number with your right leg in front.

Lock your elbows.

Hold your shoulders down and back. You should try to create as much space between your shoulders and your ears as you can.

Brace your core.

Your left foot should be in front of your right one.

Don't allow the bar to move forward as you squat.

Your arms should be straight.

Keep your torso upright for the entire movement.

Bend the knee of your front leg.

Your rear knee should nearly touch the floor.

THE BEST CALF EXERCISE YOU'VE NEVER DONE
Farmer's Walk on Toes

This exercise not only works your calves but also improves your cardiovascular fitness. Choose the heaviest pair of dumbbells that allows you to perform the exercise for 60 seconds. If you feel like you could have gone longer, grab heavier weights on your next set.

Keep your head up.

Stick your chest out.

Stand as tall as you can.

Walk on the balls of your feet.

A

- Grab a pair of heavy dumbbells and hold them at your sides at arm's length.

B

- Raise your heels and walk forward (or in a circle) for 60 seconds.

227

Quads & Calves

THE BEST STRETCH FOR YOUR QUADRICEPS
Kneeling Hip Flexor Stretch

Why it's good: This stretch loosens the muscles at the top of your thigh. When these muscles are tight, they pull your pelvis forward, which increases stress on your lower back and decreases the range of motion of your hips.

Make the most of it: Hold this stretch for 30 seconds on each side, then repeat twice for a total of three sets. Perform this routine daily, and up to three times a day if you're really tight.

Contract your left glute (butt).

Brace your abs.

Reach as far behind you as you can.

Hold this position.

You should feel this stretch here.

A
- Kneel down on your left knee, with your right foot on the floor and your right knee bent 90 degrees.
- Reach up with your right hand as high as you can.

B
- Bend your torso to your right.

C
- Rotate your torso to the right as you reach with your right hand as far behind you as you can. Hold this position for the prescribed length of time.
- Kneel on your right knee, switch arms, and repeat.

10

Percentage reduction in the risk of groin injury for every degree that you increase your hip range of motion, according to a study in the *Journal of Science and Medicine in Sport.*

THE BEST STRETCHES FOR YOUR CALVES

Straight-Leg Calf Stretch

Why it's good: It emphasizes your gastrocnemius.

Make the most of it: Hold this stretch for 30 seconds on each side, then repeat twice for a total of three sets. Perform this routine daily, and up to three times a day if you're really tight.

A

- Stand about 2 feet in front of a wall in a staggered stance.
- Place your hands on the wall and lean against it.
- Shift your weight to your back foot until you feel a stretch in your calf. Hold for the prescribed length of time.
- Switch leg positions and repeat.

Keep your arms straight.

Place your left foot in front of your right.

You should feel this stretch here.

Bent-Leg Calf Stretch

Why it's good: It emphasizes your soleus.

Make the most of it: Hold this stretch for 30 seconds on each side, then repeat twice for a total of three sets. Perform this routine daily, and up to three times a day if you're really tight.

A

- Perform this the same as the straight-leg calf stretch, only move your back foot forward so the toes of that foot are even with the heel of your front foot.
- Bend both knees until you feel a comfortable stretch just above the ankle of your back leg.

You should feel this stretch here.

Keep your heels down.

SAVE YOUR ANKLES
Researchers at the University of North Carolina found that people who sprain their ankles don't have the same range of motion in those joints as do folks who stay healthy. Tight gastrocnemius and soleus muscles limit ankle motion.

Quads & Calves

BUILD PERFECT QUADS AND CALVES

Try these workouts from Kelly Baggett, performance coach and co-owner of Transformation Clinics in Springfield, Missouri. The quadriceps routine is a create-your-own workout that's designed to increase the size and strength of your thighs. The calf workout is a personal favorite of Kelly's, since as he says, "You can do it anytime, anyplace." That includes your living room.

The Quad Workout

What to do: Choose one movement from Exercise Group A and one movement from Exercise Group B. For Exercise A, do four sets of 6 to 8 repetitions, resting for 3 minutes between sets. For Exercise B, do two sets of 10 to 12 repetitions for each leg, resting for 2 minutes between sets. Complete this workout once or twice a week.

EXERCISE GROUP A
Dumbbell squat (page 203)

Goblet squat (page 204)

Dumbbell front squat
(page 204)

Barbell squat (page 198)

Barbell squat with
heels raised (page 201)

Barbell front squat
(page 199)

EXERCISE GROUP B
Dumbbell reverse lunge
(page 217)

Barbell reverse lunge
(page 213)

Dumbbell Bulgarian
split squat (page 210)

Barbell Bulgarian
split squat (page 208)

Single-leg squat (page 196)

Pistol squat (page 197)

The Calf Workout

What to do: Do one set of each exercise, in the order shown and without resting. For each exercise, complete as many repetitions as you can. One note: Perform the exercises as directed in this chapter, only skip the dumbbells—the routine is designed to be done with just your body weight. Complete the workout twice a week.

EXERCISES
Single-leg calf raise
(page 225)

Single-leg bent-knee
calf raise (page 225)

Single-leg donkey raise
(page 225)

Chapter 9:
Glutes & Hamstrings
THE MUSCLES YOU CAN'T IGNORE

Glutes
& Hamstrings

Anytime you're standing, the muscles of your glutes and hamstrings are working. Trouble is, most of us are spending more and more of our days sitting—whether in front of a computer or 46-inch plasma. The impact of so much chair time: Our hip muscles not only become weak, they forget how to contract. This is especially true for your glutes. And that's a shame, since your glutes are your body's largest and perhaps most powerful muscle group.

What's more, when either your glutes or hamstrings are weak, it disrupts the muscular balance of your body, which can cause pain and injuries in your knees, hips, and lower back. The solution? Make working your glutes and hamstrings a top priority, using the exercises in this chapter.

Bonus Benefits

Greater calorie burn! Since the glutes are your biggest muscle group, they're also one of your top calorie burners.

Better posture! Weak glutes can cause your hips to tilt forward. This puts more stress on your spine. It also pushes your lower abdomen outward, making your belly stick out.

Healthier knees! Your anterior cruciate ligaments (ACLs) rely on your hamstrings to help them stabilize your knees. Having a strong set of hamstrings can help your ACLs do their job and lower your risk of injury.

Meet Your Muscles

Gluteus Medius and Gluteus Minimus
You have two other glute muscles: your gluteus medius [2] and gluteus minimus [3]. These assist your gluteus maximus in raising your thigh out to the side. They also rotate your thigh outward when your leg is straight, and inward when your hip is bent.

Hamstrings
The muscles known collectively as your hamstring [4] are actually three separate muscles: the biceps femoris [A], semitendinosus [B], and semimembranosus [C]. Their primary functions are to bend your knee and to help your gluteus maximus extend your hip. The biceps femoris also helps rotate your thigh outward; the semimembranosus and semitendinosus help rotate it inward.

Gluteus Maximus
You could just call the gluteus maximus [1] your butt muscle. That's because it creates the shape of your rear end. It's working anytime you raise your thigh out to your side, rotate your leg so that your foot is pointing outward, or thrust your hips forward. So if you're in a sitting or squatting position, your gluteus maximus helps you stand up by straightening your hips. As a result, it's working in most lower-body exercises, but particularly during the deadlift, hip raise, and reverse hip raise.

Did You Know?
The tendons of a pig's hamstring muscle can be used to suspend a ham during curing, which explains the origin of the muscle's name.

MUSCLE MISTAKE
You Work Your Quads Harder Than Your Hamstrings

A study in the *American Journal of Sports Medicine* found that 70 percent of athletes with recurrent hamstring injuries suffered from muscle imbalances between their quadriceps and hamstrings. After correcting the imbalances by strengthening the hamstrings, every person in the study went injury-free for the entire 12-month follow-up. Now that's strong medicine.

In this chapter, you'll find 62 exercises that target the muscles of your glutes and hamstrings. Throughout, you'll notice that certain exercises have been given the designation Main Move. Master this basic version of a movement, and you'll be able to do all of its variations with flawless form.

HIP RAISES

These exercises target the muscles of your glutes and hamstrings. What's more, they require you to activate your abdominal and lower-back muscles in order to keep your body stable—so they double as great core exercises.

MAIN MOVE
Hip Raises

A

• Lie faceup on the floor with your knees bent and your feet flat on the floor.

Make sure you're pushing with your heels. To make it easier, you can position your feet so that your toes rise off the floor.

Place your arms out to your sides at 45-degree angles, your palms facing up.

GET YOUR BUTT IN GEAR

If your hamstrings cramp when you perform the hip raise, it's often a sign that your glutes are weak. That's because your hamstrings are having to work extra hard to keep your hips raised. For best results, raise your hips and hold them that way for 3 to 5 seconds per repetition. Twice a week, do two or three sets of 10 to 12 reps.

B

- Raise your hips so your body forms a straight line from your shoulders to your knees.
- Pause for up to 5 seconds in the up position, then lower your body back to the starting position.

15

Minutes of exercise it takes to improve your mood, according to a study in the *Journal of Sports and Exercise Psychology*.

Push against the floor with your heels, not your toes.

Squeeze your glutes as you lift your hips.

Glutes & Hams | HIP RAISES

VARIATION #1
Weighted Hip Raise
- Place a weight plate on your hips and perform the exercise.

VARIATION #2
Hip Raise with Knee Press-Out
- Place a 20-inch mini-band just above your knees, and keep your knees from touching each other as you perform the movement.

Pushing outward against a band increases the activation of your gluteus maximus and gluteus medius.

VARIATION #3
Hip Raise with Knee Squeeze

A
- Place a rolled-up towel or an Airex pad between your knees, and hold it there as you perform the movement.

B
- Don't allow the pad to slip as you raise your hips until your body forms a straight line from your shoulders to your knees.

TRAINER'S TIP
Pay attention as you raise your hips: If your knees tend to fall outward as you do the exercise, you probably have weak hip adductors, or groin muscles. Keeping a towel or cushion from falling to the floor as you do the exercise helps strengthen these inner-thigh muscles.

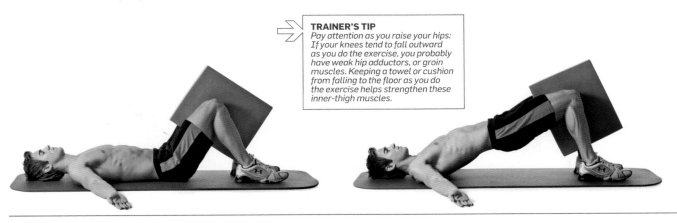

VARIATION #4
Marching Hip Raise
- Raise your hips and hold them that way.

- Lift one knee to your chest, lower back to the start, and lift your other knee to your chest. Continue to alternate back and forth.

VARIATION #5
Hip Raise with Feet on a Swiss Ball
- Perform the movement with your lower legs placed on a Swiss ball.

VARIATION #6
Marching Hip Raise with Feet on a Swiss Ball

A
- Place your feet flat on a Swiss ball.

B
- Lift one knee to your chest, lower back to the start, and lift your other knee to your chest. Continue to alternate back and forth.

Don't allow your hips to sag.

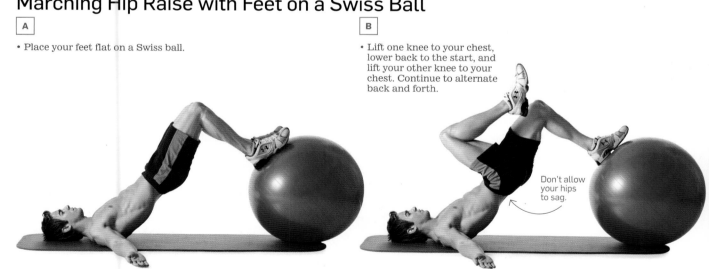

Glutes & Hams | HIP RAISES

MAIN MOVE
Single-Leg Hip Raise

A

- Lie faceup on the floor with your left knee bent and your right leg straight.
- Raise your right leg until it's in line with your left thigh.

Place your arms out to your sides at 45-degree angles to your torso, your palms facing up.

B

- Push your hips upward, keeping your left leg elevated.
- Pause, then slowly lower your body and leg back to the starting position.
- Complete the prescribed number of repetitions with your left leg, then switch legs and do the same number with your right leg.

Your right leg stays in line with your left thigh when you raise your hips.

Your body should form a straight line from your shoulders to your knees.

You can raise your toes to make sure you're pushing from your heel.

VARIATION #1
Single-Leg Hip Raise with Knee Hold

- Bring one knee toward your chest and hold it there as you perform the exercise.

TRAINER'S TIP
Holding one knee helps ensure you're using your glutes to raise your hips—and not your lower back muscles.

VARIATION #2
Single-Leg Hip Raise with Foot on a Bosu Ball

- Place your left foot on the Bosu ball.
- Raise your hips, lower, and repeat.

VARIATION #3
Single-Leg Hip Raise with Foot on Step

- Position your butt against a 6-inch step.
- Place your left foot on the step.
- Raise your hips, lower, and repeat.

VARIATION #4
Single-Leg Hip Raise with Foot on Bench

- Place your left heel on a bench, with your butt on the floor.
- Raise your hips, lower, and repeat.

VARIATION #5
Single-Leg Hip Raise with Foot on a Foam Roller

Placing your foot on a foam roller forces your stabilizer muscles to work harder to prevent the roller from moving forward or back.

- Place your left foot on a foam roller.
- Raise your hips, lower, and repeat.

VARIATION #6
Single-Leg Hip Raise with Foot on a Medicine Ball

Placing your foot on a medicine ball forces your stabilizer muscles to work harder to prevent the ball from moving forward or back, or from side to side.

- Place your left foot on a medicine ball.
- Raise your hips, lower, and repeat.

241

Glutes & Hams | HIP RAISES

VARIATION #7
Hip Raise with Head on a Bosu Ball
• Place your head and upper back on a Bosu ball.

Elevating your upper body increases the demand on your glutes.

VARIATION #8
Single-Leg Hip Raise with Head on a Bosu Ball
• Place your head and upper back on a Bosu ball, and hold your right leg in the air so that it's in line with your left thigh.

VARIATION #9
Hip Raise with Head on a Swiss Ball
• Place your head and upper back on a Swiss ball.

Performing this exercise on a Swiss ball forces your core to work harder in order to keep the ball from moving forward and back, or from side to side.

VARIATION #10
Single-Leg Hip Raise with Head on a Swiss Ball
• Place your head and upper back on a Swiss ball, and lift right leg in the air so that it's in line with your left thigh.

MAIN MOVE
Swiss-Ball Hip Raise and Leg Curl

A

- Lie faceup on the floor and place your lower legs and heels on a Swiss ball.

Place your arms out to your sides at 45-degree angles to your torso, your palms facing up.

B

- Push your hips up so that your body forms a straight line from your shoulders to your knees.

C

- Without pausing, pull your heels toward you and roll the ball as close as possible to your butt.

- Pause for 1 or 2 seconds, then reverse the motion, by rolling the ball back until your body is in a straight line. Lower your hips back to the floor.

hips in line with the rest of your body as you pull the ball toward you.

Muscle Moves

When doing the standard Swiss-ball hip raise and leg curl, your feet should point up. But by turning them in or out, you can change the part of your hamstrings that is targeted.

VARIATION #1
Swiss-Ball Hip Raise and Leg Curl with Toes Out
Place your lower legs on the ball with your heels touching and your toes pointing outward.

Turning your feet out emphasizes the hamstring muscles on the outside portion of your leg.

VARIATION #2
Swiss-Ball Hip Raise and Leg Curl with Toes In
Place your lower legs on the ball with your heels about shoulder-width apart and your toes pointing toward each other.

Turning your feet in emphasizes the hamstring muscles on the inside portion of your leg.

243

VARIATION #3
Single-Leg Swiss-Ball Hip Raise and Leg Curl

A

- Raise your right leg in the air so that it's a few inches off the ball, nearly in line with your left thigh.

Place your arms out to your sides at 45-degree angles to your torso, your palms facing up.

B

- Push your hips up so that your body forms a straight line from your shoulders to your knees.

Brace your core.

Squeeze your glutes as you lift your hips.

C

- Without pausing, pull your left heel toward you and roll the ball as close as possible to your butt.

You should really feel this in your right hamstring.

MAIN MOVE
Sliding Leg Curl

A

- Lie faceup on the floor and place each heel on a Valslide with your knees bent and your heels near your butt.

Brace your core and squeeze your glutes as you lift your hips.

B

- Keeping your hips in line with your torso, slide your heels out until your legs are straight.
- Reverse the movement back to the starting position.

Your body should form a straight line from your shoulders to your knees.

VARIATION
Single-Leg Sliding Leg Curl

A

- Raise your left leg in the air so that it's in line with your right thigh, and hold it that way as you perform the exercise.

B

- Keeping your hips in line with your torso, slide your heel out until your leg is straight.

Your body should form a straight line from your shoulders to your knees.

MUSCLE MISTAKE
You Only Do Machine Leg Curls

The machine leg curl requires you to flex your knees, a movement that is one of the jobs of your hamstrings. However, the main function of your hamstrings is to extend or push your hips forward, as you do in straight-leg deadlifts and hip raises. What's more, another type of leg curl—the Swiss-ball hip raise and leg curl—requires both knee flexion and hip extension. So it's a better choice than the classic machine version, too.

Glutes & Hams | HIP RAISES

MAIN MOVE
Reverse Hip Raise

A

- Lie chest down on the edge of a bench or Roman chair so that your torso is on the bench but your hips aren't.

Your legs should be nearly straight.

B

- Lift your legs until your thighs are in line with your torso.
- Pause, then lower to the starting position.

Squeeze your glutes as you lift your hips.

25

Minutes of weight training that actually improved the effectiveness of a subsequent flu shot, according to a study in *Brain, Behavior, and Immunity*. Scheduled to get pricked? Do your workout 6 to 12 hours beforehand.

VARIATION #1
Bent-Knee Reverse Hip Raise

• Start with your knees bent 90 degrees, and then straighten them as you raise your hips.

VARIATION #2
Swiss-Ball Reverse Hip Raise

• Instead of lying on a bench, lie on a Swiss ball and place your hands flat on the floor.

VARIATION #3
Bent-Knee Swiss-Ball Reverse Hip Raise

A

• Instead of lying on a bench, lie on a Swiss ball and place your hands flat on the floor.

B

• Straighten your legs as you raise your hips.

247

BENT-KNEE DEADLIFTS

These exercises target the muscles of your glutes and hamstrings, along with scores of others. In fact, because deadlifts strongly activate your quadriceps, core, back, and shoulder muscles, too, they're among the best total-body exercises you can do.

MAIN MOVE
Barbell Deadlift

A

- Load the barbell and roll it against your shins.
- Bend at your hips and knees and grab the bar with an overhand grip, your hands just beyond shoulder width.

B

- Without allowing your lower back to round, pull your torso back and up, thrust your hips forward, and stand up with the barbell.
- Squeeze your glutes as you perform the movement.
- Lower the bar to the floor, keeping it as close to your body as possible.

Your hips should be slightly higher than your knees.

Your lower back should be slightly arched, not rounded.

Your arms should be straight.

As you lift the bar, keep it as close to your body as possible.

TRAINER'S TIP
You can also perform the deadlift and wide-grip deadlift while standing with each foot on a 25-pound weight plate. This increases the distance you have to lift the weight, challenging your muscles even more.

VARIATION #1
Wide-Grip Barbell Deadlift

A

- Use an overhand grip that's about twice shoulder width.

B

- Once standing, reverse the movement and slowly lower the bar back to the floor.

THE ULTIMATE DEADLIFT?
Using a wider grip provides three bonus benefits: (1) It increases the demand on your upper-back muscles, (2) forces your forearm and hand muscles to work harder, and (3) boosts your range of motion.

This exercise is also called a snatch-grip deadlift, since you grasp the bar with the same grip that Olympic weightlifters use when performing the snatch.

VARIATION #2
Single-Leg Barbell Deadlift

- Place the instep of one foot on a bench that's about 2 feet behind you.
- Complete the prescribed number of reps with your right foot on the bench, then do the same number with your left foot on the bench.

VARIATION #3
Sumo Deadlift

- Stand with your feet about twice shoulder-width apart and your toes pointed out at an angle.
- Grasp the center of the bar with your hands 12 inches apart and palms facing you.

MAIN MOVE
Dumbbell Deadlift

A

- Set a pair of dumbbells on the floor in front of you.
- Bend at your hips and knees, and grab the dumbbells with an overhand grip.

B

- Without allowing your lower back to round, stand up with the dumbbells.
- Lower the dumbbells to the floor. (If you can't lower the dumbbells all the way to the floor while keeping a slight arch in your lower back, stop just above the point where it starts to round.)

1,008

Most weight, in pounds, ever deadlifted in competition.

As you rise, pull your torso back and up.

Thrust your hips forward.

Keep your chest up.

Your arms should be straight, and your lower back slightly arched, not rounded.

VARIATION #1
Single-Arm Deadlift

A

- Use just one dumbbell for this version of the exercise. Place the dumbbell on the floor next to your right ankle. If you can't pick up the dumbbell while keeping a slight arch in your lower back, start the exercise just above the point where your lower back starts to round. (As shown in the photo.)

B

- Complete the prescribed number of repetitions with the weight in your right hand, then do the same number with it in your left.

This exercise is also called the suitcase deadlift, since it's the same movement you use to pick up luggage.

VARIATION #2
Single-Leg Dumbbell Deadlift

A

- Grab a pair of light dumbbells and stand on your left foot.
- Lift your right foot behind you and bend your knee so your right lower leg is parallel to the floor.

B

- Bend forward at your hips, and slowly lower your body as far as you can, or until your right lower leg almost touches the floor.
- Pause, then push your body back to the starting position.
- Complete the prescribed number of reps while standing on your left leg, then do the same number on your right leg.

Pull your shoulders back and stick your chest out.

Keep your head up.

Don't round your lower back.

Bend your knee 90 degrees.

251

STRAIGHT-LEG DEADLIFTS

These exercises target the muscles of your glutes and hamstrings. They also work your core, especially the muscles of your lower back. One other benefit: They can help improve the flexibility of your hamstrings, since they stretch those muscles every time you lower the weight.

MAIN MOVE
Barbell Straight-Leg Deadlift

A

- Grab a barbell with an overhand grip that's just beyond shoulder width, and hold it at arm's length in front of your hips.

Push your chest out.

Brace your core.

Your knees should be slightly bent.

Set your feet hip-width apart.

TRAINER'S TIP
To lift your torso back to the starting position, squeeze your glutes and thrust your hips forward. This ensures you're engaging your hip muscles, instead of relying more on your lower back.

B

- Without changing the bend in your knees, bend at your hips and lower your torso until it's almost parallel to the floor.
- Pause, then raise your torso back to the starting position.

Don't round your lower back. It should stay naturally arched as you lower your body.

Keep your core stiff throughout the entire movement.

Glutes & Hams | STRAIGHT-LEG DEADLIFTS

VARIATION #1
Single-Leg Barbell Straight-Leg Deadlift
- Perform the movement while balanced on one leg, instead of two.
- Complete the prescribed number of repetitions with the same leg, then do the same number on your other leg.

VARIATION #2
Barbell Good Morning
- Instead of holding the barbell at arm's length in front your body, position it across your upper back and hold it with an overhand grip.

VARIATION #3
Split Barbell Good Morning

A

- Position the barbell across your upper back and hold it with an overhand grip.
- Stand about a foot in front of a 6-inch step, and place your left heel on it.

B

- Keeping your lower back naturally arched, bend forward at your hips as far as you comfortably can.
- Pause, then raise your torso back to the starting position.

Brace your core.

Your right knee should be slightly bent.

Don't round your lower back.

Your left leg should be completely straight.

VARIATION #4
Single-Leg Barbell Good Morning

- Position the barbell across your upper back and hold it with an overhand grip.
- Perform the movement while balanced on one leg, instead of two.

Pull your shoulders back so that the bar rests comfortably on the shelf created by your shoulder blades.

VARIATION #5
Zercher Good Morning

- Position the barbell in the crooks of your arms, and hold it tightly against your body as you do the movement.

You can also wrap a towel around the bar or use a bar pad for cushioning.

To secure the bar, squeeze your forearms to your upper arms.

VARIATION #6
Seated Barbell Good Morning

A

- Sit upright on a bench and hold a barbell across your upper back.

Set your feet wide and keep them flat on the floor.

B

- Keeping the natural arch in your lower back, bend forward at your hips and lower your torso as far as you comfortably can.
- Pause, then raise your torso back to the starting position.

Keep your core tight.

Glutes & Hams | STRAIGHT-LEG DEADLIFTS

MAIN MOVE
Dumbbell Straight-Leg Deadlift

A

- Grab a pair of dumbbells with an overhand grip, and hold them at arm's length in front of your thighs.
- Stand with your feet hip-width apart and your knees slightly bent.

Brace your core.

B

- Without changing the bend in your knees, bend at your hips, and lower your torso until it's almost parallel to the floor.
- Pause, then raise your torso back to the starting position.

Your back should stay naturally arched throughout the entire movement.

As you lower the weight, keep the dumbbells as close to your body as possible.

2
Times better people did on cognitive tests after exercising while listening to music compared to sweating in silence, according to an Ohio State University study.

VARIATION #1
Single-Leg Dumbbell Straight-Leg Deadlift

A

- Perform a dumbbell straight-leg deadlift while balanced on one leg, instead of two.

B

- Complete the prescribed number of repetitions with the same leg, then do the same number on your other leg.

Your right leg should stay in line with your body.

VARIATION #2
Rotational Dumbbell Straight-Leg Deadlift

A

- Grab a light dumbbell in your right hand and stand on your left foot with your knee slightly bent.
- Lift your right foot off the floor and bend your knee slightly.

B

- Without changing the bend in your left knee, bend at your hips and lower your torso as you rotate it to the left and touch the dumbbell to your left foot.
- Pause, then raise your torso back to the starting position.
- Complete the prescribed number of repetitions standing on your left foot, with the weight in your right hand. Then do the same number on your right foot, with the weight in your left hand.

Keep your core tight.

Hold the dumbbell so that it hangs vertically.

Glutes & Hams | STRAIGHT-LEG DEADLIFTS

MAIN MOVE
Back Extension

A

- Position yourself in the back-extension station and hook your feet under the leg anchors.
- Keeping your back naturally arched, lower your upper body as far as you comfortably can.

Don't allow your lower back to round.

Cross your arms over your chest.

B

- Squeeze your glutes and raise your torso until it's in line with your lower body.
- Pause, then slowly lower your torso back to the starting position.

Your shoulder blades should be pulled together.

You should have a natural arch in your lower back.

Single-Leg Back Extension

A

- Position yourself in the back-extension station with just one foot hooked under the leg anchors.

Keep your core braced.

B

Don't hyperextend your back; raise until your body forms a straight line.

258

MAIN MOVE
Cable Pull Through

A

- Attach a rope handle to the low pulley of a cable machine.
- Grab an end of the rope in each hand and stand with your back to the weight stack.
- Bend at your hips and knees and lower your torso until it's at about a 45-degree angle to the floor.

B

- Thrust your hips forward and raise your torso back to the starting position.

Your arms should stay straight for the entire movement.

Keep your lower back naturally arched throughout the entire movement.

Squeeze your glutes as you push your hips forward.

Your knees should be slightly bent.

Set your feet shoulder-width apart.

STEPUPS

These exercises target the muscles of your glutes and hamstrings. That's because you have to push your hips forward forcefully to perform the movements. Stepups also work your quadriceps, since they require you to straighten your knee against resistance.

MAIN MOVE
Barbell Stepup

A

- Stand in front of a bench or step, and place your left foot firmly on the step.

B

- Press your left heel into the step and push your body up until your left leg is straight.
- Then lower your body back down until your right foot touches the floor, and repeat.
- Complete the prescribed number of repetitions with your left leg, then do the same number with your right leg.

Pull your shoulders back so that the bar rests comfortably on the shelf created by your shoulder blades.

The step should be high enough that your knee is bent at least 90 degrees.

Your left foot stays in this position for the entire exercise.

Keep your right foot elevated.

VARIATION
Barbell Lateral Stepup

A

- Stand with your left side next to a step, and place your left foot on the step.

B

- Push your body up as you would for a standard barbell stepup. Then lower yourself back down. Complete the prescribed number of reps with your left leg, then do the same number with your right leg.

Keep your torso upright as you lift your body.

Make sure that your right foot is parallel to your left foot when you touch down.

Glutes & Hams | STEPUPS

MAIN MOVE
Dumbbell Stepup

A

- Grab a pair of dumbbells and hold them at arm's length at your sides. Stand in front of a bench or step, and place your left foot firmly on the step.

- The step should be high enough that your knee is bent 90 degrees.

B

- Press your left heel into the step and push your body up until your left leg is straight and you're standing on one leg on the bench, keeping your right foot elevated.

- Lower your body back down until your right foot touches the floor. That's one repetition.

- Complete the prescribed number of repetitions with your left leg, then do the same number with your right leg.

VARIATION #1
Lateral Dumbbell Stepup

A

- Grab a pair of dumbbells and stand with your left side next to a step.
- Place your left foot on the step.

B

- Press your left foot into the bench and push your body up until both legs are straight.
- Lower back down to the starting position.
- Complete the prescribed number of reps with your left leg, then do the same number with your right leg.

Make sure that your right foot is parallel to your left foot when you touch down.

VARIATION #2
Crossover Dumbbell Stepup

A

- Grab a pair of dumbbells and stand with your left side next to a step.
- Place your right foot on the step.

B

- Press your right foot into the bench and push your body up until both legs are straight.
- Lower your body back down to the starting position.
- Complete the prescribed number of reps with your right leg, then do the same number with your left leg.

Your right leg should cross in front of your left leg.

HIP ABDUCTION These exercises target your hip abductors, primarily a hip muscle called the *gluteus medius.*

MAIN MOVE
Standing Cable Hip Abduction

A

- Attach an ankle strap to the low pulley of a cable station, and then place the strap around your left ankle.

- Stand with your right side facing the weight stack.

- Let your left leg cross in front of your right leg. (You should be standing far enough away from the machine that the cable remains taut.)

Stand tall; don't slump.

Place your hand on a sturdy object for support.

Your left leg should be nearly straight.

- Without changing the bend in your knee, raise your left leg out to your left side as far as you can.

- Pause, then slowly return to the starting position.

- Complete the prescribed number of repetitions with your left leg, then turn around and do the same number with your right leg.

5

Weeks it takes to make exercise a habit, according to a study from the University of Sheffield in England.

Glutes & Hams

THE BEST EXERCISE YOU'VE NEVER DONE
Single-Arm Dumbbell Swing

This movement works your hamstrings and glutes explosively. That means you'll target your very important fast-twitch muscle fibers. These are the fibers that atrophy fastest with age and that are crucial in almost every activity you do—even simply raising yourself out of a chair. So you might say this exercise will help keep your body young. It also works your core, quadriceps, and shoulder muscles, making it a great move for anyone who's short on training time.

A

- Grab a dumbbell with an overhand grip and hold it in front of your waist at arm's length. (You can also do the exercise two handed, holding the dumbbell with both hands.)

- Bend at your hips and knees and lower your torso until it forms a 45-degree angle to the floor.

- Swing the dumbbell between your legs.

B

- Keeping your arm straight, thrust your hips forward, straighten your knees, and swing the dumbbell up to chest level as you rise to standing position.

- Now squat back down as you swing the dumbbell between your legs again.

- Swing the weight back and forth forcefully.

BONUS EXERCISE!

Kettlebell Swing

- Perform the same movement while grasping a kettlebell instead of a dumbbell.

Keep your lower back slightly arched.

Your arm should swing up from your momentum.

Push your hips back.

Swing the dumbbell between your legs.

Set your feet wider than shoulder-width apart.

THE BEST STRETCH FOR YOUR HAMSTRINGS
Standing Hamstring Stretch

Why it's good: It stretches your hamstrings from both your hip and your knee. Bending your knee more increases the stretch near your hip; keeping it straight increases the stretch at your knee.

Make the most of it: Hold this stretch for 30 seconds on each side, then repeat two times. Do the routine daily, and up to three times a day if you're really tight.

A

- Place your left foot on a bench or secure chair.
- Your left leg should be completely straight.
- Your right leg should be slightly bent.
- Stand tall with your back naturally arched.
- Place your hands on your hips.

B

- Without rounding your lower back, bend at the hips and lower your torso until you feel a comfortable stretch, and hold that position for the prescribed amount of time.

Rotating your toes outward emphasizes the inner portion of your hamstring; rotating your toes inward emphasizes the outer portion.

You should feel this stretch here.

Glutes & Hams

THE BEST STRETCH FOR YOUR GLUTES
Lying Glute Stretch

Why it's good:
It loosens your glutes. When these muscles are tight, you may be more likely to experience lower back pain.

Make the most of it: Hold this stretch for 30 seconds on each side, then repeat twice for a total of three sets. Perform this routine daily, and up to three times a day if you're really tight.

A

- Lie faceup on the floor with your knees and hips bent.
- Cross your left leg over your right so that your left ankle sits across your right thigh.

B

- Grab your left knee with both hands and pull it toward the middle of your chest until you feel a comfortable stretch in your glutes.

You should feel the stretch here.

Turn the page to learn how to
BUILD THE PERFECT BACKSIDE

Glutes & Hams

BUILD THE PERFECT BACKSIDE

Sculpt your glutes and hamstrings with this 4-week workout program from Mike Robertson, CSCS, co-owner of Indianapolis Fitness and Sports Training.

While this routine is designed to work your entire lower body—including your quadriceps—as well as your core, its main focus is on the muscles on the backs of your thighs. This helps to shore up the long-time weaknesses that contribute to poor posture and, as a result, often lead to back pain and a less-attractive physique. And, of course, because you're working your big lower-body muscles, you'll burn a ton of calories. So as a bonus, this workout will help melt your middle, too.

For a training plan that works your entire body, combine the "Build the Perfect Backside" routine with the "Build Perfect Shoulders" upper-body workout on page 144. Simply do this lower-body workout on the day after you do the upper-body workout.

What to do: Do each workout once a week, resting for at least 2 days between sessions. So you might do Workout A on Tuesday and Workout B on Friday. Perform the warmup before each workout. It's designed to help improve your flexibility and also prepare your muscles for the work that's about to come. Note that in each workout, the number of repetitions you perform increases each week. This helps ensure that you're continually challenging your muscles.

Warmup

Alternate back and forth between these movements without resting. Hold each exercise for 30 seconds before moving on to the other. Complete a total of three sets of each.

Kneeling hip flexor stretch (page 228)
Hip raise (page 236)

Workout A

EXERCISE	WEEK 1			WEEK 2			WEEK 3			WEEK 4		
	SETS	REPS	REST	SETS	REPS	REST	SETS	REPS	REST	SETS	REPS	REST
Barbell straight-leg deadlift (page 252)	2	8	90	3	8	90	3	10	90	3	12	90
Dumbbell split squat (page 209)	2	8	90	3	8	90	3	10	90	3	12	90
Single-leg barbell straight-leg deadlift (page 254)	2	8	90	3	8	90	3	10	90	3	12	90
Back extension (page 258)	2	8	60	3	8	60	3	10	60	3	12	60
Barbell rollout (page 292)	2	8	60	3	8	60	3	10	60	3	12	60

Workout B

EXERCISE	WEEK 1			WEEK 2			WEEK 3			WEEK 4		
	SETS	REPS	REST	SETS	REPS	REST	SETS	REPS	REST	SETS	REPS	REST
Braced squat (page 194)	2	8	90	3	8	90	3	10	90	3	12	90
Cable pull through (page 259)	2	8	90	3	8	90	3	10	90	3	12	90
Dumbbell stepup (page 262)	2	8	90	3	8	90	3	10	90	3	12	90
Swiss-ball hip raise and leg curl (page 243)	2	8	60	3	8	60	3	10	60	3	12	60
Plank (page 278)	2	8	60	3	8	60	3	10	60	3	12	60

Chapter 10: Core

YOUR CENTER OF ATTRACTION

Core

I f the number of infomercial products is any indication, people spend more money on their abs than on any other muscle group. And why wouldn't they? Your abs—or more specifically, your core, which also includes the muscles of your lower back and hips—are involved in every single movement you do. And not just in the gym. If it weren't for your core muscles, you wouldn't even be able to stand or sit upright.

Of course, all of this usually has little to do with most guys' desire for abs that show. Their true motivation is that a visible six-pack is highly appealing to the opposite sex. Perhaps that's because defined abs are an outward sign of a healthy, fit body. The take-home message: Sculpting a rock-solid midsection makes your body not only look better, but work better, too.

Bonus Benefits

Live longer! A Canadian study of more than 8,000 people over 13 years found that those with the weakest abdominal muscles had a death rate more than twice that of the people with the strongest midsections.

Lift more! A stronger core supports your spine, making your entire body more structurally sound. That allows you to use heavier weights on every exercise.

A pain-free back! California State University researchers found that when men followed a 10-week core workout program, they experienced 30 percent less back pain.

Meet Your Muscles

Abdominals

There's no doubt that the most popular abs muscle is the rectus abdominis [1], also known as the six-pack. Despite its nickname, this muscle actually consists of eight segments that are separated by a dense connective tissue called fascia [A]. This muscle is one of those that counteract the pull of the muscles that extend your lower back, helping to keep your spine stable. Its other main duty is to pull your torso toward your hips. That's why you can work this muscle by doing situps and crunches. However, the best way to train your rectus abdominis—and your core as a whole—is with spinal stability exercises, such as the plank and side plank.

The abs muscles on the sides of your torso are the external obliques [2] and internal obliques [3]. These muscles help bend your torso to your side, help rotate your torso to your left and right, and perhaps most important, actually act to resist your torso from rotating. So rotational exercises such as the kneeling rotational chop train these muscles, as do antirotation exercises like the kneeling stability chop.

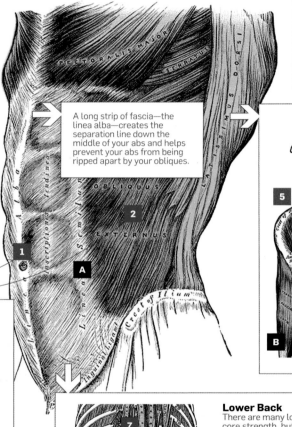

A long strip of fascia—the linea alba—creates the separation line down the middle of your abs and helps prevent your abs from being ripped apart by your obliques.

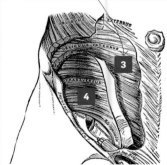

Your deepest abdominal muscle is the transverse abdominis [4]. This muscle lies beneath your rectus abdominis and obliques, and its job is to pull your abdominal wall inward—as when you're sucking in your gut.

YOUR CORE, DEFINED

While it's common to use the words *core* and *abs* interchangeably, it's not entirely accurate. That's because the term *core* actually describes the more than two dozen abdominal, lower-back, and hip muscles that stabilize your spine to keep your torso upright. What's more, your core muscles allow you to bend your torso forward, back, and from side to side, as well as rotate. As a result, your core is critical in everything you do—except, perhaps, sleeping.

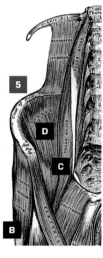

Hips

A group of muscles on the fronts of your hips, known as your hip flexors [5], also play a valuable role in core strength. The reason: They originate on either your spine or pelvis, an area that you might call the ground floor of your core. A number of muscles qualify as hip flexors, but the main ones are the tensor fascia latae [B], psoas [C], and iliacus [D]. As the name suggests, these muscles allow you flex your hips. To visualize, imagine raising your upper legs toward your chest. You can target these muscles with exercises such as the reverse crunch and the hanging leg raise.

Lower Back

There are many lower-back muscles that contribute to your core strength, but for simplicity's sake, the main ones are your erector spinae (shown as sacropsinalis) [6], multifidus [7], and quadratus lumborum [8]. Collectively, these muscles help keep your spine stable and also allow it to bend backward and to the side. They're best trained with stability exercises such as the plank, side plank, and the prone cobra, and also with any exercise that requires you to bend or pull.

What's more, even though your gluteus maximus is technically a hip muscle—and was covered in depth in Chapter 9—it's also worth mentioning here. That's because it's attached to your lower back by connective tissue and, therefore, works in conjunction with your other core muscles.

Core | STABILITY EXERCISES

In this chapter, you'll find more than 100 exercises that target the muscles of your core. You'll notice that certain exercises have been designated as a Main Move. Master this basic version of an exercise, and you'll be able to do all its variations with flawless form.

STABILITY EXERCISES

These exercises improve your ability to stabilize your spine. This is essential for lower-back health and peak performance in any sport. But don't worry: Stability exercises are also highly effective at working the abdominal muscles that are most visible— including the ones that make up your six-pack.

MAIN MOVE
Plank

- Start to get into a pushup position, but bend your elbows and rest your weight on your forearms instead of on your hands.

- Your body should form a straight line from your shoulders to your ankles.

- Brace your core by contracting your abs as if you were about to be punched in the gut.

- Hold this position for 30 seconds—or as directed—while breathing deeply.

IF YOU CAN'T HOLD THE PLANK POSITION FOR 30 SECONDS, *hold for 5 to 10 seconds, rest for 5 seconds, and repeat as many times as needed to total 30 seconds. Each time you perform the exercise, try to hold each repetition a little longer so that you reach your 30-second goal with fewer repetitions. Want more options? Try the 45-degree plank, the kneeling plank, or the quadruped, and work your way up to the plank.*

Squeeze your glutes.

If you were to place a broomstick on your back, it should make contact with your head, upper back, and butt.

Your elbows should be directly under your shoulders.

MUSCLE MISTAKE
You Think Crunches Make You Thin

Researchers at the University of Virginia found that it takes 250,000 crunches to burn 1 pound of fat—that's 100 crunches a day for 7 years. So simply working the muscles buried beneath your gut won't give you a six-pack. Your best strategy for fat loss is to work all of the muscles of your body, spending most of your time training the big muscles of your lower body and back. That's because the more muscles you work, the more calories you burn.

279

Core | STABILITY EXERCISES

VARIATION #1
45-Degree Plank
- Place your forearms on a bench instead of on the floor.

The plank is easier when you place your elbows on a bench, since you don't have to support as much of your body weight.

Your elbows should be placed so that your arms and torso form a 90-degree angle.

VARIATION #2
Kneeling Plank
- Instead of performing the exercise with your legs straight, bend your knees so that they help support your body weight.

Your body should form a straight line from your shoulders to your knees.

VARIATION #3
Elevated-Feet Plank
- Place both feet on a bench.

Elevating your feet increases the difficulty of the exercise.

VARIATION #4
Single-Leg Elevated-Feet Plank
- Place one foot on a bench and hold your other foot a couple of inches above it. Switch legs each set.

VARIATION #5
Extended Plank
- Place your weight on your hands (as you would for a pushup) and position them 6 to 8 inches in front of your shoulders.

The farther your hands are in front of you, the harder the exercise.

VARIATION #6
Wide-Stance Plank with Leg Lift
- Move your feet out wider than your shoulders, and hold one foot a few inches off the floor. Switch legs each set.

VARIATION #7
Wide-Stance Plank with Diagonal Arm Lift

- Move your feet out wider than your shoulders, instead of placing them close together.

- Raise and straighten your right arm—with your thumb pointing up—and hold it diagonally in relation to your torso.

- Hold for 5 to 10 seconds and switch arms. That's one rep.

VARIATION #8
Wide-Stance Plank with Opposite Arm and Leg Lift

- Move your feet out wider than your shoulders.

- Hold your left foot and your right arm off the floor for 5 to 10 seconds, then switch arms and legs and repeat. That's one rep.

When you raise your arm and leg, focus on holding your hips and torso in place.

VARIATION #9
Swiss-Ball Plank

- Place your forearms on a Swiss ball and your feet on a bench.

TWICE THE ABS WORKOUT
Canadian researchers determined that your abs work nearly twice as hard when you do a plank on a Swiss ball instead of on the floor.

VARIATION #10
Swiss-Ball Plank with Feet on Bench

- Place your forearms on a Swiss ball.

Putting your feet in on the bench raises your feet to the same level as your elbows, similar to how you would be on the floor—only the instability of the Swiss ball makes it harder to hold your position.

Core | STABILITY EXERCISES

MAIN MOVE
Quadruped

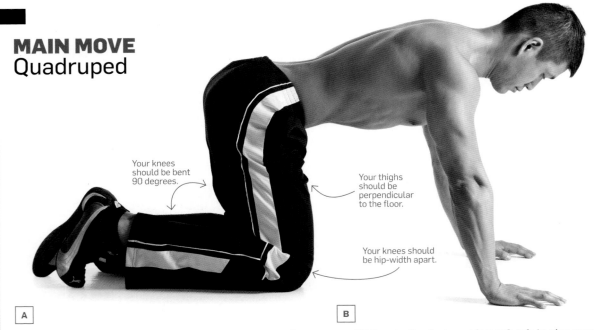

Your knees should be bent 90 degrees.

Your thighs should be perpendicular to the floor.

Your knees should be hip-width apart.

A

- Get down on your hands and knees with your palms flat on the floor and shoulder-width apart.
- Relax your core so that your lower back and abdomen are in their natural positions.

B

- Without allowing your lower back to rise or round, brace your abs as if you were about to be punched in the gut. Hold your abs tight for 5 to 10 seconds, breathing deeply throughout the exercise. That's one repetition.

VARIATION #1
Fire Hydrant In-Out

A

- Without allowing your lower-back posture to change, raise your right knee as close as you can to your chest. (Your knee may not move forward much.)

B

- Keeping your right knee bent, raise your thigh out to the side without moving your hips.

C

- Kick your raised right leg straight back until it's in line with your torso. That's one rep.

VARIATION #2
Quadruped with Leg Lift

- Without allowing your lower-back posture to change, raise and straighten your left leg until it's in line with your body. Hold for 5 to 10 seconds.
- Return to the starting position. Repeat with your right leg. Continue to alternate back and forth.

Brace your abs.

VARIATION #3
Bird Dog

- Brace your abs, and raise your right arm and left leg until they're in line with your body. Hold for 5 to 10 seconds.
- Return to the starting position. Repeat with your left arm and right leg. Continue to alternate back and forth.

Try to keep your hips and lower back still, even as you switch arms and legs.

Swiss-Ball Opposite Arm and Leg Lift

- Lie belly-side down with your navel over the center of a Swiss ball.
- You should be on the balls of both feet, with your hands placed flat on the floor.
- Brace your abs, and raise your right arm and left leg until they're in line with your body and hold that position for a few seconds.
- Return to the starting position. Repeat with your left arm and right leg. Continue to alternate back and forth.

Cat Camel

- Position yourself on your hands and knees.
- Gently arch your lower back—don't push—then lower your head between your shoulders and raise your upper back toward the ceiling, rounding your spine. That's one repetition.
- Move back and forth slowly, without pushing at either end of the movement.

Floss Away Back Pain

The cat camel may look funny, but slowly flexing and extending your spine in small ranges of motion is a great way to prepare your core for any activity. What's more, this movement can help prevent back pain because it "flosses" the nerves of your lower back as they exit your spinal canal. This helps keep the nerves from becoming pinched, lowering your risk of painful conditions such as sciatica. It can also help free a nerve that's already impinged. A good routine: Do 5 to 10 reps.

Core | STABILITY EXERCISES

MAIN MOVE
Side Plank

A

- Lie on your left side with your knees straight.
- Prop your upper body up on your left elbow and forearm.

B

- Brace your core by contracting your abs forcefully as if you were about to be punched in the gut.
- Raise your hips until your body forms a straight line from your ankles to your shoulders.
- Breathe deeply for the duration of the exercise.
- Hold this position for 30 seconds (or as directed). That's one set.
- Turn around so that you're lying on your right side and repeat.

IF YOU CAN'T HOLD THE SIDE PLANK FOR 30 SECONDS, *hold for 5 to 10 seconds, rest for 5 seconds, and repeat as many times as needed to total 30 seconds. Each time you perform the exercise, try to hold each repetition a little longer, so that you reach your 30-second goal with fewer repetitions.*

Place your right hand on your hip.

Your head should stay in line with your body.

Keep your hips raised and pushed forward.

Position your elbow under your shoulder.

VARIATION #1
Modified Side Plank
• Bend your knees 90 degrees.

Bending your knees reduces the amount of your body weight that you have to lift.

VARIATION #2
Rolling Side Plank
• Start by performing a side plank with your right side down. Hold for 1 second or 2 seconds, then roll your body over onto both elbows—into a plank—and hold for a second. Next, roll all the way up onto your left elbow so that you're performing a side plank facing the opposite direction. Hold for another second or two. That's one repetition. Make sure to move your entire body as a single unit each time you roll.

VARIATION #3
Side Plank with Feet on Bench
• Place both feet on a bench.

Elevating your feet increases the difficulty.

VARIATION #4
Side Plank with Feet on Swiss Ball
• Place both feet on a Swiss ball.

The instability of the Swiss ball forces your core to work even harder.

VARIATION #5
Single-Leg Side Plank
• Raise your top leg as high as you can and hold it that way for the duration of the exercise.

Keep your core braced.

VARIATION #6
Side Plank with Knee Tuck
• Lift your bottom leg toward your chest and hold it that way for the duration of the exercise.

Don't drop your hips or round your lower back.

Core | STABILITY EXERCISES

VARIATION #7
Side Plank with Reach Under

- Lift your body into a side plank, and start with your right arm raised straight above you so that it's perpendicular to the floor.

- Reach under and behind your torso with your right hand, then lift your arm back up to the starting position. That's one rep.

Keeping your abs braced, rotate your torso to your right as you reach behind you with your right arm.

VARIATION #8
Plyometric Side Plank

- Raise your top leg slightly, and move it forward and back at an even tempo.

Moving your leg back and forth increases the challenge to your core by forcing you to stabilize your weight under conditions of varying force and movements.

Before attempting this exercise, you should be able to hold the side plank for 60 seconds.

VARIATION #9
Side Plank and Row

- Attach a handle to the low pulley of a cable machine and grab it with your right hand.

- Brace your core and raise your body into a side plank.

Your arm should be straight.

- Bend your elbow and pull the handle to your rib cage, keeping your hips pushed up and forward.

- Slowly straighten your arm back out in front of you. That's one repetition.

Resist the urge to rotate at the hips or shoulders.

The cable should be taut.

T-Stabilization

A

- Assume a pushup position.
- Your body should form a straight line from your head to your ankles.

Brace your core.

B

- Keeping your arms straight and your body rigid, shift your weight onto your left arm and rotate your torso up and to the right until you're facing sideways.
- Pause for 3 seconds, then lower back down to the starting position.
- Rotate to your left. That's one rep.
- Continue to rotate back and forth.

Keep your core stiff as you rotate from side to side.

Do You Measure Up?

Researchers in Finland found that people with poor muscular endurance in their lower backs are 3.4 times more likely to develop lower-back problems than those who have fair or good endurance. And turns out, a side-plank test is one of the best ways to gauge this endurance. Simply perform a side plank for as long as you can without allowing your hips to drop or drift backward. A good score: 60 seconds. If you don't meet this standard, start focusing more on your core.

MAIN MOVE
Mountain Climber

A

- Assume a pushup position with your arms completely straight.

Your body should form a straight line from your head to your ankles.

Brace your core.

B

- Lift your right foot off the floor and slowly raise your knee as close to your chest as you can.
- Touch the floor with your right foot.
- Return to the starting position.
- Repeat with your left leg. Alternate back and forth for 30 seconds.

Don't change your lower-back posture as you lift your knee.

VARIATION #1
Mountain Climber with Hands on Bench
- Place your hands on a bench, then alternate raising each knee.

VARIATION #2
Mountain Climber with Hands on Medicine Ball
- Place your hands on a medicine ball, then alternate raising each knee.

VARIATION #3
Mountain Climber with Hands on Swiss Ball
- Place your hands on a Swiss ball, then alternate raising each knee.

VARIATION #4
Mountain Climber with Feet on Valslides
- Place each foot on a Valslide and bring one knee toward your chest by sliding your foot forward.

As in the standard mountain climber, you can also perform this move with your hands on a bench, Swiss ball, or medicine ball.

VARIATION #5
Cross-Body Mountain Climber
- Raise your right knee toward your left elbow, lower, and then raise your left knee to your right elbow.

VARIATION #6
Cross-Body Mountain Climber with Feet on Swiss Ball
- With your feet on a Swiss ball, raise one knee toward your left elbow, lower, then raise the other knee.

Swiss-Ball Rollout

A

- Sit on your knees in front of a Swiss ball and place your forearms and fists on the ball.

Keep your core braced.

Your elbows should be bent about 90 degrees.

Your lower back should be naturally arched.

B

- Slowly roll the ball forward, straightening your arms and extending your body as far as you can without allowing your lower back to "collapse."

- Use your abdominal muscles to pull the ball back to your knees.

Don't let your hips sag.

Keep your core braced.

Barbell Rollout

A

- Load a barbell with a 10-pound plate on each side and affix collars.

- Kneel on the floor and grab the bar with an overhand, shoulder-width grip.

- Your shoulders should start over the barbell.

B

- Slowly roll the bar forward, extending your body as far as you can without allowing your hips to sag.

- Use your abdominal muscles to pull the bar back to your knees.

Stiffen your core and squeeze your glutes to keep your lower back from collapsing.

Your shoulders should start over the barbell.

MAIN MOVE
Slide Out

A

- Kneel on the floor and place both hands on a Valslide.

Keep your body rigid.

Your hands should be under your shoulders.

B

- Slowly push the Valslide forward, extending your body as far as you can without allowing your hips to sag.
- Use your abdominal muscles to pull your hands back to below your shoulders.

VARIATION
Single-Arm Slide Out

A

- Place each hand on a Valslide and assume a pushup position with your arms completely straight and your legs extended.

Your body should form a straight line from your head to your ankles.

B

- Slide your right hand out in front of you as you bend your left arm to lower your body.
- Slowly push the Valslide forward, extending your body as far as you can without allowing your hips to sag.
- Your body should remain rigid for the entire movement.
- Repeat with your left hand. Alternate back and forth with each repetition.

Core | STABILITY EXERCISES

Lateral Roll

A

- Lie with your upper back placed firmly on a Swiss ball.
- Raise your hips so that your body forms a straight line from your knees to your shoulders.
- Hold a pole or broomstick, with your arms straight out from your sides.

B

- Without allowing your hips or arms to sag, roll across the Swiss ball as far as you can, taking tiny steps with your feet.
- Reverse directions and roll as far as you can to the other side.

Keep your core braced.

Don't drop your hips.

Static Back Extension

A

- Position yourself in the back-extension station and hook your feet under the leg anchors.
- Raise your torso until it's in line with your lower body.
- Hold this position for 60 seconds, or until you can't maintain perfect form.

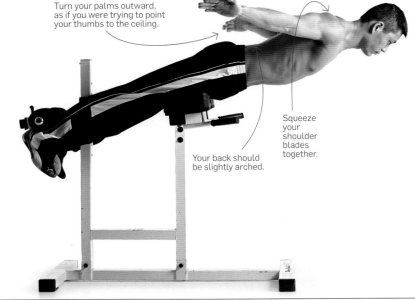

Turn your palms outward, as if you were trying to point your thumbs to the ceiling.

Squeeze your shoulder blades together.

Your back should be slightly arched.

Prone Cobra

A

- Lie facedown on the floor with your legs straight and your arms next to your sides, palms down.

B

- Contract your glutes and the muscles of your lower back, and raise your head, chest, arms, and legs off the floor.

- Simultaneously rotate your arms so that your thumbs point toward the ceiling. At this time, your hips should be the only parts of your body touching the floor. Hold this position for 60 seconds.

IF YOU CAN'T HOLD THE PRONE COBRA FOR 60 SECONDS, *hold for 5 to 10 seconds, rest for 5 seconds, and repeat as many times as needed to total 60 seconds. Each time you perform the exercise, try to hold each repetition a little longer so that you reach your 60-second goal with fewer repetitions. If the exercise is too easy, you can hold light dumbbells in your hands when you do it.*

Hold your legs off the floor.

Squeeze your glutes.

Hold your chest off the floor.

Cable Core Press

A

- With a hand-over-hand grip, grab a handle attached to the mid pulley of a cable station.

- Stand with your right side facing the weight stack and spread your feet about shoulder-width apart, your knees slightly bent.

- Step away from the stack so the cable is taut. Hold the handle against your chest and brace your abs.

B

- Slowly press your arms in front of you until they're completely straight, pause for a second, and bring them back.

- Do all your reps, then turn around and work your other side.

THE OBJECTIVE OF THIS EXERCISE IS TO PREVENT ROTATION. *So if you're hiking up your hip or rotating your shoulders, you're using too much weight. Squeeze your abs, keep your chest up and shoulders back, and move your arms at a slow and steady pace.*

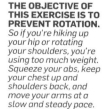

Core | STABILITY EXERCISES

MAIN MOVE
Kneeling Stability Chop

A

- Attach a rope handle to the high pulley of a cable station. Kneel down next to the handle so that your right side faces the weight stack.
- With both hands, grasp the rope with an overhand grip.
- Your shoulders should be turned toward the rope, but your belly button should be pointing forward.

Grasp the rope at arm's length, just in front of your left shoulder.

Your hands should be about 18 inches apart.

Brace your core.

Squeeze your glutes.

B

- Keep your torso upright for the entire movement.
- Without moving your torso, pull the rope past your left hip.
- Reverse the movement to return to the starting position.
- Complete the prescribed number of repetitions toward your left side, then kneel with your left side facing the weight stack and do the same number of reps toward your right side.

Move only your arms and shoulders to pull the rope down and across your body.

Don't rotate your torso.

Keep your arms straight.

VARIATION #1
Half-Kneeling Stability Chop

A

- Kneel down so that your outside knee is on the floor but your inside knee is bent 90 degrees, with your inside foot flat on the floor.

Your torso should be → upright.

Inside knee →

B

- Without moving your torso, pull the rope to your outside hip.

Don't bend your arms to pull the rope down.

Keep your core stiff.

← Outside knee

VARIATION #2
Standing Stability Chop

A

- Perform the movement standing in a staggered stance, your inside foot in front of your outside foot.

Your arms should be straight.

Bend your knee slightly. →

B

- Without moving your torso or bending your arms, pull the rope past your outside hip.

Your belly button should point forward.

Core | STABILITY EXERCISES

MAIN MOVE
Kneeling Stability Reverse Chop

A

- Attach a rope handle to the low pulley of a cable station. Kneel down next to the handle so that your right side faces the weight stack.
- With both hands, grasp the rope with an overhand grip.
- Your shoulders should be turned toward the rope, but your belly button should be pointing forward.

B

- Keep your torso upright for the entire movement.
- Without moving your torso, pull the rope past your left shoulder.
- Reverse the movement to return to the starting position.
- Complete the prescribed number of repetitions toward your left side, then kneel with your left side facing the weight stack and do the same number of reps toward your right side.

Move only your shoulders and arms to pull the rope up and across your body.

Grasp the rope at arm's length in front of your right hip.

Brace your core.

Squeeze your glutes.

Keep your arms straight.

Your hands should be about 18 inches apart.

Don't move your torso.

VARIATION #1
Half-Kneeling Stability Reverse Chop

A

- Kneel down so that your inside knee is on the floor but your outside knee is bent 90 degrees, with your outside foot flat on the floor.

Tighten your core.

B

- Without moving your torso, pull the rope past your outside shoulder.

Keep arms straight from start to finish.

Your belly button should point forward.

VARIATION #2
Standing Stability Reverse Chop

A

- Perform the movement standing in a staggered stance, your outside foot in front of your inside foot.

Bend your knee slightly.

B

- Without moving your torso, pull the rope past your outside shoulder.

Keep your torso upright.

Don't bend your arms to pull the rope up.

ROTATIONAL EXERCISES

These exercises target all of your abdominal muscles, with an emphasis on your obliques. They also help your abs work in conjunction with the muscles of your lower back and hips so that you can rotate your body with more power. These movements are ideal for anyone who plays tennis, softball, or golf, since they improve your ability to throw and swing explosively.

10

Number of additional reps people could complete while listening to their favorite music on an MP3 player, according to a study from the College of Charleston.

MAIN MOVE
Russian Twist

A

- Sit on the floor with your knees bent and your feet flat.
- Hold your arms straight out in front of your chest with your palms together.
- Lean back so your torso is at a 45-degree angle to the floor.

Rotate without raising or lowering your torso.

B

- Brace your core and rotate to the right as far as you can.

C

- Pause, then reverse your movement and twist all the way back to the left as far as you can.

VARIATION #1
Weighted Russian Twist

A

- With both hands, hold the ends of a dumbbell, the sides of a weight plate, or a medicine ball as you perform the movement.

Your arms should be straight.

Hold your torso at a 45-degree angle for the entire movement.

B

- Brace your core, and rotate your torso to the right as far as you can.

Keep your feet flat on the floor.

C

- Rotate to the left as far as you can.

VARIATION #2
Elevated-Feet Russian Twist

A

- Raise your feet a few inches off the floor and hold them there as you perform the movement

Brace your core.

Your knees should be bent.

B

- Rotate your torso to the right.

Don't drop your feet.

C

- Rotate your torso to the left.

VARIATION #3
Cycling Russian Twist

A

- Lift your legs so they're elevated but parallel with the floor.
- Extend your left leg and twist to the right as you pull your right knee to your chest. Don't let your legs touch the floor at any point during the move.

B

- Rotate to the left as you raise your left knee and straighten your right leg.

VARIATION #4
Swiss-Ball Russian Twist

A

- Lie with your middle and upper back placed firmly on a Swiss ball.
- Raise your hips so that your body forms a straight line from your knees to your shoulders.
- Hold your arms straight out in front of your chest with your palms together.

GET ON THE BALL!
A study published in the Journal of Strength and Conditioning Research *found that people who do exercises such as the Swiss-ball Russian twist build midsections that are four times more stable than those who do no Swiss-ball work.*

B

- Brace your core and roll your upper body to the right as far as you can.

Don't drop your hips, but allow them to rotate naturally.

C

- Reverse your movement and roll all the way back to the left as far as you can.

MAIN MOVE
Hip Crossover

A

- Lie faceup on the floor with your arms straight out from your sides, palms facing up.
- Raise your legs off the floor so that your hips and knees are bent 90 degrees.

Your thighs should be perpendicular to the floor.

This exercise is also known as the lower-body Russian twist and the windshield wiper.

Your lower legs should be parallel to the floor.

B

- Brace your abs and lower your legs to the right as far as you comfortably can without lifting your shoulders off the floor.

C

- Reverse the movement all the way to the left. Continue to alternate back and forth.

Don't allow your shoulders to raise off the floor.

Keep your core braced.

Core | ROTATIONAL EXERCISES

VARIATION
Swiss-Ball Hip Crossover

A

- Hold a Swiss ball between your lower legs and the backs of your thighs.

B

- Brace your abs and lower your legs to your right as far as you can.

Squeeze the ball between your legs.

C

- Reverse the movement all the back to the left.

Keep your shoulders on the floor.

> **BUILD A BULLET-PROOF BODY**
> *Core exercises like hip crossovers and planks can keep you healthy. Medicine & Science in Sports & Exercise reports that researchers tracked college basketball and track athletes before their seasons and found that those who suffered lower-body injuries had 32 percent less core strength than those who avoided such injuries. Strong stabilizing muscles in the hips, lower back, and abdominal areas provided safe foundations for the injury-free players.*

Dumbbell Chop

A

- Grab a dumbbell and hold it with both hands above your right shoulder.
- Rotate your torso to your right.

Your arms should be straight.

Brace your core.

B

- Swing the dumbbell down and to the outside of your left knee by rotating to the left and bending at your hips.
- Reverse the movement to return to the start.
- Complete the prescribed number of reps toward your left side, then do the same number on your right side, holding the dumbbell over your left shoulder.

Set your feet shoulder-width apart.

Don't round your lower back.

Medicine-Ball Side Throw

A

- Grab a medicine ball and stand sideways about 3 feet from a brick or concrete wall, your left side closer to the wall.

- Hold the ball at chest level with your arms straight, and rotate your torso to your right.

B

- Quickly switch directions and throw as hard as you can against the wall to your left.

- As the ball rebounds off the wall, catch it and repeat the movement.

- Complete the prescribed number of repetitions, then do the same number with your right side facing the wall, throwing from your left.

30

Percentage more control that golfers had on the putting green after an 11-week workout plan that included rotational medicine-ball exercises.

Your arms should be straight and parallel to the floor.

Brace your core.

Allow your hips to rotate naturally.

Your feet should be shoulder-width apart and your knees slightly bent.

Pivot so that both feet turn in the direction you're tossing the ball.

Core | ROTATIONAL EXERCISES

MAIN MOVE
Kneeling Rotational Chop

A

- Attach a rope handle to the high pulley of a cable station. Kneel down next to the handle so that your right side faces the weight stack.

- Rotate your body to grip the rope with both hands.

- Your torso should be turned toward the cable machine.

B

- Keep your torso upright for the entire movement.

- In one movement, pull the rope down and past your left hip as you simultaneously rotate your torso.

- Reverse the movement to return to the starting position.

- Complete the prescribed number of repetitions to your left side, then do the same number with your left side facing the stack, pulling toward your right.

Your hands should be about 18 inches apart.

Brace your core.

Keep your arms straight.

Don't round your lower back.

Allow your torso to rotate as you pull the rope down and across your body.

VARIATION #1
Standing Split Rotational Chop
- Perform the movement standing in a staggered stance, your inside foot in front of your outside foot.

Stiffen your core.

Your knees should be bent.

VARIATION #2
Standing Rotational Chop
- Perform the movement while standing with your feet shoulder-width apart.

Pivot to your left as you pull the cable down and to your left.

Bend your knees slightly.

Your feet should be angled toward the weight stack.

VARIATION #3
Half-Kneeling Rotational Chop

A

- Kneel down so that your outside knee is on the floor but your inside knee is bent 90 degrees with your inside foot flat on the floor.

Don't bend your arms as you pull the rope down and across your body.

B

- Pull the rope past your outside hip.

Keep your core braced.

MAIN MOVE
Kneeling Rotational Reverse Chop

A

- Attach a rope handle to the low pulley of a cable station. Kneel down next to the handle so that your right side faces the weight stack.
- Brace your core and rotate your body to grip the rope with both hands.
- Your shoulders should be turned toward the cable machine.

B

- Keep your torso upright for the entire movement.
- In one movement, pull the rope past your left shoulder as you simultaneously rotate your torso to the left.
- Reverse the movement to return to the starting position.
- Complete the prescribed number of reps to your left side, then do the same number with your left side facing the stack, rotating to your right.

Grasp the rope at arm's length in front of your right hip.

Your hands should be about 18 inches apart.

Don't round your lower back.

Keep your arms straight.

Allow your torso to rotate as you pull the rope up and across your body.

VARIATION #1
Standing Split Rotational Reverse Chop

- Perform the movement standing in a staggered stance, your outside foot in front of your inside foot.

VARIATION #2
Standing Rotational Reverse Chop

- Perform the movement while standing with your feet shoulder-width apart.

Brace your core.

Bend your knees slightly.

Pivot to your left as you pull the cable up and to your left.

Your knees should be bent.

Your feet should be angled toward the weight stack.

VARIATION #3
Half-Kneeling Rotational Reverse Chop

A

- Kneel down so that your inside knee is on the floor but your outside knee is bent 90 degrees with your outside foot flat on the floor.

B

- Pull the rope past your outside shoulder.

Keep your torso upright.

Don't bend your arms as you pull the rope up and across your body.

TRUNK FLEXION EXERCISES

These exercises target your rectus abdominis, a.k.a. your six-pack muscles. They also work your internal and external obliques.

MAIN MOVE
Situp

A

- Lie faceup on the floor with your knees bent and feet flat.

Place your fingertips behind your ears.

Your elbows should be in line with your body.

23

Percent reduction in heart disease risk linked to doing just 30 minutes of weight training a week, according to a Harvard University study.

MUSCLE MISTAKE
You Do Situps to Protect Your Back

While these exercises work well for building your ab muscles, they require you to round your lower back repeatedly. This can actually contribute to lower-back problems in some people, as well as aggravate pre-existing damage. So if you already have back pain, you should avoid these exercises. And as a general rule, make stability exercises the backbone of your core workout, since they've been shown to be beneficial to spinal health.

B

- Raise your torso to a sitting position.
- The movement should be fluid, not jerky—if it's the latter, you need to use a variation that's easier.
- Slowly lower your torso back to the starting position.

Keep your elbows pulled back.

Raise your torso until you're sitting upright.

Keep your feet flat on the floor.

Core | TRUNK FLEXION EXERCISES

VARIATION #1
Negative Situp

- Sit with your feet flat on the floor and your legs bent—as if you had just performed a situp—and slowly lower your body.

> *During a negative situp, try to lower your torso at the same rate from start to finish. If you can't control your speed, identify the point at which you start to collapse and hold just above that point for 5 seconds on each repetition.*

Keep your elbows pulled back.

VARIATION #2
Modified Situp

- Hold your arms completely straight next to your body, raised just a bit so that they're parallel to the floor.

Keep your arms parallel to the floor for the entire movement. (They'll rise off the floor as your body does.)

VARIATION #3
Crossed-Arms Situp

 A

- Perform the situp with your arms crossed in front of your chest.

B

- Contract your abs and curl your torso upward.

Raise your torso to a sitting position.

VARIATION #4
Weighted Situp

• Perform the situp while holding a weight plate across your chest.

Hold the weight plate tight against your chest.

VARIATION #5
Alternating Situp

• As you raise your torso, rotate it to the left so that your left elbow touches your left knee. Lower, and on the next situp, rotate to the other side so that your right elbow touches your right knee.

Alternate the side you twist to each repetition.

VARIATION #6
Decline Situp

A

• Position your feet under the leg anchors of a decline bench, and lie flat on your back.

B

• Raise your torso to a sitting position.

Don't pull your head forward as you raise your body. If you can't help it, the exercise is too hard for you.

Core | TRUNK FLEXION EXERCISES

MAIN MOVE
Crunch

A

- Sit on the floor with your knees bent and your feet flat on the floor.
- Place your fingertips behind your ears, and pull your elbows back so that they're in line with your body.

B

- Raise your head and shoulders and crunch your rib cage toward your pelvis.
- Pause, then slowly return to the starting position.

Don't pull your head forward.

VARIATION #1
Crossed-Arms Crunch
- Perform the crunch with your arms crossed in front of your chest.

Crunch your rib cage toward your pelvis.

Keep your feet flat on the floor.

VARIATION #2
Weighted Crunch
- Perform the crunch while holding a weight plate across your chest.

Hold the weight plate tight against your chest.

VARIATION #3
Wrist-to-Knee Crunch
- Lie faceup with your hips and knees bent 90 degrees so that your lower legs are parallel to the floor.

- Place your fingers on the sides of your forehead.

- Lift your shoulders off the floor and hold them there.

- Twist your upper body to the right as you pull your right knee in as fast as you can until it touches your left wrist. Simultaneously straighten your left leg.

- Return to the starting position and repeat to the right.

VARIATION #4
Raised-Legs Crunch
- Lie on your back with your hips bent 90 degrees and your legs straight.

- Hold your arms straight above your chest.

- Reach for your toes by crunching your head and shoulders off the floor.

- Lower your head and shoulders to the starting position.

Your legs should point toward the ceiling.

Core | TRUNK FLEXION EXERCISES

MAIN MOVE
V-Up

A

- Lie faceup on the floor with your legs and arms straight.
- Hold your arms straight above the top of your head.

Your arms should be in line with your body.

B

- In one movement, simultaneously lift your torso and legs as if you're trying to touch your toes.
- Lower your body back to the starting position.

Keep your head in line with your body; don't crane your neck forward.

Your torso and legs should form a V.

Your legs should be straight.

VARIATION #1

Medicine-Ball V-Up

A

- Hold a medicine ball as you do the exercise.

B

- In one movement, lift your torso and legs as your bring the ball toward your feet.

Your arms should be straight.

VARIATION #2

Modified V-Up

A

- Lie faceup on the floor with your legs straight and your arms at your sides.

B

- In one movement, quickly lift your torso into an upright position as you pull your knees to your chest.
- Lower your body back to the starting position.

Keep your arms parallel to the floor.

Hold your arms slightly off the floor, your palms facing down.

Core | TRUNK FLEXION EXERCISES

MAIN MOVE
Swiss-Ball Crunch

A

- Lie with your hips, lower back, and shoulders in contact with a Swiss ball.
- Place your fingertips behind your ears, and pull your elbows back so that they're in line with your body.

B

- Raise your head and shoulders and crunch your rib cage toward your pelvis.
- Pause, then slowly return to the starting position.
- Don't allow your hips to drop as you crunch up.

Keep your elbows pulled back.

Your feet should be flat on the floor.

Don't strain your neck forward.

VARIATION #1
Weighted Swiss-Ball Crunch

A

- Hold a weight plate across your chest.

B

- Raise your head and shoulders off the ball.

Hug the weight tight against your chest.

Crunch your rib cage toward your pelvis.

MAIN MOVE
Medicine-Ball Slam

A

- Grab a medicine ball and hold it above your head.

B C

- Reach back as far as you can, then slam the ball to the floor in front of you.

VARIATION #1
Single-Leg Medicine-Ball Slam
- Stand on one leg as you perform the exercise.

Your arms should be slightly bent.

Throw the ball at the floor forcefully.

Set your feet shoulder-width apart.

Kneeling Cable Crunch

A

- Attach a rope handle to the high pulley of a cable station, and kneel with your back to the weight stack.
- Drape the rope around your neck and hold an end against your chest with each hand.

B

- Crunch your rib cage toward your pelvis.
- Pause, then slowly return to the starting position.

Standing Cable Crunch

A

- Attach a rope handle to the high pulley of a cable station, and stand with your back to the weight stack.
- Drape the rope around your neck and hold an end against your chest with each hand.
- Your elbows should be pointing straight down to the floor.

B

- Crunch your rib cage toward your pelvis.
- Pause, then slowly return to the starting position.

Your elbows should point toward the floor.

Your knees should be slightly bent.

Train Your Abs—Fast

Scientists in Spain found that performing abdominal exercises at a fast tempo activates more muscle than doing them slowly. That's because to increase your rate of movement, your muscles have to generate higher amounts of force, say the researchers. Their recommendation: Do as many reps as you can in 20 seconds. You'll target your fast-twitch muscle fibers, which are the ones with the greatest potential for size and strength.

321

HIP FLEXION EXERCISES

These exercises target your hip flexors and your external obliques. They also work many of your other core muscles, including your rectus abdominis.

MAIN MOVE
Reverse Crunch

A

- Lie faceup on the floor with your palms facing down.
- Bend your hips and knees 90 degrees.

Hold your feet together.

B

- Raise your hips off the floor and crunch them inward.

Your knees should move toward your chest.

Imagine that you are emptying a bucket of water that's resting on your pelvis.

Your hips and lower back should raise up off the floor.

C

- Pause, then slowly lower your legs until your heels nearly touch the floor.

Don't change the bend in your knees from start to finish.

VARIATION #1
Swiss-Ball Reverse Crunch

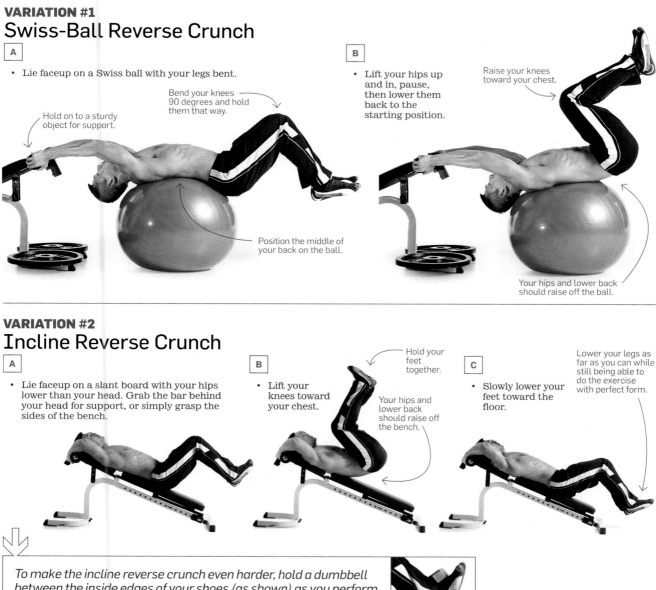

A

- Lie faceup on a Swiss ball with your legs bent.

Bend your knees 90 degrees and hold them that way.

Hold on to a sturdy object for support.

Position the middle of your back on the ball.

B

- Lift your hips up and in, pause, then lower them back to the starting position.

Raise your knees toward your chest.

Your hips and lower back should raise off the ball.

VARIATION #2
Incline Reverse Crunch

A

- Lie faceup on a slant board with your hips lower than your head. Grab the bar behind your head for support, or simply grasp the sides of the bench.

B

- Lift your knees toward your chest.

Hold your feet together.

Your hips and lower back should raise off the bench.

C

- Slowly lower your feet toward the floor.

Lower your legs as far as you can while still being able to do the exercise with perfect form.

To make the incline reverse crunch even harder, hold a dumbbell between the inside edges of your shoes (as shown) as you perform the exercise. Keep your feet together, and the dumbbell won't fall.

Core | HIP FLEXION EXERCISES

MAIN MOVE
Foam-Roller Reverse Crunch on Bench

A

- Lie faceup on a bench and hold a foam roller between the backs of your ankles and thighs.
- The fronts of your thighs should be facing your chest.
- Grasp the sides of the bench, next to your head.

Squeezing the foam roller between your legs deactivates your hip flexors, forcing your abdominal muscles to do more work.

B

- Raise your hips and bring your knees toward your shoulders without releasing the roller.
- Pause, then lower.

Raise your hips and lower back.

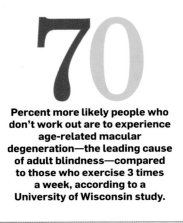

70

Percent more likely people who don't work out are to experience age-related macular degeneration—the leading cause of adult blindness—compared to those who exercise 3 times a week, according to a University of Wisconsin study.

VARIATION #1
Foam-Roller Reverse Crunch with Dumbbell

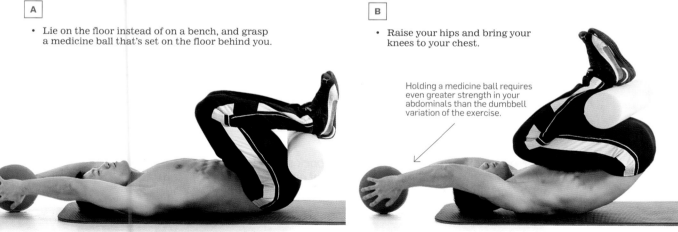

A

- Lie on the floor instead of on a bench, and grasp a heavy dumbbell that's set on the floor behind you.

B

- Raise your hips and bring your knees to your chest.

Because the dumbbell is less secure than the bench (it weighs less), this variation forces your abdominals to work harder than the Main Move.

VARIATION #2
Foam-Roller Reverse Crunch with Medicine Ball

A

- Lie on the floor instead of on a bench, and grasp a medicine ball that's set on the floor behind you.

B

- Raise your hips and bring your knees to your chest.

Holding a medicine ball requires even greater strength in your abdominals than the dumbbell variation of the exercise.

Swiss-Ball Pike

A

- Assume a pushup position with your arms completely straight.
- Position your hands slightly wider than and in line with your shoulders.
- Rest your shins on a Swiss ball.
- Your body should form a straight line from your head to your ankles.

B

- Without bending your knees, roll the Swiss ball toward your body by raising your hips as high as you can.
- Pause, then return the ball to the starting position by lowering your hips and rolling the ball backward.

Your hands should be below your shoulders.

Don't round your lower back.

Push your hips toward the ceiling.

MAIN MOVE
Hanging Leg Raise

A

- Grab a chinup bar with an overhand, shoulder-width grip, and hang from the bar with your knees slightly bent and feet together. (If you have access to elbow supports—sling-like devices that hang from the bar—you may prefer to use those.)

B

- Simultaneously bend your knees, raise your hips, and curl your lower back underneath you as you lift your thighs toward your chest.
- Pause when the fronts of your thighs reach your chest, then slowly lower your legs back to the starting position.

- Maintain an upright torso, and simply raise one leg as far as you can without allowing your other leg to pull forward. Pause, then slowly lower back to the starting position and repeat with your other leg. Alternate back and forth.

If you're strong enough to perform this exercise, you shouldn't have to lean backward. In fact, your shoulders should remain in place or round forward slightly.

Don't simply bend your knees and lift your legs up. Instead, imagine scooping your hips up and pulling them toward you.

Core | HIP FLEXION EXERCISES

Hanging Hurdle

A

- Place a bench under and perpendicular to a chinup bar.
- Hang from the bar with your legs to one side of the bench, feet together and knees slightly bent.

B

- Without changing the bends in your knees or elbows, lift your legs over the bench to the opposite side.
- Repeat back and forth for 10 to 15 seconds.

A GOOD CHALLENGE:
Work up so that you can do two sets of 60 seconds, with 60 to 90 seconds of rest between sets.

Medicine-Ball Leg Drops

A

- Lie faceup on the floor and squeeze a light medicine ball between your ankles.
- Keep your legs nearly straight and hold them directly above your hips.

B

- Allow your legs to drop straight down as far as possible without touching the floor. (It should feel like you're "throwing on the brakes.")
- In the same motion, return your legs to the starting position as fast as possible. That's one rep.

Keep the same bend in your knees from start to finish.

Brace your core.

In a pinch, a basketball can work in place of the medicine ball.

Your feet shouldn't touch the floor.

SIDE FLEXION EXERCISES These exercises target your internal and external obliques, the muscles on the sides of your torso. They also hit your quadratus lumborum, a lower-back muscle that helps you bend to the side.

Side Crunch

A

- Lie faceup with your knees together and bent 90 degrees.
- Without moving your upper body, lower your knees to the right so that they're touching the floor.
- Place your fingers behind your ears.

B

- Raise your shoulders toward your hips.
- Pause for 1 second, then take 2 seconds to lower your upper body back to the starting position.

Don't strain your neck by pulling forward with your head.

Overhead Dumbbell Side Bend

A

- Hold a pair of dumbbells over your head, in line with your shoulders, with your arms straight.

B

- Without twisting your upper body, slowly bend directly to your left side as far as you can.
- Pause, return to an upright position, then bend to your right side. Alternate back and forth with each repetition.

Lock your elbows.

Brace your core.

Hold your arms in position as you lower your torso.

Hanging Oblique Raise

A

- Grasp a chinup bar with an overhand grip and hang from it at arm's length.
- Lift your legs until your hips and knees are bent at 90-degree angles.

B

- Raise your right hip toward your right armpit.
- Pause, then return to the starting position and lift your left hip toward your left armpit. Alternate back and forth with each repetition.

Your lower legs should be nearly parallel to the floor.

Swiss-Ball Side Crunch

A

- Lie sideways on a Swiss ball and brace your left foot against a wall or against a heavy object. Place your fingers behind your ears.

B

- Lift your shoulders and crunch sideways toward your hip.
- Pause, then return to the starting position.
- Complete the prescribed number of reps on that side, then do the same number on your other side.

Allow your torso to wrap around the ball.

Cross your right leg over your left, and place your right foot flat on the floor.

Core

THE BEST CORE EXERCISE YOU'VE NEVER DONE
Core Stabilization

Instead of rotating your core to move a weight, this exercise moves the weight around your core. Constantly shifting the location of the load forces your core muscles to perpetually adjust in order to keep your body stable. This not only builds your abs, but also more closely mimics the way your core muscles have to fire when you're playing sports— giving you an edge anytime you step on the court.

A

- Sit on the floor with your knees bent.
- Hold a weight plate straight out in front of your chest.
- Lean back so your torso is at a 45-degree angle to the floor, and brace your core.

Don't round your lower back.

Your feet should be flat on the floor.

B

- Without moving your torso, rotate your arms to the left as far as you can. Pause for 3 seconds.

Keep your core braced.

Your arms should stay straight.

C

- Rotate your arms to the right as far as you can.
- Pause again, then continue to alternate back and forth for the allotted time. A good goal: 30 seconds.

Your belly button should point straight ahead at all times.

Hold your torso in place.

THE BEST STRETCH FOR YOUR CORE
Half-Kneeling Rotation

Why it's good: Long hours of sitting at a desk or in front of a steering wheel can reduce the ability of your upper spine to rotate and bend to the side. This can lead to rounded shoulders and a hunched posture. This stretch increases the mobility of your upper spine, improving your posture as well as enhancing your rotation for sports such as golf, tennis, and softball.

Make the most of it: Hold this stretch for 5 seconds per repetition, and do 15 repetitions. Do a total of three sets. Perform this routine daily, and up to three times a day if you're really tight.

A

- Hold a broomstick across your upper back.
- Kneel down on your left knee and bend your right knee 90 degrees, with your right foot flat on the floor.
- Brace your abs and hold them that way.

Your torso should be upright.

B

- Keeping your back naturally arched, rotate your left shoulder toward your right knee. Hold that position for the prescribed amount of time.
- Return to the starting position. That's one repetition.
- Complete the prescribed number of reps toward your right side, then switch knee positions and do the same number to your left side.

Keep your core braced.

Core

BUILD PERFECT ABS

Work your abs like never before, with these cutting-edge core routines from Tony Gentilcore, CSCS. Tony is the cofounder of Cressey Performance in Hudson, Massachusetts, and a frequent guest host of an always informative Internet podcast called The Fit-Cast. (Check it out at http://fitcast.com.) Each of the three workouts he's provided sculpts your six-pack by forcing your abs to resist rotation and work double time to keep your spine stable.

How to do the workouts: Choose one of the three routines and perform the exercises in the order shown, using the prescribed sets, reps, and rest periods. Do the exercises as a circuit, completing one set of each in succession. Once you've done one set of each exercise, repeat the entire circuit two more times. For best results, complete this workout twice a week. After 4 weeks, try one of the other routines.

Workout A

EXERCISE 1: Cable core press (page 295)
Do 10 repetitions for each side, then rest for 30 to 45 seconds and move on to the next exercise.

EXERCISE 2: Reverse crunch (page 322)
Do 12 repetitions, then rest for 30 to 45 seconds and move on to the next exercise.

EXERCISE 3: Barbell rollout (page 292)
Do 8 repetitions, then rest for 60 seconds and repeat the entire circuit one time.

Workout B

EXERCISE 1: Kneeling stability chop (page 296)
Do 8 repetitions for each side, then rest for 30 to 45 seconds and move on to the next exercise.

EXERCISE 2: Swiss-ball plank (page 281)
Hold for 30 seconds, then rest for 30 to 45 seconds and move on to the next exercise.

EXERCISE 3: Swiss-ball rollout (page 292)
Do 8 repetitions, then rest for 60 seconds and repeat the entire circuit one time.

Workout C

EXERCISE 1: Single-arm cable chest press (page 58)
Do 10 repetitions for each side, then rest for 30 to 45 seconds and move on to the next exercise.

EXERCISE 2: Standing stability chop (page 297)
Do 10 repetitions for each side, then rest for 30 to 45 seconds and move on to the next exercise.

EXERCISE 3: Rolling side plank (page 285)
Hold each position for 5 seconds, then rest for 60 seconds and repeat the entire circuit one time.

BONUS ABS WORKOUT!

For each routine, perform the exercises in the order shown, using the prescribed sets, reps, and rest periods. The Level 1 routine is the easiest, and a good place for beginners to start; the Level 3 routine is the most difficult. For best results, complete this workout twice a week. If you start with the Level 1 workout, do it for 3 or 4 weeks, then progress to Level 2, and so forth.

LEVEL 1

1. Plank (page 278)
Hold the plank for 30 seconds. Rest for 30 seconds and repeat once.

2. Mountain climber with hands on bench (page 289)
Each time your raise your knee toward your chest, pause for 2 seconds, and then slowly lower your leg back to the start. Alternate your legs back and forth for 30 seconds. Rest for 30 seconds and repeat once.

3. Side plank (page 284)
Hold the plank for 30 seconds. Rest for 30 seconds and repeat once.

LEVEL 2

1. Elevated-feet plank (page 280)
Hold the plank for 30 seconds. Rest for 30 seconds and repeat once.

2. Mountain climber with hands on Swiss ball (page 289)
Each time your raise your knee toward your chest, pause for 2 seconds, and then slowly lower your leg back to the start. Alternate your legs back and forth for 30 seconds. Rest for 30 seconds and repeat once.

3. Side plank with feet on bench (page 285)
Hold the plank for 30 seconds. Rest for 30 seconds and repeat once.

LEVEL 3

1. Extended plank (page 280)
Hold the plank for 30 seconds. Rest for 30 seconds and repeat once.

2. Swiss-ball jackknife (page 290)
Do two sets of 15 reps, resting for 30 seconds between sets.

3. Single-leg side plank (page 285)
Hold the plank for 30 seconds. Rest for 30 seconds and repeat once.

BONUS WORKOUT: SAVE YOUR BACK IN 7 MINUTES

To reduce your chances of a back attack, try this workout from Stuart McGill, PhD, professor of spine biomechanics at the University of Waterloo, and author of *Low Back Disorders*. This 7-minute (or less) workout increases the endurance of your deep back and abdominal muscles, to improve spine stability and ultimately reduce lower-back stress. Do this routine once a day, every day. Simply perform the exercises as a circuit, doing one set of each movement without rest in between.

Cat camel (page 283)
Do five to eight repetitions.

McGill curlup (page 291)
Hold the curlup position for 7 or 8 seconds, then lower momentarily. That's one repetition. Do four repetitions, then switch legs and repeat.

Side plank (page 284)
Hold the side-plank position for 7 or 8 seconds, then lower your hips for a moment. That's one repetition. Do four or five repetitions, then switch sides and repeat.

Bird dog (page 283)
Hold the bird-dog position for 7 or 8 seconds, then lower your arm and leg momentarily. That's one rep. Do four repetitions, then switch arms and legs and repeat.

Chapter 11: Total Body

LOOK GREAT, ALL OVER

Total
Body

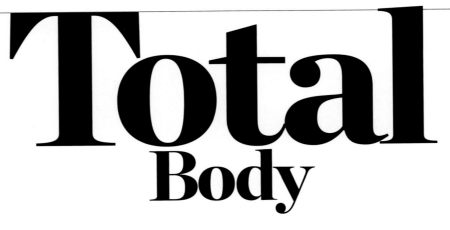

You might say exercises that work your total body are ideal for anyone who doesn't like to work out. Why? Because they target several large muscle groups at once, so you can accomplish an intense heart- and lung-pumping workout—that torches calories and stokes your metabolism—with fewer exercises and in less time than ever before. Of course, for those same exact reasons, total-body moves are also great for those who *do* love to work out.

In this chapter, you'll find 18 total-body exercises. Some will look familiar, since they're combinations of exercises from previous sections. Others will seem novel. But there's one trait they all share: These movements are among the fastest ways to burn fat and build total-body muscle.

Bonus Benefits

An athletic body! Total-body exercises improve your coordination and balance. So you'll be more graceful in every activity—from tennis to running to beach volleyball.

A healthier heart! The combination exercises will convince you that the term *cardio* doesn't just apply to aerobic exercise.

Greater strength! Full-body exercises require muscles all over your body to fire simultaneously. This enhances your strength from head to toe, helping eliminate the weaknesses that may be holding you back.

COMBINATION EXERCISES

Most of these exercises are combinations of movements that appear in other chapters. Each exercise works the muscles of your upper body, lower body, and core, and is a great addition to any fat-loss workout.

Barbell Front Squat to Push Press

A

- Hold the bar with an overhand grip that's just beyond shoulder width.
- Raise your upper arms until they're parallel to the floor.
- Set your feet shoulder-width apart.

B

- Keeping your upper arms parallel to the floor, push your hips back, bend your knees, and lower your body as far as you can.

C

- Simultaneously push your body back to the start as you press the bar over your head.

Stand as tall as you can.

Allow the bar to roll back so that it's resting on your fingers, not on your palms.

Push the weight up until your arms are completely straight.

Keep your elbows and upper arms raised.

Don't round your lower back.

Total Body | COMBINATION EXERCISES

Barbell Straight-Leg Deadlift to Row

A

- Grab a barbell with an overhand grip and hold it at arm's length in front your thighs.
- Stand with your feet shoulder-width apart and your knees slightly bent.

Bend your knees slightly and maintain that bend throughout the lift.

Set your feet shoulder-width apart.

B

- Keeping your back naturally arched, bend at your hips and lower torso until it's nearly parallel to the floor.

Don't round your lower back.

C

- Pull the bar to your upper abs.
- Pause, then reverse through each step of the movement to return to the starting position.

Squeeze your shoulder blades together.

Dumbbell Straight-Leg Deadlift to Row

A

- Let a pair of dumbbells hang at arm's length in front of your hips.

Your palms should face your thighs.

B

- Bend at your hips and lower your torso into a bent-over position.

Keep your lower back naturally arched.

C

- Pull the dumbbells to the sides of your torso.

Row the weights up without moving your torso.

Thrusters

A
- Grab a pair of dumbbells and hold them next to your shoulders, your palms facing each other.
- Stand tall with your feet shoulder-width apart.

TRAINER'S TIP
Initiate the movement by pushing your hips backward, then bend your knees and lower your body as far as possible. (The deeper you squat, the better.)

B
- Lower your body until the tops of your thighs are at least parallel to the floor.

Keep your torso as upright as possible throughout the movement.

C
- Push your body back to a standing position as you press the dumbbells directly over your shoulders.
- Lower the dumbbells back to the starting position.

Dumbbell Hammer Curl to Lunge to Press

A
- Grab a pair of dumbbells and hold them at arm's length next to your sides, your palms facing each other.
- Stand tall with your feet hip-width apart.

Keep your torso upright for the entire movement.

B
- Step forward with your left leg and lower your body until your front knee is bent at least 90 degrees.
- As you lunge, curl the dumbbells.

Your back knee should nearly touch the floor.

C
- Press the dumbbells directly above your shoulders.

Your arms should be straight.

D
- Push yourself back to the start, then lower the weights and repeat.

MUSCLE MISTAKE
You Don't Use Total-Body Moves to Define Your Muscles

Big mistake. Whether a muscle is visible or not primarily depends on how much fat is covering it. And because total-body exercises burn more calories than isolation exercises such as biceps curls and triceps extensions, multi-muscle movements are far more valuable for helping to define your arms. The reason: You simply can't choose the location of the fat you burn, no matter what exercise you do.

Total Body | COMBINATION EXERCISES

Single-Arm Stepup and Press

A

- Grab a dumbbell and hold it in your left hand, just outside your shoulder, your palm facing your shoulder.
- Place your right foot on box or a step that's about knee height.

Brace your core.

B

- Push down with your right heel, and step up onto the box as you push the dumbbell straight above your left shoulder.
- To return to the starting position, lower your left foot back to the floor.
- Complete the prescribed number of repetitions with your right foot on the box and the weight in your left hand, then switch arms and legs and do the same number of reps.

Straighten your arm completely.

Your left leg should be held in the air.

Single-Arm Reverse Lunge and Press

A

- Grab a dumbbell with your left hand, and hold it next to your left shoulder, your palm facing in.

2

Times more fat people lost when they trained their entire body 3 days a week, compared to working each muscle group only once a week, according to University of Alabama scientists.

B

- Step backward with your left leg and lower your body into a reverse lunge as you simultaneously press the dumbbell straight above your shoulder.
- To return to the starting position, lower the dumbbell as you push yourself back up. That's one rep.
- Complete all your reps, then switch arms and legs and repeat.

Your arm should be straight.

Side Lunge and Press

A

- Grab a pair of dumbbells and stand with your feet hip-width apart.
- Press the dumbbells over your head so that your arms are straight.

Brace your core.

B

- Step to your right and lower your body into a side lunge as you lower the right dumbbell to your shoulder.
- Reverse the movement and push yourself back to the start.

Keep your torso as upright as possible.

Turkish Getup

Lock your elbow.

A

- Lie faceup with your legs straight.
- Hold a dumbbell in your left hand with your arm straight above you.

Don't take your eyes off the dumbbell at any time.

Roll onto your right side and prop yourself up on your right elbow.

Place one flat foot on the floor.

B **C** **D**

- Simply stand up, while keeping your arm straight and the dumbbell above you at all times.

Push yourself to a kneeling position.

E

- Once standing, reverse the movement to return to the starting position.
- Complete the prescribed number of reps, then do the same number with your right hand holding the weight.

Total Body | POWER EXERCISES

POWER EXERCISES

These exercises target your fast-twitch muscle fibers, the ones with the greatest potential for size and strength. Your goal should be to perform each of these movements as quickly as possible, while maintaining control of the weight at all times. If you play sports, these exercises are ideal for enhancing your ability to produce power, a combination of strength and speed that's the key to jumping higher, sprinting faster, and throwing farther.

Barbell High Pull

A

- Load the barbell with a light weight and roll it against your shins.
- Grab the bar with an overhand grip that's just beyond shoulder width.
- Bend at your hips and knees to squat down.
- Raise your chest and hips until your arms are straight.

B

- Pull the bar as high as you can by explosively standing up as you bend your elbows and raise your upper arms.
- You should rise up on your toes.
- Reverse the movement to return to the starting position.

Pull your torso backward.

Your lower back should be slightly arched.

Thrust your hips forward forcefully.

You should rise up on your toes.

Barbell Hang Pull

A

- Start with the bar just below knee height.

Don't round your lower back.

B

- Pull the bar as high as you can.

Push your hips forward.

Dumbbell Hang Pull

A

- Grab a pair of dumbbells with an overhand grip and hold them just below knee height.

Set your feet shoulder-width apart.

B

- Explosively pull the dumbbells upward.

Bend your elbows and pull the weights.

In one movement, straighten your hips, knees, and ankles.

Olympic Lifts for Everyone

Consider the barbell high pull and the other power exercises in this chapter to be simplified versions of the Olympic lifts used in the weight-lifting competitions you see at the Summer Games. While the Olympic lifts are quite technical and hard to learn, the high pull and jump shrug provide similar benefits with a much lower degree of difficulty. The reason: They require the same basic pulling movements but eliminate the "catch" phase, which yields little in terms of muscle work and is what makes these exercises so complicated.

Total Body | POWER EXERCISES

Barbell Jump Shrug

A

- Grab a barbell with an overhand grip that's just beyond shoulder width.

- Bend at your hips and knees until the barbell hangs just below your knees.

Your lower back should be slightly arched.

B

- Simultaneously thrust your hips forward, shrug your shoulders forcefully, and jump as high as you can.

- Land as softly as you can, and reset.

Keep your arms straight.

Keep the bar close to your body.

18

Percentage more power that men generated during the jump shrug than during the power clean that is the gold standard of Olympic lifts, according to University of Wisconsin researchers.

Wide-Grip Jump Shrug

- Use an overhand grip that's about twice shoulder width.

Thrust your hips forward.

Jump as high as you can.

The bar should hang just below your knees.

Dumbbell Jump Shrug

- Grab a pair of dumbbells and let them hang at arm's length, your palms facing your sides.

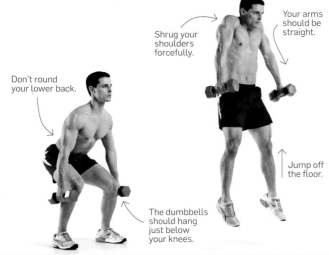

Your arms should be straight.

Shrug your shoulders forcefully.

Don't round your lower back.

Jump off the floor.

The dumbbells should hang just below your knees.

Single-Arm Dumbbell Snatch

A

- Grab a dumbbell with an overhand grip.
- Bend at your hips and knees to squat down until the weight is centered between your feet, your arm straight.

Your lower back should be slightly arched.

Drive your heels into the floor.

B

- In a single movement, try to throw the dumbbell at the ceiling—without letting go of it.

Your feet should be slightly wider than shoulder-width apart.

Bend your arm and raise your elbow as high as you can.

C

- Allow your forearm to rotate up and back from the momentum of the lift, until your arm is straight and your palm is facing forward.
- Pull your body under the weight.

Keep the dumbbell as close to your body as possible at all times.

You should be thrusting the dumbbell upward so forcefully that you rise up on your toes.

Push your hips forward.

Single-Arm Hang Snatch

- Instead of starting from the floor, hold the dumbbell just below knee height.

Single-Arm Kettlebell Snatch

- Substitute a kettlebell for a dumbbell.

Power Up Your Workout

Try a doing a power move before a traditional strength exercise. For instance, perform a single-arm snatch or jump shrug before squats, or explosive pushups before standard pushups. In a study published in the *Journal of Strength and Conditioning Research*, people who did a squat after a power exercise performed better in the squat than those who skipped the explosive movement. The researchers speculate that performing a power exercise causes chemical changes within the muscle fiber, stimulating a greater number of nerves to be activated during the second exercise.

349

Chapter 12:
Fat Loss Exercises
SWEAT, SCULPT, AND SHRED

Fat Loss
Exercises

L et's start with the obvious: Just about every exercise in this book can help you burn calories and lose fat. From pushups to squats to lunges to total body movements, there are hundreds of great options.

But new variations of these exercises—as well as some old classics—are becoming highly popular for their ability to send your heart rate through the roof with relatively light weights. Or no weights at all. Which makes them fantastic for use in fast-paced conditioning workouts that torch calories at a blistering rate.

So when I set out to create a new chapter for the revised edition of this book, the theme was a no-brainer: exercises that help you blast fat faster than ever. And on the pages that follow, you'll find more than 100 that'll do just that.

Bonus Benefits

Greater endurance! Many of these fat-loss exercises allow you to go all-out for 30 to 60 seconds at a time—a highly effective way to improve your stamina.

A rock-solid core! Nearly every one of these movements challenges your abs and glutes as you incinerate calories.

Workouts you'll love! It's almost impossible to get bored with so many options of *seriously* fun, fast-moving exercises.

Fat Loss Exercises

In this chapter, you'll find 114 exercises that are tremendous calorie-burners. Each movement is labeled as "total body," "cardio" (usually fast-moving exercises that elevate heart rate), or with a target muscle group—or a combination of those terms. Use these labels to determine how to best use an exercise within a routine (see Chapter 16: The Best New Fat Loss Workouts).

TOTAL BODY VERSUS CARDIO: WHAT'S THE DIFF?

Just like in Chapter 11: Total Body, every exercise in this chapter counts as "cardio." But if the movement presents a significant challenge to both your upper and lower body, it's labeled "total body." If it's a faster-moving exercise with a focus on elevating your heart rate—but requires little or no weights—it's labeled "cardio." Some movements—burpees!—are a bit of a tossup. Simply use the labels as a general guide—that's all they're intended to be.

The Genius Way to Use These Exercises

Imagine if your workout gave your body exactly what it needed. It can do just that with a workout technique called heart rate interval training, says Alwyn Cosgrove, co-owner of Results Fitness in Santa Clarita, California. Here's how it works: Instead of pre-determining how long you work and rest for a particular exercise, you let your heart rate tell you how long you do each. (You'll need a heart rate monitor, of course.) "I work until my heart reaches 85 percent of max, and then rest until it reaches 65 percent of max," says Cosgrove. This allows you to automatically adjust your routine for your body's abilities on any given day. Cosgrove likes to rotate between four exercises—pretty much any will work—but you could choose do more movements, or fewer. Once you complete one round of each exercise, just repeat the process for as many rounds as you can complete in a given time period—say, 20 minutes.

Fat Loss Exercises

MAIN MOVE
Burpee
TOTAL BODY

A

- Stand with your feet about twice shoulder-width apart and your hands at your sides.

B

- Simultaneously squat down and place your hands on the floor as you kick your legs back.

C

- Land so that you're in the top position of a pushup.

Your hands and feet shouldn't be touching the floor at the same time.

TRAINER'S TIP
Positioning your feet wide apart makes it easier for you to bend over at your hips. This can help prevent strain on your lower back, making the exercise more comfortable to do.

Your body should form a straight line from your head to your ankles.

Your toes may point out about 15 to 30 degrees.

Straighten your legs, with your weight on your toes.

Your arms should be straight.

D

- Optional: Skip step C, and instead go right into the down position of a pushup, shown here.

E

- In one movement, jump your feet up toward your shoulders as you simultaneously push off the floor with your hands and land in a squat position.

F

- Push yourself back up to a standing position.

10

Number of fast-paced burpees that rev your metabolism as much as a 30-second sprint, according to a study from the American College of Sports Medicine.

Don't let your hips sag.

Tuck your elbows toward your sides.

Keep your core stiff

To make it harder, you can jump up from the squat position instead of simply standing up.

Your arms and hands should be out in front of your body.

Your upper thighs should be parallel to the floor.

Fat Loss Exercises

Low-Box Burpee
TOTAL BODY

A
- Stand facing a box or sturdy object.

The box should be high enough so that you can squat down and place your hands on it without rounding your lower back.

B
- Bend at your hips and knees and place your hands on the box.

C
- Jump your legs back and lower your body into the down position of a pushup. (To make it easier, you can skip the pushup, and keep your arms straight as you kick your legs back.)

The higher the box, the easier the pushup will be.

Squeeze your glutes.

Single-Leg Burpee
TOTAL BODY

- Perform this movement just like a low-box burpee, only lift one foot off the floor and hold it in the air the entire time.

Holding one leg in the air forces your core to work harder.

Don't let your hips rotate as you jump back.

F

- Jump your legs back up near the box, landing with your feet spread wide apart.

G

- Stand or jump up to return to the starting position.

Placing your hands on a box reduces the distance you have to bend down, making this a great option if you have limited mobility or experience low-back discomfort when doing the standard version.

VARIATION #3
Single-Arm Burpee
TOTAL BODY

- Do this movement just like a low-box burpee, only lift one hand off the box and hold it in the air the entire time. (Fair warning: Most people should skip the actual pushup!)

When you kick your legs back, your feet should be spread wide apart.

VARIATION #4
Mobility Burpee
TOTAL BODY

- Get into pushup position with your arms straight.

- Lift your right foot, bend your knee, and place your right foot as close as you comfortably can to your right hand.

- Drive your right heel into the floor and push your body up to a standing position. Reverse the movement to the pushup position, and repeat with your left leg.

Stand up tall with good posture.

Don't let your hips sag.

Your foot should be outside of your hand.

Squeeze your glutes as you step forward.

VARIATION #5
Bottom Burpee
TOTAL BODY

- Lower into the down position of a pushup. (If that's too hard, you can start from the up position of the pushup.)

- In one movement, jump your feet up toward your shoulders as you simultaneously push off the floor with your hands and land in a squat position. Reverse the movement and repeat.

Squeeze your glutes.

Push your chest out and up.

VARIATION #6
Reverse Burpee
TOTAL BODY

- Start in pushup position, but with your hands out in front of your shoulders.

- Slowly walk your hands back toward your feet until you're in a position where you can jump up.

- Quickly explode upward.

Reach for the sky as you jump.

Your body should form a straight line from your head to your ankles.

Take little steps with your hands as you push your hips upward.

VARIATION #7
Burpee to Thruster
TOTAL BODY

- Grasp a pair of hex dumbbell handles and set yourself in pushup position.

- Optional: lower into the down position of a pushup.
- Jump your feet forward so that they land next to the dumbbells.

- Drop into a deep squat, and then curl the dumbbells to your shoulders.

- In one movement, push your body to a standing position as you explosively press the dumbbells above your head.

Your arms should be completely straight.

Pressing the weights above your head targets your shoulders and triceps.

When you jump forward, don't lift the dumbbells off the floor.

Focus on lifting your chest upward.

As you curl, sit back even more into the squat.

Stiffen your core.

Your arms should be straight.

MAIN MOVE
Hollow Body Hops
CARDIO

- Stand tall with your hands on your hips.
- Focus on creating tension throughout your whole body by contracting your muscles. That's the key to this exercise.
- Hop in place while maintaining that muscle tension.

Slightly crunch your hips toward your pelvis as you stiffen your core.

Tightly squeeze your glutes and quadriceps.

Pretend you are trying to crack a nut between your ankles.

Make it harder by placing your hands behind your head, or even harder by raising your arms above your head. See variations 1 and 2.

VARIATION #1
Hollow Body Hops with Hands Behind Head
CARDIO

Forward-and-Back Hops
CARDIO
- Stand facing a line, and hop back and forth over it.
- Move quickly while staying as close to the line on each hop as possible.

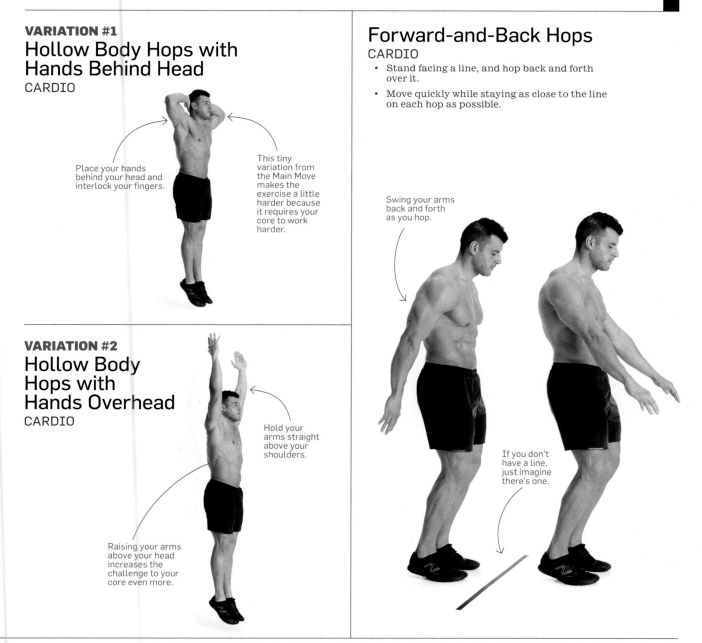

Place your hands behind your head and interlock your fingers.

This tiny variation from the Main Move makes the exercise a little harder because it requires your core to work harder.

VARIATION #2
Hollow Body Hops with Hands Overhead
CARDIO

Hold your arms straight above your shoulders.

Raising your arms above your head increases the challenge to your core even more.

Swing your arms back and forth as you hop.

If you don't have a line, just imagine there's one.

Fat Loss Exercises

Side-to-Side Hops
CARDIO

- Stand with your side facing a line, and hop back and forth over it.

Use short, quick hops and try to minimize the time your feet are in contact with the floor.

Squat Hops
CARDIO + QUADRICEPS

- Stand on the balls of your feet and lower your body into a squat.
- While holding the squat position, hop up and down.

Raise your heels.

Your feet should be slightly wider than shoulder-width apart.

Don't round your lower back.

Holding the squat position makes this a great way to challenge your quadriceps and glutes.

Skater Hops
CARDIO + GLUTES/HAMSTRINGS

A

- Stand on your left leg, with your left leg bent and your right leg raised behind you.
- Position your arms to the left of your body as shown.

MAKE IT HARDER
- *Increase the distance that you hop.*
- *Increase the height that you hop.*
- *Decrease the time your foot is on the floor.*
- *Bend your front knee more, so that your body stays lower.*
- *Do very short hops, but at a faster speed.*

If you have trouble with balance, tap your raised foot on the floor behind you.

Stay low as you hop. (Imagine that you're hopping back and forth in a tunnel.)

B

- Push off the floor and hop a couple of feet to your right, landing on your right foot with your right knee bent and your left leg raised behind you.

Swing your arms to your right as you hop, mimicking the motion of a speed skater.

Bench Hops
CARDIO

A

- Stand next to a bench and place your hands on it.
- Place your feet together.
- Grasp the outside of the bench.

B

- Keeping your hands in place, hop over the bench.

C

- Land on the opposite side and immediately hop back.

MAIN MOVE
Low Box Runners
CARDIO

A

- Stand with the ball of your left foot on a low box or step.

B

- In one movement, quickly switch feet and arm positions. Repeat back and forth.

A

- Stand with your right side facing a low box or step, your right foot on the box and your left foot on the floor.

B

- In one movement, hop sideways across the box, so that your left foot is on the box and your right foot is on the floor. Repeat back and forth.

Your left arm should be swung behind you.

Your right arm should be bent and out in front of you, as if you were sprinting.

Your right foot should be a few inches away from the box, heel raised.

Remember: Opposite arm and leg move forward with each rep.

MAIN MOVE
Seal Jacks
CARDIO

- Stand with your feet and hands together.
- Simultaneously kick your legs out to your sides as you pull your arms back. Reverse the movement and repeat back and forth.

Squeeze your shoulder blades together as you pull your arms back.

Your arms should be out to your sides.

Your arms should be straight in front of your body at shoulder height.

The Simplest Fat Loss Workout Ever

Try this seal jack pyramid workout from famed strength and conditioning coach Dan John, author of *Never Let Go*. It can work with just about any variation of the exercise. Do as many jacks as you can in 10 seconds, and rest for an equal amount of time. Next, do as many jacks as you can in 20 seconds, and rest for 20 seconds. Then do 30 seconds of jacks followed by 30 seconds of rest. Now work your way back down the pyramid, starting with 30 seconds (then 20 and 10). Repeat three times for a great 12-minute fat-frying routine you can do anywhere, anytime.

Fat Loss Exercises

VARIATION #1
Seal to Predator Jacks
CARDIO

- As you kick your legs out, drop into a squat.

Pull your arms back wide and squeeze your shoulder blades together.

Stand tall with your chest out.

The tops of your thighs should be parallel to the floor.

VARIATION #3
Jumping Jacks with a Mini-Band
CARDIO

- Place a light mini-band just above your ankles.
- Simultaneously kick your legs out to your sides as you raise your arms to shoulder level. Reverse the movement and repeat back and forth.

Your palms should be facing the floor.

Keep the bend in your elbow as you raise your arms.

Bend your elbows 90-degrees.

Stand with your feet far enough apart that there's tension in the band.

The band targets your glutes.

VARIATION #2
Modified Seal Jacks
CARDIO

A

- Stand with your feet and hands together.

Your arms should be straight.

B

- Step your left leg out wide to the side and tap your toes on the floor.
- Simultaneously pull your arms back so that they're in line with your body.

Your palms should face forward.

C

- Step back to the starting position.

D

- Step out to the side with your right leg. Reverse the movement to the starting position, and continue to alternate back and forth.

WHY GO SLOW?
This "slow" version of the classic jumping jack is ideal if you have joint or mobility problems or are just starting a fitness program.

Keep your torso upright with your shoulders pulled back.

VARIATION #4
Cross-Body Jacks
CARDIO

- Kick your legs and arms out to your sides, as you would for a seal jack.
- When you jump, bring your legs and arms back toward your body, crossing your legs and arms over one another.

Alternate the limb that crosses over in front each repetition.

VARIATION #5
Star Jacks
CARDIO

- Stand in a quarter-squat with your feet together.
- Jump up as you kick your legs out and swing your hands upward. Land and repeat.

Lean forward at your hips.

Place your hands near your knees.

Your arms and legs should form a "star."

Fat Loss Exercises

VARIATION #6
Dumbbell Split Raise Jacks
CARDIO + SHOULDERS

- Grab a pair of light dumbbells and stand on the balls of your feet in a staggered stance, your right foot in front of your left.
- Now switch leg positions by jumping forward with your left foot and back with your right.
- As you switch leg positions, swing one dumbbell forward and the other dumbbell backward.

Raise the front dumbbell to shoulder height.

Swing the dumbbell in the opposite direction as your same side leg. So, as your left leg jumps forward, your right arm swings forward.

Your feet should be a couple of feet apart.

VARIATION #7
Dumbbell Lateral Raise Jacks
CARDIO + SHOULDERS

- Stand tall while holding a pair of dumbbells at your sides.
- Kick your feet out to your sides as you raise the dumbbells. Reverse the movement and repeat.

Your palms should be facing the floor.

Lift the dumbbells to shoulder height.

Position your feet close together.

VARIATION #8
Dumbbell Curl Jacks
CARDIO + BICEPS

- Hold a pair of light dumbbells next to your sides, with your palms facing each other.
- Curl the dumbbells to your shoulders as you jump one foot forward and one foot back. Reverse the movement to the starting position, and then repeat, this time jumping forward and back with the opposite feet.

Stand as tall as you can.

Don't hunch forward.

Your front leg should be bent in semi-squat position.

VARIATION #9
Dumbbell Overhead Press Jacks
CARDIO + SHOULDERS

- Hold a pair of light dumbbells in front of your shoulders, with your knuckles pointing to the ceiling.
- Press the dumbbells overhead as you kick your legs out the sides.

Your palms should be facing each other.

Your arms should be completely straight.

369

Fat Loss Exercises

VARIATION #10
Dumbbell Chest Press Jacks
CARDIO + CORE + SHOULDERS

- Hold a pair of light dumbbells in front of your chest, the thumb side of your hands pointing up.
- Press the dumbbells straight in front of your chest as you kick your legs out to the sides.

Your palms should be facing each other.

Your upper arms should be next to your sides with your elbows bent 90 degrees.

VARIATION #11
In-and-Out Squats
CARDIO + QUADRICEPS

- Stand with your feet about hip-width apart and lower your body into a squat.
- While holding the squat position, jump your feet out so that they're beyond shoulder-width. Reverse the movement and repeat back and forth.

Keep your chest up as you jump back and forth.

Don't round your lower back.

VARIATION #12
Band Jack Curls
CARDIO + BICEPS

- Place your feet on a continuous loop resistance band.
- Grasp the band with both hands next to your sides.
- Curl the band upward as you jump your feet out to your sides. Reverse the movement and repeat.

Your palms should be facing each other.

Keep your torso upright.

Adjust your hand placement so that you feel slight tension in the band.

Your feet should be about shoulder-width apart.

VARIATION #13
Band Jack Presses
CARDIO + SHOULDERS

- Grasp the band with both hands in front of your shoulders.
- Press the band overhead as you jump your feet out.

Your palms should face away from your body.

Your arms should be completely straight.

VARIATION #14
Band Jack Pull-Aparts
CARDIO + UPPER BACK

- Hold a continuous loop resistance band with both hands in front of your chest.
- Pull your arms back as far as you can as you jump your feet out to the sides.

Your arms should be nearly straight.

Squeeze your shoulder blades together.

Your palms should face the floor.

Fat Loss Exercises

MAIN MOVE
Stepup Jump
GLUTES/HAMSTRINGS

A

- Place your right foot on a sturdy box or step that's about knee height.

B

- Drive your right heel into the box and jump up explosively.

Cock your arms behind you as you prepare to jump.

Forcefully swing your arms upward.

C

- Land as softly as you can in the starting position and immediately jump again. Do all your reps and then repeat with your left foot on the box.

You can make it easier by using a lower box.

VARIATION
Alternating Stepup Jump
GLUTES/HAMSTRINGS

- Place your right foot on the box and your left leg on the floor.
- Jump up so that you land with your left foot on the box and your right foot on the floor.

Squeeze your glutes.

Switch legs in mid-air.

Try to land as softly as you can.

Seated Squat Jump
QUADRICEPS

A

- Sit tall on a sturdy box or step that's about knee height.

B

- Explosively drive your heels into the floor and jump as high as you can. Land softly and slowly lower back to the starting position.

13 Calories per minute burned when people did eight 20-second rounds of all-out jump squats interspersed with 10 seconds of rest, according to a study from Auburn University at Montgomery.

Hold your arms straight out in front of you.

Your thighs should be parallel to the floor.

As you jump, forcefully swing your arms behind you.

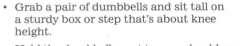

MAIN MOVE
Box Thrusters
TOTAL BODY

A

- Grab a pair of dumbbells and sit tall on a sturdy box or step that's about knee height.

- Hold the dumbbells next to your shoulders.

B

- In one movement, drive your heels into the floor and push your body to a standing position as you explosively press the dumbbells above your head. Lower and repeat.

Your arms should be completely straight.

Your palms should be facing each other.

The press portion of the lift targets your shoulders, triceps, and quadriceps.

Your feet should be about shoulder-width apart.

VARIATION #1
Single-Arm Dumbbell Thrusters
TOTAL BODY

- Hold a dumbbell next to your chest and lower your body into a squat.
- In one movement, push your body to a standing position as you press the dumbbell over your head.

As you press, rotate your forearm outward so that your palm faces forward at the top.

Your palm should be facing your body.

Your arm should be straight.

The top of your thighs should be parallel or lower to the floor.

Your elbow should be bent and tucked close to your side.

VARIATION #2
Split Stance Thrusters
TOTAL BODY

- Hold a pair of dumbbells in front of your shoulders and lower your body into a split squat position.
- Simultaneously push your body up to a standing position as you press the dumbbells over your head. Lower and repeat. Do all your reps, then switch legs.

Your palms should be facing each other.

Your arms should be completely straight.

Your torso should be upright.

Your front knee should be bent 90 degrees.

Fat Loss Exercises

VARIATION #3
Squat Curl to Thruster
TOTAL BODY

A

- Grab a pair of dumbbells and set your feet wider than shoulder-width apart.
- Lower your body into a squat and hold the dumbbells at arm's length between your legs.

Keep your lower back naturally arched.

B

- Bend your elbows and curl the dumbbells to your shoulders.

Curling the weights targets your biceps.

C

- In one movement, push your body to a standing position as you press the dumbbells over your head. Reverse the movement and repeat.

Your palms should be facing each other.

VARIATION #4
Kettlebell Goblet Thrusters
TOTAL BODY

- Hold a kettlebell next to your chest and lower your body into a squat.
- In one movement, push your body to a standing position as you press the kettlebell over your head.

Your arms should be as straight as possible.

Grasp the horns of the kettlebell.

The top of your thighs should be parallel or lower to the floor.

VARIATION #5
Stepup Thrusters
TOTAL BODY

- Grab a pair of dumbbells and hold them in front of your shoulders, your palms facing each other.
- Place your right foot on a sturdy box or step, with your weight shifted onto it.
- In one movement, drive your right foot into the box and push your body upward as you press the dumbbells over your head.
- Lower back to the starting position. Do all your reps, then switch legs and repeat.

Your arms should be completely straight.

Performing thrusters on a step emphasizes your glutes.

You should be on the ball of your left foot.

Keep your left foot off the box.

VARIATION #6
Wall Ball
TOTAL BODY

- Hold a medicine ball next to your chest and lower your body into a squat.
- In one movement, push your body to a standing position as you toss the ball upward.
- Catch the ball as you lower back into the squat and repeat.

Perform the movement in front of a wall to better guide the ball.

Squeeze your glutes forcefully as you push upward.

Goblet Clean to Squat to Press
TOTAL BODY

A

- Stand with your feet slightly beyond shoulder-width apart and place a dumbbell between your heels.
- Push your hips back, bend your knees, and grasp the top head of the dumbbell with both hands.

B

- In one movement, forcefully stand up as you rotate your hands under the head of the dumbbell.

C

- Lower your body into a squat.

D

- Push your body up as you press the dumbbell above your head. Squat down, lower the dumbbell back to the floor, and repeat.

Pull your shoulders down and hold them that way.

Hold the dumbbell close to your chest.

Push your chest out and up.

Keep your torso as upright as you can.

The tops of your thighs should be at least parallel or lower to the floor.

Sumo Deadlift to Curl to Press
TOTAL BODY

A

- Grab a pair of dumbbells and hold them at arm's length in front of your thighs.
- Stand with your feet about twice shoulder-width apart.

B

- Bend at your hips and knees, and lower your torso as far as you can without rounding your lower back.

C

- In one movement, stand up straight as you curl the dumbbells to your shoulders.

D

- Press the dumbbells over your head. Reverse the movement and repeat.

Your arms should be as straight as possible.

The curl targets your biceps.

Keep your lower back naturally arched.

Your palms should be facing each other.

Squeeze your glutes forcefully and hold them that way as you press.

The overhead press works your shoulders and triceps.

Your toes should point out at a 15- to 30-degree angle.

Reverse Lunge to Stepup
GLUTES/HAMSTRINGS

A
- Stand behind a box or step that's about knee height.

B
- Step back with your right leg and lower your body into a lunge.

C
- With your right leg, take a big step and place your right foot onto the box.

D
- Drive your right heel into the box and push your body upward until your right leg is straight.
- Reverse the movement to the starting position. Do all your reps and repeat with your left leg.

Your left arm should be pulled back behind you.

Your right arm should be bent and in front of your body.

Keep your torso upright.

Your arms should switch positions as your leg positions change.

Bend your left knee and lift it as high as you can.

Stepup to Hip Hinge
GLUTES/HAMSTRINGS

A

- Place your right foot on a sturdy box or step that's about knee height.

B

- Drive your right heel into the box and push your body upward until your right leg is straight.

C

- Keeping your lower back naturally arched, bend at your hips and lower your torso as far as you comfortably can. Reverse the movement to the starting position. Do all your reps and repeat with your left leg.

Hold your left foot in the air.

Don't round your lower back.

Your right knee should be slightly bent.

Reach down and try to touch the box.

381

Stepup to Curl to Press
TOTAL BODY

A
- Grab a pair of dumbbells and place your right foot on a sturdy box or step that's about knee height.

B
- Drive your right heel into the box and push your body upward until your right leg is straight.

C
- Curl the dumbbells toward your shoulders.

D
- Press the dumbbells above your head.

Your arms should be completely straight.

Stand tall with good posture.

Adding a curl works your biceps.

Pressing the weights over your head targets your shoulders and triceps.

MAIN MOVE
Metabolic Up-Downs
CARDIO

- Kneel on the floor on both knees.
- Lift your right knee and place your right foot on the floor in front of you.
- Press your right foot into the floor and push your body to a standing position. Reverse the movement to return to the starting position, and repeat with your left leg.

Try to be as "tall" as you can in the kneeling position.

Squeeze your glutes tightly.

Don't lean forward or back.

Your front shin should be nearly vertical.

Your feet should be about hip-width apart.

Fat Loss Exercises

Sandbag Up-Downs
TOTAL BODY

- Hold a sandbag over one shoulder and perform the movement.

Push your hips forward as you stand.

Dig your toes into the floor.

Drive your heel into the floor.

Split Squat Shoulder Raise
TOTAL BODY

- Grab a pair of dumbbells and lower your body into a split squat position, holding the weights at your sides.

- Simultaneously press your front heel into the floor and push your body up to a standing position as you raise the dumbbells to shoulder level. Lower and repeat.

Raising your arms works your shoulders.

Your palms should be facing the floor.

Your front knee should be bent 90 degrees.

Your torso should be upright.

The split squat targets your quadriceps.

Squat Press
TOTAL BODY

- Hold a dumbbell with both hands next to your chest and lower your body into a squat.
- Push the dumbbells straight out from your chest.

Your elbows should be bent and tucked next to your sides.

Pressing the weight out challenges both your core and your shoulders.

Your arms should be completely straight.

Your thighs should be parallel to the floor.

Duck Walk
QUADRICEPS

- Lower your body into a squat and hold that position as you walk forward and backward.

TRAINER'S TIP
To make it harder, you can hold a pair of kettlebells or dumbbells at arm's length between your legs. (Don't round your back or bend over any further than the bodyweight version.)

Keep your torso as upright as possible.

Your thighs should be parallel to the floor.

With each step, your back toes should be about even with your front heel.

Dumbbell Discus
TOTAL BODY

A

- Grab a light dumbbell in your right hand and stand in a deep staggered stance, your right foot in front of your left foot.
- Lean forward at your hips, bend your front knee, and lower your torso until it's at about a 45-degree angle with the floor.
- Lock the dumbbell behind your hips.

B

- In one movement, pivot both feet about 180 degrees as you quickly swing the dumbbell out and up so that meets your free hand in front of your face. Reverse the movement and repeat. Do all your reps and switch sides.

Keep your arm nearly straight for the entire movement.

Your lower back should be naturally arched.

Put your weight on your front foot.

Raise your torso until it's upright.

Stop the motion of the weight with your free hand.

Lift your back heel as you pivot.

Straighten your front leg.

Dumbbell Shotput
TOTAL BODY

A

- Hold a light dumbbell in front of your right shoulder and stand in a staggered stance, your right foot in front of your left.

- Bend forward at your hips and lower your torso until it's at about a 45-degree angle with the floor.

B

- In one movement, pivot both feet about 180 degrees as you explosively rotate your body and press the dumbbell out and up. Reverse the movement and repeat. Do all your reps and switch sides.

Your palm should be facing your opposite arm.

Lean forward without rounding your lower back.

Bend your front knee.

Push your foot into the floor.

As you turn, swing your free arm back.

Push your hips forward and raise your torso.

Press the dumbbell at a 45-degree angle from your body.

Your arm should be completely straight.

As you pivot, lower your heel and straighten your front leg.

Pivot on the ball of your foot.

Lawn Mower Pull
TOTAL BODY

A

- Grab a light dumbbell in your left hand and stand in a staggered stance, your right foot in front of your left.
- Lower your torso until it's at nearly parallel to the floor and let the dumbbell hang straight down from your shoulder.

B

- In one movement, quickly pivot 180 degrees as you explosively pull the dumbbell to your shoulder. Reverse the movement and repeat. Do all your reps and switch sides.

The pulling motion targets your upper back and biceps.

Don't round your lower back.

Bend your front leg.

Shift your weight onto your front foot.

Raise your back heel.

Raise your torso to an upright position.

As you pull the dumbbell, imagine that you're starting a lawn mower.

Dumbbell Piston Push-Pulls

CARDIO + BACK + BICEPS

A

- Grab a dumbbell with both hands and lower your torso until it's nearly parallel to the floor.
- Let the dumbbell hang straight down from your shoulders.

B

- Without moving your torso, bend your arms and pull the dumbbell to your rib cage. Lower by pushing the dumbbell back to the starting position. Continue to push and pull continuously until you've done all your reps.

Lean forward at your hips.

Keep your lower back naturally arched.

Don't raise or lower your upper body.

Bend your knees.

Interlock your fingers around the dumbbell handle.

Your feet should be just beyond shoulder-width apart.

MAIN MOVE
Skier Swing

CARDIO + GLUTES/HAMSTRINGS

A

- Grab a pair of dumbbells and set your feet about hip-width apart.
- Lean forward at your hips and swing the dumbbells backward.

B

- Squeeze your glutes, thrust your hips forward, and swing the dumbbells up to chest level. Reverse the motion and repeat, swinging the dumbbells back and forth.

Your arms should be straight.

Crunch your abs at the top of the movement.

Squeeze your glutes.

Straighten your knees as you swing the weights forward.

Don't round your lower back.

Your knees should be slightly bent.

VARIATION #1
Bodyweight Skier Swing
CARDIO + GLUTES/HAMSTRINGS

- Without weights, bend at your hips and swing your arms forcefully upward as you rise to a standing position.

- As you progress, allow your feet to leave the floor an inch or two on the upward swing.

VARIATION #2
Overhead Skier Swing
CARDIO + GLUTES/HAMSTRINGS

- Swing the weights past chest level and all the way up until they're straight above your shoulders.

Keep your lower back naturally arched.

Your hips should be completely extended (so that they're in line with your upper body).

From here, thrust your hips forward.

Hold this position for a second or two before you swing the weights back down.

VARIATION #3
Staggered Skier Swing
CARDIO + GLUTES/HAMSTRINGS

- Stagger your feet, one foot in front of another. Do all your reps and switch foot positions.

Squeeze your glutes.

Your back toes should line up with your front heel.

VARIATION #4
Rocker Skier Swing
CARDIO + GLUTES/HAMSTRINGS

- Instead of thrusting your hips forward as you swing the weights, "sit back" into a quarter squat position. Rock back and forth as you swing the dumbells.

Keep your lower back naturally arched.

Drop your hips down.

Your torso should become more upright as you sit back.

The counterweight of the dumbells is what allows you to sit back.

VARIATION #5
Dumbbell Clean
CARDIO + GLUTES/
HAMSTRINGS + BICEPS

- As you swing the weights upward, bend your arms and pull the dumbbells to your shoulders.

Don't round your lower back.

Your palms should be facing each other.

VARIATION #6
Reverse Lunge with Single-Arm Swing
CARDIO + GLUTES/HAMSTRINGS

A

- Grab a light dumbbell in your right hand and stand with your feet hip-width apart.
- Let the dumbbell hang at arm's length next to your side.
- Step back into a lunge with your right leg.

B

- In one movement, push your body back to a standing position as you swing the dumbbell upward until it's above your right shoulder. Reverse the movement and repeat.

Keep your arm straight.

Your knee should be bent 90 degrees.

Swing the dumbbell up in a wide arc.

Your palm should be facing your side.

MAIN MOVE
Kettlebell Swing
CARDIO + GLUTES/HAMSTRINGS

A

- Stand about 2 feet behind a kettlebell, bend forward at your hips, and grasp the kettlebell handle with both hands.

- You should look like you're going to hike the kettlebell between your legs. (Which is what you're going to do.)

B

- Keeping your back naturally arched, swing the kettlebell between your legs.

C

- Thrust your hips forward and swing the kettlebell to chest height. Continue to swing the kettlebell back and forth (between position B and position C).

20

Number of calories people burned per minute when doing kettlebell swings with a 16-kilogram kettlebell, according to a University of Wisconsin study.

Don't round your lower back.

Your feet should be about shoulder-width apart.

Tilt the kettlebell toward you.

Contract your glutes forcefully.

Pack your shoulders by pulling them down and slightly back. Hold that way as you swing.

Hinge at your hips so that your butt goes back as you lower your torso.

Your knees should be slightly bent.

The kettlebell should pass close to your crotch, not down by your knees.

Keep your shoulders packed.

Allow the momentum of your hip thrust to swing your arms upward. You are not actively raising them.

Your hips should be pushed forward.

Crunch your rib cage down and brace your core to create a "standing plank."

The kettlebell should feel "weightless" in the position.

Squeeze your glutes and quads tightly.

Your arms and legs should be straight.

394

VARIATION
Kettlebell Shuffle Swing
CARDIO + GLUTES/HAMSTRINGS

- As you swing the kettlebell upward, step your left foot to your right.
- As the kettlebell swings toward your hips, step your left foot back out. On the next rep, step your right foot to your left, and then back out. Continue to alternate back and forth.

Keep your lower back naturally arched.

THE SECRET TO A BETTER SWING
Hold the "standing plank" position as long as you can—even as you swing the kettlebell back toward your body. In fact, famed Russian kettlebell expert and StrongFirst Chairman Pavel Tsatsouline says to imagine you're playing chicken with the kettlebell and your crotch. The idea is to stay upright as long as possible and at the very last moment, bend forward to allow the kettlebell to swing between your legs. This ensures that the kettlebell stays high and protects your lower back.

Step one foot toward the other so that your feet are close together.

Goblet Clean
CARDIO + GLUTES/HAMSTRINGS + SHOULDERS

A

- Stand with your feet slightly beyond shoulder-width apart and place a kettlebell between your heels.
- Bend at your hips and knees and lower your torso until you can grasp the kettle-bell handle with both hands.

B

- In one movement, stand up as you bend your arms and pull the kettlebell to your chest, rotating your hands around the handle.

Pull your shoulders down into their sockets (toward your hips).

Keep your lower back naturally arched.

Squeeze your glutes tightly.

You should be holding the kettlebell at its horns.

Your arms should be straight.

Your feet should be slightly wider than shoulder-width apart.

Your legs should be straight.

Fat Loss Exercises

MAIN MOVE
Sandbag Lunge with Rotation
CARDIO + GLUTES/HAMSTRINGS

A

- Grasp the handles of a sandbag with each hand and step back with your left leg into a reverse lunge, your right leg forward.
- Rotate the sandbag so that you're holding it at arms' length on the right side of your body.

B

- Push your body to a standing position as you rotate the sandbag in front of you.

C

- Continue to rotate the sandbag to your left as you step back with your right leg.

Your torso should be upright.

Squeeze your glutes tightly.

Try to resist twisting your upper body even as you allow the sandbag to rotate to your left.

You should be facing forward.

Your front knee should be bent at least 90 degrees.

VARIATION
Sandbag Lunge with Rotational Swing
CARDIO + GLUTES/HAMSTRINGS + CORE

- In one movement, forcefully swing the sandbag up and out in front of you as you move from lunging to standing to lunging. Then immediately reverse the motion and continue to swing the bag back and forth as you lunge.

Keep your core braced for the entire movement.

Your arms should be straight.

Try to keep your belly button facing forward.

MAIN MOVE
Rack Carry
TOTAL BODY

- Grab a pair of dumbbells and hold them in front of your chest as you walk forward, backward, or even laterally with perfect posture.

Holding the weights in the "rack" position increases the challenge to your upper back and biceps.

Your palms should be facing your chest.

Keep your chest up.

Bend your elbows and hold them tight to your body.

How to Carry the Load

Carries look simple—and they are. But they're also a truly fantastic training tool that work your shoulders, upper back, core, biceps, forearms, glutes, and really, just about every part of your body. They'll also elevate your heart rate and improve your conditioning.When you do a carry, imagine that you're performing a "standing plank." You want to stand tall with perfect posture, pull your shoulders down—and hold them that way—and brace your core. Use a short stride, your feet about 12 inches apart. To get the most out of this awesome exercise, use the following basic guidelines from strength coach Dan John. To build strength, choose heavy weights that you can only carry for about 50 feet. To target endurance, walk with a weight that you're able to hold for about 300 feet. Or work on a mix of both qualities, by using a load that's challenging for about 150 feet. (It might sound obvious, but just in case it's not: You don't have to walk the entire distance in a straight line; simply turn around whenever you run out of room.)

Fat Loss Exer-ises

VARIATION #1
Overhead Carry
TOTAL BODY + CORE + SHOULDERS

- Hold dumbbells over your head as you walk.

Your arms should be completely straight.

Don't lean forward or back.

Holding the load overhead forces your core and shoulders to work harder.

VARIATION #2
Single-Arm Carry
TOTAL BODY

- Hold a dumbbell in one hand next to your side as you walk.
- Perform for an equal amount of time or distance on each side.

Pull your shoulder down and slightly back.

Don't allow the weight to cause you to lean in any direction.

Holding a weight on just one side of your body forces your obliques to work overtime in order to keep your body upright.

VARIATION #3
Single-Arm Rack Carry
TOTAL BODY

- Hold a dumbbell in one hand next to your chest.

Position your arm tight to your body.

Your palm should be facing your chest.

VARIATION #4
Single-Arm Overhead Carry
TOTAL BODY

- Hold a dumbbell in one arm above your head as you walk.

Your arm should be completely straight.

To help with balance and posture, position your free arm away from and slightly out in front of you.

VARIATION #5
High-Low Carry
TOTAL BODY

- Hold a heavy dumbbell next to your side and a lighter dumbbell above your head.

Focus on maintaining perfect posture as you walk.

VARIATION #6
Flexed Arm Carry
TOTAL BODY

- Grab a pair of dumbbells and hold them with bent arms as you walk.

The flexed position really challenges your biceps.

Hold your upper arms next to your sides.

Bend your elbows 90 degrees.

VARIATION #7
Kettlebell Goblet Carry
TOTAL BODY

- Grasp a kettlebell with both hands and hold it next to your chest as you walk.

Hold the horns of the kettlebell.

Pull your shoulders down and back.

VARIATION #8
Kettlebell Bottoms-Up Carry
TOTAL BODY

- Position a kettlebell upside down and hold it with one hand as you walk. (This is much harder than it looks!)

Your wrist should be straight.

Bend your elbow.

The bottoms-up position requires mental focus and strong forearms—so that your wrist doesn't bend.

VARIATION #9
Sandbag Carry
TOTAL BODY

- Hold a sandbag over one shoulder as you walk. Repeat for an equal distance on the other side.

Keep your torso upright with your chest out.

399

MAIN MOVE
Pushup Jacks
CARDIO + CORE + CHEST

A

- Get into the top position of a pushup.

Your body should form a straight line from your head to your ankles.

Your arms should be straight.

Your feet should be close together.

Brace your abdominals and hold them that way for the duration of this exercise.

Place your hands under your shoulders.

B

- As you bend your elbows and lower your body to the floor, jump your legs out to beyond shoulder-width apart. Reverse the movement and repeat.

Pull your shoulders down toward your feet.

Keep your core stiff.

Your chest should almost touch the floor.

As you lower your body, pull your upper arms toward your sides.

Your feet should be spread wide apart.

MAKE IT HARDER
As you jump your feet wide, also jump your hands out. Push up explosively and jump them both back to the starting position.

VARIATION #1
Plank Jacks
CARDIO + CORE
- Without moving your arms, jump your feet out wide, and then back close. Repeat back and forth.

Your body should form a straight line from your head to your ankles.

Your torso should remain stiff.

Your feet should be close to each other.

Your feet should be beyond shoulder-width apart.

VARIATION #2
Deadstop Pushup
CHEST
- Get into the top position of a pushup, and lower your body all the way to the floor.
- Raise your hands off the floor as high as you can, hold for a second, then press your hands into the floor, and push yourself back up to the starting position.

Push your upper back toward the ceiling.

Brace your core.

Contract your glutes tightly.

Squeeze your shoulder blades together.

Your body should be resting on the floor.

The Best New Way to Do a Pushup

The deadstop pushup is my new favorite way to do a pushup. I first read about it from a strength coach named Rob Shaul, CSCS, owner of Strong, Swift, and Durable in Jackson Hole, Wyoming. Here's why I like it so much: Raising your hands off the floor at the bottom of the exercise forces you to come to a complete stop and eliminates the stretch reflex—or elasticity—in your muscles. (It also prevents you from cheating!) This requires you to generate more force to push your body back to the top with each repetition, which will make you stronger and help you burn more calories. Give it a try: You're guaranteed to feel the difference immediately.

Fat Loss Exercises

MAIN MOVE
Blast-Off Pushup
CHEST

A

- Get into the top position of a pushup.
- Without rounding your lower back, bend your knees and push your hips back as far as you can.

B

- Push forward and down into the bottom position of a pushup. Then push your hips backward again and repeat.

Keep your lower back naturally arched.

Your arms should be straight.

Don't let your hips sag.

VARIATION
Blast-Off Plank
CORE

A

- Get into the top position of a pushup.

B

- Without rounding your lower back, bend your knees and push your hips back as far as you can. Then push your body back to the starting position and repeat.

Squeeze your glutes.

Don't round your lower back.

Your arms should be straight.

MAIN MOVE
Bucking Hops
CARDIO + CORE

A

- Get down on all fours and place your hands on the floor so that they're slightly wider than and in line with your shoulders.
- Raise your knees a couple of inches off the floor.

B

- Jump your feet off the floor as if you're "bucking" like a horse. Land in the starting position as softly as you can.

Keep your lower back flat.

Dig your toes into the floor.

Brace your core and keep it stiff as you buck.

Your weight should be on your hands.

Your legs should be straight.

VARIATION
Donkey Kicks
CARDIO + CORE

- Perform the same movement as the bucking hop, only kick your legs away from your body as you buck.
- Bring your legs back toward your body and land in the starting position.

MAIN MOVE
Plank Tap to Hand
CARDIO + CORE

A

- Get into the top position of a pushup, with your hands underneath your shoulders.

B

- Keeping your body still, lift your left hand off the floor and tap your right hand. Return to the starting position, and then lift your right hand and tap your left. Continue to alternate back and forth.

TRAINER'S TIP
You can do plank taps at a fast tempo, but before you speed up, make sure you've perfected your form. Keep your core stiff and don't allow your hips or torso to sag or rotate.

Your body should form a straight line from your head to your ankles.

Spread your feet wide for more stability.

Squeeze your glutes and thighs tightly.

Brace your core and hold it that way for the duration of this exercise.

Don't let your hips sag or pike.

Resist allowing your body to rotate as you move your hands back and forth.

VARIATION #1
Plank Tap to Elbow
CARDIO + CORE
- Touch one elbow and then the other.

VARIATION #2
Plank Tap to Shoulder
CARDIO + CORE
- Touch one shoulder and then the other.

VARIATION #3
Plank Tap to Hip
CARDIO + CORE
- Touch one hip and then the other.

VARIATION #4
Plank Tap to Knee
CARDIO + CORE
- Touch one knee and then the other.

Raise your hips without rounding your lower back.

Use your anchored hand to push your body backward.

VARIATION #5
Low Box Plank Hand Taps
CARDIO + CORE
- Touch the box with one hand and then the other.

VARIATION #6
Low Box Plank Stepper
CARDIO + CORE
- Place your left hand on a low box and then your right hand. Step down with your left and then your right. Repeat, only this time, start with your right hand. Continue to repeat back and forth.

Fat Loss Exercises

Single-Leg Plank Walkout
CARDIO + CORE

- Stand tall on your left leg.
- Bend forward and place your hands on the floor.
- Keeping your right foot in the air, walk your hands out until you're at least in a high plank position.

Ideally, your hands will be beyond your head. Walk them out as far as you can while maintaining perfect form.

Your body should form a straight line from your head to your ankles.

Hold your right foot in the air.

Bend your knee only as much as you need to.

Your hips should not sag.

Brace your core forcefully.

Plank Walkup
CARDIO + CORE

- Position your body in a low plank, your forearms on the floor.
- Keeping your body stiff, place your right hand on the floor.
- In one movement, straighten your right arm as you simultaneously place your left hand on the floor and straighten your left arm. Reverse the movement by placing your right forearm on the floor and then your left. Repeat, this time starting with your left hand.

Place your right hand under your shoulder.

Your arms should be completely straight.

Make your body stiff as a board and hold it that way as you move up and down.

Pushup to Side Plank Transfer
CARDIO + CORE

A

- Get into the top position of a push-up—a high plank—with your hands underneath your shoulders.

B

- Lift your left hand and place your left forearm on the floor.

C

- Roll onto your left elbow as you rotate your entire body upward into a side plank. Reverse the movement to the high plank, and repeat by rolling onto your right elbow. Continue to transfer back and forth.

Your feet should be about hip-width part.

Brace your core.

Bend your right elbow.

Your forearm should be perpendicular to your body.

Lift your right arm straight above your shoulder.

Your hips and torso should move together as one unit.

Alligator Crawl
CARDIO + CORE

- Get into the down position of a pushup, your chest nearly touching the floor.

- Without changing your body position, "walk" forward by taking small steps with your hands and feet.

Squeeze your glutes.

To make it easier, perform the same movement, but in the up position of the pushup, with your arms straight.

Don't let your hips sag or pike.

Stiffen your core.

MAIN MOVE
Bear Crawl
CARDIO + CORE

- Get down on all fours and place your hands on the floor so that they're slightly wider than and in line with your shoulders.

- Raise your knees a couple of inches off the floor.

- Without changing your posture, crawl forward by taking a small "step" with your right hand and left foot. Continue to crawl by stepping with your left hand and right foot, and repeating back and forth.

- You can also walk backward or side-to-side for an even greater challenge.

TRAINER'S TIP
As you crawl, your back should look flat, like a tabletop. One challenge to help you perfect your form: Have a partner place an object such as a cone on your lower back. Your goal: Keep your torso and hip movement so minimal that the cone doesn't fall off as you crawl.

Keep your lower back flat.

Stay low and steady: Don't raise or rotate your hips as you crawl.

Your arms should be straight.

VARIATION #1
High Bear Crawl
CARDIO + CORE

- Perform a bear crawl, only pike your hips and hold them that way as you move.

Compared to the standard version of the exercise, the high bear crawl emphasizes greater mobility at your hips and shoulders and increases the challenge to your upper body.

VARIATION #2
Bear Crawl to Explosive Pushup

- From the bear crawl position, kick your legs out and drop your body into the down position of a pushup.

- Push your body up as you explosively jump your legs back into the bear crawl position. Take two steps and then do another pushup.

Your body should form a straight line from head to ankles.

VARIATION #3
Bear Crawl to Row to Donkey Kick
CARDIO + CORE

A

- Get into a bear crawl position, but while grasping a pair of dumbbells.

Your back should look like a tabletop.

B

- Crawl two steps forward and then row one weight to the side of your torso, lower it, and then row the other dumbbell.

Don't allow your hips to rotate as you row.

Pull the dumbbell toward your rib cage.

C

- Do a donkey kick by kicking your legs away from your body. Return to the bear crawl position, and repeat.

MAIN MOVE
Crab Walk
CARDIO

- Sit upright on the floor with your feet flat and your hands on the floor next to your sides.
- Put your weight on your hands and raise your hips a couple of inches off the floor.
- Now walk forward or backward quickly by taking small steps with your feet and hands. (You can also crab walk laterally.)

You'll find this exercise also challenges your shoulders and triceps.

Don't round your lower back.

Your fingers should be pointing to the side, away from your body.

VARIATION
High Crab Walk
CARDIO + CORE + GLUTES/ HAMSTRINGS

- Get into a crab walk position, but push your hips upward until they're in line with your body and hold them that way was you walk. (You'll have to move more slowly than you do in the regular crab walk.)

Don't crane your neck by trying to look up; keep your head in line with your body.

Compared to the standard version of the exercise, the high crab walk works your glutes and core harder.

Squeeze your glutes tightly.

Situp to Hipup
CORE + GLUTES/HAMSTRINGS

A

- Lie faceup on the floor with your arms straight above your shoulders.

Your palms should be facing up.

B

- In one movement, bring your arms forward, place your hands next to your hips, and sit upright with your feet flat.

Squeeze your glutes tightly.

C

- Thrust your hips up until they're in line with your torso. Reverse the movement and repeat.

Your body should form a straight line from your head to your knees.

Bridge to Press to Pullover
CORE + GLUTES/HAMSTRINGS + BACK

A

- Grab a pair of dumbbells and lie faceup on the floor.
- Position your upper arms next to your sides, with your elbows bent 90 degrees.

Your palms should face each other.

B

- Thrust your hips upward so that they're in line with your upper body.

Squeeze your glutes tightly and hold them that way.

C

- Press the dumbbells above your shoulders.

Your arms should be straight.

D

- Keeping your arms nearly straight, lower the dumbbells behind you toward the floor. Reverse the movement and repeat.

Fat Loss Exercises

MAIN MOVE
Plyo Hip Thrust
CARDIO + CORE + GLUTES/ HAMSTRINGS

- Lie faceup on the floor with your knees bent and your feet flat on the floor.
- Explosively thrust your hips upward so that your feet rise off the floor.

Stiffen your core and hold it that way as you thrust.

Squeeze your glutes forcefully.

Your hips should be fully extended so that they're in line with your torso.

VARIATION
Plyo Single-Leg Hip Thrust
CARDIO + CORE + GLUTES/ HAMSTRINGS

- Perform a plyo hip thrust, but hold one foot off the floor. Do all your reps and switch legs and repeat.

The foot of your working leg should leave the floor.

MAIN MOVE
Landmine Squat
QUADRICEPS

- Grasp the end of the barbell with both hands and stand with your feet slightly wider than shoulder-width apart.

- Push your hips back, bend your knees, and lower your body until the tops of your thighs are at least parallel to the floor.

SEEK OUT A LANDMINE
The landmine is a unique fitness tool in which you slide the end of a barbell into a metal sleeve. Once inserted, you can move the bar in any direction—up and down, side to side, or rotationally. This makes it easier to use than a classic barbell and allows you to perform unique exercise variations that challenge your body in new ways. Many gyms now have landmines, but you can also buy your own at online fitness retailers such as performbetter .com and roguefitness.com.

Keep your torso as upright as possible.

Step back enough so that your body is slightly leaning forward.

413

Fat Loss Exercises

■

MAIN MOVE
Battle Ropes Up-Down Waves
CARDIO + CORE

- With each hand, grasp the ends of a battle rope and stand in a quarter-squat position.
- Moving almost exclusively at your forearms, shake the rope up and down quickly to create continuous waves.

10

Calories per minute that battle-rope exercises burned in a study at the College of New Jersey.

Lean forward slightly without rounding your lower back.

Your arms should be slightly bent and stay that way.

Your upper arms should hardly move.

Keep your torso still.

Your feet should be slightly wider than shoulder-width apart.

VARIATION #1
Battle Ropes Alternating Waves
CARDIO + CORE

- Raise one arm while lowering the other so that the waves alternate.

Keep your lower back naturally arched.

VARIATION #2
Battle Ropes Squat Hold Waves
CARDIO + CORE

- Perform battle ropes up-down waves while holding a squat position.

Your thighs should be nearly parallel to the floor.

Your body shouldn't move from the squat position.

Make waves by raising and lowering your forearms.

Chapter 13: Warmup Exercises

MOVES THAT REALLY MATTER

Warmup
Exercises

You're probably tempted to flip past this chapter. After all, who has time to warm up?

The answer is everyone. You see, over the years, fitness experts have discovered that doing the right movements before a workout is like turning on the power to your muscles. Scientists believe that exercises known as dynamic stretches—what you might think of as calisthenics—appear to enhance the communication between your mind and muscles, allowing you to achieve peak performance in the gym. Translation: more muscle and faster fat loss. Surely, that isn't something you want to miss out on.

That's why this chapter provides a library of exercises that you can perform before any workout. Besides activating your muscles, the movements that have been chosen will also improve your flexibility, mobility, and posture—all critical factors for keeping your body both young and injury-free. All of this and it'll only require 5 to 10 minutes of your time.

But wait, there's more! You'll find a section on foam-roller exercises, too. These are movements that help ensure your muscles are functioning like they're supposed to. The best part: They can be done at any time—whether it's at the gym as part of your workout or after dinner on your living room floor. Just consider it the regular muscle maintenance you need to keep your body moving like a well-oiled machine.

Warmup Exercises

In this chapter, you'll find 49 exercises that help prepare your muscles for just about any activity, while also improving your flexibility and mobility.

Jumping Jacks

- Stand with your feet together and your hands at your sides.
- Simultaneously raise your arms above your head and jump up just enough to spread your feet out wide.
- Without pausing, quickly reverse the movement and repeat.

Kick your legs out to the sides quickly.

Split Jacks

- Stand in a staggered stance, your right foot in front of your left.
- Simultaneously jump back with right foot and forward with your left as you swing your right arm forward and above your shoulder and swing your left arm back.
- Continue to quickly switch legs back and forth as you raise and lower your arms.
- Repeat as many times as you can in 30 seconds.

Scissor-kick your legs back and forth.

Warmup Exercises

Squat Thrusts

- Stand with your feet shoulder-width apart and your arms at your sides.
- Push your hips back, bend your knees, and lower your body as deep as you can into a squat.
- Kick your legs backward, so that you're now in a pushup position.
- Then quickly bring your legs back to the squat position.
- Stand up quickly and repeat the entire movement.

As you squat down, place your hands on the floor in front of you, shifting your weight onto them.

If you want a greater challenge, do a pushup here.

Wall Slide

- Lean your head, upper back, and butt against the wall.
- Place your hands and arms against the wall in the "high-five" position, your elbows bent 90 degrees and your upper arms at shoulder height.
- Keeping your elbows, wrists, and hands pressed into the wall, slide your elbows down toward your sides as far as you can. Squeeze your shoulder blades together.
- Slide your arms back up the wall as high as you can while keeping your hands in contact with the wall.
- Lower and repeat.

Don't allow your head, upper back, or butt to lose contact with the wall.

Hold for 1 second.

When your hands start to lose contact with the wall, slide your arms back down again.

THE BENEFIT
Enhances the function of your shoulder blades, which can help improve posture and shoulder health.

Hand Crossover

- Hold your arms so that, together, they form a straight line and a 45-degree angle with the floor.
- Your right arm should be raised, with your palm facing forward and your thumb pointing up.
- Your left arm should be held low, with your palm facing behind you and your thumb pointing down.
- Bring your arms across your body as if they were swapping positions, only keep the palm of each hand facing the same direction it was in the starting position.
- Alternate back and forth, gradually increasing the speed of the crossovers, so that you're loosely and quickly swinging your arms across your body. Do all your reps, then switch the starting and repeat.

Palm facing behind you, thumb up.

Palm facing forward, thumb up.

Palm facing behind you, thumb down.

Palm facing forward, thumb down.

THE BENEFIT *Improves the mobility of your shoulders.*

Neck Rotations

- Stand tall with your feet shoulder-width apart.
- Roll your neck in a circular motion to the left 10 times (or as prescribed).
- Reverse directions, rolling in a circular motion to the right 10 times.

THE BENEFIT
Enhances the mobility of your neck.

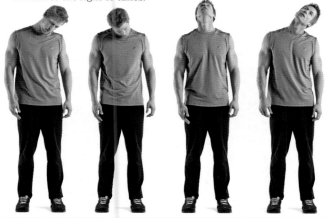

Side-Lying Thoracic Rotation

- Lie on your left side on the floor, with your hips and knees bent 90 degrees.
- Straighten both arms in front of you at shoulder height, palms pressed together.
- Keeping your left arm and both legs in position, rotate your right arm up and over your body and rotate your torso to the right, until your right hand and upper back are flat on the floor.
- Hold for 2 seconds, then bring your right arm back to the starting position.
- Complete the prescribed number of reps, then turn over and do the same number for your other side.

THE BENEFIT
Loosens the muscles of your middle and upper back.

Your arm and shoulder should touch the floor.

Thoracic Rotation

- Get down on on all fours.
- Place your right hand behind your head.
- Brace your core.
- Rotate your upper back downward so your elbow is pointed down and to your left.
- Raise your right elbow toward the ceiling by rotating your head and upper back up and to the right as far as possible.
- Complete the prescribed number of reps, then do the same number on your left.

Bracing your abs—as if you were about to be punched in the gut—ensures that the rotation takes place at your upper back, and not your lower back.

THE BENEFIT
Enhances the mobility of your upper back, which can help improve posture.

Reach, Roll, and Lift

- Kneel down and place your elbows on the floor, allowing your back to round.
- Your elbows should be bent 90 degrees.
- Your palms should be flat on the floor.
- Slide your right hand forward until your arm is straight.
- Rotate your right palm so that it's facing up.
- Raise your right arm as high as you can.
- Do all your reps, then repeat with your left arm.

THE BENEFIT
Enhances the mobility of your shoulders and upper back.

Turn your palm up.

Lift your arm.

Warmup Exercises

Bent-Over Reach to Sky

- Keeping your lower back naturally arched, bend at your hips and knees and lower your torso until it's almost parallel to the floor.

- Let your arms hang straight down from your shoulders, palms facing each other.

- Brace your core.

- Rotate your torso the right as you reach as high as you can with your right arm.

- Pause, then return and reverse the movement to your left. That's one rep. (For even greater benefit, touch your toes between reps.)

THE BENEFIT *Enhances the mobility of your upper back.*

Keep your arms straight for the entire movement.

Set your feet shoulder-width apart.

Shoulder Circles

- Stand tall with your feet placed shoulder-width apart.

- Without moving any other part of your body, roll your shoulders backward in a circular motion 10 times.

THE BENEFIT *Enhances the mobility of your shoulders.*

Over-Under Shoulder Stretch

- Simultaneously reach behind your head with your right hand and behind your back with your left hand, and clasp your fingers together. Hold for 10 to 15 seconds.

- Release, and repeat with your left hand behind your head and your right hand behind your back

Can't touch your hands together? Hold a towel with one hand and grab onto it with the other hand.

THE BENEFIT *Loosens your rotator cuff and enhances shoulder mobility.*

Arm Circles

- Stand tall, holding your arms straight out to your sides, so that they're parallel to the floor.
- Start by making small circles with your arm progressing to bigger circles. Do 10 reps forward, and 10 reps backward.

THE BENEFIT
Enhances the mobility of your shoulders.

Stand as tall as you can.

Low Side-to-Side Lunge

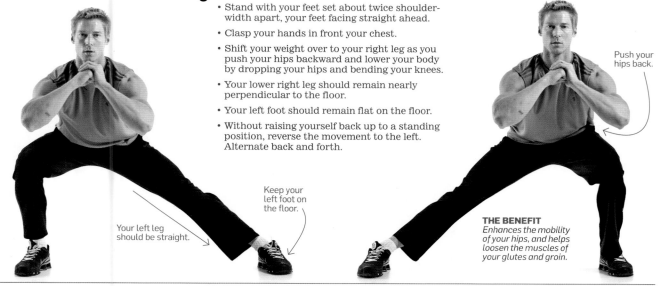

- Stand with your feet set about twice shoulder-width apart, your feet facing straight ahead.
- Clasp your hands in front your chest.
- Shift your weight over to your right leg as you push your hips backward and lower your body by dropping your hips and bending your knees.
- Your lower right leg should remain nearly perpendicular to the floor.
- Your left foot should remain flat on the floor.
- Without raising yourself back up to a standing position, reverse the movement to the left. Alternate back and forth.

Your left leg should be straight.

Keep your left foot on the floor.

Push your hips back.

THE BENEFIT
Enhances the mobility of your hips, and helps loosen the muscles of your glutes and groin.

Warmup Exercises

Reverse Lunge with Reach Back

- Stand tall with your arms hanging at your sides.
- Brace your core and hold it that way.
- Lunge back with your right leg, lowering your body until your left knee is bent at least 90 degrees.
- As you lunge, reach back over your shoulders and to the left.
- Reverse the movement back to the starting position.
- Complete the prescribed number of repetitions with your left leg, then step back with your left leg and reach over your right shoulder for the same number of reps.
- Keep your torso upright for the entire movement.

Always reach over the same-side shoulder as your lead leg.

THE BENEFIT *Enhances the mobility of your hips and upper back, and helps the chain of muscles between your hips and shoulders better function together.*

Lunge with Diagonal Reach

- Grab a light dumbbell in your left hand and hold it in the "high-five" position—your upper arm perpendicular to your body and your elbow bent 90 degrees.
- Lunge forward with your right leg, lowering your body until your right knee is bent at least 90 degrees.
- As you lunge, rotate your torso to the right and reach across your body with your left arm, almost as if you were trying to put the dumbbell in your right back pocket.
- Reverse the movement back to the starting position.
- Do all your reps and repeat with your right arm, lunging with your left leg.

Brace your core and keep your torso as upright as you can.

THE BENEFIT *Enhances the mobility of your hips, and helps the chain of muscles between your hips and shoulders function better together.*

Reverse Lunge with Twist and Overhead Reach

- Stand tall with your arms hanging at your sides and your palms facing the side of your thighs.
- Brace your core.
- Step backward with your right leg, and lower your body until your left knee is bent at least 90 degrees.
- As you lunge, rotate your torso to your left as you reach high with both hands.
- Return to the starting position.
- Complete the prescribed number of repetitions with your right leg stepping back and your torso rotating left, then step back with your left leg and rotate right for the same number of reps.

THE BENEFIT *Loosens your thigh, hip, and oblique muscles.*

Keep your torso upright as you rotate.

Lunge with Side Bend

- Stand tall with your arms hanging at your sides.
- Step forward with your right leg, and lower your body until your right knee is bent at least 90 degrees.
- As you lunge, reach over your head with your left arm as you bend your torso to your right.
- Reach for the floor with your right hand.
- Return to the starting position.
- Complete the prescribed number of reps, then lunge with your left leg and bend to your left for the same number of reps.

Overhead Lunge with Rotation

- Hold a broomstick above your head with your hands about twice shoulder-width apart.
- Your arms should be completely straight.
- Step forward with your right leg and lower your body until your right knee is bent at least 90 degrees.
- As you lunge, rotate your upper body to the right.
- Reverse the movement back to the starting position.
- Complete the prescribed number of reps, then do the same number with your left leg, rotating to your left.

THE BENEFIT
Loosens your thigh, hip, and oblique muscles.

Brace your core and hold it that way.

Keep your torso upright.

Bend toward the same side as your lead leg.

Keep your core stiff.

THE BENEFIT
Loosens your thigh, hip, and oblique muscles.

Elbow-to-Foot Lunge

- Stand tall with your arms at your sides.
- Brace your core, and lunge forward with your right leg.
- As you lunge, lean forward at your hips and place your left hand on the floor so that it's even with your right foot.
- Place your right elbow next to the instep of your right foot (or as close as you can), and hold for 2 seconds.
- Next, rotate your torso up and to the right and reach as high as you can with your right hand.
- Now, rotate back and place your right hand on the floor outside your right foot, then push your hips upward. That's one rep.
- Step forward with your left leg and repeat.

THE BENEFIT
Loosens your quadriceps, hamstrings, glutes, and groin.

THE WORLD'S GREATEST STRETCH? *That's what Mark Verstegen, the famed strength coach who popularized this movement, calls the elbow-to-foot lunge.*

Warmup Exercises

Inchworm

- Stand tall with your legs straight and bend over and touch the floor.
- Keeping your legs straight, walk your hands forward.
- Then take tiny steps to walk your feet back to your hands. That's one repetition.

If you can't reach the floor with your legs straight, bend your knees just enough so you can. As your flexibility improves, try to straighten them a little more.

THE BENEFIT
Loosens your thigh, hip, and oblique muscles.

Walk your hands out as far as you can without allowing your hips to sag.

Keep your core braced.

Sumo Squat to Stand

- Stand tall with your legs straight and your feet shoulder-width apart.
- Keeping your legs straight, bend over and grab your toes. (If you need to bend your knees you can, but bend them only as much as necessary.)
- Without letting go of your toes, lower your body into a squat as you raise your chest and shoulders up.
- Staying in the squat position, raise your right arm up high and wide. Then raise your left arm.
- Now stand up.

Inverted Hamstring

- Stand on your left leg, your knee bent slightly.
- Raise your right foot slightly off the floor.
- Without changing the bend in your left knee, bend at your hips and lower your torso until it's parallel to the floor.
- As you bend over, raise your arms straight out from your sides until they're in line with your torso, your palms facing down.
- Your right leg should stay in line with your body as you lower your torso.
- Return to the start. Complete the prescribed number of reps on your left leg, then do the same number on your right.

THE BENEFIT
Loosens your quadriceps, hamstrings, glutes, groin, and lower back.

Your arms should be straight.

Keep your chest and head up.

Raise one arm straight above your shoulder, and then the other.

Keep your lower back naturally arched.

Your arms should form a T with your body.

THE BENEFIT
Loosens your hamstrings.

Lateral Slide

- Stand with your feet just beyond shoulder width.

- Push your hips back, bend your knees, and lower your body until your hips are just slightly higher than your knees.

- Shuffle to your left by taking a step to your left with your right foot and then one with your left foot. Slide about 10 feet.

- Slide back to your right.

- Repeat for 30 seconds, or as prescribed.

You should be in an athletic stance.

← Your feet should be just beyond shoulder width. →

THE BENEFIT
Improves the rotational and side-to-side mobility of your hips.

Walking High Knees

- Stand tall with your feet shoulder-width apart.

- Without changing your posture, raise your left knee as high as you can and step forward.

- Repeat with your right leg. Continue to alternate back and forth.

THE BENEFIT
Loosens your glutes and hamstrings.

Don't round your lower back.

Walking Leg Cradles

- Stand with your feet shoulder-width apart and your arms at your sides.

- Step forward with your left leg as you lift your right knee and grasp it with your right hand and grasp your right ankle in your left hand.

- Stand up as tall as you can while you gently pull your right leg toward your chest.

- Release your leg, take three steps forward, and repeat by raising your left knee. Continue to alternate back and forth.

Pull your leg toward your chest.

THE BENEFIT
Loosens your glutes and hamstrings.

Walking Knee Hugs

- Stand with your feet shoulder-width apart and your arms at your sides.

- Step forward with your right leg, bend your knee, and lean forward slightly at your hips.

- Lift your left knee toward your chest, grasping it with both hands just below your kneecap. Then pull it as close to the middle of your chest as you can, while you stand up tall.

- Release your leg, take three steps forward, and repeat by raising your right knee. Continue to alternate back and forth.

THE BENEFIT
Loosens your glutes and hamstrings.

Don't round your lower back.

Warmup Exercises

Lateral Stepover

- Stand with your right side facing a bench.
- Lift your right knee in front of you, then rotate your thigh to step over the bench.
- Follow with your left leg.
- As soon as your left leg touches the floor, reverse the movement, back to the other side. That's one rep.

THE BENEFIT
Enhances the mobility of your thighs and hips.

Lateral Duck Under

- Set a barbell in a squat rack or Smith machine a little higher than waist level.
- Stand with your left side next to the bar.
- Take a long stride under the bar, and shift your weight toward your left leg as you squat low to duck under the bar in one movement.
- Rise to a standing position on the other side of the bar.
- Reverse the movement to return to the starting position.

THE BENEFIT
Enhances the mobility of your thighs and hips.

You don't actually need a bench or a bar to perform the lateral stepover or duck under. Just imagine there's one there and perform the move.

Lying Side Leg Raise

- Lie on your left side with your legs straight, your right leg on top of your left. Brace your left upper arm on the floor, and support your head with your left hand.

- Keeping your knee straight, raise your left leg as high as possible in a straight line.

- Lower your leg back to the starting position.

THE BENEFIT
Loosens your hip adductors, or groin.

Walking Heel to Butt

- Stand tall with your arms at your sides.

- Step forward with your left leg, then lift your right ankle toward your butt, grasping it with your right hand.

- Pull your ankle as close to your butt as you can.

- Release your ankle, take three steps forward, and repeat by raising your left ankle.

THE BENEFIT
Loosens your quadriceps.

MUSCLE MISTAKE
You Only Do Slow, Static Stretches

That's so 20th century. Here's why: Static stretches—the kind you learned in grade school—boost your flexibility in a specific posture at a slow speed. So they're beneficial for improving your general range of motion and for loosening tight muscles that can contribute to poor posture. (Static stretches appear throughout the book, one for each muscle group.)

Dynamic stretches, on the other hand, give you the flexibility you need when your muscles stretch at fast speeds and in various body positions, such as during weight training and when you play sports. Dynamic stretches also excite your central nervous system and increase blood-flow and strength and power production. So they're the ideal warmup for any physical activity. That's why they constitute most of the movements in this chapter. And it's also why you should regularly do *both* dynamic and static stretches. That way, your body will benefit from the best of both modes.

Lying Straight Leg Raise

- Lie faceup on the floor with your legs straight.

- Keeping both knees straight, raise your right leg upward as far as possible. (Imagine that you're trying to kick a ball that's hanging over your body.)

- Complete the prescribed number of reps with your right leg, then do the same number with your left leg.

THE BENEFIT
Loosens your hamstrings.

Keep your leg straight.

Your non-working leg should remain flat on the floor.

Warmup Exercises

Forward-and-Back Leg Swings

- Stand tall and hold on to a sturdy object with your left hand.

- Brace your core.

- Keeping your right knee straight, swing your right leg forward as high as you comfortably can.

- Swing your right leg backward as far as you can. That's one rep.

- Swing back and forth continuously. Complete all your reps, then do the same with your left leg.

Keep your torso upright and stiff for the entire movement.

THE BENEFIT
Loosens your hamstrings and glutes.

Side-to-Side Leg Swings

- Stand tall and hold on to a sturdy object with both hands.

- Keeping your left knee straight, swing your left leg as high out to the side as you comfortably can.

- Swing your leg back toward your body so that it crosses in front of your right leg. That's one rep.

- Swing back and forth continuously until you complete the prescribed number of reps, then do the same with your right leg.

Keep your leg as straight as you can.

THE BENEFIT
Loosens your hip adductors, or groin, and your outer hips.

Walking High Kicks

- Stand tall with arms hanging at your sides.

- Keeping your knee straight, kick your right leg up—reaching with your left arm out to meet it—as you simultaneously take a step forward. (Just imagine that you're a Russian soldier.)

- As soon as your right foot touches the floor, repeat the movement with your left leg and right arm. Alternate back and forth.

THE BENEFIT
Loosens your glutes and hamstrings.

Prone Hip Internal Rotation

- Lie facedown on the floor with your knees together and bent 90 degrees.

- Without allowing your hips to rise off the floor, lower your feet straight out to the sides as far as you comfortably can. Hold for 1 or 2 seconds, then return to the starting position.

THE BENEFIT
Loosens the muscles of your outer thighs and hips.

Groiners

- Get into pushup position.

THE BENEFIT
Loosens your hip adductors, or groin, and enhances hip mobility.

- Bring your right foot forward, place it next to your right hand (or as close as you can), and lower your hips for a brief moment.

- Return to the start, and repeat with your left leg.

Push your hips down.

Raise your chest and head up.

Warmup Exercises

Ankle Circles

- Stand tall on one foot, and raise your left thigh until it's parallel to the floor. Clasp your hands under your left knee to support your leg.

- Without moving your lower leg, rotate your ankle clockwise. Each circle is one repetition.

- Complete all your reps, then do the same number in a counterclockwise direction. Repeat with your right leg.

THE BENEFIT
Enhances the mobility of your ankles.

Ankle Flexion

- Place the balls of your feet on a surface that's about 2 inches high, with your heels on the floor.

- Stand tall with your legs nearly straight.

- Bend your knees and shift your weight forward until you feel a stretch in the backs of your heels. Hold for 2 or 3 seconds, then return to the starting position. That's one repetition.

THE BENEFIT
Enhances the mobility of your ankles.

Bend your knees.

Your heels should be on the floor.

Supine Hip Internal Rotation

- Lie faceup on the floor with your knees bent 90 degrees.

- Your feet should be flat on the floor and about twice shoulder-width apart.

- Without allowing your feet to move, lower your knees inward as far as you comfortably can. Hold for 1 or 2 seconds, then return to the starting position.

THE BENEFIT
Loosens the muscles of your inner thighs and hips.

Your feet should remain stationary.

434

FOAM-ROLL EXERCISES

You might liken these foam-roller exercises to a deep massage. By rolling the hard foam over your thighs, calves, and back, you'll loosen tough connective tissue and decrease the stiffness of your muscles. This helps enhance your flexibility and mobility and keeps your muscles functioning properly. As a result, foam-rolling exercises are valuable both before and after a hard workout, and really, anytime you have the opportunity. Want to multitask? Pull out the foam roller while you're watching TV.

At first, you may find foam rolling to be uncomfortable. This will be especially true for the muscles that need it most. The more it hurts; the more you need to roll. The good news: Roll regularly, and you'll notice that your muscles will become a little less tender with every subsequent session. For each muscle that you work, slowly move the roller back and forth over it for 30 seconds. If you hit a point that's particularly tender, pause on it for 5 to 10 seconds.

Your main objective: Focus on foam rolling the muscles that need it the most. Trust me, you'll know which ones those are as soon as you start experimenting with the exercises that follow. You can buy your own 36-inch foam roll at most fitness-equipment stores. But in a pinch, you can substitute a basketball, tennis ball, or a section of PVC pipe.

Hamstrings Roll

- Place a foam roller under your right knee, with your leg straight.
- Cross your left leg over your right ankle.
- Put your hands flat on the floor for support.
- Keep your back naturally arched.
- Roll your body forward until the roller reaches your glutes. Then roll back and forth.
- Repeat with the roller under your left thigh.

Start at your knee.

Roll to the bottoms of your glutes.

IF THAT'S TOO HARD, *perform the movement with both legs on the roller.*

Glutes Roll

- Sit on a foam roller, with it positioned on the back of your right thigh, just below your glutes.
- Cross your right leg over the front of your left thigh.
- Put your hands flat on the floor for support.
- Roll your body forward until the roller reaches your lower back. Then roll back and forth.
- Repeat with the roller under your left glutes.

Start just below your glutes.

Roll to your lower back.

Warmup Exercises

Iliotibial-Band Roll

- Lie on your left side and place your left hip on a foam roller.
- Put your hands on the floor for support.
- Cross your right leg over your left, and place your right foot flat on the floor.
- Roll your body forward until the roller reaches your knee. Then roll back and forth.
- Lie on your right side and repeat with the roller under your right hip.

Start at your hip.

WHEN THAT BECOMES TOO EASY, *place your right leg on top of your left instead of bracing it on the floor.*

Roll to your knee.

ROLL AWAY TENSION
Your iliotibial band—commonly called the IT band—is a tough strip of connective tissue that runs down the side of your thigh, starting on your hip bone and connecting just below your knee. When it comes to foam rolling, you'll probably find this tissue is one of the most sensitive areas that you can roll over, perhaps due to high tension in the band. You should make it a priority, though: Over time, an overly tense IT band can lead to knee pain.

Calf Roll

- Place a foam roller under your right ankle, with your right leg straight.
- Cross your left leg over your right ankle.
- Put your hands flat on the floor for support.
- Keep your back naturally arched.
- Roll your body forward until the roller reaches the back of your right knee. Then roll back and forth.
- Repeat with the roller under your left calf.

IF THAT'S TOO HARD, *perform the movement with both legs on the roller.*

Start at your ankle.

Roll to your knee.

Quadriceps-and-Hip-Flexors Roll

- Lie facedown on the floor with a foam roller positioned above your right knee.
- Cross your left leg over your right ankle and place your elbows on the floor for support.
- Roll your body backward until the roller reaches the top of your right thigh.
- Then roll back and forth.
- Repeat with the roller under your left thigh.

IF THAT'S TOO HARD, *perform the movement with both thighs on the roller.*

Start at your knee.

Roll to the top of your thigh.

Groin Roll

- Lie facedown on the floor.
- Place a foam roller parallel to your body.
- Put your elbows on the floor for support.
- Position your right thigh nearly perpendicular to your body, with the inner portion of your thigh, just above the level of your knee, resting on top of the roller.
- Roll your body toward the right until the roller reaches your pelvis. Then roll back and forth.
- Repeat with the roller under your left thigh.

Start just above your knee.

Roll to your pelvis.

Upper-Back Roll

- Lie faceup with a foam roller under your mid back, at the bottoms of your shoulder blades.
- Clasp your hands behind your head and pull your elbows toward each other.
- Raise your hips off the floor slightly.
- Slowly lower your head and upper back downward, so that your upper back bends over the foam roller.
- Raise back to the start and roll forward a couple of inches—so that the roller sits higher under your upper back—and repeat.
- Roll forward one more time and do it again. That's one rep.

To start, set the roller at the bottoms of your shoulder blades.

Lower-Back Roll

- Lie faceup with a foam roller under your mid back.
- Cross your arms over your chest.
- Your knees should be bent, with your feet flat on the floor.
- Raise your hips off the floor slightly.
- Roll back and forth over your lower back.

Start at your mid back.

Roll to the top of your glutes.

Shoulder-Blades Roll

- Lie faceup with a foam roller under your upper back, at the tops of your shoulder blades.
- Cross your arms over your chest.
- Your knees should be bent, with your feet flat on the floor.
- Raise your hips so they're slightly elevated off the floor.
- Roll back and forth over your shoulder blades and your mid and upper back.

Start at the tops of your shoulder blades.

Roll to the bottoms of your shoulder blades.

Warmup Exercises

CREATE YOUR OWN WARMUP

Besides the movements shown in this chapter, many of the exercises that appear elsewhere in this book also double as great warmup moves. They've been included here in order to give you a full roster of exercises to choose from. (For convenience, the appropriate page number follows the exercise.) To create your own 5-minute warmup, use these guidelines from Mike Wunsch, CSCS, director of fitness programs at Results Fitness in Santa Clarita, California. Simply choose your moves from the categories that follow, using the accompanying

CATEGORY 1
Choose one movement from this list exercises.

Hand crossover (page 422)

Wall slide (page 422)

Reach, roll, and lift (page 423)

Pushup plus (page 64)

CATEGORY 2
Choose one movement from this list exercises.

Floor Y raise (page 86)

Floor T raise (page 88)

Incline Y raise* (page 86)

Incline T raise* (page 88)

Incline W raise* (page 90)

Incline L raise* (page 89)

Swiss-ball Y raise* (page 86)

Swiss-ball T raise* (page 88)

Swiss-ball W raise* (page 90)

Swiss-ball L raise* (page 89)

CATEGORY 3
Choose one movement from this list of exercises.

Side-lying thoracic rotation (page 423)

Thoracic rotation (page 423)

Bent-over reach to sky (page 424)

CATEGORY 4
Choose three movements from this list of exercises—one from each category.

QUADRICEPS AND HIP ADDUCTORS (GROIN)

Walking heel to butt (page 431)

Supine hip internal rotation (page 434)

Groiners (page 433)

Side-to-side leg swings (page 432)

HAMSTRINGS

Walking high knees (page 429)

Walking knee hugs (page 429)

Walking high kicks (page 433)

Lying straight leg raise (page 431)

Forward-and-back leg swings (page 432)

GLUTES AND HIP ABDUCTORS (OUTER HIPS)

Hip raise (page 236)

Single-leg hip raise with knee hold (page 241)

Lateral band walks (page 267)

Walking leg cradles (page 429)

Prone hip internal rotation (page 433)

Clamshell (page 267)

Lying side leg raise (page 431)

*For these exercises, use the form shown, but perform the movement without the dumbbells.

directions. You can either do 5 to 10 reps of each exercise or perform each one for 30 seconds. Do the movements in a circuit, completing one set of each exercise without resting. *One additional option:* If you can't get to the gym or don't have time for your regular workout, do this warmup as a quickie bodyweight routine. Use the same directions for each category, only choose three exercises—instead of just one—from Category 6, and do as many sets of the three exercises in Category 7 as you have time for.

CATEGORY 5

Choose any Core exercise in Chapter 10, from the section labeled "Stability Exercises." For example, any version of the plank, side plank, or mountain climber.

CATEGORY 6

Choose one to three movements—as time allows—from this list of exercises.

Jumping jacks (page 421)

Split jacks (page 421)

Squat thrusts (page 422)

CATEGORY 7

Choose three movements—one of each movement type—from this list of exercises. So you'll select one side-to-side movement, one forward and back movement, and one rotational movement.

SIDE-TO-SIDE MOVEMENTS

Low side-to-side lunge (page 425)

Lateral slide (page 429)

Lateral stepover (page 430)

Lateral duck under (page 430)

Dumbbell side lunge* (page 221)

FORWARD AND BACK MOVEMENTS

Prisoner squat (page 192)

Body-weight squat (page 190)

Dumbbell lunge* (page 216)

Reverse dumbbell lunge* (page 217)

Dumbbell crossover lunge* (page 219)

Reverse dumbbell crossover lunge* (page 219)

Inverted hamstring (page 428)

Inchworm (page 428)

Elbow-to-foot lunge (page 427)

Sumo squat to stand (page 428)

ROTATIONAL MOVEMENTS

Reverse lunge with reach back (page 426)

Lunge with diagonal reach (page 426)

Lunge with side bend (page 427)

Reverse lunge with twist and overhead reach (page 426)

Overhead lunge with rotation (page 427)

Chapter 14:
The Best Workouts for Everything
YOUR COMPLETE GUIDE TO TRANSFORMING YOUR BODY

Here are the blueprints for the body you want.

Whether your goal is to pack on pounds of muscle, sky-rocket your strength, or lose your gut for good, there's a workout for you. In fact, there are lots of workouts. That's because I've enlisted the world's top fitness experts to create cutting-edge plans for just about everything—a bigger bench, faster fat loss, even your wedding day. There's also a workout for every lifestyle. Too busy for the gym? Try an intense 15-minute routine. Always on the road? There's a body-weight workout you can do in your room. Never picked up a weight before? The Get-Back-in-Shape Workout on page 444 is what you need.

Simply choose one of the plans that follow, then use the instructions on page 443 to make sure you do it right. (And for even more routines, downloaded straight to your iPhone, check out the *Men's Health Workouts* app from the iTunes store.) If you have additional questions, you're likely to find the answers in Chapter 2.

Now get to work. Your new body is waiting.

Best Workouts for Everything

Before You Start:
What You Need to Know

**Use these instructions to ensure you understand
how to do each workout in this chapter.**

How to Do These Workouts

• Always perform the exercises in the order shown.

• When you see a number without a letter next to it—such as "1" or "4"—perform the exercise as a straight set. That is, do one set of the exercise, rest for the prescribed amount of time, and then do another set. Complete all sets of this exercise before moving on to the next.

• When you see a number with a letter next to it—such as "2A"—it indicates that the exercise is to be performed as part of a group of exercises. (A group of exercises all share the same number, but will each have a different letter, for example: 1A, 1B, and 1C.) Do one set of the exercise, rest for the prescribed amount of time, and then do one set of the next exercise in the group. For instance, if you see 2A and 2B in a workout, complete one set of Exercise 2A, rest for the prescribed amount of time, then do one set of Exercise 2B, and rest again. Repeat until you've completed all of your sets for each exercise. Follow this procedure regardless of how many exercises are in a group.

• You'll notice that sometimes the prescribed rest period is actually "0"—zero seconds. That means you're not to rest between movements; move directly to the next exercise.

• When a duration (for example, 30 seconds) is given for the number of reps, simply perform the exercise for the prescribed time. So if it's a plank or side plank, hold the position for the duration of the set. If it's an exercise in which you normally do repetitions, complete as many reps as you can in the given time period.

• The acronym AMAP stands for *as many as possible*. So when AMAP is indicating the number of repetitions you should do, it means that you're to complete as many repetitions as you can. When it's indicating the number of sets you do, complete as many sets as you can in the given time frame.

• The acronym ALAP stands for *as little as possible*. So when ALAP is indicating your rest period, it means that you're to rest only as long as you feel you need. Basically, catch your breath and get back to work.

Best Workouts

The Get-Back-in-Shape Workout Phase 1: Weeks 1 to 4

Whether you've never lifted weights before or you just haven't made time for exercise lately, this 12-week plan, from Joe Dowdell, CSCS, was created with you in mind. It's designed to blast fat and build muscle, while taking into account that you're not yet in peak condition. And it does all of this while targeting the weaknesses brought on by a sedentary lifestyle—the kind that often slow your results and lead to frustration. So you'll not only transform your body, you'll do it faster than ever.

About the Expert
Joe Dowdell, CSCS, is co-owner of Peak Performance in New York City. Joe makes his living training celebrities, professional athletes, and cover models and is widely recognized as one of the best strength coaches in the world. (Search for his new book at amazon.com.)

How to Do This Workout
• Do the Weight Workout 3 days a week, resting for at least a day after each session. So you might lift weights on Monday, Wednesday, and Friday.
• Do the Cardio Workout twice a week, on the days in between your Weight Workouts. So you might do your cardio sessions on Tuesday and Thursday. (If you can't find time to exercise 5 days a week, just do the Cardio Workout immediately following two of your weight workouts.)
• Prior to each Weight Workout, complete the warmup.
• Questions? Flip back to page 443, where you'll find complete instructions for performing all of the workouts.

Warmup

EXERCISE	SETS	REPS	REST
1A. Side-lying thoracic rotation (page 423)	1	5	0
1B. Body-weight lunge (page 217)	1	4	0
1C. Low side-to-side lunge (page 425)	1	4	0
1D. Hip raise with knee press-out (page 238)	1	10–12	0
1E. Plank (page 278)	1	4–6	0
1F. Swiss-ball W raise (page 90)	1	8–10	0

For the plank and the prone cobra, hold the position for 1 second, then relax momentarily and repeat. That's one repetition.

Workout

If the barbell squat is too hard, substitute a body-weight squat.

EXERCISE	SETS	REPS	REST
1A. Barbell squat (page 198)	2–3	10–12	1 min
1B. Pushup (page 34)	2–3	10–12	1 min
2A. Hip raises with feet on a Swiss ball (page 236)	2–3	10–12	1 min
2B. Cable row to neck with external rotation (page 95)	2–3	10–12	1 min
3A. Reverse crunch (page 322)	2–3	10–12	1 min
3B. Prone cobra (page 295)	2–3	10–12	1 min

If you have difficulty with the pushup, choose a variation that's easier—such as the modified pushup or incline pushup—but still challenging.

Cardio Workout

THE PLAN

Warm up by walking on a treadmill at an easy pace—about 30 to 50 percent of your best effort—for 3 to 5 minutes. Then do this interval workout:
- Raise the incline on the treadmill until you're exercising at an intensity that's 40 to 60 percent of your best effort. Go for 2 minutes.
- Lower the incline back to 0 percent and go for 2 more minutes. That's one set.
- Do a total of three sets, then cool down for 3 to 5 minutes, walking at an easy pace.
- During the course of this 4-week phase, try to work up to a total of five sets.

The Get-Back-In-Shape Workout
Phase 2: Weeks 5 to 8

How to Do This Workout

• Do the Weight Workout three days a week, resting for at least a day after each session. So you might lift weights on Monday, Wednesday, and Friday.
• Do the Cardio Workout three times a week, on the days in between each Weight Workout. For your first two workouts, perform the Interval Workout. For the last workout, do the Aerobic Workout. So you might do the Interval Workout on Tuesday and Thursday, and the Aerobic Workout on Saturday.
• Prior to each Weight Workout, complete the warmup.
• Questions? Flip back to page 443, where you'll find complete instructions for performing all of the workouts.

Warmup

EXERCISE	SETS	REPS	REST
1A. Hip crossover (page 303)	1	5	0
1B. Elbow-to-foot lunge (page 427)	1	4	0
1C. Body-weight side lunge (page 221)	1	4	0
1D. Clamshell (page 267)	1	8–10	0
1E. Side plank (page 284)	1	4–6	0
1F. Swiss-ball T raise (page 88)	1	8–10	0

Workout

EXERCISE	SETS	REPS	REST
1A. Dumbbell split squat (page 209)	2–3	10–12	1 min
1B. Dumbbell bench press (page 52)	2–3	10–12	1 min
2A. Swiss-ball hip raise and leg curl (page 243)	2–3	10–12	1 min
2B. Band-assisted chinup (page 98)	2–3	10–12	1 min
3A. Side crunch (page 332)	2–3	8–10	1 min ←
3B. Bird dog (page 283)	2–3	8–10	1 min ←

For the side crunch, hold the up position of each crunch for 2 seconds.

For the side plank (in the warmup) and bird dog, hold the position for 1 second, then relax momentarily and repeat. That's one repetition.

Cardio Workout

THE PLAN

Warm up by walking on a treadmill at an easy pace—about 30 to 50 percent of your best effort—for 3 to 5 minutes. Then do one of these workouts, performing the Interval Workout on your first and second cardio day each week, and do the Aerobic Workout on your third cardio day.

INTERVAL WORKOUT

- Increase the treadmill speed to an intensity that's 65 to 75 percent of your best effort. Go for 60 seconds.
- Lower the speed to 3.5 miles per hour and go for 2 minutes. That's one set.
- Do a total of four sets, then cool down for 3 to 5 minutes, walking at an easy pace.
- Try to work up to a total of six sets during the course of this 4-week phase.

AEROBIC WORKOUT

- Increase the treadmill speed or incline until you're exercising at an intensity that's 40 to 60 percent of your best effort. Go at that pace for 15 minutes.
- During the course of this 4-week phase, try to work up to 25 minutes.

The Get-Back-in-Shape Workout
Phase 3: Weeks 9 to 12

How to Do This Workout

• Alternate between Workout A and Workout B three days a week, resting for at least a day between each session. So if you plan to lift on Monday, Wednesday, and Friday, you'd do Workout A on Monday, Workout B on Wednesday, and Workout A again on Friday. The next week, you'd do Workout B on Monday and Friday, and Workout A on Wednesday.

• Do the Cardio Workout three times a week, on the days in between Weight Workouts. For your first two workouts, perform the Interval Workout. For the last workout, do the Aerobic Workout. So you might do the Interval Workout on Tuesday and Thursday, and the Aerobic Workout on Saturday. Note that you do Interval Workout A for the first 2 weeks (weeks 9 and 10), then transition to Interval Workout B for the last 2 weeks (weeks 11 and 12).

• Prior to each workout, complete the warmup.

• Questions? Flip back to page 443, where you'll find complete instructions for performing all of the workouts.

Warmup

EXERCISE	SETS	REPS	REST
1A. Cat camel (page 283)	1	5–6	0
1B. Elbow-to-foot lunge (page 427)	1	4	0
1C. Walking knee hugs (page 429)	1	5	0
1D. Lateral band walks (page 267)	1	10–12	0
1E. Inchworm (page 428)	1	3–5	0
1F. Swiss-ball Y raise (page 87)	1	8–10	0

Workout A

EXERCISE	SETS	REPS	REST
1A. Barbell deadlift (page 248)	3	8–10	1 min
1B. Incline dumbbell bench press (page 54)	3	8–10	1 min
2A. Partial single-leg squat (page 197)	3	8–10	1 min
2B. Kneeling supported neutral-grip dumbbell row (page 80)	3	8–10	1 min
3A. Hammer curl to press (page 161)	3	8–10	1 min
3B. Swiss-ball crunch (page 318)	3	8–10	1 min

Workout B

EXERCISE	SETS	REPS	REST
1A. Dumbbell stepup (page 262)	3	10–12	1 min
1B. Dumbbell bench press (page 52)	3	10–12	1 min
2A. Barbell straight-leg deadlift (page 252)	3	8–10	1 min
2B. Rear lateral raise (page 83)	3	10–12	1 min
3A. Dumbbell lying triceps extension (page 168)	3	8–10	1 min
3B. Back extension (page 258)	3	8–10	1 min

Cardio Workout

THE PLAN

Perform the appropriate Interval Workout on your first and second cardio day each week, and do the Aerobic Workout on your third cardio day.

INTERVAL WORKOUT A

- Increase the treadmill speed you're exercising at to an intensity that's 70 to 80 percent of your best effort. Go for 45 seconds.
- Lower the speed to 3.5 miles per hour and go for 2 minutes. That's one set.
- Do a total of five sets, then cool down for 3 to 5 minutes, walking at an easy pace.
- Try to work up to a total of seven sets during the course of this 4-week phase.

INTERVAL WORKOUT B

- Increase the treadmill speed you're exercising at to an intensity that's 70 to 80 percent of your best effort. Go for 30 seconds.
- Lower the speed to 3.5 miles per hour and go for 90 seconds. That's one set.
- Do a total of six sets, then cool down for 3 to 5 minutes, walking at an easy pace.
- Try to work up to a total of eight sets during the course of this 4-week phase.

AEROBIC WORKOUT

- Increase the treadmill speed or incline until you're exercising at an intensity that's 40 to 60 percent of your best effort. Go at that pace for 25 minutes.
- During the course of this 4-week phase, try to work up to 30 minutes at an effort of 60 percent.

The Best Workouts for a Crowded Gym

You should never have to wait in line at the gym. And these three workout plans—all designed to build muscle and burn fat—ensure you won't have to.

About the Expert
Craig Ballantyne, MS, CSCS, has been a fitness advisor to *Men's Health* for nearly a decade. Based in Toronto, Craig is the owner of TurbulenceTraining.com, one of the most popular and effective online training programs.

Workout Plan 1

How to Do This Workout

• The only equipment you need: one pair of dumbbells. This routine is designed so that you won't have to even change the amount of weight you use from one move to the next.

• Do each workout (Workout A, Workout B, and Workout C) once a week, resting for at least a day after each session.

• Questions? Flip back to page 443, where you'll find complete instructions for performing all of the workouts.

Workout A

EXERCISE	SETS	REPS	REST
1A. Dumbbell bench press (page 52)	4	8	1 min
1B. Kneeling supported neutral-grip dumbbell row (page 80)	4	8–12	1 min
2A. Incline dumbbell bench press (page 54)	3	5	0
2B. Dumbbell squat (page 203)	3	12	1 min

Workout B

EXERCISE	SETS	REPS	REST
1A. Dumbbell split squat (page 209)	4	8	1 min
1B. Single-arm dumbbell shoulder press (page 122)	4	12	1 min
2A. Dumbbell straight-leg deadlift (page 256)	3	10	0
2B. Single-arm dumbbell swing (page 268)	3	15–20	1 min

Workout C

EXERCISE	SETS	REPS	REST
1A. Dumbbell stepup (page 262)	4	8	1 min
1B. Lying supported neutral-grip dumbbell row (page 80)	4	12	1 min
2A. Standing dumbbell curl (page 156)	4	10	0
2B. Lying dumbbell triceps extension (page 168)	4	12	1 min

The Best Workouts for a Crowded Gym

Workout Plan 2

How to Do This Workout

• This unique 45-minute workout is designed so that you stay at each station for 10 minutes, using the same weight the entire time. This keeps you in one place and working hard for the whole session, with no need to change exercises or weights.

• Do each Weight Workout (Workout A, Workout B, and Workout C) once a week, resting for at least a day after each session. So you might do Workout A on Monday, Workout B on Wednesday, and Workout C on Friday. Follow these guidelines:

• For Exercise 1 in each workout, choose the heaviest weight that allows you to complete 10 to 12 repetitions. This is the weight you'll use for each set that you perform.

• Set a timer for 10 minutes.

• Do three repetitions, rest for 10 seconds, and repeat. Continue in this manner until you can't complete all three reps. Then increase your rest by 10 seconds, so that you're resting for

20 seconds after each three-repetition set. When you're once again unable to complete three reps, increase your rest to 30 seconds, and so on. Follow this procedure until your 10 minutes are up. That's your cue to move on to the next exercise.

• Use these same guidelines for Exercise 2 and Exercise 3.

• Each week, increase the weight you use for each exercise by 5 to 10 pounds.

• For Exercises 4 and 5, simply choose one core exercise (Chapter 10) and one arm exercise (Chapter 7). Do two sets of 10 to 12 reps of each using the heaviest weight that allows you to complete all of your repetitions. Rest for 60 seconds between sets. One *caveat*: If you choose a core exercise such as the plank or side plank, hold the position for 30 seconds.

• Do the Cardio Workout immediately after each Weight Workout.

• Questions? Flip back to page 443, where you'll find complete instructions for performing all of the workouts.

About the Expert
Nick Nilsson is the vice president of BetterU, Inc., an online personal-training company. Nick has a degree in kinesiology and has been a personal trainer for more than a decade.

Workout A

EXERCISE

1. Dumbbell bench press (page 52)

2. Chinup (page 96)

3. Barbell squat (page 198)

4. Core exercise: your choice (Chapter 10)

5. Arm exercise: your choice (Chapter 7)

Workout B

EXERCISE

1. Dumbbell split squat (page 209)

2. Barbell bench press (page 46)

3. Barbell row (page 76)

4. Core exercise: your choice (Chapter 10)

5. Arm exercise: your choice (Chapter 7)

Workout C

EXERCISE

1. Barbell deadlift (page 248)

2. Pushup (page 34)

3. Barbell front squat (page 199)

4. Core exercise: your choice (Chapter 10)

5. Arm exercise: your choice (Chapter 7)

Cardio Workout

THE PLAN

- You can perform this workout on a treadmill, on a stationary bike, or outside on the sidewalk or a track. Do it for a total of 10 minutes.
- Exercise at an intensity that's about 90 percent of your best effort. Go for 30 seconds.
- Rest for 30 seconds. Then repeat until your 10 minutes are up.

The Best Workouts for a Crowded Gym

Workout Plan 3

How to Do This Workout
• To perform this 8-week workout program, you don't need a bench or a squat rack—just a little space.
• Do this workout 3 days a week, resting for at least a day after each session. So you might lift weights on Monday, Wednesday, and Friday.
• Questions? Flip back to page 443, where you'll find complete instructions for performing all of the workouts.

Weeks 1 to 4
Warmup

EXERCISE	SETS	REPS	REST
1A. Body-weight side lunge (page 221)	1	12	0
1B. Wall slide (page 422)	1	12	0
1C. Inchworm (page 428)	1	10	0

If you can't do at least eight repetitions of the two-medicine-ball pushup, substitute a variation that does allow you to complete that many.

Workout

EXERCISE	SETS	REPS	REST
1A. Two-arm medicine-ball pushup (page 40)	3	AMAP	0
1B. Dumbbell row (page 78)	3	10–12	0
1C. Dumbbell front squat (page 204)	3	10	60–90 sec
2A. Swiss-ball pike (page 328)	2–3	10–15	0
2B. Single-leg hip raise (page 240)	2–3	12–15	60–90 sec

About the Expert
Stephen Cabral, CSCS, owns the Stephen Cabral Studio fitness center in Boston and is a fitness consultant for the MTV reality show *Made*.

Weeks 5-8
Warmup

EXERCISE	SETS	REPS	REST
1A. Groiners (page 365)	1	24	0
1B. Seated dumbbell external rotation (page 136)	1	12	0
1C. Medicine-ball slam (page 320)	1	12	0

Workout

EXERCISE	SETS	REPS	REST
1A. Dumbbell push press (page 121)	3	8	0
1B. Pushup and row (page 43)	3	10–12	0
1C. Dumbbell Bulgarian split squat (page 210)	3	10	60–90 sec
2A. Dumbbell chop (page 304)	2–3	12	0
2B. Prone cobra (page 295)	2–3	12–15	60–90 sec

For the prone cobra, hold the position for 1 second, then relax momentarily and repeat. That's one repetition.

Best Workouts

The Ultimate Fat-Loss Workout
Phase 1: Weeks 1 to 4

If you're ready to blast your belly, use this intense 12-week fat-loss plan from Bill Hartman, PT, CSCS. It not only torches calories during your workout but also unleashes a flood of fat-burning hormones that supercharge your metabolism for hours after you're done training. So your body's fat-frying furnace runs on high all day long, even when you're sitting on the couch. And that's the secret to losing your gut for good.

About the Expert
Bill Hartman, PT, CSCS, is a physical therapist and strength coach in Indianapolis. Bill is a top fitness advisor to *Men's Health* and the co-owner of Indianapolis Fitness and Sports Training.

How to Do These Workouts

• Do each Weight Workout (Workout A, Workout B, and Workout C) once a week, resting for at least a day after each session. So you might do Workout A on Monday, Workout B on Wednesday, and Workout C on Friday.

• Do the Cardio Workout three times a week, on the days in between your Weight Workouts. So you might do your cardio sessions on Tuesday, Thursday, and Saturday.

• Questions? Flip back to page 443, where you'll find complete instructions for performing all of the workouts.

Workout A

EXERCISE	WEEK 1			WEEK 2			WEEK 3			WEEK 4		
Workout A	SETS	REPS	REST	SETS	REPS	REST	SETS	REPS	REST	SETS	REPS	REST
1A. Barbell stepup (page 260)	2	15	75 sec	3	12	75 sec	3	10	75 sec	2	10	75 sec
1B. Dumbbell bench press (page 52)	2	15	75 sec	3	12	75 sec	3	10	75 sec	2	10	75 sec
2A. Dumbbell row (page 78)	2	15	75 sec	3	12	75 sec	3	10	75 sec	2	10	75 sec
2B. Scaption (page 129)	2	15	75 sec	3	12	75 sec	3	10	75 sec	2	10	75 sec
3A. Seated dumbbell external rotation (page 136)	2	15	30 sec	2	12	30 sec	2	10	30 sec	2	10	30 sec
3B. Plank (page 278)	2	8	30 sec	2	10	30 sec	2	12	30 sec	2	10	30 sec

For the plank and side plank, hold the position for 5 seconds, then relax momentarily and repeat. That's one repetition.

Cardio Workout

THE PLAN

In your first Cardio Workout, exercise continuously for 40 minutes at a pace that's 65 to 70 percent of your best effort. This could be walking on a treadmill that's set to an incline; walking, running, or cycling outside; riding a stationary bike; or even swimming. In each subsequent workout, increase the time you're exercising by 5 minutes. So you'll go for 45 minutes in your second workout, 50 minutes in your third workout, and so on.

The Ultimate Fat-Loss Workout
Phase 1: Weeks 1 to 4

Workout B

EXERCISE	WEEK 1			WEEK 2			WEEK 3			WEEK 4		
	SETS	REPS	REST	SETS	REPS	REST	SETS	REPS	REST	SETS	REPS	REST
1A. Barbell split squat (page 206)	2	15	75 sec	3	15	75 sec	3	12	75 sec	2	12	75 sec
1B. Pushup (page 34)	2	12	75 sec	3	10	75 sec	3	8	75 sec	2	10	75 sec
2A. Inverted row (page 72)	2	12	75 sec	3	10	75 sec	3	8	75 sec	2	10	75 sec
2B. Combo shoulder raise (page 129)	2	12	75 sec	3	10	75 sec	3	8	75 sec	2	10	75 sec
3A. Lying external rotation (page 138)	2	12	30 sec	3	10	30 sec	3	8	30 sec	2	10	30 sec
4. Side plank (page 284)	2	8	30 sec	2	10	30 sec	2	12	30 sec	2	10	30 sec

Workout C

EXERCISE	WEEK 1			WEEK 2			WEEK 3			WEEK 4		
	SETS	REPS	REST	SETS	REPS	REST	SETS	REPS	REST	SETS	REPS	REST
1A. Barbell stepup (page 260)	2	12	75 sec	3	10	75 sec	3	8	75 sec	2	10	75 sec
1B. Dumbbell bench press (page 52)	2	12	75 sec	3	10	75 sec	3	8	75 sec	2	10	75 sec
2A. Dumbbell row (page 78)	2	12	75 sec	3	10	75 sec	3	8	75 sec	2	10	75 sec
2B. Scaption (page 129)	2	12	75 sec	3	10	75 sec	3	8	75 sec	2	10	75 sec
3A. Seated dumbbell external rotation (page 136)	2	12	30 sec	2	10	30 sec	3	8	30 sec	2	10	30 sec
3B. Plank (page 278)	2	8	30 sec	2	12	30 sec	2	12	30 sec	2	10	30 sec

The Ultimate Fat-Loss Workout
Phase 2: Weeks 5 to 8

Workout A

EXERCISE	WEEK 1			WEEK 2			WEEK 3			WEEK 4		
	SETS	REPS	REST	SETS	REPS	REST	SETS	REPS	REST	SETS	REPS	REST
1A. Wide-grip barbell deadlift (page 249)	3	8	1 min	3	10	1 min	4	8	1 min	3	10	1 min
1B. Barbell bench press (page 46)	3	8	1 min	3	10	1 min	4	8	1 min	3	10	1 min
2A. Cable row (page 92)	3	8	1 min	3	10	1 min	4	8	1 min	3	10	1 min
2B. Cable diagonal raise (page 139)	3	8	1 min	3	10	1 min	4	8	1 min	3	10	1 min
3. Swiss-ball rollout (page 292)	3	12	30 sec	3	10	30 sec	3	12	30 sec	3	10	30 sec

Workout B

EXERCISE	WEEK 1			WEEK 2			WEEK 3			WEEK 4		
	SETS	REPS	REST	SETS	REPS	REST	SETS	REPS	REST	SETS	REPS	REST
1A. Dumbbell squat (page 203)	3	8	75 sec	3	10	75 sec	4	8	75 sec	3	10	75 sec
1B. Decline pushup (page 36)	3	12	75 sec	3	10	75 sec	4	8	75 sec	3	10	75 sec
2A. Lat pulldown (page 102)	3	8	75 sec	3	10	75 sec	4	8	75 sec	3	10	75 sec
2B. Bent-arm lateral raise and external rotation (page 128)	3	12	75 sec	3	10	75 sec	4	8	75 sec	3	10	75 sec
3. Single-leg side plank (page 285)	3	8	30 sec	3	10	30 sec	3	12	30 sec	3	10	75 sec

For the single-leg side plank, hold the position for 5 seconds, then relax momentarily and repeat. That's one repetition.

Workout C

EXERCISE	WEEK 1			WEEK 2			WEEK 3			WEEK 4		
	SETS	REPS	REST	SETS	REPS	REST	SETS	REPS	REST	SETS	REPS	REST
1A. Wide-grip barbell deadlift (page 249)	3	8	1 min	3	8	1 min	4	6	1 min	3	8	1 min
1B. Barbell bench press (page 46)	3	8	1 min	3	8	1 min	4	6	1 min	3	8	1 min
2A. Cable row (page 92)	3	10	1 min	3	8	1 min	4	6	1 min	3	8	1 min
2B. Cable diagonal raise (page 139)	3	10	1 min	3	8	1 min	4	6	1 min	3	8	1 min
3. Swiss-ball rollout (page 292)	3	8	30 sec	3	10	30 sec	3	12	30 sec	3	10	30 sec

Cardio Workout

THE PLAN

- You can perform this workout on a treadmill, on a stationary bike, or outside on the sidewalk or a track.
- Exercise at an intensity that's 90 to 95 percent of your best effort. Go for 30 seconds.
- Slow down until your intensity is about 50 percent of your best effort and go for 2 minutes. That's one set.
- Use the schedule below to progress from week to week. Note that Workout A is the Cardio Workout you do the day after you do Weight Workout A, Workout B is the Cardio Workout you do the day after you do Weight Workout B, and so on.
- In Week 3 and Week 4, do all of your sets, rest for 5 to 10 minutes, and then repeat that same number of sets one more time. For example, for Workout A in Week 3, you'll do four sets, rest, and then do four more sets.

WORKOUT	WEEK 1	WEEK 2	WEEK 3	WEEK 4
A	4	5	4, 4	5, 5
B	5	6	5, 5	6, 6
C	4	5	4, 4	5, 5

The Ultimate Fat-Loss Workout
Phase 3: Weeks 9 to 12

Workout A

EXERCISE	WEEK 1			WEEK 2			WEEK 3			WEEK 4		
	SETS	REPS	REST	SETS	REPS	REST	SETS	REPS	REST	SETS	REPS	REST
1A. Barbell squat (page 198)	3	15	1 min	3	12	45 sec	4	10	45 sec	3	8	30 sec
1B. Incline dumbbell bench press (page 54)	3	15	1 min	3	12	45 sec	4	10	45 sec	3	8	30 sec
2A. Underhand-grip lat pulldown (page 104)	3	15	1 min	3	12	45 sec	4	10	45 sec	3	8	30 sec
2B. Reverse dumbbell lunge (page 217)	3	15	1 min	3	12	45 sec	4	10	45 sec	3	8	30 sec
3A. Cable face pull with external rotation (page 108)	3	15	1 min	3	12	45 sec	4	10	45 sec	3	8	30 sec
3B. Swiss-ball jackknife (page 290)	3	8	30 sec	3	10	30 sec	3	12	30 sec	3	10	30 sec

Workout B

EXERCISE	WEEK 1			WEEK 2			WEEK 3			WEEK 4		
	SETS	REPS	REST	SETS	REPS	REST	SETS	REPS	REST	SETS	REPS	REST
1A. Dumbbell lunge (page 216)	3	12	1 min	3	10	45 sec	4	8	45 sec	3	10	30 sec
1B. T-pushup (page 41)	3	12	1 min	3	10	45 sec	4	8	45 sec	3	10	30 sec
2A. Barbell row (page 76)	3	12	1 min	3	10	45 sec	4	8	45 sec	3	10	30 sec
2B. Incline Y raise (page 86)	3	12	1 min	3	10	45 sec	4	8	45 sec	3	10	30 sec
3. Standing rotational chop (page 307)	3	12	30 sec	3	10	30 sec	3	8	45 sec	3	10	30 sec

Workout C

EXERCISE	WEEK 1			WEEK 2			WEEK 3			WEEK 4		
	SETS	REPS	REST	SETS	REPS	REST	SETS	REPS	REST	SETS	REPS	REST
1A. Barbell squat (page 198)	3	12	1 min	3	10	45 sec	4	8	45 sec	3	10	30 sec
1B. Incline dumbbell bench press (page 54)	3	12	1 min	3	10	45 sec	4	8	45 sec	3	10	30 sec
2A. Underhand-grip lat pulldown (page 104)	3	12	1 min	3	10	45 sec	4	8	45 sec	3	10	30 sec
2B. Reverse dumbbell lunge (page 217)	3	12	1 min	3	10	45 sec	4	8	45 sec	3	10	30 sec
3A. Cable face pull with external rotation (page 108)	3	12	1 min	3	10	45 sec	4	8	45 sec	3	10	30 sec
3B. Swiss-ball jackknife (page 290)	3	8	30 sec	3	10	30 sec	3	12	30 sec	3	10	30 sec

Cardio Workout

THE PLAN

- You can perform this workout on a treadmill, on a stationary bike, or outside on the sidewalk or a track.
- Exercise at an intensity that's 90 to 95 percent of your best effort. Go for 30 seconds.
- Slow down until your intensity is about 50 percent of your best effort and go for 2 minutes. That's one set.
- Use the schedule below to progress from week to week. Note that Workout A is the Cardio Workout you do the day after you do Weight Workout A, Workout B is the Cardio Workout you do the day after you do Weight Workout B, and so on.
- In Week 3 and Week 4, do all of your sets, rest for 5 to 10 minutes, and then repeat that same number of sets one more time. For example, for Workout A in Week 3, you'll do five sets, rest, and then do five more sets.

WORKOUT	WEEK 1	WEEK 2	WEEK 3	WEEK 4
A	5	6	5, 5	6, 6
B	6	7	6, 6	5, 5, 5
C	7	8	5, 5	5

The Beach-Ready Workout
Phase 1: Weeks 1 and 2

This 8-week plan is designed to help even lifelong skinny guys gain a mountain of muscle. How? By making you strong, says trainer Vince DelMonte, who created the workout. After all, he points out, how many guys do you see with small chests who can bench 275 pounds? The answer is not many. So use his total-body training program to spike your strength, and you'll supersize your muscles—from head to toe.

How to Do This Workout

• For Phases 1 and 3, do each workout (Workout A, Workout B, and Workout C) once a week, resting for at least a day after each session. So you might do Workout A on Monday, Workout B on Wednesday, and Workout C on Friday.

• For Phases 2 and 4, do Workout A and Workout B once a week, on consecutive days. Then rest a day or two, and do Workout C and Workout D on consecutive days. Rest for a day or two again, and start over the following week. So you might do Workout A on Monday, Workout B on Tuesday, Workout C on Thursday, and Workout D on Friday.

• Note that in each phase you'll do more sets and more repetitions. The idea is to start each exercise with the heaviest weight that allows you to complete all your sets and repetitions in Phase 1, and use that same amount of weight in each subsequent phase. So if you use 185 pounds for the barbell squat in Phase 1, you'll use that same weight for the barbell squat in Phases 2, 3, and 4—you'll just be doing more sets and reps.

• You can also substitute exercises as needed, as long as the alternatives you use are similar to what's prescribed. For example, you can do the dumbbell bench press instead of the barbell bench press, or choose a variation of the crunch or situp for the Swiss-ball crunch.

• Make sure that you always use a weight that challenges you to complete all of your repetitions. For example, when you're to do 30 repetitions of the Swiss-ball crunch, you shouldn't feel like you could complete 10 more reps when the set is complete. If it's too easy, simply hold a weight plate across your chest to increase the difficulty.

About the Expert
Vince DelMonte is the author of *No-Nonsense Muscle Building*, the number-1 ranked muscle-building e-book. Vince has a degree in kinesiology from the University of Western Ontario and is a former skinny guy who has packed on more than 40 pounds of muscle using his get-strong to get-big method.

Workout A

EXERCISE	SETS	REPS	REST
1. Barbell squat (page 198)	4	4	2–3 min
2A. Barbell bench press (page 46)	4	4	90 sec
2B. Barbell row (page 76)	4	4	90 sec
3A. Dumbbell shrug (page 133)	4	4	30 sec
3B. Standing barbell calf raise (page 224)	4	4	30 sec

Workout B

EXERCISE	SETS	REPS	REST
1A. Dumbbell lunge (page 216)	4	12–15	90 sec
1B. Barbell straight-leg deadlift (page 252)	4	12–15	90 sec
2A. Dip (page 44)	4	AMAP	30 sec
2B. Chinup (page 96)	4	AMAP	30 sec
3. Swiss-ball crunch (page 318)	3	30	1 min

Workout C

EXERCISE	SETS	REPS	REST
1. Barbell deadlift (page 248)	4	4	2–3 min
2A. Dumbbell shoulder press (page 120)	4	4	90 sec
2B. Wide-grip pullup (page 99)	4	4	90 sec
3A. Barbell shrug (page 130)	2	20	30 sec
3B. Standing barbell calf raise (page 224)	2	20	30 sec

The Beach-Ready Workout
Phase 2: Weeks 3 and 4

Workout A

EXERCISE	SETS	REPS	REST
1. Barbell squat (page 198)	5	5	2–3 min
2. Barbell straight-leg deadlift (page 252)	5	5	2–3 min
3. Barbell curl (page 76)	5	5	2–3 min
4A. Barbell shrug (page 130)	3	30	30 sec
4B. Barbell calf raise (page 224)	3	30	30 sec

Workout B

EXERCISE	SETS	REPS	REST
1A. Dumbbell bench press (page 52)	5	5	90 sec
1B. Barbell row (page 76)	5	5	90 sec
2. Dumbbell shoulder press (page 120)	5	5	2–3 min
3. Swiss-ball crunch (page 318)	3	30	1 min

Workout C

EXERCISE	SETS	REPS	REST
1. Barbell deadlift (page 248)	5	5	2–3 min
2. Dumbbell lunge (page 216)	5	5	2–3 min
3. Close-grip bench press (page 47)	5	5	2–3 min
4A. Barbell shrug (page 130)	3	30	30 sec
4B. Barbell calf raise (page 224)	3	30	30 sec

Workout D

EXERCISE	SETS	REPS	REST
1A. Incline dumbbell bench press (page 54)	5	5	90 sec
1B. Cable row (page 92)	5	5	90 sec
2. Dumbbell shoulder press (page 120)	5	5	2–3 min
3. Swiss-ball crunch (page 318)	3	30	1 min

Best Workouts

The Beach-Ready Workout
Phase 3: Weeks 5 and 6

Workout A

EXERCISE	SETS	REPS	REST
1. Barbell squat (page 198)	6	6	2–3 min
2A. Barbell bench press (page 46)	6	6	90 sec
2B. Barbell row (page 76)	6	6	90 sec
3A. Lateral raise (page 126)	3	15	30 sec
3B. Barbell calf raise (page 224)	3	15	30 sec

Workout B

EXERCISE	SETS	REPS	REST
1A. Dumbbell lunge (page 216)	4	8-12	90 sec
1B. Barbell straight-leg deadlift (page 252)	4	8-12	90 sec
2A. Dip (page 44)	4	AMAP	30 sec
2B. Chinup (page 96)	4	AMAP	30 sec
3. Swiss-ball crunch (page 318)	3	30	1 min

Workout C

EXERCISE	SETS	REPS	REST
1. Barbell deadlift (page 248)	6	6	2–3 min
2A. Dumbbell shoulder press (page 120)	6	6	90 sec
2B. Wide-grip pullup (page 99)	6	6	90 sec
3A. Barbell shrug (page 130)	3	15	30 sec
3B. Barbell calf raise (page 224)	3	15	30 sec

The Beach-Ready Workout
Phase 4: Weeks 7 and 8

Workout A

EXERCISE	SETS	REPS	REST
1. Barbell squat (page 198)	7	7	2–3 min
2. Barbell straight-leg deadlift (page 252)	7	7	2–3 min
3. Barbell curl (page 154)	7	7	2–3 min
4A. Barbell shrug (page 130)	3	30	30 sec
4B. Barbell calf raise (page 224)	3	30	30 sec

Workout B

EXERCISE	SETS	REPS	REST
1A. Dumbbell bench press (page 52)	7	7	90 sec
1B. Barbell row (page 76)	7	7	90 sec
2. Dumbbell shoulder press (page 120)	7	7	2–3 min
3. Swiss-ball crunch (page 318)	3	30	1 min

Workout C

EXERCISE	SETS	REPS	REST
1. Barbell deadlift (page 248)	7	7	2–3 min
2. Dumbbell lunge (page 216)	7	7	2–3 min
3. Close-grip bench press (page 47)	7	7	2–3 min
4A. Barbell shrug (page 130)	3	30	30 sec
4B. Barbell calf raise (page 224)	3	30	30 sec

Workout D

EXERCISE	SETS	REPS	REST
1A. Incline dumbbell bench press (page 54)	7	7	90 sec
1B. Cable row (page 92)	7	7	90 sec
2. Barbell shoulder press (page 116)	7	7	2–3 min
3. Swiss-ball crunch (page 318)	2	20	1 min

Best Workouts

Best Workouts

The Wedding Workout
Phase 2: Weeks 5 to 8

Workout A

For the wide-stance plank with opposite arm and leg lift, hold the position for 5 seconds, then lower your arm and leg to the floor. That's one repetition. Alternate the arm and leg you raise for each repetition.

EXERCISE	SETS	REPS	REST
1A. Explosive pushup (page 42)	5	AMAP	10 sec
1B. Elevated-feet inverted row (page 74)	5	AMAP	10 sec
1C. Reverse dumbbell lunge (page 217)	5	12–15	10 sec
1D. Single-leg Swiss-ball hip riase and leg curl (page 244)	5	15–20	10 sec
1E. Wide-stance plank with opposite arm and leg lift (page 281)	5	8–10	10 sec
1F. High box jump (page 195)	5	30	1 min

Workout B

EXERCISE	SETS	REPS	REST
1A. Floor inverted shoulder press (page 123)	5	AMAP	10 sec
1B. Chinup (page 96)	5	AMAP	10 sec
1C. Barbell stepup (page 260)	5	12–15	10 sec
1D. Dumbbell hang pull (page 347)	5	12–15	10 sec
1E. Barbell rollout (page 292)	5	12–20	10 sec
1F. Squat thrusts (page 422)	5	30–50	1 min

Workout C

EXERCISE	SETS	REPS	REST
1A. Single-arm shoulder press (page 122)	5	5	1 min
1B. Pullup (page 99)	5	5	1 min
2A. Pistol squat (page 197)	5	5	1 min
2B. Single-arm kettlebell or dumbbell snatch (page 268)	5	5	1 min
3. Squat thrusts (page 422)	1	100	ALAP

For the squat thrusts, set a stopwatch and do 100 repetitions as fast as possible, taking breaks as needed. So you might perform 32 reps, rest for 20 to 30 seconds, do another 20 reps, then rest again. Continue in this manner until you've completed all 100 reps. Then stop the clock. Record the elapsed time, and try to beat it the next time you repeat the workout.

Cardio

THE PLAN

Jump rope two times a week, on days when you don't perform a Weight Workout. One turn of the rope is equal to one repetition. Do 100 repetitions forward and 100 repetitions backward. Then do 90 reps forward, 90 reps back; 80 reps forward, 80 reps back, and so on, until you complete 10 reps forward, and 10 reps back. Set a stopwatch at the beginning of the workout, and record how long it takes you to complete the routine. Try to complete the workout in less time each session.

The Vertical-Jump Workout

This high-flying plan from strength coach Kelly Baggett is designed to add 4 to 10 inches to your vertical. It uses traditional exercises like the barbell squat to strengthen the muscles you use to jump. And just as important, it incorporates plyometrics—the box jump and depth jump—to teach those same muscles to to fire faster. The upshot: You'll raise your game to all new heights.

About the Expert
Kelly Baggett is the co-owner of Transformation Clinics in Springfield, Missouri. Kelly is the author of *The Vertical Jump Development Bible*, the most complete guide to jumping higher that you're ever likely to see.

Phase 1: Weeks 1 to 4

Workout A

EXERCISE	SETS	REPS	REST
1. Kneeling hip flexor stretch (page 228)	1	30-sec hold	0
2. Reverse hip raise (page 246)	2	15	1 min
3. Jump rope	3	1 min	1 min
4. Barbell deadlift (page 248)	1	5	3 min
5. Dumbbell Bulgarian split squat (page 210)	2	8	3 min
6. Standing barbell calf raise (page 224)	3	20	90 sec

Workout B

EXERCISE	SETS	REPS	REST
1. Kneeling hip flexor stretch (page 228)	1	30-sec hold	0
2. Reverse hip raise (page 246)	2	15	1 min
3. Jump rope	3	1 min	1 min
4. Barbell squat (page 198)	3	5	3 min
5. Swiss-ball hip raise and leg curl (page 243)	3	8	90 sec
6. Standing barbell calf raise (page 224)	3	20	90 sec

If the Swiss-ball hip raise and leg curl is too easy, use the single-leg version of the exercise (page 244).

How to Do This Workout
• Use this program 3 days a week. In Phase 1, alternate between Workout A and Workout B, resting for at least a day after each session. So if you plan to lift on Monday, Wednesday, and Friday, do Workout A on Monday, Workout B on Wednesday, and Workout A again on Friday. The next week, do Workout B on Monday and Friday, and Workout A on Wednesday. In Phase 2, always do Workout A on Monday and Friday, and Workout B on Wednesday.
• Questions? Flip back to page 443, where you'll find complete instructions for performing all of the workouts.

Phase 2: Weeks 5 to 8

Workout A

EXERCISE	SETS	REPS	REST
1. Kneeling hip flexor stretch (page 228)	1	30-sec hold	0
2. Reverse hip raise (page 246)	2	15	1 min
3. Jump rope	3	1 min	1 min
4. Depth jump (page 195)	6	3	1 min
5. Barbell jump squat (page 202)	4	8	90 sec

Workout B

EXERCISE	SETS	REPS	REST
1. Kneeling hip flexor stretch (page 228)	1	30-sec hold	0
2. Reverse hip raise (page 246)	2	15	1 min
3. Jump rope	3	1 min	1 min
4. Depth jump (page 195)	6	3	1 min
5. Barbell squat (page 198)	3	5	3 min
6. Swiss-ball hip raise and leg curl (page 243)	3	8	90 sec ←

If the Swiss-ball hip raise and leg curl is too easy, use the single-leg version of the exercise (page 244).

The Scrawny-to-Brawny Workout

This old-school muscle-building plan is all about the basics: heavy weights and hard work. That's the proven formula for packing on size, says strength coach Zach Even-Esh. Add slabs of muscle to your frame with his time-tested workout.

How to Do This Workout

• Do each workout (Workout A, Workout B, and Workout C) once a week, resting for at least a day in between sessions.

• For any exercise with a rep range that starts with the largest number, use a pyramid method. That is, if 10 to 5 repetitions are prescribed (10-5), start with 10 reps for your first set and then increase the weight and do fewer reps in each subsequent set. Your end goal: Do your last one or two sets with the heaviest weight that allows you to complete the lowest number of pre-scribed reps. (In the case of 10-5, you'd want to 5 reps in your last two sets, with the heaviest load you can handle.)

• Questions? Flip back to page 443, where you'll find complete instructions for performing all of the workouts.

About the Expert
Zach Even-Esh has a master's degree in health education and is the owner of Underground Strength Gym, a hard-core athletic training center in Edison, New Jersey.

Workout A

EXERCISE	SETS	REPS	REST
1. Single-arm dumbbell snatch (page 349)	3	10–5	1 min
2. Rear lateral raise (page 83)	3	10	30 sec
3. Lateral raise (page 126)	3	10	30 sec
4A. Barbell curl (page 154)	3	6–10	0
4B. Dip (page 44)	3	AMAP	0
5. Wrist curl (page 176)	2	AMAP	30 sec
6A. Swiss-ball jackknife (page 290)	1	15	0
6B. Medicine-ball V-up (page 317)	1	15	0
6C. Plank (page 278)	1	30-sec hold	0
6D. Side plank (page 284)	1	30-sec hold	0

Workout B

EXERCISE	SETS	REPS	REST
1. Barbell squat (page 198)	5	10–5	90 sec
2. Barbell deadlift (page 248)	3	3	90 sec
3. Walking dumbbell lunge (page 217)	2	20	90 sec
4. Single-arm dumbbell swing (page 268)	2	10	1 min
5. Single-leg standing dumbbell calf raise (page 226)	3	10–20	0

For the walking dumbbell lunge, each step forward counts as one repetition. So you'll do 10 reps for each leg.

Workout C

EXERCISE	SETS	REPS	REST
1A. Barbell bench press (page 46)	5	10–3	0
1B. Pullup (page 99)	5	AMAP	0
2A. Incline dumbbell bench press (page 54)	3	10–5	0
2B. Kneeling supported neutral-grip dumbbell row (page 80)	5	12–6	0
3A. Barbell shrug (page 130)	3	15–10	0
3B. Pushup (page 34)	3	AMAP	0
4A. Barbell rollout (page 292)	1	10	0
4B. Weighted situp (page 313)	1	15	0
4C. Swiss-ball jackknife (page 290)	1	15	0
4D. Crunch (page 314)	1	AMAP	0

Best Workouts

The Best Sports Workout

Workout C

EXERCISE	WEEK 1			WEEK 2			WEEK 3		
	SETS	REPS	REST	SETS	REPS	REST	SETS	REPS	REST
1A. Single-arm kettlebell swing (page 268)	3	5	1 min	3	5	1 min	3	5	1 min
1B. Cable core press (page 295)	2	12	1 min	2	14	1 min	2	16	1 min
2A. Single-leg squat (page 196)	2	8	1 min	3	8	1 min	3	8	1 min
2B. Inverted row (page 72)	2	15	1 min	3	15	1 min	3	15	1 min
2C. Side plank (page 284)	2	30-sec hold	30 sec	2	40-sec hold	30 sec	2	50-sec hold	30 sec
3A. Lat pulldown (page 102)	2	15	30 sec	2	15	30 sec	2	15	30 sec
3B. Dumbbell lunge (page 216)	2	8	30 sec	2	12	30 sec	2	15	30 sec
3C. Swiss-ball hip raise and leg curl (page 243)	2	8	30 sec	2	10	30 sec	2	12	30 sec
3D. Half-kneeling stability chop (page 297)	2	8	30 sec	2	8	30 sec	2	8	30 sec

Workout D

EXERCISE	WEEK 1			WEEK 2			WEEK 3		
	SETS	REPS	REST	SETS	REPS	REST	SETS	REPS	REST
1A. Close-grip bench press (page 47)	2	8	1 min	3	8	1 min	3	8	1 min
1B. Swiss-ball rollout (page 292)	2	20	1 min	2	30	1 min	2	40	1 min
2A. Combo shoulder raise (page 129)	2	10	1 min	2	10	1 min	2	10	1 min
2B. Wall slide (page 422)	2	10	0	2	12	0	2	14	0
2C. Plank (page 278)	2	30-sec hold	30 sec	2	40-sec hold	30 sec	2	50-sec hold	30 sec
3A. Mountain climber (page 288)	2	10	1 min	2	12	1 min	2	14	1 min
3B. Incline Y-T-W-L (page 86)	2	8	1 min	2	10	1 min	2	12	1 min
3C. Standing cable hip adduction (page 222)	2	10	1 min	2	12	1 min	2	14	1 min
3D. Cable core press (page 295)	2	8	1 min	2	8	1 min	2	8	1 min

The Best Three-Exercise Workouts

Build muscle fast with these "three and out" workouts from Bill Hartman, PT, CSCS. They include only what Hartman calls "big" exercises—those that work multiple muscle groups. There's one exercise for your lower body, and pushing and pulling exercises for your upper body. Do all three for the best results in the least amount of time.

How to Do These Workouts
• Choose one exercise from each category: Big Lower Body, Big Pull, and Big Push.
• Perform the three exercises as a circuit, doing one set of each in succession, resting as prescribed.
• Complete a total of four or five circuits, 3 days a week. Rest at least a day between sessions.

Exercise 1

BIG LOWER BODY

• Do six to eight repetitions.
• Rest for 75 seconds.
• Move on to Exercise 2.

Barbell squat (page 198)

Dumbbell squat (page 203)

Barbell front squat (page 199)

Goblet squat (page 204)

Barbell deadlift (page 248)

Dumbbell deadlift (page 250)

Barbell split squat (page 206)

Dumbbell split squat (page 209)

Exercise 2

BIG PULL

• Do six to eight repetitions.
• Rest for 75 seconds.
• Move on to Exercise 3.

Chinup (page 96)

Pullup (page 99)

Mixed-grip chinup (page 100)

Barbell row (page 76)

Dumbbell row (page 78)

Cable row (page 92)

Lat pulldown (page 102)

30-degree lat pulldown (page 104)

Exercise 3

BIG PUSH

• Do six to eight repetitions.
• Rest for 60 seconds.
• Go back to Exercise 1, and repeat until you've completed four or five circuits.

Barbell shoulder press (page 116)

Dumbbell shoulder press (page 120)

Barbell push press (page 118)

Barbell bench press (page 46)

Dumbbell bench press (page 52)

Incline barbell bench press (page 50)

Incline dumbbell bench press (page 54)

Weighted pushup (page 37)

The Big Bench Press Workout

When was the last time you added 20 pounds to your bench press? How about 30? Well, this workout, designed by world-class powerlifter Dave Tate, will help you do just that—and maybe more. In fact, Tate says that the average guy should expect to increase his maximum bench press by 20 to 50 pounds in just 8 weeks on this program.

The Secret

You'll use a method developed at Westside Barbell, one of the premier powerlifting clubs on the planet. It features fast lifting with light weights one day—called the speed workout— and low-rep, heavy lifting on the other (the maximum-effort workout). The speed workout helps teach your muscles to blow through their sticking point. The maximum-effort workout builds the strength you need to push the bar the last few, tough inches. This combination will have you packing on the plates in the no time.

How to Do This Workout

• Do each workout (Workout A and Workout B) once a week, resting for at least 3 days after each session. So you might do Workout A on Monday and Workout B on Friday. Use one of the days in between to do a lower-body workout, like the "Build the Perfect Backside Workout" in Chapter 9.

• Questions? Flip back to page 443, where you'll find complete instructions for performing all of the workouts.

About the Expert
Dave Tate is the founder and CEO of Elite Fitness Systems in London, Ohio, and a longtime contributor to *Men's Health*. He not only touts a personal best of 610 pounds in the bench press but has also completed a 935-pound squat and a 740-pound deadlift.

Workout A: Speed

EXERCISE	SETS	REPS	REST
1. Barbell bench press (page 46)	9	3	45 sec
2. Close-grip barbell bench press (page 47)	2–3	5	2–3 min
3. EZ-bar lying triceps extension (page 164)	3	8	1 min
4. Barbell row (page 76)	5	5	2 min
5. Dumbbell shoulder press (page 120)	3	8	1 min
6. Reverse EZ-bar curl (page 153)	1	10	0

For the barbell bench press, use a weight that's about half of what you can lift one time. Press the weight as fast as possible each time. Try to complete each three-repetition set in 3 1/2 seconds or less. Rest for 45 seconds after each set, and alternate your grip every three sets—so that your hands are about 16, then 20, then 24 inches apart.

Workout B: Maximum Effort

EXERCISE	SETS	REPS	REST

1. Bench press: your choice

For the bench press, choose one of the three bench press variations listed in the exercise menu below. (Switch to a different one every 2 weeks.) Start by lifting the empty bar for three repetitions as a warmup. Rest for 45 seconds. Add 20 to 40 pounds and do another three repetitions. Continue this way until a three-repetition set feels difficult. Then add weight, but do only one repetition instead of three, and increase your rest between sets to 2 minutes. Work up to the weight you can lift only one time. Keep track of this record, and try to break it during each maximum-weight workout. Important note: Always use a spotter.

	SETS	REPS	REST
2. Dumbbell lying triceps extension (page 168)	5	10	60–90 sec
3. Triceps pressdown (page 173)	5	10	60–90 sec
4. Dumbbell row (page 78)	5	10	60–90 sec
5. Front raise (page 124)	5	10	60–90 sec

Exercise Menu
- Towel or board press (page 48)
- Barbell floor press (page 49)
- Barbell pin press (page 49)

The Time-Saving Couples Workout

This fat-burning plan is designed so that you can work out with your spouse but still ensure that you get the results you want. The weight workouts are performed in a circuit. You can do them simultaneously, or if you're sharing the same equipment, perform them follow-the-leader style, with one of you completing the first exercise before the other starts. After you've finished the main workout, you can then choose an optional workout that allows you to customize your routine for the body you want.

How to Do This Workout

• Do each Weight Workout (Workout A, Workout B, and Workout C) once a week, resting for at least a day after each session. So you might do Workout A on Monday, Workout B on Wednesday, and Workout C on Friday.

• Prior to each Weight Workout, complete the warmup.

• Each Weight Workout is designed to last 10 minutes. Simply do as many sets of each exercise as you can in that time frame. Note that you'll be performing the exercises in a circuit. So complete one set of the first exercise, then move immediately to the second exercise, and so on. Stop your workout when you run out of time.

• After each Weight Workout, you can also choose one of the 4-Minute Add-On Workouts. These are optional, so do them only if you have time. They're designed to both burn fat and give a little extra attention to the muscles that you may want to show off. As a result, you'll find there are different routines for men and women (although you can choose from any of them).

• Do the Cardio Workout twice a week, on the days in between your Weight Workouts. So you might do your cardio sessions on Tuesday and Thursday. (If you can't find time to exercise 5 days a week, just do the Cardio Workout immediately following two of your Weight Workouts.)

• Questions? Flip back to page 443, where you'll find complete instructions for performing all of the workouts.

About the Expert
Ed Scow, CPT, is the owner of ELS Massage and Personal Training in Lincoln, Nebraska. Ed specializes in helping busy men and women lose fat and get fit fast.

Weight Workouts
Warmup

EXERCISE	SETS	REPS	REST
1A. Jumping jacks (page 421)	1	15	0
1B. Prisoner squat (page 192)	1	10	0
1C. Pushup (page 34)	1	8	0

Workout A

EXERCISE	SETS	REPS	REST	DURATION
1A. Incline dumbbell bench press (page 54)	AMAP	8	0	8 min
1B. Dumbbell row (page 78)	AMAP	8	0	
1C. Single-arm dumbbell swing (page 268)	AMAP	8	0	
2. Squat thrusts (page 422)	AMAP	20 sec	10 sec	2 min

• This workout is split into two separate routines. One routine lasts 8 minutes and the other is to be performed for 2 minutes. Simply do as many sets of each exercise as you can in the given time frame.

• For the 8-minute routine, you'll be performing the three exercises in an 8-minute circuit. So complete one set of the first exercise, then move immediately to the second exercise, and so on. When time is up, move on to the 2-minute routine.

• For the 2-minute routine, you'll simply do one exercise. Do as many reps as you can in 20 seconds, rest for 10 seconds, then repeat until you run out of time.

Best Workouts

The Time-Saving Couples Workout

Workout B

EXERCISE	SETS	REPS	REST	DURATION
1A. Thrusters (page 343)	AMAP	8	0	
1B. Rear lateral raise (page 83)	AMAP	8	0	
1C. Pushup (page 34)	AMAP	12	0	10 min
1D. Reverse dumbbell lunge (page 217)	AMAP	8	0	
1E. Mountain climber (page 288)	AMAP	30 sec	0	

Workout C

EXERCISE	SETS	REPS	REST	DURATION
1A. Elbows-out dumbbell row (page 78)	AMAP	10	0	
1B. Incline dumbbell bench press (page 54)	AMAP	10	0	
1C. Squat thrusts (page 422)	AMAP	8	0	10 min
1D. Dumbbell push press (page 120)	AMAP	10	0	
1E. Single-arm dumbbell swing (page 268)	AMAP	12	0	

4-Minute Add-On Workouts for Men
Option 1: Arms and Core

EXERCISE	SETS	REPS	REST	DURATION
1A. Standing dumbbell curl (page 156)	AMAP	20 sec	10 sec	
1B. Squat thrusts (page 422)	AMAP	20 sec	10 sec	
1C. Dumbbell lying triceps extension (page 168)	AMAP	20 sec	10 sec	4 min
1D. Squat thrusts (page 422)	AMAP	20 sec	10 sec	

Option 2: Hips, Arms, and Core

EXERCISE	SETS	REPS	REST	DURATION
1A. Close-hands pushup (page 38)	AMAP	20 sec	10 sec	
1B. Single-arm dumbbell swing (page 268)	AMAP	20 sec	10 sec	
1C. Hammer curl to press (page 161)	AMAP	20 sec	10 sec	4 min
1D. Single-arm dumbbell swing (page 268)	AMAP	20 sec	10 sec	

Option 3: Arms and Core

EXERCISE	SETS	REPS	REST	DURATION
1A. Swiss-ball jackknife (page 290)	AMAP	20 sec	10 sec	
1B. Hammer curl (page 158)	AMAP	20 sec	10 sec	
1C. Swiss-ball jackknife (page 290)	AMAP	20 sec	10 sec	4 min
1D. Dumbbell lying triceps extension (page 168)	AMAP	20 sec	10 sec	

The Time-Saving Couples Workout

4-Minute Add-On Workouts for Women
Option 1: Hips, Triceps, and Core

EXERCISE	SETS	REPS	REST	DURATION
1A. Hip raise with feet on a Swiss ball (page 239)	AMAP	20 sec	10 sec	
1B. Mountain climber (page 288)	AMAP	20 sec	10 sec	4 min
1C. Dumbbell lying triceps extension (page 168)	AMAP	20 sec	10 sec	
1D. Mountain climber (page 288)	AMAP	20 sec	10 sec	

Option 2: Hips, Thighs, and Core

EXERCISE	SETS	REPS	REST	DURATION
1A. Swiss-ball jackknife (page 290)	AMAP	20 sec	10 sec	
1B. Swiss-ball hip raise and leg curl (page 243)	AMAP	20 sec	10 sec	4 min
1C. Swiss-ball jackknife (page 290)	AMAP	20 sec	10 sec	
1D. Split jump (page 211)	AMAP	20 sec	10 sec	

Option 3: Hips, Thighs, Shoulders, and Arms

EXERCISE	SETS	REPS	REST	DURATION
1A. Dumbbell squat (page 203)	AMAP	20 sec	10 sec	
1B. Single-arm dumbbell swing (page 268)	AMAP	20 sec	10 sec	4 min
1C. Hammer curl to press (page 161)	AMAP	20 sec	10 sec	
1D. Single-arm dumbbell swing (page 268)	AMAP	20 sec	10 sec	

The 16-Minute Cardio Workout

THE PLAN

- You can perform this workout on a treadmill, on a stationary bike, or outside on the sidewalk or a track.
- Start by going at an easy pace—about 30 percent of your best effort—for 4 minutes. Then do this interval workout:
- Exercise at an intensity that's about 80 percent of your best effort. Go for 30 seconds.
- Slow down until your intensity is about 40 percent of your best effort and go for 60 seconds. That's one set. Do 6 sets.
- Once you've completed all of your sets, slow down to 30 percent of your best effort and go for 3 minutes.

The Best Body-Weight Workouts

You don't need a gym membership to sculpt a great body. In fact, you don't even need equipment. Build muscle and burn fat anywhere with these super-simple body-weight workouts.

Workout 1

EXERCISE	SETS	REPS	REST
1. Body-weight Bulgarian split squat (page 210)	3	10–12	1 min
2A. Pushup (page 34)	3	12–15	1 min
2B. Hip raise (page 236)	3	12–15	1 min
3A. Side plank (page 284)	3	30-sec hold	30 sec
3B. Floor Y-T-I raises (pages 86–91)	3	10	30 sec

If any of the first four exercises are too hard, feel free to substitute the variation of the movement that allows you to perform the prescribed number of reps. Likewise, if you find an exercise is too easy, use a harder variation instead.

For the floor Y-T-I raises, do 10 repetitions of each letter. That is, do 10 reps of the floor Y raise, followed by 10 reps of the floor T raise and 10 reps of the floor I raise.

Workout 2

EXERCISE	SETS	REPS	REST
1. Iso-explosive jump squat (page 194)	4	6–8	1 min
2A. Iso-explosive pushup (page 42)	3	6–8	1 min
2B. Single-leg hip raise (page 238)	3	12–15	1 min
3A. Inverted shoulder press (page 123)	3	AMAP	1 min
3B. Prone cobra (page 295)	2	1-min hold	1 min

For the iso-explosive jump squat and the iso-explosive pushup, make sure to hold the down position for 5 seconds each repetition.

Workout 3

EXERCISE	SETS	REPS	REST
1A. Jumping jacks (page 421)	2–5	30 sec	0
1B. Prisoner squat (page 192)	2–5	20	0
1C. Close-hands pushup (page 38)	2–5	20	0
1D. Walking lunge (page 217)	2–5	12	0
1E. Mountain climber (page 288)	2–5	10	0
1F. Inverted hamstring (page 428)	2–5	8	0
1G. T-pushup (page 41)	2–5	8	0
1H. Run in place	2–5	30 sec	0

The first time you try this routine, do two sets of each exercise. In future workouts, work your way up to five sets for each.

Best Workouts

The Best 15-Minute Workouts

Ready to start sculpting a leaner, stronger body? It won't take you long. Just three 15-minute weight workouts a week can double a beginner's strength, report scientists at the University of Kansas. What's more, unlike the average person, who quits a new weight-training program within a month, 96 percent of the participants in the study easily fit the quickie workouts into their lives. You can do the same, with the 10 workouts that follow—all of which are designed to build muscle while melting fat.

Workout 1

EXERCISE	SETS	REPS	REST
1A. Barbell squat (page 198)	3	15	0
1B. Pushup (page 34)	3	AMAP	0
1C. Hip raise (page 236)	3	12–15	0
1D. Dumbbell row (page 78)	3	10–12	0
1E. Plank (page 278)	3	30-sec hold	0

Workout 2

EXERCISE	SETS	REPS	REST
1A. Swiss-ball hip raise and leg curl (page 243)	3	AMAP	0
1B. Pushup plus (page 64)	3	AMAP	0
1C. Swiss-ball jackknife (page 290)	3	AMAP	30 sec
2A. Chinup (page 96)	2–3	AMAP	30 sec
2B. Dumbbell shoulder press (page 120)	2–3	8–10	30 sec

Before You Start

If any of the body-weight exercises in these workouts are too hard or too easy, feel free to substitute the variation of the movement that allows you to perform the prescribed number of reps. Remember, each set should challenge your muscles to the point where you start to struggle but don't quite reach complete failure. (See Chapter 2 for a more detailed explanation on this concept.)

And make no mistake: These workouts aren't easy. They're fast paced and intense. So if they're too hard when you first start, go ahead and take longer rest between sets, and finish as much of the workout as you can in the 15 minutes. In each subsequent workout, try to do a little more, until you're able to complete the entire routine.

How to Do These Workouts

• Option 1: Choose a workout and do it three times a week, resting for at least a day after each session. After 2 or 3 weeks, switch to a new workout.
• Option 2: Choose two workouts and alternate between them 3 days a week. Always rest for at least a day after each session. So you might do Workout 1 on Monday and Friday, and Workout 2 on Wednesday. The following week, you'd do Workout 2 on Monday and Friday, and Workout 1 on Wednesday. After 4 weeks, it's time to choose two new workouts.

Workout 3

EXERCISE	SETS	REPS	REST
1. Single-arm reverse lunge and press (page 344)	3	10–12	1 min
2A. Chinup (page 96)	3	AMAP	0
2B. Side plank (page 284)	3	30-sec hold	0
2C. Pushup (page 34)	3	AMAP	45 sec

Workout 4

EXERCISE	SETS	REPS	REST
1A. Single-arm dumbbell swing (page 268)	3	12	30 sec
1B. Pushup and row (page 43)	3	12	30 sec
2A. Thrusters (page 343)	2	12	30 sec
2B. Swiss-ball jackknife (page 290)	2	12–15	30 sec

The Best 15-Minute Workout

Workout 5

EXERCISE	SETS	REPS	REST
1. Side lunge and press (page 345)	3	10–12	1 min
2A. Single-leg dumbbell row (page 79)	3	12–15	0
2B. Single-leg hip raise (page 240)	3	AMAP	0
2C. T-pushup (page 41)	3	AMAP	30 sec

Workout 6

EXERCISE	SETS	REPS	REST
1A. Overhead dumbbell lunge (page 219)	3	10–12	0
1B. Single-arm neutral-grip dumbbell row and rotation (page 82)	3	10–12	0
1C. Single-arm stepup and press (page 344)	3	10–12	0
1D. Pushup (page 34)	3	AMAP	0
1E. Prone cobra (page 295)	3	30-sec hold	60

Workout 7

EXERCISE	SETS	REPS	REST
1. Wide-grip barbell deadlift (page 249)	4	5	90 sec
2A. Incline dumbbell bench press (page 54)	2	10–12	0 sec
2B. Swiss-ball Russian twist (page 302)	2	10–12	0 sec
2C. Dumbbell lunge (page 216)	2	10–12	1 min

Workout 8

EXERCISE	SETS	REPS	REST
1A. Barbell good morning (page 254)	3	8	0
1B. Dumbbell bench press (page 52)	3	8	0
1C. Body-weight squat (page 190)	3	30 sec	0
1D. Dumbbell row (page 78)	3	10	0
1E. Mountain climber (page 288)	3	30 sec	15 to 30 sec

Workout 9

EXERCISE	SETS	REPS	REST
1A. Dumbbell deadlift (page 250)	4	6	0
1B. Jump rope	4	45-sec	0
1C. Dumbbell push press (page 121)	4	6	0
1D. Jump rope	4	45-sec	1 min

Workout 10

EXERCISE	SETS	REPS	REST
1. Barbell front squat (page 199)	3	6-8	1 min
2A. Barbell row (page 76)	3	6-8	0
2B. Core stabilization (page 334)	3	30-sec	0
2C. Single-arm dumbbell swing (page 268)	3	10–12	0
2D. Decline pushup (page 36)	3	AMAP	30 sec

Best Workouts

The Spartacus Workout

Ever wonder how Hollywood actors get in such incredible shape? It's not rocket science. But it is exercise science. So when executives at Starz asked me to create a training plan for the cast of the network's new show, *Spartacus*—in preparation for the program's January 2010 premiere—I knew exactly who to consult: Rachel Cosgrove, one of the world's top fitness experts who's known industry-wide for her ability to meld the latest in muscle and fat loss science to achieve stunning results.

For the actors in Spartacus, we mixed old-school training equipment—such as sandbags and kettlebells—with modern variations of classic exercises, like T-pushups and the dumbbell lunge and rotation. All of which were designed to mimic the movements a Spartan warrior would need in training and in battle. (To see a video of the cast working out, go to MensHealth.com/Spartacus.) For you, we've tweaked the exercises to make the workout more gym-friendly, while keeping it every bit as effective. The final product: A cutting-edge circuit routine that will strip away fat, define your chest, arms, and abs, and send your fitness levels soaring. So you'll sculpt the lean, muscular, and athletic-looking body of a Spartan warrior—while getting in the best shape of your life.

About the Expert
Rachel Cosgrove, CSCS, is the co-owner of Results Fitness in Santa Clarita, California and a top fitness advisor to both *Men's Health* and *Women's Health*.

How to Do This Workout

• Do this workout three days a week. You can do it as your primary weight workout, or as a "cardio" workout on the days between your regular weight workout. This approach will help you speed fat loss even more.

• Perform the workout as a circuit, doing one set of each exercise—or "station"—in succession. Each station in the circuit lasts for 60 seconds. Do as many repetitions as you can in that duration, then move on to the next station in the circuit. Give yourself 15 seconds to transition between stations, and rest for 2 minutes after you've done one circuit of all 10 exercises. Then repeat 2 times. If you can't go for the entire minute on the bodyweight exercises, go as long as you can, rest for a few seconds, then go again until your time at that station is up.

• Prior to each workout, complete a 5 to 10 minute warmup. Use the "Create Your Own Warmup" guide in Chapter 13 to design your routine.

STATION 1

Goblet squat (page 204)

STATION 2

Mountain climber (page 288)

STATION 3

Single-arm dumbbell swing (page 268)

STATION 4

T-push up (page 41)

STATION 5

Split jump (page 211)

STATION 6

Dumbbell row (page 78)

STATION 7

Dumbbell side lunge and touch (page 221)

STATION 8

Pushup position row (page 43)

For the Pushup Position Row, refer to the Pushup and Row on page 43. Simply do the row portion of the exercise, without the pushup.

STATION 9

Dumbbell lunge and rotation (page 219)

STATION 10

Dumbbell push press (page 121)

Chapter 15:
The Best Cardio Workouts

FINISH STRONG, EVERY TIME

Let's
clear something up:

The term *cardio* doesn't just mean "aerobic exercise." After all, *cardio* is really short for *cardiovascular conditioning*. And the fact is, weight training and sprints are highly beneficial to your heart and lungs, too. So you'll see plenty of great cardio routines throughout this entire book.

But in the pages that follow, you'll find a dozen more fast, unique workouts that may forever change the way you think about cardio. Whether you want to bust out of your rut, train for a 10-K, or just finish in a flurry, you'll find there's a cutting-edge plan for you.

8 World-Class Ways to Run Faster

If you're tired of long, boring runs, try these short speed workouts from Ed Eyestone, MS, a two-time Olympic marathoner and head coach of the Brigham Young University men's cross-country team. These routines not only help break up the monotony, they'll boost your speed and endurance to an all-time high. A great way to mix them up: Do one of the first three workouts early in the week, then choose a second from numbers 4 through 7 later in the week, at the track. Do the last run on the weekend.

1. Tempo Run

What: A fuel-injected version of your 4-mile jog, run at a "comfortably hard" pace.

Why: Tempo runs train your body to clear the waste products that cause your muscles to "burn" and thereby force you to slow down. As a result, you can go harder, longer.

How: Estimate your fastest 3-mile time (think back to your best recent 5-K). Calculate the pace per mile and add 30 seconds to it. So if you think the fastest you can run 3 miles is 24 minutes—that's an 8-minute pace—try for a tempo pace of 8 minutes, 30 seconds per mile for your 4-mile run.

Tip: Be precise. Wear a watch.

2. Tempo 1,000s

What: A series of 1,000-meter runs at your tempo pace, with rest in between.

Why: Short tempo runs help you maintain a strict pace, and the brief recoveries keep your effort level high.

How: Run at your 4-mile tempo pace (determined in #1, tempo run) for 1,000 meters—that's about $2\frac{1}{2}$ times around a track—then rest for 60 seconds before repeating. Start with a total of six 1,000-meter intervals and progress to 10, adding one each time you perform the workout.

Tip: If you'd prefer, measure in time instead of distance. Perform each interval for $3\frac{1}{2}$ minutes before resting.

3. Step-Down Fartlek

What: *Fartlek* is Swedish for "speed play," meaning you accelerate and slow down according to how you feel. (How European!)

Why: In a step-down fartlek, the intervals are more structured (how American!) and become harder at the end of your run. Working hard when you're tired will make you faster when you're fresh.

How: Start at a pace that's about 75 percent of your full effort and go for 5 minutes. Then slow down to about 40 percent effort for 5 minutes. Continue this fast-then-slow pattern, but shorten the hard-running segment by a minute each time, while increasing your speed. By the last 1-minute burst, you should be almost sprinting.

Tip: Each week, add 1 minute to your

first segment—but keep doing the same step-down sequence—until your first interval is 10 minutes.

4. Mile Repeats

What: Hard 1-mile runs with rest in between. The ultimate training tool for the serious runner.

Why: The length and intensity of mile repeats force you to work at the edge of your aerobic limit, giving you the endurance and mental toughness you need to run hard for long periods of time.

How: Run three or four 1-mile intervals at your 5-K race pace. After each mile, rest for 4 minutes.

Tip: Budget your effort so that you run each quarter mile at the same pace.

5. 800 Repeats

What: Hard runs with jogging recoveries.

Why: Running at your maximum aerobic capacity is a great way to improve it.

How: Warm up till you're sweating. Subtract 10 seconds from your mile-repeat pace and maintain that speed for 800 meters (twice around the track). After each 800-meter run, jog once around the track before repeating.

Tip: Start with only four intervals per session and add one each workout until you can comfortably do eight.

6. 400 Repeats

What: Hard runs with jogging recoveries.
Why: You'll be training to finish strong.
How: Run at your fastest 1-mile pace. (So if your personal record, or PR, for

the mile is 7 minutes, you'll want to perform each 400-meter interval in 105 seconds, or 1:45.) After each 400-meter run, jog for 1 or 2 minutes, then repeat. Start with a six-interval workout and add one interval each time you go to the track, until you reach 10.

Tip: Do the math before you start. And warm up first!

7. In-and-Outs

What: Fast 200-meter runs alternating with not-so-fast 200-meter runs for 2 miles total.

Why: This workout forces you to recover on the go, allowing you to train at higher overall intensity for a longer distance than you otherwise could.

How: At your mile PR pace, run 200 meters, then slow down so it takes you 10 seconds longer to complete the next 200 meters. Continue to alternate between these speeds until you've run 2 miles.

Tip: If you slow by more than 2 seconds in either your fast or slow segment, run at a light pace until you finish the entire 2 miles.

8. Fast-Finish Long Run

What: A long run with a speed surge in the second half.

Why: You'll train your body to go long and finish hard.

How: Double your regular easy run. Do the first half at your normal pace, and at the midway point, pick up the pace by 5 to 10 seconds per mile.

Tip: Stash or carry water to help you in that second half.

The Ultimate 10-K Plan

Kick tail in your next 10-K with this 8-week speed plan from Len Kravitz, PhD, associate professor of exercise science at the University of New Mexico. It uses the Pledge of Allegiance—that's right, the Pledge you recited in grade school—to help you run faster than ever before. In a University of Wisconsin-Lacrosse study, researchers found that a person's ability to recite the Pledge of Allegiance—all 31 words—while running is a highly accurate gauge of intensity. Learn how to use it strategically, and you'll ensure that you run at the ideal pace every single workout, whether it's a long, easy run or high-intensity intervals. The end result: You'll turn in your best 10-K time ever.

The Science of Speed

Before we get to the Pledge, a lesson in lactate threshold. Lactate is your body's buffering agent for the acid that builds up in your legs and causes them to burn during a run. (This "acid" is commonly thought of as lactic acid, but scientists no longer think that's true.) The faster you run, the faster your acid levels rise. At a certain point, there's too much acid to neutralize, and you have to slow down. This is when you've crossed your lactate threshold.

You can also think of your lactate threshold as the fastest pace you can run that allows you to start and finish at the same speed without feeling any burn. So by pushing your lactate threshold higher, you'll be able to run faster, longer. That's where the Pledge of Allegiance comes in: It's the tool that will help you raise your threshold.

Training Days

In this program, you'll run 3 or 4 days a week and vary the distance and intensity of the workouts. Follow the guidelines below for performing each workout at the ideal intensity.

Volume training. On volume days, you have just one goal: Log the miles. Volume training is designed to develop your ability to perform prolonged exercise, as well as to prepare your muscles and joints for the repeated impact of running. Run at a pace that allows you to recite the Pledge of Allegiance easily.

Maximal steady-state training. Do these runs as close to your lactate threshold as possible. Maximal steady-state training simulates race pace and improves your body's ability to clear speed-limiting acid from your blood and muscles. Run at a pace that allows you to recite the Pledge of Allegiance with difficulty, in spurts of only three or four words at a time.

Interval training: You'll intersperse short bouts of running that are above your lactate threshold with longer periods of running that fall below it. Intervals train your body to tolerate high amounts of acid. Start by running at your volume-training intensity for 5 minutes. Then increase your speed until you can't recite a single word of the Pledge. Maintain this pace for 30 seconds, then slow down to your starting pace for the next 3 minutes, before beginning another 30-second high-intensity stint. Start with five intervals and try to do more each workout, while shortening the recovery periods.

The Multi-Level 10-K Plan

Determine which program is appropriate for your level of fitness, then use the chart below as a guide for your day-by-day workout calendar. Next to each mileage amount is a corresponding letter that indicates whether you perform volume training (V), maximal steady-state training (M), or interval training (I) that day. Complete the entire plan, then repeat it to continue to push your fitness level higher.

Beginner: Follow the Beginner program if you perform aerobic exercise or sports up to 2 or 3 days a week.

Advanced: Do the Advanced plan if, on 3 or more days each week, you run for at least 20 minutes or 2 miles.

WEEK		Monday	Tuesday	Wednesday	Thursday	Friday	Saturday	Sunday
Week 1	Beginner	2 miles (V)	Rest	2.5 miles (V)	Rest	3 miles (V)	Rest	3.5 miles (V)
	Advanced	3 miles (V)	Rest	3.5 miles (V)	Rest	4 miles (V)	Rest	4.5 miles (V)
Week 2	Beginner	Rest	4 miles (V)	Rest	4 miles (V)	Rest	4 miles (V)	Rest
	Advanced	Rest	5 miles (V)	Rest	5 miles (V)	Rest	5 miles (V)	Rest
Week 3	Beginner	4.5 miles (V)	Rest	4.5 miles (V)	Rest	4.5 miles (V)	Rest	5 miles (V)
	Advanced	5.5 miles (V)	Rest	5.5 miles (M)	Rest	5.5 miles (V)	Rest	6 miles (V)
Week 4	Beginner	Rest	5 miles (M)	Rest	5 miles (V)	Rest	5.5 miles (V)	Rest
	Advanced	Rest	6 miles (V)	Rest	5 miles (M)	Rest	6 miles (V)	5 miles (I)
Week 5	Beginner	4 miles (V)	Rest	4.5 miles (M)	Rest	4.5 miles (V)	Rest	4.5 miles (V)
	Advanced	Rest	6.5 miles (V)	Rest	5 miles (M)	Rest	6 miles (V)	5 miles (I)
Week 6	Beginner	Rest	5 miles (I)	Rest	6 miles (V)	Rest	5 miles (M)	6 miles (V)
	Advanced	Rest	7 miles (V)	Rest	5 miles (M)	Rest	6 miles (V)	5 miles (I)
Week 7	Beginner	Rest	5 miles (I)	Rest	6 miles (V)	Rest	5 miles (M)	6 miles (V)
	Advanced	Rest	7 miles (M)	Rest	6 miles (V)	Rest	5 miles (I)	6 miles (V)
Week 8	Beginner	Rest	5 miles (V)	Rest	4 miles (V)	Rest	Rest	Race
	Advanced	Rest	6 miles (V)	Rest	5 miles (V)	Rest	Rest	Race

The Fastest Cardio Workouts of All Time

Strapped for time? Try these novel cardio workouts used by top strength coach Alwyn Cosgrove, CSCS, and his team at Results Fitness in Santa Clarita, California. They're actually called metabolic circuits, and they're designed to challenge your cardiovascular system and speed fat loss just like hard sprints do. The big difference: You can do these routines in your basement. What's more, they also improve your aerobic capacity, just like jogging a few miles at a moderate pace. These workouts, however, take a fraction of the time, since you exercise far more intensely.

Medley Conditioning

Do one set of each exercise below in the order shown. Perform each exercise for 15 seconds, then rest for 15 seconds. Perform as many circuits as you can in 5 minutes. One note: For the dumbbell jump squat, lower your body until your thighs are at least *parallel* to the floor each repetition, then jump as high as you can.

- **Sprints or stairclimbing**
  Rest
- **Dumbbell jump squat** (page 204)
  Rest
- **Dumbbell chop** (page 305)
  Rest
- **Single-arm dumbbell or kettlebell swing** (page 268)
  Rest

Finishers

These are quickie cardio routines that you can do at the end of each workout. They're called finishers not just because they're a great way to finish off an exercise session but also because they'll help you finish off your fat.

THE LEG MATRIX

Do one set of each exercise without resting, and keep track of how long it takes to complete the circuit. Then rest for twice that duration, and repeat once. When you can finish the circuit in 90 seconds, skip the rest.

- **Body-weight squat** (page 190): 24 reps
- **Body-weight alternating lunge** (page 217): 12 reps with each leg
- **Body-weight split jump** (page 211): 12 reps with each leg
- **Body-weight jump squat** (for fat loss) (page 194): 24 reps

SQUAT SERIES

Do one set of each exercise without resting. That's one round. Complete a total of three rounds.

- **Body-weight jump squat** (for fat loss) (page 194): Do as many reps as you can in 20 seconds.
- **Body-weight squat** (page 190): Do as many reps as you can in 20 seconds.
- **Isometric squat:** Lower your body until your thighs are parallel to the floor. Hold that position for 30 seconds.

COUNTDOWNS

Alternate back and forth between two exercises (choose either option 1 or option 2), without resting. In your first round, do 10 repetitions of each exercise. In your second round, do 9 reps. Then do 8 reps in your third round. Work your way down as far as you can go. (If you get to zero, you're done.) Each week, raise the number of reps you start with by one—so in your second week, you'll begin your "countdown" with 11 reps.

Option 1
- Single-arm dumbbell swing (page 268)
- Squat thrusts (page 422)

Option 2
- Body-weight jump squat (for fat loss) (page 194)
- Explosive pushup (page 42)

Chapter 16:
The Best New Fat Loss Workouts
TAKE YOUR FITNESS TO THE NEXT LEVEL

The most popular

movement in fitness is the rise of metabolic conditioning workouts. Think: CrossFit and Insanity, as well as countless other brands and programs.

Years ago, everyone just called this circuit training. The difference is that the approach to these routines is far better than it's ever been. You might describe it as a strategic fusion of high-intensity intervals and resistance training, a combination that's shown to be an incredibly potent formula for torching calories fast.

And there's no one better at creating these kinds of workouts than B.J. Gaddour, the fitness director for *Men's Health* and creator of the 21-Day MetaShred (available on DVD at 21DayMetaShred.com).

Gaddour is a master at creating body-shredding routines that max out your calorie burn. And in the pages that follow, he gives you more than 40 new fat-blasting workouts—plus the blueprints for creating your own cutting-edge routines.

You'll discover how to choose the right moves and the right intensity for the best results. And you'll have the power to customize your workout for the time you have. Whether you want a quick and simple 5- to 10-minute routine or an all-out 30-minute gut-buster, you'll know exactly what to do.

The Best One-Exercise Fat Torchers

Can you really get a great fat-burning workout with just one exercise? Absolutely. As strength coach Alwyn Cosgrove says, "Running is just one exercise, but no one questions that when it comes to burning fat." But you don't have to take our word for it. After you try one of B.J. Gaddour's "EMOM" routines, you'll be a believer.

The approach is simple: You'll choose one exercise and perform a round of that movement every minute on the minute (EMOM!) for as many minutes as you want to train. "Beyond incinerating calories and boosting stamina, these workouts provide a beautiful blend of strength and conditioning and are also unmatched for mental training," says Gaddour.

1. Choose Your Exercise

You can use almost any movement, but here are Gaddour's top choices. With these options alone, you have more than 20 different workouts, but you can literally create hundreds of routines when you experiment with all the exercise variations in this book. Note that there are two categories: Rep-based exercises (you'll do a certain number of reps) and distance-based exercises (you'll crawl, lunge, walk, or run a certain distance).

TOP REP-BASED EMOM EXERCISES		TOP DISTANCE-BASED EMOM EXERCISES	
Goblet squat (page 204)	Hammer curl to press (page 159)	Carry (page 397-399)	Walking lunge (page 217)
Skier swing or kettlebell swing (page 390 or 394)	Burpee (page 354)	Bear crawl (page 408)	Hill sprints
Pushup (page 34)	Skater hops (page 363)	Crab walk (page 410)	Stair sprints
Dumbbell clean (page 393)	Thrusters (page 343)	Duck walk (page 385)	Lateral slide (page 429)
Dumbbell push press (page 121)	Chinup, pullup, or inverted row (page 98, 99, or 96)	Sprints	Alligator crawl (page 407)

2. Use the Right Strategy

Option A: Determine your reps. For most exercises, a good repetition per minute goal is 10 to 20 reps, but use the guidelines below to better gauge range.

- Ten reps works better for slower moves like squats or pushups, and 20 reps works better for faster moves like swings or skater jumps.

- For pure cardio exercises—like seal jacks or battle rope up-down waves— you can go as high as 50 to 100 reps per minute.

- For really challenging moves like pullups, you can go as low as 5 reps EMOM. (If you go lower, the routine won't be as effective for fat loss.)

Option B: Determine your distance. Select a distance that you can complete in about 20 seconds if you go all out. This ensures that even as you slow—due to fatigue—there will still be time to rest during the remainder of each minute.

3. Set Your Goal

Decide how many total rounds you want to do or how long you want to exercise. A general guideline: Complete anywhere from 10 to 30 rounds for a 10- to 30-minute workout. Besides simply doing one exercise the entire time, you can also do three separate 10-minute routines, choosing a different movement for each segment.

4. Do One Set Every Minute on the Minute

Start a timer and do your target number of reps. Complete all your reps in less than 1 minute, and rest for any time that's left over. That's one round. The faster you finish your reps, the more time you'll have to rest. When the timer hits 1 minute, repeat the procedure, and continue until you've completed all your rounds.

5. Keep Getting Better

Progress from session to session by using heavier weights or by increasing your rep per minute goal. You can also swap in a harder variations of the same exercise, like moving from a regular pushup to a feet-elevated pushup.

The Best Fat Loss Circuits

Prepare to build and burn: In the section below, fitness expert B.J. Gaddour will show you how to create your own cutting-edge fat loss circuits. That's because he's sharing two very simple, but highly effective "plug-and-play" templates. The result: You can choose exercises you like the most while customizing the routine to get the results you want.

1. Choose Your Template

For each template, simply fill the slots by selecting an exercise from each category.

5-EXERCISE TEMPLATE	6-EXERCISE TEMPLATE
1. Glutes/Hamstrings Exercise	1. Core Exercise
2. Chest or Shoulders Exercise	2. Glutes/Hamstrings Exercise
3. Quadriceps Exercise	3. Chest or Shoulders Exercise
4. Back Exercise	4. Quadriceps Exercise
5. Cardio, Core, or Total Body Exercise	5. Back Exercise
	6. Cardio or Total Body Exercise

- **Glutes and Hamstrings:** Choose any glutes/hamstrings exercise from Chapter 9 or any exercise labeled "Glutes/Hamstrings" in Chapter 12.
- **Chest or Shoulders:** Choose any chest exercise from Chapter 4, any shoulder exercise from Chapter 5, or any exercise labeled "Chest" or "Shoulders" in Chapter 12.
- **Quadriceps:** Choose any quadriceps exercise from Chapter 8 or any exercise labeled "Quadriceps" in Chapter 12.
- **Back:** Choose any back exercise from Chapter 5, or any exercise labeled "Back" from Chapter 12.
- **Cardio:** Choose any exercise labeled "Cardio" from Chapter 12.
- **Core:** Choose any core exercise from the section labeled "Stability Exercises" in Chapter 10 or any exercise labeled "Core" from Chapter 12.
- **Total Body:** Choose any total-body exercise from Chapter 11 or any exercise labeled "Total Body" from Chapter 12.

2. Select Your Work-to-Rest-Ratio

For any workout, choose what's called your work-to-rest ratio. This is how long you'll exercise during each set and how long you'll recover between each set. The work-to-rest ratio determines the training effect that you get from the workout.

For example, in a 15:45 work-to-rest ratio, you'll exercise for 15 seconds and rest for 45 seconds. This emphasizes power. If your work-to-rest ratio is 45:15, you'll exercise for 45 seconds and rest for 15 seconds, a strategy that emphasizes endurance. You'll note that the work-to-rest ratios you see here are all designed as 1-minute increments. That keeps timing simple.

There are specific benefits to each work-to-rest ratio, but in the circuit format that Gaddour uses, all options are fantastic for conditioning and fat loss. So try different methods to experience the benefits and find your favorites.

Here, you'll find a basic guide to three categories of work-to-rest ratios. While examples of three specific ratios—15:45, 30:30, and 45:15—are used, they're just that: examples. For each of the examples shown, you can make the work a little longer and the rest a little shorter (or vice versa) and experience a slightly different training effect.

A great approach: Do three workouts a week, but use a different work-to-rest ratio each time. You may be surprised which work-to-rest ratio that you like—or your body responds to—the best.

POWER

Work-to-Rest Ratio: 15:45

Why it works: Every set is short—just 15 seconds. But don't confuse "short" with "easy." The idea is to go hard—and make every rep count. You want to move fast, but without getting sloppy.

You should use moderate to heavy weights and perform each exercise explosively—that is, as fast as possible while maintaining proper form. By doing so, you'll target your fast-twitch muscles fibers, the ones with the most potential for gains in size and strength. These are the fibers that make you stronger, faster, and more athletic.

Even more important, they're also what you might call your "anti-aging" muscle fibers. (See page 5.)

While the work periods are short, the rest periods are comparatively long: 45 seconds. Why? Because even though your fast-twitch fibers can generate more force than your slow-twitch fibers, fast-twitch muscles fatigue considerably faster and take longer to recover. So the longer rest gives these fibers ample time to recover between sets. That way, you'll get the most out of each and every exercise.

STRENGTH

Work-to-Rest Ratio: 30:30

True strength isn't just about how much weight you can squat. It's about creating a strong body, from head to toe. It's about eliminating your weak spots and improving your mobility. And it's about going hard, even when you're tired.

This approach helps you accomplish all of that. That's because you'll keep your muscles under tension for a moderate period of time, while using relatively heavy weights.

It will simultaneously pump up your muscles and heart rate for a workout that builds your strength, triggers muscle growth, and boosts your metabolism.

One clarification: By "heavy" weights, we're talking about a weight that's challenging for *you*. Ideally, you want to be able to work for the entire 30 seconds, but feel like you only have a rep or two left by the time the set comes to an end. So you may have to experiment a bit to zero in on the most challenging weight. If you do a set and it seems too easy, don't sweat it. After all, you're still burning calories. Just up the weight in the next round.

ENDURANCE
Work-to-Rest Ratio: 45:15

If you want to sweat buckets and "feel the burn," you'll love this approach. The reason: With this work-to-rest ratio, you'll keep your muscles under tension for an extended period of time. Plus, when you do exercises like squats and pushups, you'll send your heart rate through the roof. Trust me, this can be *tough*. Let's just say you'll quickly learn to relish your rest periods.

The benefit: You'll not only annihilate calories, but with this type of training, you'll trigger your muscles to create more mitochondria. Mitochondria are tiny powerhouses in your muscles cells that produce energy. So the more mitochondria you have, the more energy you can produce. And the more energy you can produce, the harder and the longer you can exercise before you run out of gas.

All of which results in a fitter body that's better prepared for anything life throws at you.

3. Do Your Workout

Perform the exercises in the order shown using the work-to-rest ratio you've chosen. Once you've done each exercise once, you've completed one round. If you're doing a 5-exercise circuit, each round lasts 5 minutes. If you're doing a 6-exercise circuit, each round lasts 6 minutes. Do as many rounds as you like depending on your time and conditioning level.

Only have 10 minutes? Just do two rounds of a 5-exercise circuit. Have less than 20 minutes? You could just complete three rounds of the 6-exercise circuit, for an 18-minute routine.

Want to do a 30-minute workout? Perform six rounds of the 5-exercise circuit or five rounds of the 6-exercise circuit.

Either template works equally as well, but you may prefer more variety in the 6-exercise circuit, or you may like that the 5-exercise circuit allows you to do more sets of each specific movement.

Note: When you use single-arm, single-leg, or single-side exercises, you'll need to do two, four, or even six total rounds so that you train both sides equally. (Alternatively, if you're using a work-to-rest ratio that requires you to exercise for longer periods—say, 40 seconds or more—you can simply switch arms, legs, or sides at the halfway mark.) See the examples below.

5-Exercise Fat Loss Circuits

15:45 CIRCUIT	
1. Kettlebell swing (page 394)	4. Medicine ball slam (page 320)
2. Explosive Pushup (Page 42)	5. Mountain climber (page 288)
3. Split jump (page 211)	

30:30 CIRCUIT	
1. Dumbbell straight-leg deadlift (page 256)	4. Pullup (page 99)
2. Dip (page 44)	5. Rack carry (page 397)
3. Goblet squat (page 204)	

45:15 CIRCUIT*	
1. Single-leg hip raise: left leg (page 240)	4. Single-arm row: left arm (page 79)
2. Single-arm bench press: left arm (page 53)	5. Side plank: left side (page 284)
3. Bulgarian split squat: left leg (page 210)	

*Do one round and then switch arms, legs, or sides and repeat for another round.

6-Exercise Fat Loss Circuit

40:20 CIRCUIT	
1. Plank tap to hand (page 404)	4. Alternating dumbbell lunge (page 217)
2. Kettlebell swing (page 394)	5. Dumbbell clean (page 393)
3. Dumbbell push press (page 121)	6. Burpee (page 354)

The Best Tabata-Style Workouts

You're about to experience a fast and furious training method known as the "Tabata Protocol." Whether you've already heard of it or it sounds completely mysterious, I'm going to show you how to use its principles to create an incredible fat-loss routine.

For background, this training method was originally used by the Japanese Olympic speed skating team, and it was named for the scientist— Izumi Tabata—who studied its amazing effect on a group of male college students. The study subjects were all fit P.E. majors, and most were members of various varsity sports teams.

It sounds too simple—and short—to work: On a special type of stationary bike, the university students did seven or eight 20-second, all-out sprints, each separated by just 10 seconds of rest.

The results were fantastic: After doing the routine 5 days a week for 6 weeks, the college kids boosted their aerobic fitness by 14 percent. By comparison, another group—who performed a steady but moderate pace on the bikes for 60 minutes—increased their aerobic fitness by only about 10 percent.

The upshot: The high-intensity 4-minute workout was more effective than an hour of moderate cycling. Even better, the Tabata participants saw a 28 percent improvement in "anaerobic capacity"—a measure of how long the subjects could exercise at their top effort. The second group saw no such improvements.

So why isn't everyone doing Tabata workouts? Well, most people would vomit—or come close to it—if they actually tried the routine that was used in the study. Plus, to burn as many calories as you might like, you need to regularly exercise longer than just 4 minutes. (The study participants literally exercised themselves to exhaustion, making additional work unlikely.)

The good news: B.J. Gaddour has a way to solve both problems—while making the Tabata method more beneficial.

Instead of doing a single mode of exercise for each sprint, Gaddour alternates between two exercises that work your muscles in different ways. This way, fatigue doesn't overtake you as quickly—such as was the case with the stationary bike. So you're still working hard for each 20-second interval, but you're spreading the challenge around. (This is why we call them "Tabata-Style Workouts" and not simply "Tabata Workouts.")

Will it improve your fitness as fast as it did for the Japanese college students? I can't say, but you'll no doubt find it highly effective.

"Whether you're short on time and need a quick workout or just want to add some extra intensity to the end of a longer session, one of these 4-minute routines will do the trick," says Gaddour.

There's more: Because you're better at managing your fatigue, you can "stack" multiple 4-minute routines together. The key is to take 1 minute of rest between every 4-minute mini-workout. This way, you're able to recover briefly between routines and give it your all each time—while creating a longer workout for greater calorie burn.

Create Your Own Tabata-Style Workout

1. Choose Your Exercises

• You should use light loads or easier exercise variations, so you can move fast and complete as many reps as possible each round.

• As a rule of thumb, Gaddour says you should be able to get at least 10 reps within every 20-second work period—unless you're doing a movement that's measured in distance, like running, rowing, or cycling.

2. Do the Workout

You can either build your routine using the templates on this page or try the pre-made sample workouts. For each routine, do the first exercise for 20 seconds, and rest for 10 seconds. Then do the second exercise for 20 seconds, and rest for another 10 seconds. Continue to alternate back and forth for 4 minutes—that's a total of eight 20-second intervals. To stack on another 4-minute routine to your session, rest 1 minute, and choose a new interval workout. If you want to keep going, just repeat the process.

Upper Body/Lower Body Template
EXERCISE 1. PUSHUP VARIATION*
EXERCISE 2. SQUAT OR SWING VARIATION

* You can also choose upper body exercises in which you can do repetitions quickly with light dumbbells, such as alternating dumbbell shoulder presses, dumbbell piston-push pulls, and alternating dumbbell rows.

Core/Cardio Template
EXERCISE 1. PLANK VARIATION
EXERCISE 2. TOTAL BODY OR CARDIO VARIATION

Sample Routines

Workout #1
Pushup (page 34)
Body-weight squat (page 190)

Workout #2
Dumbbell piston push-pulls (page 389)
Skier swing (page 390)

Workout #3
1. Plank jacks (page 401)
2. Seal jacks (page 365)

Workout #4
1. Mountain climber (page 288)
2. Skater hop (page 363)

Workout #5
1. Low box plank hand taps (page 405)
2. Low box runners (page 364)

The Best Fat-Frying Flows

This unique style of workout comes straight from fitness expert B. J. Gaddour. The idea is that you seamlessly move between two or more exercises with little or no rest between them. The approach is not only simple, but it also *feels good* and allows you to keep moving almost perpetually for 10 to 30 minutes straight. And that makes it great for burning calories and fat. Give it a shot: I'm pretty sure you'll love it.

How to Do It

Follow the instructions for each of the routines below. For any "hold," simply maintain the prescribed position for the recommended time. (Or go by feel, holding for shorter or longer periods of time.) The "hold" position is usually the part of the movement that's the hardest.

1. Isometric Plank Holds

Flow from one position to the next every 10 to 15 seconds for 5 to 20 minutes.

- **Plank** (page 278)
- **Side plank:** left side (page 284)
- **Side plank:** right side (page 284)
- **Hip raise hold:** top position (page 236)

2. Isometric Squat Holds

For each exercise, hold the bottom position of the movement for 10 to 15 seconds. Try to move seamlessly from one exercise into the next for 5 to 20 minutes.

- **Bodyweight squat hold** (page 190)
- **Split squat hold:** left leg forward (page 209)
- **Split squat hold:** right leg forward (page 209)
- **Side lunge hold:** left leg bent (page 221)
- **Side lunge hold:** right leg bent (page 221)

3. Total Body Isometric Flow

Flow between the exercises every 10 to 15 seconds. If that's too hard, you can modify the routine by holding the top position of the pushup and the bottom position of the pullup. If you don't have access to a pullup bar, just flow between the pushup hold and the squat hold.

- **Pushup hold:** bottom position (page 34)
- **Squat hold:** bottom position (page 190)
- **Pullup hold:** top position (page 99)

4. Burpee and Hang Flow

Perform as many burpees (page 354) as you can with perfect technique. The moment your form starts to deteriorate or you have to slow down due to fatigue, hang from a pullup bar for as long as you can (with your arms completely straight) to recover. Each time you do that is one round. Complete 5 to 10 total rounds or set a clock for 10 to 30 minutes and flow for time. Make this routine harder by doing pullups instead of hangs.

5. Swings and Pushups Flow

Perform as many skier (page 390) or kettlebell swings (page 394) as you can with perfect form. The moment your form starts to deteriorate or you have to slow down due to fatigue, perform pushups (page 34) to recover. Each time you do that is one round. Complete 5 to 10 total rounds or set a clock for 10 to 30 minutes and flow for time. Make this routine easier by doing plank holds instead of pushups.

The Greatest Fat Burning Workout You've Never Tried

Besides being a great fat-burning workout, these Weight Loss Wheels are tremendous for improving cardiovascular fitness, says fitness expert B.J. Gaddour.

The concept is simple: A wheel consists of a hub and multiple spokes. The hub is the main move that you start with and return to over and over. It's typically a higher-speed exercise that's cardio-intensive and works most of your body. This keeps your heart rate high for the duration of your workout.

The spokes are accessory moves that you sprinkle in throughout the routine to target specific muscles. You might say this allows you to train for strength right in the middle of your cardio workout. "In my opinion, this strategy leads to unparalleled fat-burning and fitness gains," says Gaddour.

How It Works

For each Weight Loss Wheel, you'll do one set of the "Hub" exercise, followed by a "Spoke" exercise. Then you'll do the Hub exercise again, followed by a different Spoke exercise. You'll continue this until you've completed five different Spoke movements. That's one Weight Loss Wheel. Here's a visual:

Hub Exercise → Spoke Exercise 1

Hub Exercise → Spoke Exercise 2

Hub Exercise → Spoke Exercise 3

Hub Exercise → Spoke Exercise 4

Hub Exercise → Spoke Exercise 5

If you want to perform multiple wheels, rest for a set period of time and repeat.

Get Started

For each exercise in the Weight Loss Wheels on the opposite page, Gaddour recommends a 30:15 work-to-rest ratio. (He's found this formula works very well.) For example, perform the Hub exercise for 30 seconds, and rest for 15 seconds. Then do Spoke Exercise #1 for 30 seconds, and rest for 15 seconds. Return to the Hub exercise, followed by Spoke Exercise #2. And so on.

After you've finished the entire Weight Loss Wheel, rest for 2 minutes, and then repeat one time, for a total of two Weight Loss Wheels. When you're done, you will have completed a 17-minute high-intensity interval workout. You can, of course, do even more wheels than that if you like.

With the Weight Loss Wheels that follow, you can try one at a time and simply repeat it as many times as desired, or stack one Weight Loss Wheel on top of another for more variety.

Weight Loss Wheels

WHEEL #1

Hub: Medicine-ball slam (page 320)

Spoke 1: Alternating reverse lunge (page 217)
Spoke 2: Blast-off pushup (page 402)
Spoke 3: Alternating lunge (page 216)
Spoke 4: Donkey kicks (page 403)
Spoke 5: Alternating side lunge (page 221)

WHEEL #2

Hub: Burpee (page 354)

Spoke 1: Plank (page 278)
Spoke 2: Hip raise (page 236)
Spoke 3: Side plank: left (page 284)
Spoke 4: Side plank: right (page 284)
Spoke 5: Bird dog (page 283)

WHEEL #3

Hub: Kettlebell swing (page 394)

Spoke 1: Goblet squat (page 204)
Spoke 2: Stepup jump: left (page 372)
Spoke 3: Stepup jump: right (page 372)
Spoke 4: Single-arm dumbbell shoulder press: left (page 122)
Spoke 5: Single-arm dumbbell shoulder press: right (page 122)

WHEEL #4

Hub: Battle ropes up-down waves (page 416)

Spoke 1: Seated squat jump (page 372)
Spoke 2: Spiderman pushup (page 39)
Spoke 3: Single-leg hip raise: left (page 240)
Spoke 4: Single-leg hip raise: right (page 240)
Spoke 5: Inverted row (page 72)

WHEEL #5

Hub: Thrusters (page 343)

Spoke 1: Seal jacks (page 365)
Spoke 2: Mountain climber (page 288)
Spoke 3: Skater hops (page 363)
Spoke 4: Bucking hops (page 403)
Spoke 5: Split jump (page 211)

Chapter 17:
The Big Chapter of
Nutrition Secrets

UNLOCK THE POWER OF FOOD

Food is power.

In fact, it has too much power over so many of us. But that's why it's liberating to know the rules of good nutrition. The first lesson: Denial won't get you lean. Instead, think about making smart food choices—ones that will allow you to enjoy great-tasting, nutrient-rich meals that fill you up *without* filling you out. Once you learn to eat smart, you take control over your body and gain the power to lose your gut, build more muscle, and improve your health with every bite you take. So dive into the nutrition secrets that follow, and harness the power of food to improve your whole life.

The Simplest Diet Ever

There's one law of weight loss that can't be avoided: You have to burn more calories than you eat. Of course, there are dozens of ways to achieve this deficit. But it doesn't need to be complicated. Case in point: The eating plan that follows. It's designed to reduce your daily intake by trading empty-calorie fare that you're likely to binge on for nutritious whole foods that fill you up. The end result is that you'll lose your gut without feeling like you're on a diet. All you have to do is take it one step at a time—it's as easy as 1-2-3.

Your Three-Step Plan

Follow these three guidelines and you'll quickly find that everything else is just details when it comes to eating for a healthy, lean body. Start with step 1 and adhere to it for 2 weeks. You're likely to find that fat starts melting off you. If it doesn't, combine the advice in step 1 with the guidelines in step 2. Still having problems? Move on to step 3 to guarantee the results you want.

Step 1: Eliminate Added Sugars

This one step is the simplest way to quickly clean up any diet. According to a USDA survey, an average American eats 82 grams of added sugars every day. That's almost 20 teaspoons, contributing an empty 317 calories. The researchers report that 91 percent of these added sugars can be attributed to intake of regular soda (33 percent), baked goods and breakfast cereals (23 percent), candy (16 percent), fruit drinks (10 percent), and sweetened milk products (9 percent), such as chocolate milk, ice cream, and flavored yogurt.

What's not on the list? Meat, vegetables, whole fruit, and eggs, along with whole-grain and dairy products that haven't been sweetened. There's your menu; now eat accordingly. Also, go ahead and have whatever you want at one meal a week—great results don't depend on being perfect 100 percent of the time.

The key message here: Don't overanalyze your diet or worry too much about the details. By simply avoiding foods that contain added sugar, you'll automatically eliminate most junk food. So your diet will instantly become healthier. And for most people, this strategy also dramatically reduces calorie intake. So you start losing weight, without counting calories or restricting entire food groups. Try it for 2 weeks. If this doesn't kickstart fat loss, move on to step 2.

Step 2: Cut Back on Starch

Starches are the main carbs in bread, pasta, and rice. And not just in the processed versions—such as white bread—but also in the 100 percent whole-grain kind. Of course, you've probably been told you actually need more of these foods. You don't. Why? For starters, too much starch messes with your blood sugar.

Here's a more in-depth explanation:

Your blood sugar can fall too low after just 4 hours of not eating. You know when this happens; you become cranky, tired, and maybe even shaky. As a result, you start craving carbohydrates, particularly in the forms of starch and sugar, both of which quickly raise blood sugar. (Protein and fat have little effect on blood sugar.)

Now, chances are, you won't just eat a small amount of starch or sugar. You'll be more likely to binge, spiking your blood sugar high and fast. This fast-rising blood sugar triggers your pancreas to release a flood of insulin, a hormone that lowers blood sugar back to normal. Unfortunately, in nearly half the population, insulin tends to "overshoot," a dysfunction that sends blood sugar crashing. This reinforces the binge, because it makes you crave sugar and starch again. See the problem?

A review from the USDA Human Nutrition Research Center at Tufts University found that consuming carbohydrates such as bread, pasta, and rice, as well as sugar, promotes an increase in total calorie consumption. But by reducing your starch and cutting out foods with added sugars, you'll better control your blood sugar and be less likely to experience the intense carb cravings that tend to derail diets.

So how much starch can you eat? It depends. As a general guideline, limit yourself to two servings a day. Consider one serving to be about 20 grams of carbohydrates—equal to about one slice of bread, one cup of hot or cold cereal,

CARBOHYDRATES . . . EXPLAINED

Simple Carbohydrates (aka Sugar)
There are many types of sugar, but the two main ones in our diet are glucose and fructose. These are known as single sugars, and they combine with each other to create double sugars, such as sucrose (better known as table sugar). Typically, most foods with sugar contain a combination of glucose and fructose. This is true whether you're eating an apple or drinking a soda.

• *Glucose:* This is your body's primary energy source. It's also the "sugar" in blood sugar. And because it's already in the form your body needs, it's quickly absorbed into your blood. As a result, glucose is the type of carbohydrate that raises blood sugar the fastest.

• *Fructose:* Unlike glucose, fructose doesn't spike blood sugar. That's because to use fructose, your body must first send it from your intestines to your liver. From there, your body converts it to glucose and stores it. However, if your liver glucose stores are already full, then the fructose is converted to fat. This is why an excess can lead to weight gain, even though it has little impact on blood sugar.

Complex Carbohydrates
The definition of these is simple: any carbohydrate that's composed of more than two sugar molecules.

• *Starch:* This is the stored form of glucose in plant foods. There's an abundance of starch in grains, legumes, and root vegetables, such as potatoes. Essentially, starch is a bunch of glucose molecules that are held together by a weak chemical bond. So when you eat it, it breaks down easily, and you're left with pure glucose. The upshot: It raises blood sugar quickly when eaten without fat or fiber.

• *Fiber:* Also called a nondigestible carbohydrate, fiber is the structural material in the leaves, stems, and roots of plants. So it's found in vegetables, fruits, and grains. Fiber is composed of bundles of sugar molecules, but unlike starch, it has no effect on blood sugar. That's because human digestive enzymes can't break the bonds that hold those bundles together. What's more, fiber slows the absorption of starch into your bloodstream and is thought to help you feel full longer after a meal.

half of a large potato, or ½ cup cooked pasta, rice, or beans. (For a more accurate measure of the starch and sugar in a food, subtract the amount of fiber from the total carbohydrates.) As a rule, emphasize the highest-fiber, least-processed versions of these foods—breads, pastas, and cereals that are made with "100 percent whole wheat"; brown rice instead of white; and whole potatoes, including the skin.

To troubleshoot even further, reduce your starches to zero to one serving on days you don't work out; ramp back up to two servings on days when you exercise intensely. The reason: You burn more carbs on the days you work out. So give your body more fuel on the days you need it, and less on the days you don't.

As for the rest of your diet, follow these guidelines.

Never restrict your produce intake.
There's a popular saying in the diet industry: "No one ever got fat from eating produce." And it's true. Most whole fruits and vegetables contain very few calories, very little starch, and a wealth of belly-filling fiber. Don't worry about needing a list to double-check which ones meet these criteria. You can just consider potatoes, beans, corn, and peas to be your starchy exceptions, and enjoy the rest as desired. Sure, other root vegetables such as squash and parsnips could also fall under your starch limitations. But chances are, you won't be eating these foods every day anyway—much less *overeating* them.

Have some protein with every meal.
Eating protein ensures that your body always has the raw material to build and maintain your muscle, even while you lose fat. What's more, University of Illinois researchers determined that dieters who eat higher amounts of protein lose more fat and feel more satisfied than those who eat the lowest amounts of the nutrient. So at every meal and snack, make a conscious effort to have a serving or two of protein in the form of yogurt, cheese, milk, beef, turkey, chicken, fish, pork, eggs, nuts, or a protein shake.

If you want a number to shoot for, the ideal amount is about 1 gram of protein per pound of your target body weight. For example, if you want to weigh 180 pounds, eat 180 grams of protein a day. Of course, that much protein can be hard for some people to swallow—or even just inconvenient. If either is the case for you, consider your minimum requirement to be about 125 grams a day. Use the following chart to guide your selections.

FOOD	PROTEIN (G)
1 EGG	6
3 OZ BEEF, PORK, CHICKEN, OR FISH	25 TO 30
8 OZ MILK OR YOGURT	9
1 OZ (1 SLICE) CHEESE	7
1 OZ NUT BUTTER, NUTS, OR SEEDS	6

Don't be afraid of fat. You won't store it if you aren't eating too many total calories. For instance, research shows that diets containing upward of 60 percent fat are just as effective for weight loss as those in which fat provides only 20 percent of the calories. (Both approaches lower your risk of heart disease.) The fact is, fat is filling and it adds flavor to your meals, both of which help you avoid feeling deprived. And that means you can eat the natural fat in meat, cheese, milk, butter, avocados, nuts, and olive oil. Because you've already cut out foods with added sugar, you've also slashed many of the junk foods that provide the overload of fat and calories in the average person's diet.

Eat until you're satisfied, not stuffed. Focusing your diet on foods that provide healthy doses of protein, fiber, and fat fills you up, keeps you satisfied, and regulates your blood sugar. This combination of benefits helps diminish your appetite and often automatically reduces the number of calories you consume, speeding fat loss. However, if you eat mindlessly, you're not likely to lose fat. So pay attention to how you feel—and don't clean your plate out of habit. In a Cornell University nutrition survey, the heaviest men said they usually stopped eating when they thought they had consumed the "normal amount"—a typical restaurant entrée, say—instead of when they started to feel full.

Step 3: Watch Your Calories

If you've slashed sugar and starch for a month and your jeans haven't yet started fitting better, your problem is simple: You're still eating too much. It could be that you don't realize that you're satisfied *until* you're stuffed. Or maybe it's just hard to break old habits. The upshot? You need portion control.

Use this strategy from Alan Aragon, MS, *Men's Health* advisor and a nutritionist in Thousand Oaks, California. Simply multiply your desired body weight by 10 to 12. Then eat that many calories a day. One note: Choose your multiplier—10, 11, or 12—by how active you are. So if your desired weight is 180 pounds and you work out 5 days a week, you'd multiply 180 by 12—giving you a target of 2,160 calories a day. Just use your best judgment; you can always further adjust your intake if you're not achieving the results you want.

To ensure that you meet your calorie target, keep a food journal for 2 weeks. For each food you eat, estimate the serving size and write it down. (Be honest; otherwise, it doesn't work.) Then log each meal and snack into the free nutrient analysis tool like the one at www.nutritiondata.com or sparkpeople.com. This not only keeps you on track but also quickly teaches you how to eyeball meals to estimate their calorie counts. You'll begin to automatically realize what an appropriate portion is for your diet. Once you reach your desired weight, you can up your calorie intake to 14 to 16 calories per pound.

HOW SUGAR HIDES

Scanning a product's ingredients list to see if it contains sugar is smart—but you may need to expand your vocabulary. Here are 20 aliases that the sweet stuff goes by—none of which include the word *sugar*.

- **Barley malt**
- **Brown rice syrup**
- **Corn syrup**
- **Dextrose**
- **Evaporated cane juice invert syrup**
- **Fructose**
- **Fruit juice**
- **Galactose**
- **Glucose**
- **Granular fruit grape juice concentrate**
- **High-fructose corn syrup**
- **Honey**
- **Lactose**
- **Maltodextrin**
- **Maple syrup**
- **Molasses**
- **Organic cane juice**
- **Sorghum**
- **Sucrose**
- **Turbinado**

NUTRITION SECRET #1

The Healthiest Foods You Aren't Eating

The real secret to eating better? Fill your diet with healthy fare that tastes good. Here are eight foods to make that task easier than ever.

Pork Chops

Taste isn't the only great thing about the pig meat in your butcher's case. Compared with other meats, pork chops contain relatively high amounts of selenium, a mineral that's linked to lower risk of cancer. Per gram of protein, pork chops pack almost five times the selenium of beef, and more than twice that of chicken. They're also loaded with riboflavin and thiamin, B vitamins that help your body more efficiently convert carbs to energy. But perhaps most important, Purdue researchers found that a 6-ounce daily serving helped people preserve their muscle as they lost weight on very low-calorie diets.

Mushrooms

Never mind that these edible fungi are more than 90 percent water—at least 700 different species are known to have a medicinal effect. Credit their metabolites, by-products that are created when mushrooms are broken down during the digestion process. Researchers in the Netherlands recently reported that metabolites have been shown to boost immunity and prevent cancer growth.

Red-Pepper Flakes

These hot little numbers may help extinguish your appetite. Dutch researchers have discovered that consuming a gram of red pepper—about $\frac{1}{2}$ teaspoon—30 minutes prior to a meal decreased total calorie intake by 14 percent. The scientists believe the appetite-reducing effect is due to capsaicin, the chemical compound that gives red peppers their heat. Emerging research suggests that capsaicin may also help kill cancer cells.

Full-Fat Cheese

Besides enhancing the flavor of broccoli, cheese is an excellent source of casein—a slow-digesting, high-quality protein that may be the best muscle-building nutrient you can eat. What's more, casein causes your body to utilize more of the bone-building calcium in cheese, according to a study in the *Journal of the American College of Nutrition*. Worried about your cholesterol? Don't be. Danish researchers found that even when men ate between seven and ten 1-ounce servings of full-fat cheese daily for 2 weeks, their LDL ("bad") cholesterol didn't budge.

Iceberg Lettuce

Conventional wisdom suggests this vegetable is nutritionally bankrupt. But that reputation is unfounded. As it turns out, $\frac{1}{2}$ head of iceberg lettuce has significantly more alpha-carotene, a powerful disease-fighting antioxidant, than either romaine lettuce or spinach. And at 10 calories per cup, you can consider it a nutritional freebie.

Scallops

These mollusks are composed almost entirely of protein. In fact, a 3-ounce serving provides 18 grams of the nutrient and just 93 calories. So it's a delicious and seemingly indulgent way to pack more protein into your diet. Clams and oysters provide a similar benefit.

Vinegar

Scientists in Sweden discovered that when people consumed 2 tablespoons of vinegar with a high-carb meal, their blood sugar was 23 percent lower than when they skipped the antioxidant-loaded liquid. They also felt fuller. Vinegar is packed with polyphenols, powerful chemicals that have been shown to improve cardiovascular health, report Arizona State University scientists. Besides combining it with olive oil for a salad dressing, you can use it to punch up your cooking: Add a splash of balsamic vinegar to mayonnaise before spreading it on a sandwich, drizzle a few tablespoons of red or white wine vinegar on a hot pan of sautéed vegetables (especially caramelized onions), or throw a shot of sherry vinegar into your next bowl of tomato soup.

Chicken Thighs

If you're bored with chicken breasts, try the thighs for a change. Sure, they have a little more fat, but that's why they taste so good. Nutritionally speaking, per ounce, thighs have just 1 more gram of fat and 11 more calories than breasts. Of course, if you judged all foods by calories per ounce, you'd end up on the celery diet. The key is portion size: If you like chicken thighs—or prime rib, for that matter—adjust the amount you eat so that it fits into your caloric budget. And don't forget that fat satisfies, so it may keep you full longer after your meal, causing you to eat less at your next.

TRACK YOUR LOSSES

Research shows that for every pound of weight you lose, you'll melt $\frac{1}{4}$ inch off your waist. See for yourself: Wrap a measuring tape around your abdomen—or have your significant other help—so that the bottom of the tape touches the tops of your hip bones. (Your navel moves as you lose weight, so targeting the hips ensures that you always take the measurement at precisely the same location.) The tape should be parallel to the floor and snug without compressing your skin.

NUTRITION SECRET #2

Fatty Foods You Can Eat Guilt-Free

As is true of other nutrients, the fat you eat shouldn't come from candy bars, cookies, and cake. Instead, it should be derived from whole, natural foods. And it's important to remember that calories still matter, too. But with that in mind, here are seven foods you can start eating again, as long as you keep the portions reasonable.

Meat with Flavor

We're talking about beef (rib eye), poultry (dark meat), and pork (bacon and ham). The fat may add calories, but it also triggers your body to produce CCK, a satiety hormone that helps you feel full longer after you've eaten. And that can reduce your calorie intake at subsequent meals.

Whole Milk

While you've probably always been told to drink reduced-fat milk, the majority of scientific research shows that drinking whole milk actually improves cholesterol levels—just not as much as drinking skim. So choose milk based on your taste preference. A lower-fat option may save you a few calories, but you shouldn't consider it a necessity if your total calories are in check. Interestingly, scientists at the University of Texas Medical Branch, in Galveston, found that drinking whole milk after lifting weights boosted muscle protein synthesis—an indicator of muscle growth—2.8 times more than drinking skim.

Butter

Downing a basket of bread slathered in butter isn't healthy. But while many nutritionists object to the number of calories that butter adds to a meal, the reality is that one pat contains just 36 calories. And research shows the fat in butter improves your body's ability to absorb fat-soluble vitamins A, D, E, and K. Butter is also ideal for cooking, especially compared with polyunsaturated fats, such as those found in vegetable oils (corn or soybean). That's because under high heat, polyunsaturated fats are more susceptible to oxidation, an effect that may contribute to heart disease, according to Canadian researchers.

Sour Cream

For years, you've been told to avoid sour cream or to eat the light version. That's because 90 percent of the dairy product's calories are derived from fat, at least half of which is saturated. Sure, the percentage of fat is high, but the total amount isn't. Consider that a serving of sour cream is 2 tablespoons. That provides just 52 calories—half the amount that's in a single tablespoon of mayonnaise—and less saturated fat than you'd get from drinking a 12-ounce glass of 2% milk. Besides, full-fat tastes far better than the light or fat-free products, which also have added carbohydrates.

Coconut

Ounce for ounce, coconut contains even more saturated fat than butter does. As a result, health experts have warned that it will clog your arteries. But research shows that the saturated fat in coconut has a beneficial effect on heart disease risk factors. One reason: More than 50 percent of its saturated fat content is lauric acid. A recent analysis of 60 studies published in the *American Journal of Clinical Nutrition* reports that even though lauric acid raises LDL ("bad") cholesterol, it boosts HDL ("good") cholesterol even more. Overall, this means it decreases your risk of cardiovascular disease. The rest of the saturated fat in a coconut is believed to have little or no effect on cholesterol levels.

Chicken Skin

No, not the battered, fried kind. But leaving the skin on a roasted chicken breast makes the meat taste better and provides half your daily requirement of selenium.

Eggs

In a recent scientific review of dozens of studies, Wake Forest University researchers found no connection between egg consumption and heart disease. And more and more research suggests the nutrients in egg yolk are beneficial to your health.

Eggs may even be the perfect diet food: Saint Louis University scientists found that people who had eggs as part of their breakfast ate fewer calories the rest of the day than those who ate bagels instead. Even though both breakfasts contained the same number of calories, the egg eaters consumed 264 fewer calories for the entire day.

The Saturated Fat Secret: Is Bad Fat Good for You?

You've probably come to believe that saturated fats are a high-fat health hazard. But do you really know the facts?

Turns out, there are more than 13 types of saturated fat. And though they've been damned as a whole by health experts for decades, some of them are actually *good* for your heart. You read right: Saturated fat is not a nutritional evil.

Take the saturated fat in beef, for example. Most of it actually decrease*s* your heart disease risk, either by lowering LDL ("bad") cholesterol or by reducing your ratio of total cholesterol to HDL ("good") cholesterol.

Let's dissect a sirloin into its various fatty acids, looking at the impact each has on your heart health. Although this analysis is specific to beef, it differs very little from in the results we'd get if we looked at chicken and turkey (think: dark meat and skin), pork (including ham and bacon), and eggs. That's because nearly all fat derived from animals is similar in composition. Dairy products, such as butter and cream, have a higher percentage of saturated fat than do beef, poultry, and pork. However, most of the saturated fat in dairy—about 70 percent—is from palmitic and stearic acids, neither of which raises heart disease risk.

MONOUNSATURATED FAT: 49%
Oleic acid: 45% [+]
Palmitoleic acid: 4% [+]

SATURATED FAT: 47%
Palmitic acid: 27% [+]
Stearic acid: 16% [0]
Myristic acid: 3% [-]
Lauric acid: 1% [+]

POLYUNSATURATED FAT: 4%
Linoleic acid: 4% [+]

+ = positive effect on cholesterol
- = negative effect on cholesterol
0 = no effect on cholesterol

So a simple analysis shows us that 97 percent of the fat in beef either has no effect on or lowers your risk for heart disease. You'll also notice, and perhaps be surprised by, the fact that the fat in beef isn't 100 percent saturated fat. That's because natural foods are typically made up of a combination of fats.

Consider lard: Because it's solid at room temperature—saturated fats are solid; unsaturated fats are liquid—it's often solely thought of as "saturated." Yet just as in beef, chicken, and pork, about 40 percent of lard's fat content is a monounsaturated fat called oleic acid. This is the very same heart-healthy fat that's found in olive oil, yet most people have never heard this fact.

But what about all the strong scientific evidence showing that saturated fat leads to heart disease? That case is actually pretty weak. The hypothesis that consuming saturated fat leads to heart disease was first proposed in the 1950s. Today, nearly 60 years later, that hypothesis has still never been proved. This despite the fact that billions of taxpayer dollars have been spent trying to prove it. For example, the Women's Health Initiative—the largest and most expensive diet study ever funded by the US government—showed that women who followed a diet low in total fat and saturated fat for an average of 8 years had the same heart disease and stroke rates as women who didn't change their eating habits. (The low-fat dieters ate 29 percent less saturated fat.)

What's more, your body is always making saturated fat. One reason: Saturated fats are part of every cell membrane in your body. They're also needed for production of hormones and serve as an important source of fuel. So even if you were to eat zero saturated fat, you'd make enough to serve these important functions. Bottom line: Saturated fat isn't poison to your body, despite what you may have been led to believe.

Of course, you don't want *too* much. Several studies indicate that higher levels of saturated fat in your blood are associated with increased risk for heart disease. Does that mean eating saturated fat boosts your chances of developing heart disease? Not likely, as long as you don't eat too many total calories overall.

In a recent study, University of Connecticut researchers compared people on a low-carb, high-fat diet—which didn't restrict saturated fat—to people following a low-fat, high-carb approach. The finding: Both groups ate fewer calories, lost weight, and lowered the amount of saturated fat in their bloodstreams. This shows the benefit of controlling your calories, regardless of the type of diet you're consuming. However, the low-carb dieters—who ate three times more saturated fat than the low-fat dieters—actually reduced their blood levels of saturated fat by twice as much. (The low-carb group also improved their HDL "good" cholesterol, and didn't raise their LDL "bad" cholesterol—a combination that lowered their risk of heart disease.)

Turns out, carbs are easily converted to saturated fat in your liver. In fact, eating carbs ramps up your liver's production of saturated fat, while consuming saturated fat itself lowers your internal production of the fat. So if you regularly *gorge* on carbs, your blood levels of the fat will likely skyrocket—even if you don't eat any saturated fat.

The take-home message: Eating too many calories is far worse for you than is consuming any specific fat or carb. And based on science, there's no good reason that whole foods containing saturated fat shouldn't be part of a healthy diet. So go ahead: Start enjoying fat again—just don't overindulge. Consider that your golden rule of eating for all foods.

PUMPKIN SEEDS: THE BEST SNACK YOU AREN'T EATING

These jack-o'-lantern waste products are the easiest way to consume more magnesium. That's important because French researchers have determined that people with the highest levels of magnesium in their blood have a 40 percent lower risk of early death than those with the lowest levels. On average, men consume 343 milligrams (mg) of the mineral daily, well under the 420 mg recommended by the Institute of Medicine.

How to eat them: Whole, shells and all. (The shells provide extra fiber.) Roasted pumpkin seeds contain 150 mg of magnesium per ounce, which will ensure you hit your daily target easily. Look for them in the snack section of your grocery store, next to the nuts and sunflower seeds.

NUTRITION SECRET #3

Health Food Frauds

Just because the label says it's good for you doesn't mean that it is. Here's how to read beyond the marketing hype.

Yogurt with Fruit at the Bottom

The upside: Yogurt and fruit are two of the healthiest foods known to man.

The downside: Corn syrup is not. But that's exactly what's used to make these products super sweet. For example, a six-ounce carton of fruit-flavored yogurt contains 32 grams of sugar, only about half of which is found naturally in the yogurt and fruit. The rest comes from corn syrup, an "added"—or what we prefer to call "unnecessary"—sugar.

The healthier alternative: Mix ½ cup plain yogurt with ½ cup fresh fruit, such as blueberries or raspberries. You'll eliminate the excess sugar while more than doubling the amount of fruit you down.

Baked Beans

The upside: Beans are packed with fiber that helps keep you full and slows the absorption of sugar into your bloodstream.

The downside: The baked kind are typically covered in a sauce made with brown and white sugars. And because the fiber is located inside the bean, it doesn't have a chance to interfere with the speed at which the sugary glaze is digested. Consider that 1 cup of baked beans contains 24 grams of sugar: about the same amount that's in an 8-ounce soft drink. Not drinking regular soda? Then you should skip the baked beans, too.

The healthier alternative: Red kidney beans, packed in water. You get the nutritional benefits of legumes, without the extra sugar. They don't even need to be heated: Just open the can, rinse off the liquid and excess salt they're stored in, and serve. Try splashing some hot sauce on top for a spicy variation.

California Roll

The upside: The seaweed it's wrapped in contains essential nutrients, such as iodine, calcium, and omega-3 fats.

The downside: It's basically a Japanese sugar cube. That's because its two other major components are white rice and imitation crab, both of which are packed with fast-digesting carbohydrates and almost no protein.

The healthier alternative: Opt for real sushi, by choosing a roll that's made with tuna or salmon. This automatically reduces the number of blood sugar–boosting carbohydrates you're eating, while providing a hefty helping of high-quality protein. Or better yet, skip the rice, too, by ordering sashimi.

Fat-Free Salad Dressing

The upside: Cutting out the fat reduces the calories that a dressing contains.

The downside: Sugar is added to

provide flavor. Perhaps more important, the removal of fat reduces your body's ability to absorb many of the vitamins found in salad vegetables. In a recent study, Ohio State University researchers discovered that people who ate a salad dressing containing fat absorbed 15 times more beta-carotene and five times more lutein—both powerful antioxidants—than when they downed a salad topped with fat-free dressing.

The healthier alternative: Choose a full-fat dressing that is made with either olive oil or canola oil, and that provides less than 2 grams of carbohydrate per serving. Or keep it simple, tangy, and completely sugar-free by shaking liberal amounts of balsamic vinegar and olive oil over your salad.

Reduced-Fat Peanut Butter

The upside: Even the reduced-fat version is packed with healthy monounsaturated fat.

The downside: Many commercial brands are sweetened with "icing sugar"—the same finely ground sugar used to decorate cupcakes. And reduced-fat versions are the worst of all because they extract the healthy fat only to infuse more icing sugar. In fact, each tablespoon of reduced-fat Skippy contains $1/2$ teaspoon of the sweet stuff. So the label might as well read, "Stick a birthday candle in me."

The healthier alternative: An all-natural, full-fat peanut butter that contains no added sugar.

Corn Oil

The upside: It's considered good for you because it contains high levels of omega-6 fatty acid—an essential polyunsaturated fat that doesn't raise cholesterol.

The downside: Corn oil contains 60 times more omega-6 than omega-3, the type of healthy fat predominantly found in fish, walnuts, and flaxseed. This is a problem because research shows that a high intake of omega-6 fats relative to omega-3 fats is associated with increased inflammation that boosts your risk of cancer, arthritis, and obesity.

The healthier alternative: Olive or canola oils, which have a much better balance of omega-6 to omega-3 fats. They also have also a greater proportion of monounsaturated fat, which has been shown to lower LDL ("bad") cholesterol.

DRINK TO YOUR BICEPS

Now you can build muscle at the office. French researchers found that men who drank small amounts of a shake containing 30 grams (g) of protein every 20 minutes for 7 hours increased muscle growth far more than those who drank all 30 g in one sitting. To mimic this strategy, combine 30 g of protein powder (1 to $1 1/2$ scoops) with 16 ounces of water and sip on it throughout your workday. You'll provide your muscles with a steady flow of raw materials for growth, and you'll be less tempted to raid the vending machine between meals.

5 Food Rules You Should Break

Foolproof your diet for good with this nutrition-myth-busting guide from *Men's Health* nutrition advisor Alan Aragon, MS.

Myth #1: High Protein Intake Is Harmful to Your Kidneys

The origin: Back in 1983, researchers first discovered that eating more protein increases your glomerular filtration rate, or GFR. Think of GFR as the amount of blood your kidneys are filtering per minute. From this finding, many scientists made the leap that a higher GFR places your kidneys under greater stress.

What science really shows: Nearly 2 decades ago, Dutch researchers found that while a protein-rich meal did boost GFR, it didn't have an adverse effect on overall kidney function. In fact, there's zero published research showing that downing hefty amounts of protein—specifically, up to 1.27 grams per pound of body weight a day—damages healthy kidneys.

The bottom line: As a rule of thumb, shoot to eat your target body weight in grams of protein daily. For example, if you are a chubby 200 pounds and want to be a lean 180, then have 180 grams of protein a day.

Myth #2: Blueberries Are Better for You Than Bananas

The origin: Studies show that, per cup, blueberries have among the highest antioxidant content of almost any fruit. So they've been marketed as superior to other fruits—especially bananas.

What science really shows: They're both good for you, in different ways. For example, per calorie, bananas have about four times as much potassium and magnesium as blueberries have. So it's not as simple as one food being superior to another; it all has to do with your perspective—and it's likely that variety is best. For instance, Colorado State University scientists found that people who consume the widest array of fruits and vegetables experience more health benefits than those who eat just as much produce from among a smaller assortment.

The bottom line: Produce is good for you. And for the most benefits, you should eat a mix of the kinds you like the best—not limit yourself based on an antioxidant ranking.

Myth #3: Red Meat Causes Cancer

The origin: In a 1986 study, Japanese researchers discovered cancer in rats that were fed heterocyclic amines, compounds that are generated from overcooking meat via high heat. Since then, some studies of large populations have suggested a potential link between meat and cancer.

What science really shows: No study

has ever found a direct cause-and-effect relationship between red-meat consumption and cancer. As for the population studies, they're far from conclusive. They rely on broad surveys of people's eating habits and health afflictions, and the resulting numbers are crunched to find trends, not causes.

The bottom line: Don't stop grilling. Meat lovers who are worried about the supposed risks of grilled meat don't need to avoid burgers and steak; rather, they should just trim off the burned or overcooked sections of the meat.

Myth #4: High-Fructose Corn Syrup (HFCS) Is More Fattening Than Regular Sugar

The origin: In 2002, University of California at Davis researchers published a well-publicized paper noting that Americans' increasing consumption of fructose, including that in HFCS, paralleled our skyrocketing rates of obesity.

What science really shows: Both HFCS and sucrose—better known as table sugar—contain similar amounts of fructose. In fact, they're almost chemically identical in that they're both composed of about 50 percent fructose and 50 percent glucose. This is why the University of California at Davis scientists determined fructose intakes from *both* HFCS and sucrose. The truth is, there's no evidence to show any differences in these two types of sugar. Both will cause weight gain when consumed in excess.

The bottom line: HFCS and regular sugar are empty-calorie carbs that should be consumed in limited amounts.

Myth #5: Salt Causes High Blood Pressure and Should Be Avoided

The origin: In the 1940s, a Duke University researcher named Walter Kempner, MD, became famous for using salt restriction to treat people with hypertension. Later, studies confirmed that reducing salt could be helpful.

What science really shows: Large-scale scientific reviews have determined there's no reason for people with normal blood pressure to restrict sodium. Now, if you are already hypertensive, you may be "salt sensitive." As a result, reducing the amount of salt you eat could be helpful. However, it's been known for 20 years that people with high BP who don't want to lower their salt intake can simply consume more potassium-rich foods to achieve the same health benefits. Why? Because it's the balance of the two minerals that matters: Dutch scientists found that a low potassium intake has the same impact on blood pressure as high salt consumption does. And turns out, the average guy consumes 3,200 milligrams (mg) of potassium a day—1,500 mg less than recommended.

The bottom line: Strive for a diet rich in potassium by eating fruits, vegetables, and legumes. For instance, spinach (cooked), bananas, and most types of beans each contain more than 400 mg of potassium per serving.

THINK BEFORE YOU EAT

Before your next snack, review your previous meal. British researchers determined that people who used this strategy ate 30 percent fewer calories than those who didn't stop to think. The theory: Simply remembering what you've already eaten makes you less likely to overindulge.

■

SPECIAL FEATURE

Workout Nutrition Secrets

Whether you want to lose fat or build muscle, you'll achieve the best results by making sure your muscles are well fed. That means consuming a healthy dose of protein around your workout. This provides your body with the raw materials to repair and upgrade your muscles, enhancing your results.

What's more, after your workout is also the best time of the day to consume carbs. Why? Well, imagine that the carbs you eat go into a bucket. When the bucket is full, the carbs overflow and are converted to fat. This is what happens in your body, with the bucket representing your muscles. But when you exercise, you burn carbs, removing them from your bucket. As a result, you have more room in which to store the carbs you eat after your workout. That makes postworkout carbs less likely to end up stored as belly fat. Just as important, these carbs help speed the repair of your muscles.

The upshot: You can strategically eat most of your daily starch and sugar immediately before or after your workout, or you can stick with protein-only pre- and postworkout snacks to keep your carb bucket close to empty and your body burning fat at full blast. Simply choose the option you like best.

Protein-Only Workout Snacks

Option #1:

A convenient shake. Prepare a protein shake (mixed with water) that provides at least 20 grams of protein. (More is fine.) When choosing a product, look for one that contains only small amounts of carbs and fat. Here are three reputable products—they all have blends of whey and casein protein—but comparable protein powders work as well.

At Large Nutrition Nitrean
Available at: www.atlargenutrition.com
Per serving (make 2 servings): 24 grams (g) protein, 2 g carbohydrate, 1 g fat

Biotest Metabolic Drive Super Protein Shake
Available at: www.t-nation.com
and www.biotest.net
Per serving (make 2 servings): 20 g protein, 4 g carbohydrate, 1.5 g fat

**MET-Rx Protein Plus Protein Powder
(46-g Metamyosyn Protein Blend)**
Available at: metrx.com
Per serving (make 1 serving): 46 g protein, 3 g carbohydrate, 1.5 g fat

Option #2:

Regular fare. Consume at least 20 grams of high-quality protein in the form of solid food.
- A small can (3.5 ounces) of tuna
- 3 to 4 ounces of lean deli meat
- A serving of any lean meat that's the size (length, width, thickness) of a deck of cards
- 3 eggs—an omelet, for instance

Protein-and-Carbs Workout Snacks

Option #1:

A convenient shake (with carbs). Prepare a shake (mixed with water or milk) that provides a blend of 40 to 80 grams of carbohydrates and at least 40 grams of whey and casein protein. When choosing a product, look for one that contains both types of protein. As for carbohydrates, this is the one time when sugar is perfectly acceptable. That's because it can be used immediately for energy during your workout, and it helps speed muscle growth after your workout. Three products that fit the criteria:

At Large Nutrition Opticen
Available at: www.atlargenutrition.com
Per serving (make 1 serving): 52 g protein, 25 g carbohydrate, 1.7 g fat

Biotest Surge Recovery
Available at: www.t-nation.com and www.biotest.net
Per serving (make 1 serving): 25 g protein, 46 g carbohydrate, 2.5 g fat

MET-Rx Xtreme Size Up
Available at: metrx.com
Per serving (make 1 serving): 59 g protein, 80 g carbohydrate, 6 g fat

Option #2:

Regular fare (that includes carbs). Take advantage of your half-empty carb bucket and enjoy a couple of servings of carbs without worrying about the impact on your waistline. Consume at least 20 grams of high-quality protein and up to 40 grams of carbohydrates from regular food. You can mix and match foods as desired, or use the general guidelines to figure out your own favorites. (Think: pizza!)

Foods that contain 20 grams of protein:
- A small can (3.5 ounces) of tuna
- 3 to 4 ounces of any kind of meat
- 3 eggs

Amounts and type of foods that contain 15 to 20 grams of carbs (you need two servings):
- 1 slice of bread
- ½ cup cooked pasta or rice
- ½ cup of cereal
- ½ medium potato
- 1 cup of berries or sliced fruit
- 1 whole apple, orange, or peach, or
- ½ large banana

Dairy foods that contain both protein and carbohydrates (per 8-ounce cup):

DAIRY FOOD	PROTEIN (G)	CARBS (G)
MILK	8	12
CHOCOLATE MILK	8	25
PLAIN YOGURT	8	12
FRUIT YOGURT	8	25
KEFIR	14	12
FLAVORED KEFIR	14	25
COTTAGE CHEESE	31	8

NUTRITION SECRET #5

Surprising Muscle Foods

Meat, fish, and eggs are packed with protein—so they're great for your muscles. But here are four not-so-obvious foods that can help you sculpt your body, too.

Almonds

Crunch for crunch, almonds are one of the best sources of alpha-tocopherol vitamin E—the form that's best absorbed by your body. That matters to your muscles because vitamin E is a potent antioxidant that can help prevent free-radical damage after heavy workouts. And the fewer hits taken from free radicals, the faster your muscles will recover and start growing. How much to munch? Two handfuls a day. A Toronto University study found that men can eat that amount daily without gaining weight.

Almonds also double as brain insurance. A study published in the *Journal of the American Medical Association* found that those men who consumed the most vitamin E—from food sources, not supplements—had a 67 percent lower risk for Alzheimer's disease than those eating the least.

Olive Oil

The monounsaturated fat in olive oil appears to act as an anticatabolic nutrient. In other words, it prevents muscle breakdown by lowering levels of tumor necrosis factor, a cellular protein linked with muscle wasting. Monounsaturated fats have also been associated with lower rates of heart disease.

Spinach

Well, spinach and just about any other vegetable or fruit. Australian researchers found that people who reduced their antioxidant intake—eating just one serving of fruit and two of vegetables daily—for 2 weeks felt as if they were exerting more effort than when exercising on a diet rich in antioxidants. It seems that eating several servings of fruits and vegetables daily can make exercise seem easier—and help you finish those last reps.

Water

Whether they're in your shins or your shoulders, muscles are approximately 80 percent water. A reduction in body water of as little as 1 percent can impair exercise performance and adversely affect recovery. For example, a German study found that protein synthesis occurs at a higher rate in muscle cells that are well-hydrated, compared with dehydrated cells. English translation: The more parched you are, the slower your body uses protein to build muscle. Plus, researchers at Loma Linda University found that people who drank at least five 8-ounce glasses of water a day were 54 percent less likely to suffer a fatal heart attack than those who drank two or fewer.

The Protein-Powder Primer

Here's your guide to navigating the supplement aisle.

The Best Ingredients: Whey and Casein

What are they? The primary proteins found in milk. In fact, about 20 percent of the protein in milk is whey, and the other 80 percent is casein.

What's the diff? Both are high-quality proteins, meaning they contain all the essential amino acids that are needed by your body. However, whey is known as a "fast protein." That's because it's quickly broken down into amino acids and absorbed into your bloodstream. This makes it a very good protein to consume after your workout, as it can be delivered to your muscles right away. Casein, on the other hand, is digested more slowly, so it's ideal for providing your body with a steady supply of smaller amounts of protein for a longer period of time—such as between meals or while you sleep. Think of it as time-release protein.

Which one? Try a blend. Either will provide your muscles with the raw materials for growth, but combining them allows you to optimize your protein intake no matter when you down a shake.

The Label Decoder

To most people, the ingredients list of a protein powder may as well be written in Sanskrit. That's because it often contains several subtypes of whey and casein protein. Here's how to read the label like a chemist.

Concentrate: The cheapest form of most proteins. It contains slightly higher amounts of fat and carbohydrate than more pure versions and can be clumpy and hard to mix by hand; however, it provides the same basic muscle-building benefits. In the case of casein, it's referred to as caseinate.

Isolate: A protein that's more pure than concentrate—meaning it contains lower amounts of fat and carbohydrate—and is also easier to mix.

Hydrosylate, or hydrolyzed protein: A protein that's been broken down into smaller fractions than are in a concentrate or isolate, allowing it to be absorbed into your bloodstream more quickly. However, when it comes to casein hydrosylate, this defeats the purpose, since the benefit of casein is that it absorbs slowly.

Micellar casein, or isolated casein peptides: An expensive but easy-to-mix protein that's nearly pure casein, ensuring slow and steady absorption.

Milk protein: An ingredient that has the composition of natural milk protein— 80 percent casein and 20 percent whey.

Egg-white protein: Like whey and casein, an excellent high-quality protein. It's sometimes called *instantized egg albumin* on the label.

FROM MEAT TO MUSCLE

How steak makes it to your biceps:

1. Your teeth pulverize the steak into smaller particles, mixing it with saliva, to form a semi-solid lump.

2. Once swallowed, the beef moves down the esophagus and empties into your stomach. Here, enzymes such as pepsin chemically break the steak into strands of amino acids. The whole mess is now more of a liquid called chyme.

3. From the stomach, the chyme passes into the small intestines. Here additional enzymes— trypsin and chymotrypsin—act on the amino acid strands to break them into even smaller parts.

4. The amino acids are then absorbed through the cells that line the wall of the intestines, reaching the bloodstream. They're now ready to be sent to your muscles via your blood vessels.

5. Once in the bloodstream, the amino acids are delivered directly to the muscle fiber via capillaries. There they aid in the repair of damaged muscle tissue. In fact, muscle protein synthesis can't occur unless amino acids are readily available—all the more reason to eat protein before you work out.

BONUS!

25 Fat-Fighting Snacks
End Mindless Eating with These Winning Combinations

Whenever you need a between-meals fix, just choose one item from each of the two categories below, mix-and-match style. Adhere to the suggested serving size, and you'll have 25 options for a balanced snack of approximately 200 calories. Each will provide you with a filling dose of protein, fat, and fiber, along with a shot of disease-fighting antioxidants.

EAT THIS...	AMOUNT	WITH THAT...	AMOUNT
ALMOND OR PEANUT BUTTER, NUTS, OR SEEDS	1 TBSP	APPLE	1 MEDIUM
PLAIN YOGURT	¾ CUP	PEACH	1 LARGE
HAM OR TURKEY SLICES	3 SLICES	CELERY*	5 STALKS
HARD CHEESE (PARMESAN OR CHEDDAR)	1 OZ/1 SLICE	BLUEBERRIES	1 CUP
2% COTTAGE CHEESE	½ CUP	BABY CARROTS*	1 CUP

*Because these are very low-calorie choices, you can double the serving size of the "Eat This" snack that you pair them with.

Index

Boldface page references indicate references indicate illustrations/photographs.
Underscored references indicate boxed text.